The Tournament's Price

The Tournament's Price

GIVEN HOFFMAN

PRESS ON
PUBLISHING

Copyright © 2020 Given Hoffman. All rights reserved. No part of this publication may be reproduced, distributed, or transmitted in any form or by any means, including photocopying, recording, or other electronic or mechanical methods, without the prior written permission of the author except in the case of a brief quotation embodied in critical reviews and certain other noncommercial uses permitted by copyright law.

Map created by BriAnn Beck and Given Hoffman.

This is a work of fiction. Names, characters, businesses, places, events, locales, and incidents are either the products of the author's imagination or used in a fictitious manner. Any resemblance to actual persons, living or dead, or actual events is purely coincidental.

Scripture taken from the New King James Version. Copyright © 1982 by Thomas Nelson, Inc. Used by permission. All rights reserved.

ISBN: 978-1-54399-784-2 (print)

ISBN: 978-1-54399-785-9 (eBook)

To my younger brother, Kaben, who has taught me so much. I will always treasure the hours we spent as children exploring the woods together.

Author's Note

There is something continually intriguing about the medieval time period. I'm still not sure what it is exactly that draws so many of us to the tales of knights and nobility. Perhaps it's the battles, weapons, castles, honor, and bravery. I personally dove deeper into medieval research several years ago because I knew Gage belonged in a medieval setting.

Accuracy in historical fiction has always mattered a great deal to me, and the fear that I might possibly misrepresent real people and times in history is why I have never dared traverse into writing historical fiction. In creating Gage's story, I allowed myself several concessions, which shifted this novel's genre instead to medieval action/adventure.

1. I chose to make the setting medieval but still fictitious.
2. I chose no particular historical dates but rather used details and research from the medieval age as a whole.
3. I took liberties within my fictitious setting and altered what would have been the typical religious styles, governments, laws, etc.

These decisions gave me the freedom to write Gage's story with many of the fascinating factors of the medieval time period but without the restrictions or fear of having to hold perfectly to history.

I hope you enjoy the medieval flavor and setting of this story.

Glossary of Terms

Arming Doublet – A padded jacket worn under armor, particularly under plate armor

Aye – "Yes"

Azure – A bright blue color

Bailey – The inner walled enclosure located at the heart of a medieval castle

Caltrop – A spiked metal device with four or more spines used to cripple mounts

Caparisoned – A covering, often displaying a coat-of-arms, designed for a horse

Couter – Armor for the elbow

Curtain Wall – A fortified wall surrounding a castle or fortress

Demesne – (də'mān) Land attached to a manor and retained by the lord for his own use

Destrier – A valuable war horse

Gauntlet – Armored gloves or thick leather gloves (thrown down to signify a challenge)

Gorget – Armor for the neck

Grand Guard – A piece of armor worn on the shoulder by jousters

Greaves – Armor worn upon the shins

Gudgeon – A small fish often caught and used as bait

Keep – A fortified tower, typically within a castle or fortress

Kipper – A servant who would retrieve armor or arms from a knight's fallen adversaries

Mayhap – "Perhaps"

Nay – "No"

None – Midafternoon, approximately 3:00 p.m.

Palfrey – A smooth gaited, quality riding horse

Pauldron – Armor for the shoulder

Prime – Early morning, approximately 6:00 a.m.

Prithee – "Please"

Rouncey – An ordinary riding horse

Rerebrace – Armor for the upper arm

Sabatons – Armor that protects the feet

Saltcellar – An elaborate standing salt dish frequently crafted of silver

Sext – Midday, approximately 12:00 p.m.

Solar – An upper chamber in a medieval house and the family's private living area

Terce – Later morning, approximately 9:00 a.m.

Tilt – The wooden barrier between jousting competitors; also, to joust

Tonsure – The shaving of the top of the head as a symbol of religious devotion

Trenchers – Large pieces of stale bread used like plates while dining

Vambrace – Armor for the forearm

Vamplate – A circular hand guard on a spear or lance

Vespers – Evening, approximately 6:00 p.m.

Character List

King Axel – King of Edelmar

Queen Irena – Queen of Edelmar

Prince Haaken – Firstborn son of King Axel and Queen Irena

    Sir Renner – Haaken's knight

    Sir Holbird – Haaken's knight and brother to Lady Cathleen

Prince Gage – Second-born son of King Axel and Queen Irena

    Allard – Gage's squire and son of Baron Roger of Ulbin

    Sir Brent – Gage's oldest knight (Sword) who knows Lady Natriece

    Sir Reid – Gage's knight (Dagger) who is interested in Lady Cathleen

    Sir Hayson – Gage's knight (Battle Axe) who loves to improve tools

    Sir Wick – Gage's youngest knight (Arrow) son of the lord of Clement

    Emerett – Gage's cook

    Old Tobin, Amos, & Morley – Gage's wagon drivers

    Badger, Mattson, Bardon, & Wellens – Gage's servants

Baron Roderick – Baron of Leland and a renown jouster

Baron James – Baron of Nardell and tournament host

Baron Elmon – Baron of Awnquera and Gage's uncle on his mother's side

Baron Roger – Gage's instructor and the baron of Ulbin

Baroness Agnes – Allard's mother, wife of Roger, and baroness of Ulbin

Lord Henry – Lord of Aro, son of Baron Roger and Allard's older brother

Novia – A friend of Gage's and Haaken's who drowned as a child

Lady Emma – (Emmie) daughter of Baron Blakely

Lady Natriece – Daughter of Lord Gregory of Veiroot, she dances with Gage

Lady Cathleen – Sister of Sir Holbird, she is interested in Sir Reid

Baron Hewitt – Baron of Duvall, firstborn son of the deceased Baron Lucas

The Blue Crow – A known thief who has been harassing the lords of Edelmar

Felix – A man who requests to travel with Gage's retinue

King Maurice – Deceased king of Delkara

Queen Marjorie – Queen mother of Delkara

King Strephon – King of Delkara, firstborn son of deceased King Maurice

Prince Thayer – Deceased second-born son of King Maurice

Manton – Gage's traveling companion

Spice Seller – A woman Gage meets at the Wallmon Inn in Clement

Kenley & Heather – Manton's friends from a manor outside of Maneo

Papermaker – Manton's friend who lives in Asplin

Marjorie, Jordan, & Derik – Manton's friends, the Coopers from Lapidus

Prior Joseph – Manton's friend, the prior of a monastery in Burnel

Ian & Wilona – Manton's friends from Ivett, relatives to the Coopers

Evan & Tilda – Chandlers from Delipp

Jack & Georgette – A couple from Claustrom, relatives to the Chandlers

Lord Hadrian – Lord of Delipp where there is the artesian well

Baron Bertram – Baron of Lyster whose coat-of-arms is a dog with a ring of keys

Moses – A mystery play performer

Arron & Michael – Manton's friends from Dinslage who Gage meets at Nikledon

Baron Selwin – Baron of Nikledon, son of the deceased Lord Terryn

Sir Jarret – The knight who detains Gage on the road outside of Nikledon

1

Coated in dirt, sweat, and the thrill of combat, Gage kicked his horse into a gallop down the tilt. He tightened his armored fingers below his lance's vamplate and lowered the shaft across his mount's neck. Focusing on his opponent, he confirmed his aim. The crowd surrounding them went silent.

Gage's breathing huffed against the inside of his helmet. His horse's hooves struck the ground, jarring his armor. Two more pounding strides, then with a rush of expectation, Gage embraced the impact.

The tip of his lance smashed into the grand guard on his opponent's shoulder. The shaft's center exploded into splinters. That same moment, Gage felt the fierce pain of Baron Roderick's lance plowing into his own armored chest.

His body rammed backward in his saddle, and he numbly dropped what was left of his shattered weapon. His head pounded, and his off-kilter weight slid him along the back of his saddle. No! He would not accept the same fate as every other knight who'd jousted against Baron Roderick. Not when he was so close.

Clamping his legs harder around his mount and gritting his teeth, Gage heaved himself back upright.

The crowd—utterly silent a moment before—erupted in cheers.

The rush of accomplishment momentarily obliterated Gage's pain. He reined in his mount and slid the sorrel—clothed in his blue-and-white coat-of-arms overlaid with a bend of gold and purple—to a sharp, dusty stop at the end of the tilt, then paraded his horse sideways.

Commoners, gentry, and nobles alike roared their approval.

Gage had the right to show off. Knighted three years early after winning a vespers tournament, he had jousted undefeated at two prior tournaments and was now one tilt away from possibly winning another.

Beneath the helmet that covered his face, Gage grinned. He flexed his numb fingers until a prickling sensation returned and then glanced at the covered platform to find his brother.

Amid the polished jewelry and lavish apparel of lords and ladies, he spotted Haaken. Five years older than Gage, Haaken had their father's wavy, light-brown hair under his crown, whereas Gage had their mother's dark curls. Standing and smiling, Haaken clapped heartily, unlike Baron James, who sat beside him with lips pursed and hands folded. Silence from James, the lord of Nardell and the tournament's host, was not a good sign. Gage could only hope the lord's disregard for the joust was due to James's unhorsing the day before and not the current tilt.

The trumpets blasted, and the crowd quieted as a herald announced the score. "His Highness, Prince Gage, hit with a broken lance—five points. Total of ten. Baron Roderick, hit with a broken lance—five points. Total of ten. Lords and ladies, gentry and common folk, you are about to witness the third and final tilt in the last joust of the tournament."

The crowd erupted once again.

Gage blinked. Their points were equal. His heart beat faster, and sweat trickled down his back. His horse snorted and pranced. Armor clanking, Gage pulled in the animal and waited for Allard, his squire, son of Baron Roger of Ulbin, to bring him a new lance. As he waited, he licked the salt from his lips and searched for Roderick through the slit in his helmet.

At the opposite end of the list, which was worn to dirt along the tilt's chest-high barrier—designed to keep jousters' horses from veering into each other—Roderick sat upon his speckled horse. Roderick's young squire waited near the tilt with a new lance, but the baron did not approach him to receive it. With the pole twice his height in hand, the squire stepped toward Roderick, as if unsure whether to take the lance to his lord or wait at the tilt. Roderick jerkily motioned the lad back and spurred his horse forward to receive his lance.

A tap against Gage's armor drew his attention to his own squire. Three years his junior, Allard's blond hair blew across blue eyes, which had silently teased Gage on many occasions. The boy offered him a lance topped with a metal coronel—a blunt, three-pronged tip designed to keep competition lances from piercing armor. Gage reached for the shaft, but Allard pulled it back.

In a voice that had not yet fully shaken its youth, Allard said, "Both you and Baron Roderick have taken every opponent each of you has jousted against this tournament. Still, Baron Roderick is considered the superior jouster." Allard cracked a broad grin. "But you and I know better. Unhorse him, Your Highness, and carry home the tournament's prize."

Grinning back, Gage replied by locking his gauntleted hand around the lance and thrusting it upward. Keeping its tip skyward, he pranced his horse to the tilt. He pulled the sorrel to a stop at its end. His breathing filled his helmet with heat, and he inhaled the smell of wet steel. Sweat stuck his hair to his forehead and neck. This was it, the moment he had waited for and always loved as a child—the last charge in the final joust of the tournament.

Gage shifted in his saddle. His legs quivered. His horse threw its head and snorted. Gage tightened the reins and adjusted his grip on his lance. He tested the shaft's weight and judged the distance down the tilt. Hitting a rider was one point. A hit with a broken lance was five points. If Roderick matched him in either, they would be even again. The only way to assure victory was to unhorse the other rider for ten points, but Gage feared the likelihood of this rested in Roderick's favor. The man never missed his mark, and though Gage had rallied his strength many times throughout the day to save his seat, his endurance was waning.

He needed to stay on his horse, and he needed a solid hit with a broken lance. If he failed either, he would lose more than this joust. Having surprised many with his talent at the tilt, he had so far jousted undefeated. But if he lost now, his previous victories would be dismissed as simply the luck of youth. He needed this win to prove he had something of his own to offer that he had earned and not just been given.

He gritted his teeth. He could do this. Closing his fingers tighter about his lance, he locked his gaze on Roderick, who pivoted his horse into position. What was he doing? Instead of raising his lance, Roderick rested it across his horse's neck. The baron also sat angled farther forward than normal, leaning his weight against his saddle's pommel. Gage questioned whether this was a tactic he didn't know about or a trick to distract him. He settled more thoroughly in his own saddle and wondered if the marshal of the list would require the baron to straighten his body and lance before the tilt.

The trumpet blasted. No yell came from the marshal. Roderick lifted his lance off his mount's neck, and the animal sprang forward.

A moment off beat, Gage spurred his own horse into a gallop. Their mounts plunged headlong down either side of the tilt. As Gage lowered his lance, it bounced. He tensed every muscle in his arms and torso. Heat burned through his body. He exhaled against the metal of his helmet, steadying his aim at Roderick's chest.

Roderick's lance wavered off course, sliding loosely down the neck of his horse. On the next hoofbeat, Gage saw red dripping onto Roderick's armored leg, and the baron lost his grip completely. Two options collided in Gage's mind: win or withdraw?

He yanked up his lance.

He didn't have to see the crowd's startled expressions or hear their murmured questions to know they were confused. He was half confused himself. The other half of him was angry. He understood admitting injury hung a knight's dignity the same as admitting defeat, but Roderick's inability to hold his lance stole the honor from any victory Gage might have had. The baron should have declared himself injured and withdrawn or else requested to proceed with the tilt despite his injury. Then any resulting disadvantage would have been void of injustice.

Angered further that Roderick would assume he would take such a victory, Gage tossed his lance aside and slid his horse to a stop mid-tilt. He spun his mount to face Roderick, who was still galloping down the tilt.

The baron's body toppled sideways, striking the top of the wooden barrier. Caught in the saddle with his horse still moving, the man's armor grated and screeched toward the tilt's end.

"Allard! Halt his horse!" Gage yelled.

Allard sprinted into the path of the baron's war horse and threw his arms wide. The animal's hooves dug into the ground. Dust billowed.

The horse stopped less than an arm's length from the squire. Gage breathed in relief. Coughing in a covering of dirt, Allard grabbed the animal's bridle.

Fearing the baron's horse might still sidestep, Gage galloped back along the tilt and grabbed hold of Roderick's armor to keep him from falling. "Roderick, can you hear me?"

Silence was the only answer. Had the blood been from something other than Baron Roderick's hand? Was the baron even breathing? With no way to know, all Gage could do was maintain his grip and await aid.

Once when he was eight years old, he'd also held tightly to someone, unsure if they were dead or alive. Cold river water had rushed about him. One arm wrapped around Novia and the other hooked over a branch, he'd kept them from continuing down river. Had he missed the branch, they would have both drowned. As it was, chilled to the bone and too scrawny and scared to attempt to use the branch to pull them out, he'd screamed for help instead. Haaken had found them and dragged them out, but Novia was already gone. Everyone said she'd likely been dead long before Gage had caught the branch, but he still wondered if she might have lived if he'd done something different.

"Your Highness, you can let go. We have him."

Realizing that Roderick's squire, two field attendants, and the marshal had arrived, Gage released his grip on Roderick's armor. Allard steered Roderick's horse away from the tilt, so the men could lower the baron to the ground.

"Baron Roderick?" The marshal raised the baron's visor.

At the sight of Roderick's pale, narrow face and closed eyes, Gage's stomach churned. He swallowed hard and felt his body become cold.

The marshal placed a hand below the baron's nose. "He's breathing."

Relief filled Gage and pushed away the fear coursing through vhim.

2

While Roderick was carried off the field, Gage explained to the marshal what he had seen and why he had withdrawn his lance. As he did, he heard the displeased murmurings of the crowd and knew they blamed him for the unsatisfying end to the tournament. More humiliating yet, the marshal responded to his words by appealing to James for a decision regarding the tournament victor, as if the result of the joust was Gage's only concern.

With Roderick in no condition to run another tilt and it being late in the day with the feast nearing, James ruled the joust complete. He raised his hands to silence the crowd's protests. "By the feast tonight, Baron Roderick's condition should be known. The ultimate victor will then be able to be determined by whatever means seems fitting, and the victor shall crown a Queen of Love and Beauty. Until then, let the feast be prepared and the festivities continue."

Gage accepted the ruling and left the tournament field to make his way to his royal pavilion. His tent was distinguished from Haaken's by the gold crescent of the second-born displayed beneath the royal bend of gold and purple overlaying Gage's blue-and-white standard.

His knights fell in around him, accompanying him to his pavilion and clearing the way for him, his horse, and Allard. Upon reaching his large blue-and-white tent, Gage handed his horse to Allard and then headed into the spacious structure.

Elaborate chairs, a broad board table, benches, four hanging lamps, a stand for his armor, and four trunks occupied the front half of the fur-lined pavilion. The second half, partially divided off by a gilded tapestry, held another chair, a large tub, a small table, and a clothing trunk. The trunk was placed at the end of a great standing bed covered in a beautifully woven bedspread and enclosed by ornate curtains.

Dumping his helmet on the board, Gage called for Sir Brent—the oldest of his four knights—to seek a messenger. Then he took some food and drink brought by one of his servants and finally allowed Allard to persuade him to stay still long enough to begin removing his armor.

Sir Brent called to him in the nobleman's tongue from just outside the pavilion's door, which had been drawn aside to let in the breeze. "Your Highness, I have a runner."

"Send him within," Gage replied, also in the nobleman's tongue, a language strictly forbidden by law for anyone not of noble birth to learn or use. The law endured from times before the division of the three kingdoms. Gage's father had long wished to abolish it, but with many lords opposing such a change, he let it remain, for it did have its benefits.

Gage faced the door as the messenger entered. A boy in undyed clothes with skin tanned almost to the color of chestnut tiptoed on dusty feet into Gage's pavilion as if afraid the furs were not meant to be walked on. The boy's wide brown eyes flicked about the rich furnishings, crossed paths with Gage's gaze, and plowed into the floor. Bowing, the boy swallowed. "Your . . . Your Highness."

Gage answered in the boy's language, the commoner's tongue. "I appreciate you coming so quickly. What's your name, lad?"

The boy's voice trembled. "Judd, son of Dan."

"Will you carry a message for me, Judd?"

"I will. I mean, yes, Your Highness." Hands knotting, the boy's gaze remained buried in the floor.

Allard, whose back was to the child, smirked while unfastening and removing the curving metal pauldron from Gage's shoulder.

Amused as well yet sympathetic, Gage tried to help the boy out. "From what I hear, the job of message running is given to bold, swift-footed lads with good memories."

The boy's brown eyes flicked up at him, then back to the floor.

Gage kept his gaze upon the boy. "My knight trusts you to carry a message for me. Therefore, I'm inclined to believe you are such a lad. Am I correct in assuming you do your job well?"

The boy's chin lifted, his feet flattened, and his shoulders straightened. "Yes, Your Highness."

Gage nodded. "Good. I seek information as to how Baron Roderick fares. Bring me more than gossip, and I shall see you are paid well."

The lad's eyes took on a luster at the mention of a good wage, and he bowed and backed toward the door. "Yes, My lord. I mean—" He turned red. "Your Highness." Cringing and bowing twice more, the boy hurriedly backed out of the tent.

Gage shook his head in amusement. "Inexperienced, yet enthusiastic," he said to Allard in the nobleman's tongue.

"Aye, and eager for money," Allard replied with a chuckle.

Gage's smile slipped away. Had he let his inexperience and enthusiasm overrule his better judgment at the final tilt? He could have spoken before the charge when he first noticed Roderick's improper positioning, and he should have. But he hadn't because the marshal didn't, and neither had Roderick, who was the seasoned jouster. Trusting they knew better, Gage had ignored his own judgment.

Not a fortnight ago he had claimed in his father's presence that he was ready to become lord of his own manor, but how did he expect to rule a household when he hesitated to speak his mind over a joust—the one thing about which he knew the most? Decisions on a manor would be far less straightforward, and even more so than now, he would bear full responsibility if he chose wrong.

Allard's voice interrupted his thoughts. "Is something amiss?"

Realizing he had neglected to lift his arms for Allard to unbuckle the rerebrace and couter covering his upper arms and elbows, Gage did so. "Nay."

Half a head shorter than him with boyish features, Allard was the closest thing he had to a younger brother. The lad eyed him, clearly doubting his answer. Gage gave in. "I was thinking about the joust and how I could have chosen differently."

Allard frowned. "You mean if you had not raised your lance?"

Before Gage could answer, the bear-like voice of Baron Roger of Ulbin accompanied his frame as it filled the pavilion's doorway. "Aye, you could have unhorsed him and won, but it would have been a skill-less and honor-less victory. But this you already know."

Gage nodded for Sir Brent to grant Baron Roger entrance.

With hair and beard matching the fox fur lining his tunic, Roger trudged inside and gruntingly seated himself on one of the benches beside Gage's silver-plated trunks. A scar drooped Roger's right eyelid. As always, he countered the hindrance by tilting back his head to capture Gage's gaze with both eyes. "One thing is certain though. If you had not raised your lance, you would have been the only one who knew how unfit Roderick was for the last tilt."

Gage frowned at the thought. "My lord—"

Roger lifted a hand. "Your obligation to address me so formally has long been surpassed, Your Highness."

"Nay," Gage protested. "How can I not show respect to the one who taught me so much?"

Roger chuckled softly. "Aye, mayhap that much I have earned, for you have indeed come a long way from the eager youth who skewered my house's standard."

In the middle of loosening a buckle on Gage's armor, Allard coughed on a laugh. Heat rose up Gage's neck in remembrance of the mishap with his lance his first day of training.

"I'll never forget Mother's expression," Allard said, attempting to keep a straight face.

Groaning, Gage wished he could put his helmet back on and hide from his memory of Lady Agnes's inquisition. He shook his head. "Prithee, I do not need to relive that day."

Roger exchanged a smirk with his son and nodded at Gage. "Aye, if I remember right, it was a beautiful spring afternoon with the wind coming from the south."

Gage covered his face with his hands. "Aye, and the standard was blowing northward. I remember." Uncovering his face, he pointed at the two of them. "If either of you dares speak of it at any gathering, I will . . ." He searched in his mind for something to deter them. "I will restrict you both to riding donkeys for the rest of your lives."

Allard displayed appropriate consternation, but only for a moment. "It could be worth it."

"I can think of something worse," Gage warned.

"Mayhap you should," Roger said with a rumbling laugh. "For you might consider what would be said by gentry and common folk alike if you were seen with your squire riding a donkey."

"Even those in the stocks would likely mock as we passed," Allard said with a tone of sincerity as he removed Gage's breastplate. He glanced at his father. "And since His Highness likes to move from place to place rather quickly, one might wonder if a donkey's pace would in the end cause him more grief than it would me."

Gage threw up his hands. "Cease! May I never hear the end of either?"

Grinning and placing the piece of armor into a trunk, Allard bowed. "I assure you, Prince Gage, your secret is safe with us."

Gage wasn't sure whether to believe Allard or wrestle him to the floor as he'd done when they were boys. They had never been fair fights, considering he was royalty and Allard wasn't, but it was a version of kinship that they had embraced regardless.

"In truth," Roger said, diverting Gage's attention, "I was amazed you learned to manage your lance so quickly and only unintentionally impaled the one item."

"Are you saying you expected me to do far worse?"

"Nay!" Roger laughed. "Simply that I am inclined to agree with your father. In the same way Haaken is skilled with the sword, you are gifted with the lance."

Glancing to where Allard had knelt to remove the greaves from his lower legs, Gage swallowed and nodded. "Thank you."

"Your Highness," Sir Brent said from the door, "your runner has returned."

"Send him within." The boy entered and bowed, and Gage switched to the commoner's tongue. "Judd, speak, please."

The boy's chest rose and fell quickly. "Baron Roderick is well. He woke soon after being moved to his pavilion. They say water and shade brought him around easily enough. His squire even told me he'll attend the feast tonight."

"Was he not injured then?" Gage asked.

"Oh, no. He was injured. During the second tilt, the vamplate of his own lance cut a deep gash above his wrist and injured two of his fingers."

"How badly?"

"Bad enough he'll hold nothing in that hand for some time, but it will heal."

Gage shook his head in amazement. "How did he think to joust a last tilt then?"

"Had I thought to ask that, I'd have brought you this answer as well."

Gage blinked. Eager indeed. "No, you've done well. Look to the knight who engaged you. He'll see you're paid." The boy departed.

"You wonder at Roderick's choice to joust the last tilt," Roger commented in the nobleman's tongue, "but I warned you he's a worthy opponent. His skill combined with what you saw today—his willingness to withstand any pain to achieve victory—has always been his strength. 'Tis precisely this unwavering audacity that has many times won him the joust often before he has even entered the list. And no doubt today, had his body not succumbed 'ere his mind allowed, he would have withstood the pain of broken fingers and completed the final tilt, as one would do in war." Roger pointed at Gage. "And consider that undefeated he remains."

Gage frowned. "Then his choice to remain in the joust despite his injury will likely be viewed as acceptable, even honorable?"

Roger nodded. "More than likely."

"Then I should not have withdrawn my lance."

"Nay, you did right."

"How?"

Roger eyed him. "You showed yourself merciful and not driven by a lust to win."

"Mayhap, but from all you have said, would I not have been considered more merciful to have covered Roderick's weakness rather than expose it? I came here to show my skill, not to disgrace a fellow jouster."

"You showed mercy when faced with weakness. There is no disgrace in that."

Gage sighed. "Aye, but will Roderick and James see it that way?"

"I suppose we can but wait and see." Grunting, Roger rose from the bench. "Now, I must be about my business."

Allard unbuckled Gage's sabatons. Lost in thought, Gage stepped out of the armored shoes. Roger paused at the door and looked back at Allard with a glint in his eyes. "Did I mention Baron Blakely will be attending tonight's feast, accompanied by his daughters?"

Allard bounced upright, the sabatons clinking together in his hands. "Emmie's coming to the feast?"

"Aye." Chuckling and winking at Gage, Roger headed out the door.

3

Having trailed the second-born prince of Edelmar from the tournament field, a man dressed as a servant stood in the shade of a tent. Before him a page was busily using the ash from a firepit to polish his lord's armor. The man bit into a stick of cured meat and evaluated the two knights across the lane guarding the prince's blue-and-white pavilion.

The completion of the joust was supposed to have chosen his new target for him, but with no ultimate victor named, he was left either with two men to rob or else the prospect of attending the feast to discover which one would end up the ultimate victor. He had stolen from Baron Roderick before, and though disgracing him a second time was more than agreeable to him, targeting the prince of Edelmar as the price for his victory would be so much more fitting.

He eyed the prince's pavilion. A baron exited and spoke with the taller of the two knights on duty. The knight laughed, and the baron headed to where an attendant held his horse.

The man, known as the Crow, frowned at the activity around him. With nearly three hundred knights and barons plus their attendants all encamped within the two settlements surrounding the list, thieving would be better left to the cover of darkness. Though daylight offered some advantages, waiting until the ultimate victor was named would mean getting to attend a feast, and him stealing the victor's winnings would offer a far more powerful statement to the Edelmarian nobility.

The Crow waited for two knights to pass, then fell into step behind a blacksmith's apprentice who trudged along swinging a bucket filled with horseshoes.

※

Gage chuckled at Allard, who paced like a nervous charger. "What if Emma's not seated near us?" Allard asked. "Was she at the joust? Maybe they just arrived. Will I get a chance to talk to her at the feast, do you think?"

"I am certain whether seated near her or not you will have ample opportunity to speak to her and probably even to dance with her." Gage stepped behind the curtained-off section of his pavilion, where a tub of water awaited him. "Though when dancing, do remember to look in her eyes and not at your feet, as your sister Sophia is always reminding you."

A frightened look crossed Allard's face. "What if I tread on her toes?"

"You will do well. Now help me out of this arming doublet, will you?"

Taking hold of the quilted linen garment, Allard helped tug off the thick damp jacket. Stripping off the rest of his sweaty underclothing, Gage immersed himself in the cool bathwater.

"Which tunic do you wish to wear to the feast?" Allard asked.

"The azure one with the argent trimmings and ermine fur."

Allard opened the clothing trunk at the end of Gage's bed and laid out the blue garment. He returned a moment later to pour the remaining bucket of water over Gage's head and hold out a towel.

"Thank you." Gage dried himself and then pulled on the clean dyed hose that Allard handed him. Gage tied them about his waist and headed to his bed to scoop up the long silver embroidered tunic edged with white fur.

"Gage!" Gage glanced at Haaken—the only person Sir Brent was permitted to simply let enter his pavilion and one of only three people who addressed him as Gage. Haaken stood just inside his pavilion's door with a look of concern on his face. Gage mirrored his expression. "What?"

"Your bruises are far worse than mine."

Gage inspected his biggest bruise—a hand-sized yellow-and-green mark on his arm where an opponent's lance had missed his grand guard the day before. He shrugged. "If I were as narrow as you and allowed to dodge my opponent's blows, I would no doubt sport fewer bruises."

"Oh, indeed! Though despite your extra bruises, little brother, I have a feeling you would still choose the joust over the mêlée."

"Can you blame me?"

"Nay, but I will blame you if you make us late to meet Father."

"Oh! I forgot we were to meet him before the feast." Gage threw on his tunic and drew the lacing tight. He snatched up his leather boots and tugged them on while hopping to where Allard had laid out the rest of his things. Strapping on his silver-plated belt with its ornamental dagger, he grabbed his matching silver vambraces. Tucking them under an elbow to buckle about his lower arms as they went, he headed past Haaken. "I am ready."

Haaken stayed where he was. "Crown?"

"Crown." Gage spun around and plowed into Allard, who had it in his hands. Gage shrugged apologetically. "Thank you." Running his fingers through his damp curls, he placed the curved silver band with its interwoven patterns of gold on his head. "There. Now I am ready."

Nodding, Haaken strode out the door. Allard scooped up his own things and hurried to follow. Gage lifted a hand. "What are you doing?"

"Coming with you, of course."

"Nay! You smell more like swine than I did." Gage pointed toward the water. "If you want the girl to dance with you, use the bath, and borrow one of my clean tunics."

"But you—"

"Use the bath," Gage repeated, seizing Allard's gaze. "Borrow what you will, and then meet me at the feast."

Grinning, Allard nodded.

Stepping into the breeze outside his pavilion, Gage paused beside his two knights amid the clamor of one of the tournament's two settlements. Each encampment was comprised of the tournament's opposing competitors and their retinues.

Not seeing his horse or attendant where they should have been in the next tent over, Gage glanced after Haaken. His brother was headed alone on foot through the settlement toward the castle of Nardell. Frowning, Gage trotted across the lane, ducked under a picket line that was void of horses, bypassed a group of knights, and hurried through the middle of four servants to catch up with him.

The day's heat had departed with the sun sinking beyond the nearby mountains, but he still wasn't thrilled about walking to Nardell. "Haaken, prithee tell me we are not traveling all the way to Nardell on foot."

Haaken chuckled. "Nay, not if we wish to arrive on time. I told our attendants to meet us at the edge of the settlement with our horses. I figured it would be less disruptive to the camp."

Gage glanced over his shoulder. That explained why Haaken was strangely alone, whereas Gage was accompanied by two of his knights. Allard had once jokingly compared each of his knights to weaponry. The two with him currently were, by Allard's description, his sword and dagger. Sir Brent was the first knight Gage had asked to join his retinue. The knight was tall, dark-haired, and solidly built, with the nature and skill of a focused protector. Sir Reid, a fine-boned, red-headed, cordial fellow, possessed an agile attention to details, with the element of surprise as his strength in battle. Both knights had fallen in behind Gage the moment he'd left his pavilion.

Gage paused beside Haaken, who had stopped to allow an assembly of horsemen followed by a squire leading a mount to clank through the lane in front of them. Dust puffed up around the horses' hooves and carried on the wind that unfurled banners beside doorways and atop pavilions.

Haaken cut in front of the dappled gray courser led by the squire. Gage followed and sidestepped a knight's attendant, who attempted to bow to them while carrying a handful of lances.

The gray courser led by the squire whinnied. Gage glanced back. The animal trotted two strides, back arched and tail high, and neighed again. Admiring the horse's build and spirit and wondering to whom it belonged, Gage didn't see the guy line rising from a protruding tent stake.

Tripping on the stake and catching his chest on the line, he grabbed it as he fell and swung himself under it. The pavilion it supported shook with his weight, but thankfully, the stake held.

Twisting upright, he heard a chuckle behind him. He glanced back to see Sir Reid and Sir Brent smirking. Knowing he'd be teased about the incident later, Gage shook his head and jogged to catch up with Haaken, who had veered down a path between smaller tents toward a more open lane. Two servants transporting buckets of water stepped out of their way and bowed.

Striding beside Haaken in the open lane, Gage glanced up to Nardell—the sixth-largest inland city in Edelmar. On its walls beacons were already being lit, and Gage knew by the time the day faded, torches would burn throughout the castle, city, and tournament encampments. During such events, curfews were rescinded, and in the light of flames festivities would continue far into the night.

He and Haaken were three tents away from the plain that stretched to the hill leading up to the city walls when a female hawker headed toward them holding up her collection of wares. Gage quickened his pace, but she had clearly been waiting for them, no doubt determined to sell them a bottle of ointment or a trinket, so she could claim even the princes of Edelmar used her goods.

She made her offers in a loud clarion voice. Gage and Haaken declined politely and strode to where their men awaited them with a cluster of horses, which were stamping their feet and flicking their tails.

Haaken swiftly mounted his bay. Heading for his own horse, Gage went to take his reins from his attendant and realized his vambraces were still tucked under his arm. He looked at Haaken apologetically. "Just a moment." With practiced fingers, he strapped the vambraces about his lower arms. Then he accepted his reins from Mattson, his attendant, and swung into his saddle.

Trained specifically for the joust, his horse had been a gift from Baron Roger a year prior, and Gage had secretly named the animal Kipper.

Their retinues mounted, and they rode out.

Gage kept Kipper collected long enough for the others to spread out, then loosened his reins. The sorrel quickly caught up to Haaken's bay. Grinning, Gage leaned into Kipper's swift pace, silently challenging Haaken's speed.

A smile tugged at Haaken's lips, and he released his own horse. The bay leapt into a gallop. Hoofbeat for hoofbeat, their horses skimmed through the high grass of the plain and up the hill.

Laughing, they pulled their horses in just before clattering through the high arch of the city's lowest gate. Followed through by their knights, they slowed for Sir Brent to ride ahead.

Sir Brent, with a sword at his hip, a royal standard in hand, and his long dark hair loose about his armored shoulders, called out before them as they wove their way toward the castle. "Make way! Make way for the princes of Edelmar!"

People scattered to the sides of the streets, and Gage and Haaken trotted past on the winding journey up through the city to Baron James's castle's gates and into its bailey.

The walled enclosure's torches were still unlit, but bustling beneath the torches in the courtyard were musicians, entertainers, and servants, all preparing for the feast. In the bailey's center under a large yew tree stood a small part of the king's retinue—two knights with attendants accompanied by twelve men-at-arms, a handful of servants, and six pack animals.

The two knights, Sir Peter and Sir Amram, looked grim and remained upon their mounts while the servants, who should have been removing packs and stabling animals, stood idle.

The saddle to the king's stately mount was empty, and its reins rested in Sir Amram's hand. Gage's eyes swept the castle's bailey, but he saw no sign of his father.

He looked again at the knights' grim faces, and his chest tightened. Something had happened.

4

Gage was about to question Sir Amram, but Haaken spoke first. "Has not Baron James offered space enough in his stables for the king's retinue?" Haaken asked as he swung off his horse.

"You have not heard?" Sir Amram replied. "Lord Borin seeks the king's aid on the coast. A merchant vessel from Ivenyhan ran aground. Her captain and crew abandoned ship and were saved, but the ship and cargo were lost. Those whose goods were onboard seek to hang the survivors as retribution. Lord Borin secured the captain and crew within his keep, but the mob refuses to see reason. Lord Borin has requested King Axel's aid and authority in hopes of avoiding bloodshed."

Gage inhaled, wincing as he flexed bruised ribs. "That is why you tarry in the yard? The king intends to ride tonight?" Sir Amram nodded.

So it had been on so many occasions. No matter his previous plans or how late the hour, their father always rode to the aid of his people.

Haaken handed his reins to his attendant. "Where is His Majesty now?"

"Within, offering his apologies to Baron James and conveying a request for further supplies."

Haaken headed toward the castle's great hall. Gage slid off Kipper and followed. Even in the fading light, he knew Haaken's stride. As firstborn, Haaken's future obligations had always been clear. Starting as a child, Haaken had ridden at their father's side to learn what it was to rule.

Gage, on the other hand, had grown up happily as second born. Sent as a boy to Ulbin to be trained by Baron Roger and now knighted, he came and went as he pleased with far fewer responsibilities than either Haaken or his father, though taking on a manor would soon change that.

Shoving the thought aside, Gage considered instead the feast that he'd now likely attend alone. He trailed Haaken through the open iron-plated doors of Nardell's great hall and in beside benches crowded close along broad plank tables.

The three rows of boards extended the full length of the hall. Between them, servants hustled about, bumping into each other as they finished placing bread trenchers and wooden goblets on the planks. Suspended overhead and stuffed with dozens of candles, four massive iron chandeliers cast a wide glow. There was no sign of their father, only Baron James's steward near the high table.

To avoid the servants, Gage strode between the hall's pillars and the right wall. The space was narrowed by candle brackets that protruded from the pillars and an extra row of benches packed along the wall for those with no place at the board. It offered the easiest route to the raised dais and the high table, which was draped in finery and graced by candelabras.

The steward caught sight of Gage and Haaken as they skirted the hall's hearth. Turning toward them, the man gestured his long fingers for a servant to await his instructions and bowed low. "How may I assist, Your Royal Highnesses?" His loud announcement of their presence drew the attention of a group of acrobats in a nearby alcove.

"We seek the whereabouts of His Majesty, King Axel," Haaken replied.

"He and my lord are in the storeroom."

They both waited, but the steward did not offer to lead them to the storeroom or to send a servant. Haaken turned and started that way himself. Gage followed reluctantly. They would have to go through the kitchen to get to the pantry and storerooms a level lower, and at that hour, the kitchens would be sweltering.

Before they reached the passage exiting the hall, a servant backed out of it, and a minstrel plucking a lute at the opening went silent and bowed. Their father and Baron James strode into the hall, followed by a line of servants carrying supplies.

James, a poor image sprawled behind his horse after being unhorses at the joust, was a much more intimidating sight as lord and host of Nardell.

Their father—Axel, King of Edelmar—wore less finery than James but bore the same commanding presence. With boots folded in the manner of a swordsman, trousers laced about his legs, plated-belt fastened over a fitted leather jerkin, a chiseled hand at rest upon his sword's hilt, and a solid gold crown secure on his head, their father exhibited no hesitation. His squared shoulders and baritone voice expressed a king's unpretentious authority, along with his strong chin and clear eyes. He appeared to rule with ease, but the gray beneath his crown spoke the true burden of his leadership.

Catching sight of them, their father strode forward, his eyes alight. "Ah, my sons. I hear you both did very well upon the tournament field."

Smiling, Haaken embraced him. "Aye, Father. We did indeed."

Gage walked into a hug, flinching when his bruises were encountered. His father stepped back, eyebrows lifting. "An acclaim won at a heavy price, it would seem. One your mother will no doubt be glad she missed."

"I was not unhorsed," Gage said. "Therefore, the price was worth paying."

His father laughed.

James, who had paused to speak with his steward, approached. "King Axel, my marshal will see to the loading of your supplies. And had I not other responsibilities to attend to, I would accompany you to the gates of Nardell. As it is, I beg your pardon and bid you a safe journey."

"Thank you for your aid."

James bowed and strode away.

Their father looked back to them and sighed. "How I wish I could stay and celebrate such an occasion with my sons. Alas, responsibility in Ivenyhan robs me of yet another night of memories."

"Let it rob me as well then, Father," Haaken said, "that I might keep you company upon the road."

Gage opened his mouth to either protest or offer to go as well, but his father spoke before he could. "Nay, stay and enjoy it. Then you both can share with me your memories of the night."

With the joust still undecided, Gage wasn't sure if he'd want to remember the night, but he forced a smile and nodded anyway.

༄

AFTER SEEING OFF their father, Haaken returned to the great hall, and Gage headed to climb a nearby tower while riders began filling the bailey. Trailing his right hand on the smooth stone of the spiral stair's central column, Gage considered how the curve was built to give advantage to right-handed swordsmen defending from above. So much in life possessed a prearranged advantage, but when it came to being royalty, that advantage came with its disadvantages as well. Though glad to be a prince and thankful his father bore well the responsibility of a kingdom, Gage wished often that his father could sometimes lay aside that responsibility.

He stepped from the tower onto the wall-walk of the castle's battlement. Four watchmen stiffened at his presence. When they noted who he was, they relaxed and left him alone to traverse the top of the castle's walls.

More riders entered the bailey below. By their coat-of-arms, Gage recognized two of them as jousters from Roderick's side of the competitors. The third was an archer who had competed against Gage's newest knight, Sir Wick. Upon Gage's request, Sir Wick had joined his retinue at the beginning of the summer. He was the youngest of Gage's knights but had a discipline and maturity that made him seem much older. Allard had likened Sir Wick to the knight's own arrows—dark on top, long in body, straight in personality, and accurate in battle. A fitting description for the lanky yet quietly confident knight.

"It's disgraceful if you ask me," Gage heard one of the jousters from Roderick's camp comment to the other. "Truly, what means other than a joust could possibly be fitting to determine the ultimate victor?"

"I agree, but what choice was left? He withdrew, and Roderick was flat on his back."

His face flushing, Gage pulled back from the edge of the walk and turned to lean into a low crenel section of the battlement. He watched riders travel from the tournament field toward the city and considered the joust once more. It wasn't the jouster's words about its end that ate at him. It was his own indecision during the joust that churned his thoughts. His mind working on this, he wandered along the wall-walk for sometime, embracing the cooler air and quiet of the autumn night.

"No wonder I could not find you." Haaken strode toward him. "I expected you to be in the midst of your fellow jousters or in the company of the barons and baronesses, charming them with your pleasing smile and engaging manner."

Gage glanced at the city below. "Not this night."

"Something amiss?" Haaken's voice held a frown.

"'Tis nothing."

Haaken folded his arms and leaned a shoulder against the merlon section of the battlement. "I am not going anywhere until you talk to me."

Appreciative but not wanting to admit it, Gage gave him a sidelong glance. "And if I refuse to answer? Would you not then have to live here?"

"You are aware, are you not, that I am the Crown Prince of Edelmar?"

Gage grinned. "Nay, only that you are my brother, whom I shall treat with the same regard as I always have."

Chuckling, Haaken eyed him. "Very well, little brother, then prithee tell me, why are you here when you have won such a victory?"

"Victory? What victory?"

"You were one tilt away from being named ultimate victor of yet another tournament."

"Aye," Gage said, "a tilt where I couched because I believed Roderick knew better than I did. Then I withdrew because I was sure he was wrong, after which I was presented with the perspective that Roderick was in fact honorable to joust the last tilt. And now James will decide by what means we are to resolve the last tilt's errors. So, nay, I do not feel like a victor."

"You jousted with honor and risked your gold to save a soul." Frustration laced Haaken's words. "There is no error in that."

A young voice interrupted from behind them. "Your Highnesses?"

Haaken sighed but turned and answered kindly. "Aye, what is it?"

The page bowed. "I was sent to inquire of His Highness, Prince Gage, on behalf of Allard, son of Baron Roger of Ulbin. The feast is to commence presently, and he seeks his instructions for the night."

Amused by Allard's use of a title, Gage figured he could at least see to it that Allard enjoyed the feast. "Inform him I am in no need of his services and that he is released to sit where he pleases."

Bowing again, the page hurried away.

With just the two of them present once more, Haaken turned back to him. "Gage, know this. You may have hesitated at the start of the tilt, but you made the right decision when it mattered."

Gage faced the city and fields below. "Mayhap, but most decisions do not offer second chances." He sighed. "And no matter which manor I take, its steward will have more experience than I do." He didn't need to say the rest. He could tell by the lowering of Haaken's gaze and the press of his lips that he understood the issue.

"But . . . during the tilt you responded in a manner unseen upon the list field," Haaken replied. "If that does not exhibit your clear ability to choose well even in moments where you might face the issue of counsel versus deference, I scarce know what would."

His eyes drifting to the darkening horizon, Gage absorbed Haaken's words as his brother continued. "If I were to venture a guess though, I do not think your judgment is what has you questioning yourself. Rather, I believe it's your own leadership in the making that intimidates you."

Gage met Haaken's gaze, fear wrapping its hand around his chest. "Haaken, what if the person everyone thinks I am is but a mask that will not survive leading?"

"Who you are is no mask," Haaken said.

"How are you so certain?"

Grinning, Haaken pinched Gage's cheek. "Perchance because it does not come off."

"Oh, indeed!" Swatting away Haaken's fingers, Gage took a swing at him. Haaken ducked. They launched into a full tussle, both laughing.

After a few good jabs and the chuckled groans of encountered bruises, Haaken managed to get behind Gage and encircle his neck and chest. Gage stilled with Haaken's arms wrapped around him. He could feel the quick rhythmic thud of life beating within them both.

Haaken's breath brushed his ear. "Walk into yonder feast with me, little brother. Let me prove who you are. For I have no doubt you will do well as lord of a manor and far more."

Swallowing a press of gratitude, Gage nodded.

5

Upon descending to the courtyard, they were met immediately by Gage's knight, Sir Brent, and two of Haaken's eight knights, Sir Renner and Sir Holbird.

"This way." Sir Renner led them across the bailey, which Gage realized no longer bustled with the arrival of gentry and nobles. He had delayed longer than he'd thought.

Sir Renner lit a lantern and passed through a door beyond the castle's keep. Inside, their knights took them along one passage into another, past several servants, and up a short flight of stairs into a quiet chamber. Sir Renner pulled aside a tapestry on the chamber's wall and ushered them down the narrow tunnel concealed behind it.

Going first, Sir Brent turned sideways to fit. Gage and Haaken followed in like manner and found themselves emerging from behind another tapestry into the alcove in the great hall where the acrobats had been earlier.

Drapes had been lowered across the alcove's entrance, and Sir Renner slipped through them into the resounding revelry of the great hall.

Waiting in the shadows, Gage exhaled and lifted his chin in preparation for their formal announcement. Trumpet blasts reverberated in the great hall.

Silence descended. Sir Brent and Sir Holbird stepped forward and pulled aside the alcove's curtains. Somewhere a herald proclaimed, "The princes of Edelmar."

Smoothing his expression into an agreeable smile, Gage strode with Haaken across the alcove's threshold and into the great hall.

All within stood. Metal and gems glinted across the mass of colors and attire in all varieties from satin to leather, elegant dresses to simple tunics, pale to painted faces, and snoods to extravagant headpieces.

Regardless of their differences, nobles, knights, entertainers, and servants alike all bowed, and then Gage and Haaken turned ceremoniously to face the dais. Baron James, with his wife beside him, motioned them to their places of honor at the high table.

Haaken stepped to his chair beside James, and Gage moved past to his place on Haaken's right beside Elmon, the Baron of Awnquera, and their mother's brother.

The trumpets blew once more, and everyone was seated. Servants approached the high table with basins and ewers in hand. The youth who extended a basin to Gage stuck out from his tunic like an orchard sapling. Gage lifted his hands over the bowl. Despite his gangly arms, the youth poured the full ewer without a tremble. Cool water flowed over Gage's skin. He scrubbed his hands and patted them dry on the towel draped over the youth's arm. "Thank you," he said in the commoner's tongue.

The boy's eyes jerked up, and for a moment they stared at one another.

"Noah!" an older servant snapped.

The lad's eyes flicked back down, and he turned to offer water to Elmon. Curious, Gage watched the boy. His footing was careful, his balance precise, and he maneuvered the dais with ease.

Turning, Gage leaned in to speak to James in the nobleman's tongue. "Who is the lad?" He gestured with his chin toward Noah.

James glanced at the youth. "Just a servant," he replied indifferently.

James's wife, a young, soft-spoken, but intensely intelligent woman, leaned toward Gage. "He is the son of our cook. A good lad, the only boy out of five children."

"Has he received any training with the sword?" Gage asked.

At mention of the sword, Haaken considered the youth. "Aye, he looks as if he would do well with one."

James picked up his wine glass. "Mayhap, but he will not be trained for it." He tipped the chalice and, finding it empty, set it down with more force than necessary.

Lady Anna leaned forward once more. "He is—"

"He is a servant," James said with sharp finality. "And a servant he will stay."

Lady Anna closed her mouth and reached for her cup, only to withdraw her hand, likely remembering her chalice had not yet been filled either.

Growling, James thrust his chair backward and shoved the tablecloth off his knees. "Enough of this waiting." He stood.

All within the great hall stilled.

James turned to the Bishop of Nardell, seated just beyond Anna. "Grace?"

For a moment the bishop stared at James, but then it seemed to abruptly dawn on him that he was being asked to bless the meal, not being asked to offer some sort of clemency for James's rudeness. In his flowing robes, the bishop quickly stood and spread his arms to embrace the hall. "Let us thank our Heavenly God."

As everyone closed their eyes, it suddenly occurred to Gage why James was irritated. Tarrying in entering the great hall had forced all within to await his and Haaken's presence. Had they been mere lords, James would likely have begun the feast without them, but instead all had been delayed on their behalf.

Heat rose up Gage's neck and filled his face. He had been the rude one, and worse, he had dragged Haaken into the same blame. He dug his fingernails into his palms. Why had he not thought of the ramifications of delaying his arrival? And why had he opened his mouth to question James about Noah, acting as if he cared to consider one servant when he had, in fact, left the entire hall waiting on him? How James must ridicule him.

Hot all over and his stomach churning, Gage tried not to squirm in his chair. Suddenly, he realized the bishop had finished praying. Gage opened his eyes, fighting to curtail his self-loathing.

A quiet chatter resumed in the hall, and in the minstrel's gallery the strumming of a lute was joined by a harp in a lively melody.

Attempting to focus on the craftsmanship of the elaborate silver saltcellar at the center of the high table, Gage avoided eye contact with those above the salt and below it. He wished he could force the thundering assault inside his chest to cease, for it made him feel that much more conspicuous.

The pantler came, placing upon the high table overflowing baskets of bread accompanied by hand-high castles formed of butter. Then the butler and his assistants filled their goblets. Conversation throughout the hall resumed with full force. The distraction and noise gave Gage some relief.

Haaken thanked each person who served him, but Gage no longer had the will to look any in the eye, let alone address them.

More servants arrived with platters heaped with cheeses, boar meat, fish, and roasted pheasants displayed around cooked and stuffed peacocks. Thankfully, the blue-green peacock fans blocked the view of large portions of the lower tables, which were now laden with their own platters of food.

Gage ate, only half tasting the seasoned meats and flavored cheeses. Beside him Elmon was busy discussing drainage and mill issues with Baron Roger, whose manor was near Elmon's beside the Apse River, which formed much of the border between them and the kingdom of Delkara. Gage found himself absorbing pieces of the two baron's conversation along with snatches from Haaken's, who conversed with James about the harvest, the state of the nearby manors, and the coming winter.

Cups were refilled, and food continued to arrive in an endless stream of soups, meats, pies, custards, fruit tarts, and puddings. Meanwhile, the noise in the great hall grew tumultuous.

"I heard King Axel rode to Ivenyhan to solve a dispute," Elmon said loudly to Gage.

Gage snagged a piece of meat with his knife and nodded. "He has indeed."

Elmon sipped from his goblet, then cradled the cup in his hands. "Your father once told me he sees conflict not as a misfortune but as a possibility to build goodwill." Elmon settled his cup and arm on the table and leaned toward Gage. Gage smiled, knowing he was in for a story.

"Years ago," Elmon said, "when we were in drought, my manor's swine waded the Apse River and crossed into Delkara. I sent men to retrieve them, but the Delkaran Baron Lucas claimed rights to my herd, which was found foraging within his demesne."

Elmon paused to pick out a tart from a nearby platter. "I sought an audience with Lucas, but he refused to see me. So, I took the matter to your father. King Axel rode to King Maurice and then to Baron Lucas, saying to speak face to face was best. After meeting with your father, Baron Lucas gave me an audience." Elmon smiled. "Not only did I receive back my herd, I gained a good friend in Baron Lucas. All thanks to your father." Elmon bit into the tart and closed his eyes in contented pleasure.

"Father has always taught us that it is best, if we can, to use words and wit over swords and fists," Gage said.

Chuckling, Haaken leaned in and completed their father's saying. "For one wins you friends, whereas the other will almost assuredly gain you enemies."

Elmon's gaze lost its pleasure. "Aye, but some choose animosity regardless."

Haaken's expression turned sympathetic. "You mourn the loss of someone?"

"Aye, Lucas's eldest son, Hewitt. I've known him since his youth, but when Lucas died of fever a year after King Maurice, Hewitt became so different. Last we spoke, he treated me with such disrespect that I would scarce have known him."

"Loss touches all differently," Haaken said. "Mayhap the son will yet find his way."

Listening to Haaken, Gage wondered if he would ever have the wisdom and compassion of his brother or his father.

6

Gage sipped from his goblet. Elmon nodded to the hall and reflected further. "You know, years ago, a fourth of those present at an Edelmarian tournament would have been Delkaran knights and lords. Even King Maurice himself used to attend." Elmon frowned. "But after losing his second-born son, King Maurice ceased coming, and slowly more and more of the barons of Delkara also declined our invitations. With them Keric disappeared on the other side of the mountains, and now 'tis unusual to find anyone but Edelmarians at a feast or tournament in Edelmar."

"I remember King Maurice at tournaments in Edelmar," Haaken said. "And the last tournament we were at in Delkara, outside of Ithera. That was a year before the shipwreck."

"Aye, the shipwreck." Elmon sighed. "Much pain has befallen the royal house of Delkara. What with their fourth child dying at birth like your little sister, their second-born son being lost at sea, and King Maurice himself perishing three years later in a riding accident. 'Tis little wonder the queen mother took ill with grief."

Haaken shook his head. "I know not how I would manage as heir to that throne."

Elmon nodded. "Strephon's rule has no doubt been a difficult one. Many said he was not ready to take the crown, but little choice was left."

"Thayer was just twelve, was he not, when he perished at sea?" Gage asked.

"Aye, he along with forty-eight other souls," Elmon said. "Only two crew members and King Maurice were saved from the ship's wreckage. 'Twas a tragic day. All three kingdoms mourned Delkara's loss, and King Maurice was never the same."

"I remember meeting Thayer," Gage said. He could still picture the scrawny prince with freckled cheeks, thick straw-colored hair, and an even thicker will. "We didn't like each other much. Though I supposed that was because neither of us had ever spent time with anyone our own age who we could not order about."

Elmon chuckled. "Aye, 'tis nothing like putting two princes together and watching them try to figure out who has the right to make the decisions."

Haaken glanced at Gage. "Good thing that has always been very clear between us."

"Oh, indeed?" Gage said.

Elmon laughed. "Here I thought you two never fought."

"Only when absolutely necessary," Haaken replied with mock seriousness.

Elmon raised his eyebrows. "Like when hunting boar I suppose?"

Gage pointed at Haaken. "He was going the wrong way."

"Not if we ever wanted to see the boar again," Haaken said.

Gage held up his hand. "I still hold if we had gone my way, we could have cut it off before the ridge."

Elmon laughed.

A quarter of an hour later, they were in the midst of discussing a hunt being hosted in a fortnight by Baron Anthony of Blakely when James stood up and motioned to the trumpeters. They lifted their long brass instruments and blew with gusto.

The illustrious timbre brought the great hall to an instant hush, followed by a quiet shuffle as all within faced the dais. Realizing what was likely coming, Gage felt the pounding in his chest return full force.

"As you are all aware," James said in the nobleman's tongue, "a victor to the tournament's joust must yet be established."

A cheer rose from the hall. James silenced it with his hands. "More so, no one has yet been named Queen of Love and Beauty. 'Tis my hope, as I am sure it is all of yours, that such can now be named. Though the victor could not be decided in the typical manner, I trust the victor here presented shall be acceptable and shall by no means diminish the honor of the joust."

The implication of James's words was clear. A decision had already been made. Gage lowered his eyes to the gnawed bones on his plate and felt his body trap his breath within him as James continued.

"A means could have been chosen to decide the victor, but upon speaking with Baron Roderick, I judged this unnecessary." James gestured. "Baron Roderick, prithee rise and come forward."

Indignant, Gage's eyes snapped to the crowded hall. He swallowed, fighting the desire to leap up and protest or else leave while he still had some dignity left.

A green hat with white feathers upon a head of graying-brown hair rose out of the masses. Gage instantly recognized Baron Roderick's narrow face. Clothed in a jade tunic, Roderick disentangled himself from the board and bench and strode toward the dais.

"Your Highness, if you grant it, Baron Roderick wishes to address you," James said.

Avoiding Haaken's gaze, for Gage could not have handled sympathy at that moment, he forced himself to his feet. Holding his posture rigid and his expression controlled, he swung his eyes to Baron Roderick. Heart pounding, he was relieved to find no expression of triumph parading across Roderick's face. Gage nodded. "I grant permission."

"Your Highness," Roderick said, his voice taut yet genuine, "you know my reputation. And in the last year you have earned your own, so mayhap you can understand why, upon being told you withdrew your lance mid-tilt, I expressed disbelief. For this I owe you my deepest apology." He bowed and stayed bent.

Flabbergasted, Gage opened his mouth. The whole hall waited. Unable to breathe, Gage was not sure how he managed, but somehow he spoke. "I accept your apology."

Roderick calmly squared his shoulders and addressed the crowd with a decisive strength that rebounded about the hall. "Baron James and I agree. No further challenge is needed to establish who rode from yonder field the ultimate victor."

Roderick lifted his right hand to show his linen-wrapped fingers and wrist. "It is obvious I could no sooner make a strike against you now than I could with a lance at the last tilt. Thus, in war, though not dead, I would at the very least be your captive. Hence, Your Highness, you are most certainly and irrefutably the ultimate victor."

Gage stood in stunned silence.

"Having conceded your victory," Roderick said, lowering his voice, "I would yet beg of you one request. Grant me the honor of naming the Queen of Love and Beauty."

Such a petition could have been seen as offensive, but with Roderick having just acknowledged his own defeat before the entire hall, the request could not in the least have been considered pompous.

It was also a relief, for Gage had not yet decided who to name. He nodded to the baron. "I do most willingly grant your request."

Roderick's eyes met his with respect. Then the baron turned to address the hall. "I name Lady Leland Queen of Love and Beauty."

Roderick's wife, Audrey, the Lady Leland, rose from the board. Taking hold of her dark maroon skirts, she made her way past the other guests, who shifted against the board. She looked like a practical woman in a simple, modest gown with a white wimple tucked about her round face. A thin gold cross necklace and a signet ring were the only adornment to her compressed frame, but a smile played at the corners of her lips. Placing her hand upon Baron Roderick's, she ascended the steps of the dais.

A castle maidservant handed a garland of lavender flowers to Roderick, who ceremoniously placed the crown upon Lady Leland's wimple. Then Baron James circled the table and, bowing, handed her a cloth-wrapped item.

Following James, Gage stopped before Lady Audrey. His insides pounded anew but this time with a surging force that made him feel broader and taller.

Lady Leland's eyes laughed at him as she unfolded the fabric to reveal a thick circle of engraved gold garnished by four blood-red rubies and divided in two by a clasp and sharpened pin. Lady Leland lifted the brooch. "To the champion and ultimate victor of the joust," she called out with gaiety, "I hereby give this prize." She pierced the fabric of Gage's tunic and pinned the brooch firmly in place upon his shoulder.

Light-headed and smiling, Gage turned to face the hall. Those within rose in waves until everyone was standing and expressing hearty exultation.

One man stood with the rest but did not cheer. Instead he took a last drink from his flagon, retrieved his knife from the table, stepped out from between the two knights from whom he had gleaned exactly the information he needed, and drifted through the tables.

Blending into the shadows by the wall, the Crow turned to once more eye the young prince of Edelmar who boldly stood at the front of the hall, basking in the praise of his victory. "Glory now, Prince," he muttered, "for you will not keep that smile long."

7

Gage returned to his seat, and James signaled to twelve acrobats, who leapt, juggled, and rolled their way into the hall. After their mesmerizing display, two more sets of entertainers came and went, and evening wore into night.

Eventually, the trestle tables were cleared and removed, and dancing began. Gage rose from the high table planning to join those below but noticed Haaken watching the dance with a regretful expression. No woman alive in Edelmar dared seize the arm of the crown prince of Edelmar and drag him into a dance, but Novia would have. She would have picked the biggest of the circles to haul Haaken into, and despite his objections, Haaken would have loved every moment of it.

She had been audacious and startling but also kind and patient. She'd been like a sister to Gage even before it had become clear she and Haaken were destined to be married. But some destinies weren't meant to be. He pictured Novia, a daisy chain in her hair, spinning in her new dress and laughing. A daisy chain that had fallen from her head later that same day and floated away as Haaken scooped her cold body out of Gage's numb grasp.

He hadn't thought he could work his way to shore without losing his grip on her or the branch and being pulled under by the river's current, but ever since that day, Gage wished he had tried. Maybe if he had gotten her out of the water sooner she'd have lived.

"Gage." Haaken's voice startled him back to the present. "What are you waiting for? This is your night to glory. Go enjoy it."

"What of you?" Gage asked quietly. "Will you enjoy it?"

Haaken swallowed before answering. "I am fine. Truly."

Gage forced a smile. "Well, in case you are in need of a diversion, mayhap something like an engrossing conversation that would allow you to avoid the dance? I have knowledge of where such can be found. A rare accomplishment I know, but I've picked up a trick or two."

Haaken eyed him in suspicious amusement. "Have you now?"

Gage leaned close to stoke a conspiratorial feel. "Aye. All you need do is speak boldly about the advantage of some method of a disputed nature within the hearing of Baron Ogden, and he will debate you strenuously till sunrise. Or you can tell my knight, Sir Hayson, you wish to know how the trebuchet could be improved. You need only nod to keep him going for hours. Or last, but no less effective, you can inform Lord Gerrard you are considering commissioning a new suit of armor and wish to know the best smiths and metals to use. He will no doubt tell you all about his own armor, for it was the journeyman smith's masterpiece." Gage grinned. "Should keep you occupied for at least the rest of the night."

"A trick or two indeed." Haaken shook his head, but his smile reached his eyes.

"Shall I find one of them for you?" Gage took a step away.

Haaken grabbed his arm. "Nay!"

Gage chuckled, and Haaken gave him a brotherly shove. "You leave me to my own diversions, little brother, or I'll tell Lord Gerrard *you're* the one interested in armor."

"Verily." Gage quickly mingled into the mass of guests. People congratulated him wherever he went, and he accepted their praise with thanks while he conversed his way across the hall.

A lofty promenade came to an end, and the dance music changed to a swifter melody. The growing throng of dancers responded with laughter to the song's quicker rhythm. Gage spotted Allard within the third circle. He was dressed in one of Gage's plainer tunics.

Gage smiled. Skipping beside Allard was spunky Emma, her hand clasped firmly in Allard's. Wisps of her honey-colored hair had come free from the confines of her golden hairnet, and her rosy, youthful face made a pretty contrast to her blue dress.

On the other side of the dancers, Baron James paused to speak to Haaken's knight, Sir Holbird. Despite the distance, Gage could tell Sir Holbird was highly displeased by whatever James was saying. Curious, Gage headed that direction but crossed paths with Baroness Agnes, Baron Roger's wife.

"Your Highness, you are not dancing?" She motioned toward the intricate pattern of twisting skirts and perfectly timed steps. "Have not any of the young ladies present caught your eye?"

Gage laughed. "Nay, not yet, but I promise I shall dance before the night is out."

Shaking her head, Lady Agnes clicked her tongue and glanced about. "Ah. There she is." Her waving hand drew over a beautiful, willowy girl in a shimmering silver dress. Gage had seen the girl in passing, for her father was Baron of Veiroot, but he had not been formally introduced to her in years.

White crystals in a dangling V graced the young woman's slender neck and matched a smaller line of crystals draped across her forehead between two silver-netted buns of sleek brown hair.

Looking pleased with herself, Lady Agnes glanced between them. "Prince Gage, prithee allow me to present to you Lady Natriece, youngest daughter of Lord Gregory. Lady Natriece, His Highness, Prince Gage." The girl dipped her head and curtsied.

Agnes sent a knowing look in Gage's direction. "Lady Natriece attends as companion to Lord Gerrard's daughter, Lady Jolene." No doubt the girl's connections to the father and sister of his knight, Sir Brent, were meant to be recommendations on her behalf. The girl raised her head.

The music of the last dance finished, and knowing the only way to free himself from Agnes's motherly focus was to dance with the girl, Gage politely offered his hand. "Lady Natriece, would you oblige me with a dance?"

The young woman's gray-green eyes flicked about the room, then back to him. Her smile tightened, and she placed her hand on his.

Gage led Natriece to the fourth circle of dancers where a space was instantly made for them. The musicians started a new tune, the melody played on a recorder.

Natriece glided into the dance with flawless poise, but she maintained such closed civility that her companionship felt like a winter's chill compared to the warmth of his status as tournament victor.

Taking her hand for a turn, Gage tried to convey his amiability by conversing with her. "What do you think of the countryside here about?"

She replied without looking at him, "I prefer Veiroot."

"Aye, I suppose the height and view of the mountains is a far cry from the foothills. It is a fair trek to Veiroot. Do you enjoy traveling?"

"Nay."

Gage optimistically tried another question. "How did you find the tournament?"

"Only tolerable."

At this, Gage quit trying to start a conversation and simply performed the dance he had practiced since childhood. When the last long note came, he breathed a silent sigh and escorted Natriece to the hall's large hearth. He left her before it, cynically wondering if its heat might thaw her disposition.

Baron James was no longer anywhere in sight. Sir Holbird was speaking instead with Lord Samuel, who had the same displeased look as the knight. Their expressions bore a sharp contrast to Lady Cathleen, Sir Holbird's younger sister, who stood four paces from the two, utterly absorbed in smiling at someone across the hall. Gage followed her gaze and found, to his amusement, his knight, Sir Reid, loitering at the end of it. Sir Reid's reddish-blond hair and mustache were neatly combed, and his lips held a playful grin.

"I'll keep a ready eye," Lord Samuel said to Sir Holbird.

"Prithee, have your men do so as well," the knight replied.

"An eye for what?" Gage asked as Lord Samuel moved away

"There is report of a wanted thief here at the feast," Sir Holbird said quietly.

"How is it a thief who is 'wanted' has been spotted yet not detained?" Gage asked.

"Truly, over the last nine months more than one lord has attempted to lay hands on him," Sir Holbird replied calmly but with aggravation in his tone. "But the Blue Crow always manages to slip away—as he seems to have done again tonight."

Gage frowned. "The Blue Crow? Why is this the first time I have heard of him?"

Sir Holbird shifted as if to block unwanted ears. "Mayhap because those aware of his thieving are less than forthcoming in their knowledge. He has stolen from a number of lords, and not one of them has succeeded in bringing him to justice. You can thus imagine their desire to not speak of him."

Gage's insides tightened. "How is it *you* know of him?"

"I was with your brother when we happened upon one such lord the day the Blue Crow stole from him. Your brother received the details of the theft. How he so kindly gets answers out of those inclined to speak to no one, I shall never comprehend, but that is how I know."

Gage was relieved it was not because Haaken had been robbed. "What does this thief look like?"

"He often changes his appearance, but there are two things he cannot alter: his blue eyes and a nick in the top of his left ear."

"Then I shall keep an eye out as well," Gage said.

Sir Holbird nodded. Silence stretched between them, and then Sir Holbird pointed with his chin, his tone morphing into amused annoyance. "Prithee, can you not do something about that one and solve at least one of my problems? He has been standing there for the last four dances."

It took Gage a moment to realize Sir Holbird was referring to Sir Reid, who tarried still at the end of Lady Cathleen's gaze. Gage mirrored Sir Holbird's frown. "Do you think he will remain so all eve?"

"Who knows? I tell you, I'm half inclined, even if he does ask to dance with her, to deny him permission upon inconvenience alone. And truly, if he makes me stand here another dance feigning ignorance of him, perchance I *will* deny him."

Gage chuckled. "I believe I can motivate him."

Sir Holbird gave him a hopeful look. "Prithee, for if he does not ask to dance with her, I shall never hear the end of it from Cathleen."

Forcing the smile from his face, Gage raised his voice to be heard by all nearby. "Sir Holbird, I see Lady Cathleen is unattended. May I seek her company for the next dance?"

Sir Holbird gave him a questioning look but answered in kind. "Aye, you may."

"Lady Cathleen?" Gage held out his hand.

Cathleen broke her gaze from Sir Reid. Apparently just realizing Gage had asked to dance with her, she opened her mouth but then closed it. She curtsied and laid her hand on Gage's even as her eyes offered an apologetic frown over his shoulder.

Turning, Gage caught Sir Reid's gaze. The knight's stifled annoyance made Gage bite back a smile. He swept Lady Cathleen into the next dance. He could tell where Sir Reid was at all times for Lady Cathleen's eyes continually wavered in that direction. In her distraction, she consistently missed dance steps.

Gage took pity on her. "My lady, I promise you, I shall place you squarely in his arms at the start of the next dance."

Missing yet another step, Cathleen looked him full in the face. Lips tight and gaze narrowed, she shook her head. "You are trying to make him jealous."

Before Gage could answer, the tempo changed. Leaving her side, he made the proper turn and noted that Sir Reid looked ready to charge the dance floor.

Gage glided back to Cathleen. "Nay, I confess, my goal was a bit more complicated than jealousy. Though it does seem to be succeeding." He released her hand, so she could spin, and he felt the corners of his mouth rise.

Cathleen spun back to him, her cheeks pink. "No doubt my brother had a hand in this."

"Mayhap, but would you rather go reprimand him or dance with my knight?" He chuckled at the look she gave him. "As I suspected. Then just smile, and thank me."

Her chin lifted, and her lips twisted. "Thank you."

"You are welcome." Taking her hand, he glided her forward and on the song's last note deposited her in front of Sir Reid.

Sir Reid's expression went from smoldering to questioning. "Do I not first need Sir Holbird's permission to dance with her?"

"Aye, and this is it!" Gage growled, incredulous. "Now dance with her 'ere someone without so generous a soul comes along and takes her from you."

The knight thrust out his hand. "My lady."

Cathleen giggled and grasped his fingers, and the two of them hurried into the next dance. Exchanging nods of success with Sir Holbird, Gage joined the same dance circle with Lady Elizabeth, Emma's older sister.

Seven dances and four partners later, Gage waved on Allard and Sir Reid and headed to the high table to find something to quench his thirst. As he drank from his goblet, he realized he hadn't seen Haaken since their conversation at the table. Leaving the dais, he searched the hall.

He found Haaken within a knot of lords gathered just inside the great hall's doors. Gage joined them. They seemed to be in the midst of a heated discussion. "He is long gone from here," Baron Ogden said, "but that does not mean he has left completely."

"Will he try to leave Nardell, do you think?" Lord Samuel asked.

"'Tis a perfect night for it," Baron Ogden commented. "The gates are wide open."

"I already sent men to guard every gate," Baron James said. "If he tries to slip through, he will be caught."

Haaken's input lacked the anger coming from the rest but contained equal force. "More likely he will stay hidden in the city and leave on the morrow, unless he already has a target chosen for tonight."

"It would be his style," Baron Roderick muttered. Despite his bandaged hand, he looked ready to take up a sword.

"Then we send men to the tournament settlements," Haaken said to James. "If he is to strike, it will likely be there."

Baron Ogden nodded. "Aye, and each of us would be wise to send extra knights to keep an eye on our own pavilions."

Haaken nodded. "The more the better."

Ogden muttered a comment, and the assembly separated.

Gage frowned at Haaken. "Not exactly the diversion I recommended for the night."

Haaken sighed. "Nor one I would have chosen, but it's worth the focus. The Blue Crow is shrewd, ruthless, and, unfortunately, quite successful. He almost always gets what he goes after, including turning servants against their masters or removing them if they get in his way."

Fear spread through Gage. "As victor, my pavilion is full of spoils, and the men I left to guard it are few in number. I would send back my retinue and go myself as soon as possible to bolster their number."

"At this hour 'tis doubtful any would make complaint of us departing," Haaken said.

Gage nodded. "Then let us make haste."

8

Leaving the streets of Nardell behind, Gage and Haaken galloped their horses across the plain with their retinues and five other knights, two of whom served Baron Roderick. Air whistled past Gage's ears and snapped Kipper's mane about his fingers.

Ahead, both settlements were alive with fire and torchlight, but large dark gaps left portions of both camps ripe for the taking. Roderick's knights divided from their company and headed for the western settlement. Gage focused his attention on the eastern settlement.

Where earlier it had been occupied by an armed force, now it looked and sounded like an outdoor tavern. Ahead of them, Sir Brent slowed his mount to safely navigate the ruckus.

Gage reined in Kipper and felt Haaken's knee bump his as they swung around a party of servants too drunk to realize the riders were the princes of Edelmar. The servants clanked their tankards, dancing and singing to ragtag music.

Gage scrutinize them as they passed and searched the shadows while veering between pavilions. Their company came out in a wider lane and faced four horsemen.

He and Sir Brent laid their hands to their weapons, but then Gage noted the riders' formation and coat-of-arms—a maroon shield with laurel leaves surrounding a fortress. They were Baron

James's men-at-arms fully armored and already on patrol in the settlement. Gage exhaled and released his dagger. His respect for James rose a notch. Still, he was eager to reach his pavilion.

He heard the hearty snoring of old Tobin within his servants' tent before he saw Sir Hayson at his pavilion's door. Beneath a sputtering oil lamp, the knight stood chatting with Emerett, Gage's cook. Gage smiled.

Of his knights, Allard had labeled Sir Hayson as the battle-ax. Short, hefty, but thoroughly effective when in use, the blond-haired and bearded Sir Hayson was most often found deriving or discussing some better method for using this or that tool or contraption, but if aroused he could be startlingly forceful in his defense of anyone or anything to which he claimed loyalty.

Relieved to find Sir Hayson and Emerett peacefully conversing and unharmed, Gage dismounted with his retinue and nodded for Haaken to ride on.

"Has something happened?" Sir Hayson asked, running his fingers through his beard. "There are patrols through the settlement, and now—"

Not pausing to explain until he was certain the Blue Crow hadn't been there, Gage pushed aside the door to his pavilion and stepped inside.

At his sudden entrance, he startled two of his servants—quiet, heavyset Bardon, who was tallying the day's winnings, and lithe Badger, who snapped up off the floor with a raised hammer in hand.

Badger jerked to a stop. Lowering the hammer he'd been using to repair a trunk hinge, he bowed. "Your Highness, forgive me, we didn't expect—"

Drawing a breath, Gage lifted his hand. "It's all right, Badger. Your reaction does you credit, not harm."

He glanced at the pile of small chests stacked beside Bardon. Gage unlatched the top one and flipped back its lid. Gold coins glinted up at him. For this tournament, each competitor had only been allowed to enter if he had either coin enough to pay his own possible ransom or horse and armor he was willing to part with. Each round, the jouster who lost paid ransom to the jouster who beat him. This guaranteed all jousters were of means, and each would gain a profit if they won two rounds or more. Having been victorious in every round, Gage had gained much and lost nothing—at least so far.

Bardon nodded to the coins. "That chest was delivered by one of Baron Roderick's knights just after you left for the feast." Gage closed and latched it.

"Your Highness, is all well?" Sir Hayson asked in the nobleman's tongue from behind Gage.

"Aye, all is well here, but it may not be elsewhere." Strapping on his sword, Gage opened the trunk that held his additional weaponry. "There is a thief possibly in the settlement," he said in the commoner's tongue.

"There's always a thief or two at a tournament," Bardon replied.

"Pickpockets, yes, but this particular thief has robbed a number of noblemen, including Baron Roderick and Baron Ogden."

At Gage's words, a shocked silence spread through his men. Long ago any thievery in the three kingdoms had been punishable by the loss of a hand. The current laws were not nearly as harsh, but theft still bore heavy consequences. Stealing food was considered a crime of need, and therefore the punishment was restricted to the thief having to work for the person he stole from for twice as many days as the food would have cost. If, however, what was stolen was goods or coin, the thief was required to make restitution triple that which was taken. If the thief could not pay this, the thief was branded on the wrist and made a slave to the person he had stolen from until his labor had fully paid the restitution. It was an effective punishment, but it only worked if the thief was caught and convicted by the testimony of at least two witnesses.

As it was, convicting the Blue Crow wouldn't be a problem, but until he was caught, it wouldn't matter how many testimonies there were or how much restitution the Blue Crow owed.

Gage stuffed a sheathed dagger into his boot, then tossed a short sword to Badger, who caught it. Gage handed a cudgel to Bardon and motioned to the chests of coins. "I want all of these cases packed into one of my larger trunks and it locked. Hide the key until I return." He left carrying a handful of additional weapons for the rest of his servants and a hunting horn for himself.

⚬⚭⚬

After confirming Haaken's pavilion was as quiet as his own, Gage rode the settlement with Sir Wick at his side. The knight's posture was relaxed, but he had bound back his dark hair and secured his bow and arrows close at hand. Gage kept his own hand on his sword's hilt, but they came across nothing more concerning in camp than the normal riffraff.

They passed Baron James's men-at-arms several times and stopped to check in with Baron Roderick and Lord Samuel. Both men reported nothing missing and no sign of the Blue Crow.

Upon completing their fourth circuit, Sir Wick's steady voice broke the silence. "Mayhap he does not plan to strike tonight."

Gage watched a servant ahead attempt a jig, only to fall backwards into the laps of his companions, who burst out laughing. "Mayhap not." Still, Gage looked at the next dark pavilion and wondered.

He relaxed only once others from the feast began to trickle back into camp. Most returned in groups of two or three, some just as drunk as the servants they had left behind. Gage nodded to Sir Wick. "Let's make our way back."

They did so, and upon returning to his pavilion, Gage noted a figure pacing at the edge of the light in front of Sir Brent and Sir Hayson, who stood guard. Probably in his thirties, the man's long oily hair fell about his angular face and caught in his untrimmed beard. His tunic, which had clearly seen better days, hung loosely about his frame, and he held his right arm against his stomach.

Swinging off Kipper and handing his reins to Mattson, Gage looked at Sir Brent.

"I told him I knew not when you would return," Sir Brent explained in the nobleman's tongue, "but he insisted on tarrying. He has made no trouble but seems anxious to speak with you."

Gage glanced at the man and noted the desperation in his brown eyes. That the man's eyes were not blue removed one concern, but it did not ease Gage's caution. He switched to the commoner's tongue. "Speak."

The man dropped to his knees and gushed words as if his life depended on them. "Please, I seek work for food. I will do whatever I can, just please, take pity upon me and let me return with you to Einhart to find work. For I have looked here, but none will have me." The man bowed his head. "Please."

Gage swallowed. The words "I seek work for food" was a plea often spoken to his parents and never ignored. If someone was starving because they lacked work, King Axel would always help them find a way to serve themselves and others. His parents believed no one should be left without work lest they find not just their stomachs empty but also their lives meaningless. If the person was incapable of physical labor, they'd still be given a task. Even if it was just to sit at the city gates and hearten with words all who passed. However, if a person wanted food but did not desire to work for it, the help offered would take a far different turn.

"What is your name?" Gage asked.

"Felix, son of John Fletcher."

"Felix, John's son, have you no master here in Nardell?"

Felix extended his right arm, and Gage noted his oddly colored, strangely coiled fingers. "I was a tanner's apprentice in Decoro, but when this happened and I could no longer use my hand, my master freed me from service and told me to seek work elsewhere. I have sought other masters, but none will have me. And though I have eaten today because of the tournament, I will starve again tomorrow."

Gage thought of Blind Amelia, who, as a child, had been left on Einhart's streets. He had been six and she seven when they first met. He would never forget seeing her dull eyes, dirty face, and gaunt, grasping hands as she called out shrilly to his parents. "Take pity, please. I'm so hungry."

His mother dismounted and drew the child to her feet. "My dear, you need not pity but love. Come, you shall eat at our table, and tomorrow I will help you find something suitable to occupy your hands, so you can gain your own food and place in this world."

Amelia was now known widely as the best basket weaver in Einhart. Her work was tighter and stronger than anyone else's because she tested her work with her hands rather than her eyes.

"You will not starve, Felix John's son," Gage said. "You may travel with us, but you should know we travel to Ulbin, not Einhart. No doubt you can search for work just as easily there."

"Thank you, Your Highness." Felix's voice held eager hope.

Gage shook his head. "I do you no favors. My men know I travel quickly and rest sparingly. If you wish to come, you must keep up. And you will work for what you eat on the way. We ride before prime."

"I will be here."

9

Gage and his men slept the night in shifts, but no one was seen prowling about, and nothing went missing. Gage embraced the light of dawn with relief but ordered his men to remain armed.

Felix, true to his word, showed up shortly after first light with a worn satchel slung over his shoulder and a stout walking stick in his good hand. Bowing respectfully, he offered to help load the carts.

"Tobin has enough help," Gage said. "See Mattson. He could perhaps use an extra hand preparing the horses."

Felix headed that way, and Gage watched Badger and Wellens carry from his pavilion his dismantled bed frame. Amid three carts used to transport Gage's camp stood old Tobin, wise with age and shriveled as a sun-dried apple. In a worn yet commanding voice, the old man gave instructions on where to place each item in the carts.

Gage's two other cart drivers, Amos and Morley, stood in the carts receiving the furniture and putting them exactly where Tobin directed. Packing went quickly. This, Gage had discovered, was because Tobin never needed to rearrange anything. Once the items had been organized to best utilize the limited space, the old man memorized their locations and packed the same way every time. Leaving his men to their tasks, Gage headed to speak with Haaken.

Haaken's pavilion was a collapsed mass of cloth on the ground when he arrived, and Haaken was already mounted beside two of his knights. "Give Father my greetings when you see him in Ivenyhan," Gage called out to him.

"You know me too well." Haaken smiled. "I would have liked to have shared your companionship as far as Aro," he added apologetically. "Another time mayhap?"

Though he had been looking forward to Haaken's company, Gage nodded. "If nothing else, we shall in a fortnight ride back from the hunt at Blakely together, or else mayhap I will see you before then in Einhart."

"Aye, it has been a while since you were home."

"Indeed, it has." Gage lifted his hand. "Safe journey. I will see you in a fortnight, if not before."

He returned to his own retinue. Flattened grass was all that remained where his pavilion had stood, and old Tobin was doing one last check of the three fully loaded carts, plucking each rope with a gnarled finger. Tugging one rope twice, the old man whistled through his chipped teeth. Wellens launched off the front of the cart and gave the end of the rope a good heave. He motioned for Tobin to test it again.

Gage mounted to the sound of the now taut rope and smiled. "Everything ready?"

Shuffling back to the front of the cart and climbing to his seat, the old man gathered his reins and nodded. "Ready."

Gage looked at the rest of his men. Most of them mounted horses or climbed aboard carts, but three were left walking: Felix, Emerett, and Badger. Their job was to help the carts through tough spots, when necessary.

"We make for Leland," Gage said in the nobleman's tongue. "Keep alert. Stay close, and hope we get there before nightfall." Normally, he didn't mind staying at an inn or even camping in a meadow or village, but this day he was determined to make it within the walls of Leland before nightfall.

◊

Gage discovered he was not the only one with this plan, for they came upon the retinue of Baron Roderick and Lady Audrey shortly after starting along the road. Their two groups merged together amiably and with silent gratefulness, for their combined numbers offered a higher assurance of them being left in peace.

Conversation flowed differently amid their mixed group, but both sides managed well enough. Gage spent the morning talking with Baron Roderick and Lady Audrey and found he quite enjoyed their company.

With solid roads, they made good time and reached a small village by midday. Baron Roderick decided to pause there and spread a meal. Gage would normally have eaten on the move but chose to stop as well in order to maintain their doubled numbers.

Dusk came upon them while they were still shy of Leland, but the glow of the rising moon lit their way into the city.

Unlike Haaken or his father, Gage did not typically seek to stay within a lord's manor, but when Roderick offered him lodging at Leland Manor, he accepted.

He was particularly glad he did when the weather turned foul during the night, drenching the land. Morning came, but the downpour kept on. Lady Audrey insisted they wait for a reprieve. Staying a second night, they rose early the next morning to find the rain had finally ceased. Despite the wet roads and gray skies, they took their leave and continued on their way.

On day two, with long stretches of the muddy road only wide enough for a single cart, Gage rode behind Sir Brent at the front of his retinue with Allard beside him. In the wood's stillness, even Mattson's conversation with Sir Reid at the back of the retinue could be heard. "Yeah, well, I wagered on Dudley in archery."

Wellens, who was driving the second cart, called back. "Bardon, which archer did you wager on for the tournament?"

"Nilson," Bardon replied humbly yet matter-of-factly.

Allard shook his head. "How does Bardon always pick the right person?" he asked in the nobleman's tongue.

Sir Brent laughed. "He pays more attention than the rest of us." He called over his shoulder in the commoner's tongue. "Sir Wick, I'll have you know I wagered on you winning."

"So did I," Badger said. "Thought for sure you'd beat Nilson that last round. You were so close."

"He's a good archer," Sir Wick replied..

"Well, don't tell him that," Sir Reid said.

They all laughed, for Nilson had been overheard boasting drunkenly at the feast that he could have done just as well blindfolded.

☙❧

GAGE LOOKED UP sometime later when Sir Brent steered his horse close. "Do you wish to eat on the move or pause to allow the men rest?" he asked in the nobleman's tongue.

Not yet hungry, Gage glanced at the sky between branches trying to decipher how much of the day had passed. Dull gray stared back at him. He turned to evaluate his men and realized somewhere in the last hour their talking had ceased. Not a good sign. He turned back to Sir Brent. "We will stop to eat."

Sir Brent nodded. "If I remember correctly, there is a good location around yonder bend."

THE SPOT WAS not much more than a few felled trees lying in a rough circle, but Gage figured it was better than standing on the road.

Mattson, Amos, and Morley saw to the horses while Wellens unloaded their sacks of provisions, generously replenished by Lady Audrey. Searching through the packs, Emerett set about choosing their meal.

Hot food was a rarity on the road, but wishing to express his gratitude for his men's efforts, Gage told Emerett that if a fire would be of use to see if Badger could get one going.

Emerett glanced at Badger. "You heard His Highness. Get a fire going."

Glad to see smiles return to his men's faces, Gage went to confer with Sir Brent and old Tobin about the distance and road conditions they had yet to travel.

As they discussed it, Tobin crouched beside his cart and drew with a stick. "We'll pass Morden's stream next where it cuts beside us. The road is higher there and usually firm. Near the meadows is sand." The old man scratched a thick line after that. "Then there's the low road in the woods. I've never known a time when it wasn't wet somewhere near that swamp. After such a rain . . ." Tobin stuck the stick into the spot. "That stretch'll be the worst of it. But if we can get through without too much delay, we should make Aro before night."

Smoke drifted to them with the sound of crackling flames. Gage glanced toward the sound. Badger sat feeding the fire. Everyone else had settled around it. Gage thanked old Tobin and moved to join them.

"Was Roderick's manor what you expected?" Sir Reid asked Gage in the nobleman's tongue when he reached the fire.

Gage frowned at the question. "Nay, not exactly. Why do you ask?"

Sir Reid glanced at Sir Hayson. "See? I am not the only one. I have always pictured Roderick living in some large, cold castle surrounded by grim-faced knights, not in such a peaceful, ordinary sort of manor."

"Aye," Allard said, perched on the log beside Sir Reid. "He seemed vastly different at his own table than the fierce warrior he is upon the list field. He was all ease and hospitality."

Gage laughed. "'Tis that not exactly as a lord should be in his own manor?" He switched to the commoner's tongue. "I may not yet have a manor of my own, but when I do I hope I am as welcoming a host as Lord and Lady Leland. Though as for food, I think Emerett here does a better job than their three cooks combined."

Grinning, Emerett took up a sharpened stick that Wellens had made for him. "Give me a moment to roast it, and you will have hot meat and melted cheese on bread." Emerett nodded to the makings. "The rest of you can help yourselves."

After a few teasing comments, Gage's men settled in to roast their food. Sir Brent and Allard worked carefully to heat every side of their meat and cheese. Sir Hayson chose a bent stick to angle his food just right into the coals, and Sir Reid got distracted and burned his food while telling Morley he should put his cheese on the inside of his meat. Meanwhile, Sir Wick gave Wellens and Badger his spot to cook their food first.

Gage glanced around. "Where's Felix?"

"He went off to relieve himself," Wellens replied.

"When?"

Wellens looked around and frowned. "A while ago."

"He disappeared for several stretches at Roderick's manor as well," Badger said.

"He told me that sometimes he just needs space to get his wits about him," Morley said. "Sounded a bit odd, but he is an odd one. Helpful enough though, I suppose."

Absorbing their words, Gage bit into the soft warmth of meat and melted cheese. If Felix wished to continue with them, he'd show up of his own accord.

They were nearly finished eating when Felix returned. The man crouched at the edge of the fire. Several of Gage's men displayed displeased looks, but Felix seemed not to notice.

Wellens thrust a roasting stick toward the man. Nodding, Felix took it, pinned it between his knees, and used his good hand to skewer cheese and meat onto it.

Gage cleared his throat. "Where have you been?"

Felix's cheeks reddened, and he lowered his gaze. "I, um. I went to ... but then I ... I got turned around." His voice sounded pained. "It took me a bit to find the road again. Forgive me, Your Highness."

Gage better understood his men's dislike for the man. Felix was an irritating mix of boldness and cowardliness. "Next time stay closer."

Head bowed, Felix nodded. "Yes, Your Highness."

Gage exchanged a look with Sir Brent and finished eating.

10

Once again on the move, they passed Morden's stream and entered the meadow and woods. Slippery puddles and waterlogged ruts slowed their progress considerably. With the carts at a crawl behind them, Gage shifted in his saddle. "Do you think it has rained at Ulbin?" he asked in the nobleman's tongue.

"At Ulbin?" Allard echoed him absently.

Gage cleared his throat. "Aye, rain at Ulbin. Allard?"

"Rain?" The squire shook himself and glanced up. "Aye, mayhap it might."

Ahead to Gage's right, Sir Brent chuckled. "One would think by his mind's absence he had been into a strong wine."

"Nay," Sir Reid said, "'Tis no wine that has him intoxicated. Rather, I would wager thoughts of a certain young lady."

Sir Brent twisted in his saddle. "Lady Emma, no doubt." Color flushed Allard's youthful face.

Sir Reid laughed. "He cannot deny it. His complexion has answered for him."

"Why should I deny it?" Allard's sharp response drifted into wistful words. "For how could I not be thinking of her? Her eyes sparkle, and her smile, it is like . . ." His voice trailed off, as if he was unable to think of anything comparable.

Gage watched Sir Reid smirk. Before the knight could tease further, Gage spoke. "I do believe, Allard, you are in good company. For I have no doubt Sir Reid has been preoccupied with his own thoughts of a certain lady."

Sir Reid grinned back. "Sir Brent? Did you not witness our handsome prince captivated by a pretty lass from Veiroot?"

"Oh, no! No." Gage shook his head. "Not captivated, captured, and not by her. I was caught by Lady Agnes, who discovered me unaccompanied and insisted Lady Natriece and I dance together." He grimaced. "I tell you, never have I encountered a dance partner so disinterested in pleasant conversation."

Sir Brent laughed, "Natriece's reserve does indeed seem an ill fit for her exquisite features, though she is reported to improve on closer acquaintance. Or so my sister Jolene claims. If you ask me though, I think her return to her father's house has only increased her reticence. This tournament is the first invitation to accompany Jolene that Natriece has accepted in almost a year. I feel sorry for the girl."

"Well, in that case, next time *you* can dance with her," Gage said. They all chuckled.

Gage turned in his saddle to check the groaning carts and searched for Felix. The man was plodding behind the second cart, his tunic flecked with mud from pushing the cart along. Glad to see the man was staying close and helping, Gage turned back to Sir Brent. "Besides, she isn't—"

Sir Brent frowned. "Did you hear that?"

Reining his mount to a stop, Gage listened. Behind him, Tobin pulled his cart to a standstill, and everyone else did the same. Ahead, through the trees, Gage heard it too—distressed young voices, a dog's sharp barking, and the panicked bleating of sheep.

Gage shifted his reins to his other hand. "Sir Wick and Sir Hayson, stay with the carts. Allard, Sir Brent, Sir Reid, with me." Closing his fingers about the ridged hilt of his sword, he urged Kipper into a gallop

With Sir Brent's horse already ahead, Kipper's speed increased. Gage felt expectation rush through him as they pounded around the bend in the road.

Moments later, he and Sir Brent pulled their mounts to a sliding stop. Allard and Sir Reid did the same. Heaving a breath, Gage released his sword.

In front of them, a young girl and a large dog worked together trying to herd a large cluster of sheep off the road and through a gap in the trees. Meanwhile, farther down the road, two boys were miserably attempting to free almost a dozen sheep from a sloppy mire. The quagmire spanned twice the width of the road and stretched more than a stone's throw down it.

Bleating in panicked persistence, the animals fought to get loose from the muddy trap while the two boys—neither of whom could have been any older than ten—tried desperately to lift a sheep and carry it to dry ground.

The girl's voice rang out in the commoner's tongue. "Wes! Fran! It's a lord on the road." Both boys looked up, their dirty faces flushed.

"He's not a lord," one of the boys said. "Can't you see his coat-of-arms?"

While still trying to keep ahold of the sheep, the other boy offered a clumsy bow. "Your Highness, our apologies. We'll have these sheep out of your way as quickly as we can." He nudged the other boy. "Fran, come on."

Looking at the mess, it was clear to Gage that if left unassisted, the two boys would fall to weariness long before they freed even one sheep. He dropped Kipper's reins and swung to the ground. "Please, allow me and my men to help." The boys exchanged wide-eyed glances.

Sir Brent dismounted beside Gage, who turned to Allard. "Ride back and tell the others they may proceed. We will undoubtedly need Tobin's experience if we are to get the carts through this mess. And we could use the extra help to get these sheep out as well."

Allard did as instructed, and Sir Reid joined Gage and Sir Brent on the ground. Gage viewed the scene, trying to determine an approach to the ensnared animals. Straight in was probably the best option. Unstrapping his sword, he buckled it onto Kipper's saddle and headed for the mud.

He got two sloshing strides in and went to take another step but found his left boot thoroughly stuck in the smelly muck. Extending his arms, he leaned forward and pulled. The mud released him with a gasping sound. Nearly falling forward, he took another hasty step and slid deeper. The muck re-submerged his boot and crept up his leg. Swallowing, Gage focused on the task at hand.

The sheep the two boys had a hold of tried to lunge away. The older of the two boys, Wes, lost his grip on the animal and fell backward with a sloppy smack. Pulling up mud-caked fingers, the boy attempted to struggle back upright but only sank deeper.

"Wait. I'll help you." Gage slogged toward the boy. Cold slime oozed down the inside of his boot. The dagger he'd stored by his ankle suddenly came to mind. It was too late to remove it. Gage heaved himself onward.

The other boy, Fran, attempted to reach Wes by leaning over the back of the sheep. The boy succeeded only in sinking the animal further and causing it to bleat all the more incessantly.

Nearing Wes, Gage stretched out his arm. "Take my hand." For a moment, the boy hesitated. Then, shaking off his mud-coated fingers, he grabbed Gage's hand. Gritty slime from the boy's fingers bit into Gage's skin. With no solid ground to brace against, Gage carefully leaned backward, using his own weight to heave Wes up.

With a slurp, the boy's body came loose, and they smacked together. Gage grabbed the boy's shoulders, steadying them both. A tremor ran through Wes's body. Gage glanced at the boy's face. "Are you all right?" He could hear his men arriving behind them and old Tobin assigning tasks.

Wes pulled free of Gage's hands. "I'm fine."

Assuming the boy's irritation was just embarrassment, Gage teased him. "Sorry, it's hard to tell under all the mud."

Wes glanced down at his coated clothes.

"Water and soap will get him clean right enough," Fran said cheerfully. "Least that's what Ma always says."

While trying to wipe the mud off his own hands, Gage noticed Wes glare at Fran. Just then Sir Brent trekked toward them. "Why don't you two let His Highness and me get this sheep?"

From up on his cart, Tobin instructed Emerett, Bardon, and Badger to collect downed wood to throw into the mire to make a track for the carts. "If we can make a path for the carts, we can also use it to get the rest of these sheep out," he explained. Meanwhile, Sir Hayson and Sir Wick helped the girl keep the rest of the sheep from bolting into the mud.

Gage nodded to Wes and Fran. "Why don't you two help the others lay wood?" As the two boys headed that way, Gage turned to Sir Brent. "Are you ready?" he asked in the nobleman's tongue.

The knight glanced at the bleating sheep, sunk to its neck. "Are you?"

"Guess we'll find out." Hunching over, Gage buried his arms around the sheep's middle and dug his fingers into the animal's gritty wool. Sir Brent encircled its hindquarters, and together they lifted.

The sheep came loose, and the moment it did, it flailed its legs. Specks of mud hit Gage in the face. Too late to close his mouth, he tasted sludge and felt grit between his teeth. He spit and clutched the animal tighter, willing it to quit struggling. It was no use.

"Can you see?" Sir Brent asked.

With his chin enveloped in wet, filthy wool and the sheep's head in his face, Gage couldn't see anything but treetops. "Nay. Tell me which direction to go."

"One step my way," Sir Brent grunted. The animal bleated in Gage's ear. "Now," Sir Brent said.

Tugging one foot loose, Gage heaved himself forward. The mud enclosed his boot. He transferred his weight to his other leg, but his foot skated forward.

"Take heed!" Sir Brent warned.

Gage tried to compensate by shifting his weight, but the mud continued to slide his feet apart. Wavering with his arms full and no way to regain his balance, he fell backward.

A hand grabbed Gage's leather jerkin and heaved him back straight. He exhaled. "Thank you."

Allard shook his head. "What would my mother and father say if the tournament victor were to arrive back in Ulbin covered head to toe in mud?"

"Only that you must have been too far away to catch me."

Allard grinned. "Never."

Gage smiled. With Allard supporting him, he managed to free his feet, and together he and Sir Brent maneuvered out of the mud and set the sheep on solid ground. The grubby, ungrateful animal trotted off to rejoin its flock, some of whom had taken their own partial dips in the mud.

Spitting grit from his mouth, Gage turned to the next trapped sheep. It stuck out its tongue, bleating, then tried to struggle forward, only to bury itself deeper in the muck. Shaking his head, Gage trudged toward the animal. Allard and Sir Brent followed.

Bracing and balancing each other, they succeeded in hauling three more sheep out onto the wood the others were laying, while Fran and Sir Reid worked their way across the mire to rescue an ewe and her small lamb from where they had sunk near its far edge.

Watching Bardon shoo their most recently rescued animal back down the road and into the herd, Gage placed his mud-caked hands on the encrusted knees of his trousers and exhaled.

Chuckling and breathing heavily, Sir Brent slapped him on the back with a muddy hand. "Only two more to go." Gage straightened and looked at the next beast.

"If we're to get the carts through, we'll need more wood," Old Tobin called.

"Wellens and I can go deeper into the forest and bring more back," Amos answered.

Gage wiped his arm across his brow and motioned to Badger. "Lend them a hand." Watching them head into the woods, it occurred to him that getting sheep out was the least of the work they had ahead of them. Sighing, he turned to Allard. "Pray, fetch me my waterskin?" he asked in the nobleman's tongue.

"Aye, and while I do, who will keep you from falling into the mud?"

Gage glanced down and chuckled. "It would make no difference now, but I promise I shall inform anyone who asks that you made a valiant attempt to save me from my fate."

Allard grinned. "And I will tell them Prince Gage of Edelmar is a good man, worth following into the mud."

Shaking his head, Gage gave Allard a push. "Get on with you."

Allard bowed and hurried past the flock's three keepers and down the road toward the six horses being looked after by Mattson.

Gage stepped back into the mud and struggled to where Wes fought to free the last sheep. Together he and the boy dragged the animal to where Sir Brent stood on the wood. The knight hefted the animal and passed it to Bardon, who carried it to dry ground.

Sir Brent extended a hand to pull Gage from the mud. Gage motioned for Wes to take the knight's offer first. The knight pulled Wes loose from the muck and then turned back to Gage. "Your Highness."

Gage gratefully locked his grimy fingers about Sir Brent's arm and felt the last clutching grasp of the mire lose its hold. Standing precariously beside Wes on the wood, he scraped mud from his hands. Someone gave a sharp whistle. Gage turned, trying to discern who had made the sound. Beside him, Wes placed both hands against Sir Brent's back and gave him a hard shove.

Sir Brent's hands flew out, but there was nothing to catch himself on. The knight's body slapped into the mud. Thrashing like a drowning man, Sir Brent furiously attempted to free himself from the muck's embrace.

Gage grabbed Wes's arm. "What in heaven's name?" He hoped to see embarrassment upon the boy's face at some misguided jest, but instead the boy's eyes locked with his with grim determination.

Across the mire a cry came from Sir Reid, who had received a similar unexpected thrust into the mud at Fran's hand. The knight came up looking as angry as a bee from a smashed hive. Fran dodged away and disappeared into the underbrush.

Still gripping Wes's arm, Gage turned on the boy, ready to shake him and demand answers. Instead, his dagger's sheath slanted, and he heard the zing of metal sliding along metal. He grabbed for Wes's opposite wrist. The boy jerked backwards with Gage's dagger in his hand. It's tip nicked Gage's skin. He yanked up his arm. Blood seeped from a small cut below his elbow.

Looking into Wes's wide eyes, Gage suppressed his outrage. "Enough~ I don't know why you have insulted me and my men this way, but you shall return my dagger this instant. You will also apologize to my men and help them out of the mud."

Wes's fingers turned white on the weapon's hilt. "No."

Gage was too angry to laugh at the boy's foolish sincerity. "Make no mistake, boy, for your insolence, you and your brother, at the very least, have earned a day in the stocks. If you beg pardon this instant, I will rescind any further sentence."

The fear in the boy's eyes disappeared under a rigid resolve. "No, you have cheated us of what is rightfully ours. You will give us what is owed us."

"What is owed you?"

"Yes, from what you have stolen," Wes replied lividly.

Dumbfounded yet unwilling to continue the discussion until Wes had been disarmed, Gage looked at Bardon and Emerett, who were behind the boy on solid ground. Emerett lifted his chin in acknowledgement and moved forward.

Gage tried to keep the boy distracted. "I'm willing to hear whatever complaints you think you have against me, but not like this." He took a careful step forward on the wood. "Give me back my dagger, and then we can talk."

"Stay where you are," Wes said, his voice rising.

Losing his patience, Gage considered going for the dagger in his boot, but Sir Brent, who had managed to struggle to his feet, slid out his own dagger. The knight mimed tossing the weapon to him. Gage nodded. Wes must have noticed, for he lifted Gage's dagger, screamed, and rushed at him.

Taken by surprise, Gage twisted to grab the boy's arm but lost his footing and slipped off the wood. His body jolted, and Gage found himself knee-deep in the mud with Wes above him, looking just as startled.

"Your Highness." Sir Brent tossed his blade. Catching the dagger, Gage swung it at Wes. The boy scrambled backward, directly into Emerett's grasp.

The cook seized the boy by the back of his neck and twisted Gage's dagger from Wes's fingers as if the boy were no more than a kitchen scullion he'd caught using a stir stick inappropriately. Wes screamed and tried to kick at him, but Emerett simply held the boy's flailing form at arm's length.

Sir Brent grunted. "Well, I guess that solves that."

"Aye," Gage said, "but what in the world?" Shaking his head, he twisted to climb up onto the wood. As he did, an arrow smacked into the mud a hand's breadth from his leg.

Infuriated, Gage reached for the arrow. "Who do these children think they are?" He yanked the arrow out of the mud. Staring at its full-length shaft and barbed metal tip, cold realization washed over him.

He opened his mouth to shout his men to arms, but it was too late.

11

A second bowstring released. Sir Brent hollered in pain and clutched his thigh where an arrow had pierced his leg.

Two commoners with bows at the ready burst from the woods in front of old Tobin's cart. They aimed for Gage and Emerett. A third archer stepped from behind a tree on the far side of the mire and drew on Sir Reid, who had just freed his red-headed self from the mud.

The zing of a sword unsheathing mixed with the baaing of the sheep. Gage twisted to see a sword-wielding peasant hack in half the stick Sir Hayson had been using to herd sheep. The commoner brought his blade's tip to bear against Sir Hayson's hefty chest. Sir Wick plowed toward them, drawing his own sword.

"Stop!" the peasant yelled at Sir Wick. "Or I'll run him through." With three sheep between them, Sir Wick stopped, his fingers clenching and unclenching his weapon's hilt.

Standing beside Tobin's cart, Bardon pulled the cudgel from his belt. "Leave him alone."

"Stay where you are," yelled the peasant.

"Release the boy!" The archer aiming at Emerett shouted.

"On your knees!" the third archer bellowed at Sir Reid from across the mire.

"Stay where you are!"

"Let him go."

"On your knees."

For a moment no one seemed sure who was in control, and then a second sharp whistle brought silence. Stepping out of the trees behind the two archers, a man with blue eyes and a nick in his left ear lowered his fingers from his mouth.

Heat swept through Gage's body, but then he saw the man behind the Blue Crow, and his blood turned to ice. Felix smiled smugly and held a sword in his good hand.

Gage couldn't breathe. He wanted to charge headlong at Felix and beat him senseless. Three days from the tournament, he had thought them safe. But the Blue Crow had bided his time. And it was no wonder with a spy in their midst. In his anger, Gage shifted his grip on Sir Brent's dagger and saw the archers' fingers pale as they tightened on their bowstrings.

The Blue Crow was a solid man with the stance of someone used to possessing power. "Tell your men to put down their weapons."

Gage glanced about at his men and realized he still had several men unaccounted for in the woods. And though Sir Brent's face was pinched with pain, he and the others looked angry enough to fight.

"Perhaps you think you might yet outmaneuver me." The Blue Crow whistled again, and on the other side of the mire where the archer had Sir Reid, a second swordsman dragged Wellens onto the road, bound and gagged.

Badger came next, blood oozing from a gash above his right eye. Amos was last. Hauled backwards, he was kicked to his knees by a third swordsman, who yanked back his head and placed a sword at his neck. Gage's stomach churned.

Sir Brent growled. "You dare ambush a prince's retinue and treat his men this way?"

"Oh, I dare much more than that," the Blue Crow answered without shifting his gaze from Gage. "Make your choice, Your Highness."

Gage looked from the arrow in Sir Brent's leg to the blood trailing down Badger's face and then to the sword at Amos's throat and the taut bowstrings aimed at himself, Sir Reid, and Emerett. There were too many possibilities to weigh in a moment, but two things he knew for certain: the Blue Crow wasn't making idle threats, and he wasn't about to back down. Swallowing hard, Gage called to his men. "Disarm yourselves."

After a long moment, Sir Wick's sword hit the ground with a thud, followed by the clank of Bardon's cudgel. Begrudgingly, Emerett dropped Gage's dagger and released Wes.

The boy exploded away and grabbed Gage's jeweled weapon. He waved it brashly at Emerett, who would no doubt have taken it from the boy a second time had there not been other legitimate threats.

On the opposite side of the mire, Sir Reid relinquished his dagger to one of the swordsman and was turned around and shoved to his knees beside Wellens.

The Blue Crow nodded. "And you, Your Highness, toss your blade to the boy."

Gage looked at Wes, the very convincing poor shepherd boy who now sauntered to the edge of the mire. He felt more like hurling Sir Brent's blade at Wes, but instead he pitched it onto the ground at the boy's feet.

Noticing then how quiet it was, Gage glanced at where the sheep, sheepdog, and shepherdess had been. They had all disappeared into the woods. He felt like such a fool. He'd been played from every direction.

"Now come and stand before me," the Blue Crow commanded. Gage curled his fingers into fists. He was being summoned like a servant.

"This is an outrage you will be hanged for!" Sir Brent yelled.

"More than one lord has threatened the same," the Blue Crow replied. "I very much doubt you will accomplish what they have not." The man's cold gaze returned to Gage. "Come, Your Highness."

His mind spinning with panic and possibilities, Gage tried to think. Being out of the mud would gain him mobility, but what would happen if he carried out the act of compliance? Would it make the situation worse or better? It occurred to him that he still had a dagger in his boot. If he stepped from the mud, would it be noticed? Maybe he could make one of them come to him. He breathed past a swelling panic of indecision. "And if I refuse?"

The Blue Crow nodded toward the opposite side of the mire. One of the swordsman stepped behind Sir Reid and swung his weapon. It sliced across the knight's back. Sir Reid screamed and fell to his stomach. The swordsman pulled back his sword to strike again.

"Stop!" Shaking, Gage looked at the Blue Crow. "Stop, I will come." He labored out of the mud, hoping the hilt of his dagger was coated thickly enough to be concealed.

His heart pounding, he stared into the cold depths of the Blue Crow's eyes and, despite the fear coursing through his body, forced himself to stand tall before the man.

The Blue Crow smiled. "The second-born prince of Edelmar slogging from the mud. A fitting place for one who so generously offers sanctuary to one hungry soul, as if that could possibly satisfy his debt to those he has cheated and enslaved."

Gage drew air. Every bit of him wanted to attack the man, but the arrow pointed at his chest kept him in place. "You are mistaken. I have neither cheated nor enslaved any man."

"The very position you hold you gained only by stolen wealth. You live off the commoners and take whatever you wish. The seizing of your tournament winnings will be just a start at repaying these debts."

Anger pulsed through Gage with so much force it hurt. "You take anything from those carts, and it will not be justice but your own thievery."

He expected the Blue Crow to hit him, but instead Felix stepped toward him. The man's once-beseeching brown eyes were filled with contempt. "Then consider it instead a ransom for your life." Felix reached out and seized the ruby brooch pinned at Gage's shoulder.

Gage dug his fingernails into his palms. Everything in him begged him to strike Felix. The man yanked the brooch loose. Forcing himself to breathe past his rage, Gage considered again the dagger in his boot and the distance between himself and Felix.

"Search him for his keys," the Blue Crow ordered.

"He does not carry his own keys," Emerett said boldly.

The Blue Crow swung his attention to the cook. "Then who does?" The man paced toward Emerett, as did the second archer. "Tell me, and you can leave here free with his silver in your purse."

Highly aware of the archer still covering him, Gage watched Emerett's face flush. The cook looked at him, fear filling his gaze. Suddenly, Gage recalled who was carrying his keys. He glanced toward the horses. Allard's face peeked over the back edge of the second cart. He held Gage's gaze, tapped a finger to his temple, and disappeared behind the cart.

Emerett's voice shook. "What you offer me I could have taken two nights ago when His Highness entrusted me with his keys, but the contents of his trunks is neither mine nor yours to take."

The Blue Crow snorted. "Why do you think you owe him your loyalty?" He turned to the group. "Why do any of you feel you owe this boy your lives? Will you profit from his success? No! You will remain his slaves." The Blue Crow looked back to Emerett. "Take what is due you."

"What you speak of is treason, not freedom," Emerett said. "And the lords of Edelmar will find you and hang you for it."

"The lords of Edelmar have tried and failed to find me, and they will continue to fail, because they are blind when it comes to their own weaknesses. And if you refuse my offer, you are as blind as they are." The Blue Crow shifted his attention to Bardon. "What of you? Will you too remain a slave to this mere boy, or will you tell me what I wish to know and come with us with silver in your purse?"

Bardon nodded across the mire to Amos, Badger, and Wellens. "When this is how you treat my friends, I would think logic would answer for me."

"I offered them the same choice I offer you. But they were fools, like this man, too stupid and senseless to seize such an opportunity. What do you think he could do to you if you turned against him? The only reason he can lord over you is because you allow him the power he wields. Be a man, and stand on your own two feet."

"In dishonor?" Emerett muttered. "Never."

Unsheathing a knife, the Blue Crow struck at Emerett. The cook ducked but not fast enough. Gasping in pain, Emerett gripped his shoulder. The Blue Crow pointed the blade in the cook's face. "Get me those keys, or the next time—"

The squeals of frightened horses rent the air. A rush of hooves followed the cracking of wood. The saddle horses tore down the road toward them. For a moment no one moved, then all present seemed to suddenly comprehend the threat the frightened, rushing animals presented.

The quick-thinking Bardon heaved himself onto Tobin's cart. Sir Hayson and the Blue Crow's swordsman dodged into the woods in the opposite direction. The Blue Crow's archer dove under Tobin's cart. Wes sprinted into the mud, no doubt thinking that would keep him safe. But Sir Wick did not have time to get out of the way, nor did the Blue Crow, who seized Emerett and held him like a shield.

The two lead horses, Gage's and Sir Hayson's, knocked over Sir Wick as they rushed by, veered around Emerett and the Blue Crow, and careened straight for the mire. Kipper balked at its edge, then leapt, thrashing his way between Sir Brent and Wes. Sir Hayson's horse followed. The other mounts were not so willing to take to the mud. Sir Wick's horse slid to a fast stop and bolted sideways.

Bashed into by the passing animal, Gage fell backward. Felix and the remaining archer fled into the underbrush to avoid being trampled by the horse.

Sir Reid's mount came up fast behind Sir Wick's horse. Gage threw up his arms and screamed to keep the animal from running right over top of him. The horse veered into Tobin's cart horse. Despite the old man's commanding, "Whoa!" the harness mare reared.

Watching the horse's legs churn above him, panic surged through Gage. He rolled to his right just as the mare landed and plunged forward, dragging the cart past him. Its wheel clipped his left elbow as it went by. Drawing a sharp breath, Gage yanked the dagger out of his boot and scrambled to his feet.

The archer, no longer covered by Tobin's cart, scurried to grab his arrows, which had been dislodged from his quiver when he dove under the cart. Regaining his feet, Sir Wick limped toward the archer before he could fit an arrow to his bow.

Where the sheep had been, Sir Hayson had taken on the swordsman. Emerett had not fared so well. He squirmed face down on the ground under the Blue Crow's knees. The Blue Crow raised his knife, about to bury it in the cook's back.

Bardon leapt from Tobin's cart and crashed into the Blue Crow. Knocking him off Emerett, Bardon sprawled atop the Blue Crow in a twisting heap of elbows and legs.

Rushing forward, Gage knelt beside Emerett. "Are you all right?"

Emerett's eyes widened. "Watch out!" He shoved Gage backwards. An arrow tore through Gage's sleeve and slapped into the road. Gage turned from it to the quivering bow string of the archer across the mire.

In the midst of the mud, Sir Brent twisted Gage's dagger from Wes's grasp. The archer on the far side adjusted his aim and released another arrow. It impacted something solid on their side of the mud. His stomach clenching, Gage twisted to look.

12

The arrow protruded from a tree trunk just to the left of Sir Hayson's head. Relief flooded Gage. Sir Hayson tucked himself more thoroughly behind a tree while maintaining his hold of the swordsman he held pinned.

The archer seized another arrow. He seemed oblivious of his companions behind him trying to catch the three horses and of Morley, who had crept from the trees and was untying Badger, Wellens, and Amos. Instead, his line of sight led straight to where Bardon had momentarily secured a position on top of the Blue Crow. Bardon's weight bore down upon the hilt of the Blue Crow's knife—an advantageous position but one that left him utterly exposed to the archer.

Gage scrambled in that direction and yelled. "Bardon, get down!"

The arrow smacked into the side of Bardon's body. Gage watched in horror as Bardon cried out and dropped sideways.

The Blue Crow squirmed out from under him and kicked Bardon away, then regained his feet and seized his knife.

Too enraged to think, Gage rushed at the Blue Crow and swung his dagger. The Blue Crow leaned backward, easily avoiding the wild slash. Straightening, the man whipped his own knife toward Gage's neck. Gage ducked sideways. The blade whooshed by his ear.

The fear of pain filled every piece of Gage but also served as an instantaneous reminder of his years of fighting practice where Roger had roared in his ear, "Do not retreat!" Springing forward, Gage stabbed at the man's stomach. His dagger caught more than fabric.

Howling, the Blue Crow grabbed Gage's right wrist with his left hand and brought his own weapon up toward Gage's forearm.

The sting of the blade sliced his skin. Gage twisted and hissed. Spinning his body under the man's left arm, he switched his dagger into his left hand and kicked backward. His foot made contact with the Blue Crow's leg.

Grunting, the Blue Crow let go and stumbled backward. Gage wielded his blade in a fast downward arch, aiming for the man's left arm. The Blue Crow heaved up his knife, deflecting Gage's blade yet somehow falling to one knee in the process. While down, the man pried something out of the mud. Gage came at him, thinking to take advantage of his vulnerability. The Blue Crow swiveled around and up, dragging Sir Wick's sword with him.

Too close to dodge its long blade, Gage blocked the force of the man's strike with his dagger. The clash of metal stung Gage's fingers and twisted his wrist.

The Blue Crow smiled and, pivoting the sword, struck again. Thoroughly outdistanced by the weapon, Gage half blocked and half dodged the blow, then quickly put space between them. The Blue Crow stayed where he was, as if trying to decide whether to pursue Gage or go after someone else.

Armed with Bardon's cudgel, Sir Wick was still focused on trying to disarm the arrow-less archer, who was utilizing his dagger and his empty bow as weapons. Meanwhile, Emerett was attempting to drag Bardon out of the battle. Neither was any more capable of taking on the Blue Crow.

Opening his arms wide, Gage thrust his chin at the man. "Come on!" he screamed. Instead of coming at him, the Blue Crow glanced across the mire and nodded. Gage jerked around.

Fear solidified his body. He had forgotten about the other archer. The man stood at the edge of the mud, an arrow already nocked on his bowstring.

Something whirled through the air and hit the archer in the stomach. The man's hands jerked, and the arrow released, flying harmlessly into the mire. Clutching the jeweled dagger sticking out from his body, the archer fell to his knees. Gage stared in shock.

Sir Brent, now weaponless but still holding Wes, pointed past Gage. "Take heed!"

Gage turned. The Blue Crow was nearly upon Emerett and Bardon. Air refilled Gage's lungs. He bellowed and charged.

With sword already raised to strike, the Blue Crow turned around and smacked the weapon hard into Gage's dagger. The impact knocked the blade from Gage's fingers. It spun and stuck into the ground. Gage tried to go after it, but the Blue Crow came at him, cutting off his path. The man continued to advance, sword outstretched.

Gage backed away from the sword's point. Three steps later, the ground slid under his feet. His breathing quickened. Behind him and across the mire, Morley yelled a warning. Metal clashed upon metal.

The Blue Crow advanced another step. Gage grabbed a branch and tried to retreat onto the wood beside him. The branch was stuck too deep. He lost his balance, and with his feet caught in the mud smacked onto his back in the muck. He attempted to paddle backward into the cold slime, but the mud closed over his arms and clung to his body. The Blue Crow stepped onto the wood above him and pressed the tip of his sword to Gage's chest. Its tip pierced his tunic and pricked his skin.

No longer aware of the clang of weapons, the shouts, or the thudding of horses' hooves, Gage perceived only the Blue Crow's callous gaze. His heart throbbed in his chest as he waited for the man to kill him. The Blue Crow snarled. "You shouldn't have resisted me." He heaved up his sword.

"For Prince Gage and Edelmar!" The cry and the thudding of hooves filled Gage's ears. In a blur, a horse and rider crashed into the Blue Crow, sending the man flying.

The mount lost its footing and stumbled through the wood into the mud. Its hooves thrashed beside Gage. He closed his eyes, fearing the animal would trample him.

The horse's struggle ceased. Gage opened his eyes to see the front legs of Allard's mount an arm's length to his right, Tobin's cart two paces past his left shoulder, and Allard's young face looking down at him with concern. "Prince Gage, are you well?"

"Aye, I believe so." Gage struggled to get up. "Where's the Blue Crow?"

Grinning, Allard nodded forward. "Knocked halfway across the mire. Tobin and Amos have him in hand."

Relieved beyond measure, Gage drew a fortifying breath and commented shakily as he attempted to extricate himself from the muck, "Here I thought I sent you to get my waterskin, not save my life."

"And I thought I warned you about the mud."

Gage smiled despite the pain coursing through his elbow and ribs. "I tried my best."

Allard skeptically tipped his head. "Could have—" An arrow slammed through Allard's body. The boy's disbelieving eyes lowered to the tip jutting from his chest. He met Gage's gaze and opened his mouth, but no words came. Soundlessly, Allard toppled from his horse.

Stunned, Gage tried frantically to catch him. His knees buckled at the boy's weight, and he collapsed into the mud with Allard's body sprawled over his lap. Gage stared into Allard's shocked face. He couldn't breathe, couldn't think, couldn't move. He wanted to scream, but even that wouldn't come.

"Stop him!" Sir Brent yelled.

The archer, who'd been with Felix and who had somehow managed to circle through the woods and mount Sir Wick's horse, hooked his bow over his shoulder and kicked the mount into a gallop, heading back the way Gage and his retinue had come. Sir Wick ran into the center of the road with a bow. Raising the weapon, the knight loosed an arrow. It found its mark in the archer's back. The archer slumped and fell from the horse.

At the sight, Gage's insides recoiled further. He looked back down at Allard's body. His lungs screamed for air, but he was incapable of obeying their demand. All sound around him faded into a faraway pinging.

He tried to brush aside Allard's blond hair but only managed to smear grime across the boy's cheek. He searched for something to wipe it away, but there was nothing clean. Allard's young, lifeless gaze stared through him.

Gage stared back into those dead eyes while every fiber of his being pounded with the furious presence of life. His vision darkened, and for a moment he thought mercifully he might die too. But then his body betrayed him and inhaled air, bringing his vision and hearing flooding back.

Agony swept through him with the strength of a pummeling storm. He bent over Allard's body, gasping, but was unable to release the tremendous press of misery swelling within him.

※

It was old Tobin who finally approached Gage, his voice gentle and breaking. "Your Highness, please come away."

Gage didn't respond. Instead, he remained staring into Allard's face. The once-grinning existence of the boy he'd grown up with and loved like a little brother was now nothing but wide eyes and a startled expression. He was gone, like Novia. There one moment and gone the next.

Tobin crouched beside Gage, his joints creaking in the descent. The old man laid a hand on Gage's shoulder and stayed with him quietly. After a bit Tobin slowly uncurled his work-worn fingers, reached out, and closed Allard's eyes.

With that connection gone, Gage lifted his head. Tobin's gaze met his. The aged brown depths held so much compassion that Gage knew if only he could embrace what they offered, he might find a way to let the pain flow out of him. But he couldn't, not without it tearing out everything else inside him. He'd been there before. He knew what it would cost him, and he couldn't do it again. So, he just stared into Tobin's eyes, hoping somehow there was a way back that didn't involve so much grief.

Old Tobin rose to his feet but stayed beside Gage. Sir Hayson spoke from three strides away. "Your Highness, the Blue Crow and his men have been secured, all but Felix. Regrettably, he escaped. As for our injured, Emerett is seeing to Sir Reid and Sir Brent, but Bardon's wound . . . Your Highness, he needs more serious attention than Emerett can provide. We need to push on."

At the knight's words, new waves of pain and anger washed through Gage. His stomach rolled. Allard was gone, but Bardon still had a chance. Gage forced himself to stand and nod, his legs shaking beneath him.

Old Tobin gripped his waist and, with surprising strength, helped him out of the mud. The old man then set about giving orders to get the carts through the mire while Sir Wick and Sir Hayson stepped in to collect Allard's body.

13

It was long after dark by the time they reached Aro, but despite the hour, news of their arrival with prisoners spread like smoke on a stiff breeze.

They had no sooner stopped their mounts at the closest inn when the baron of Aro, Lord Henry, rode into its yard followed by a dozen men-at-arms. Henry was the eldest son of Baron Roger, and Allard's brother.

In the light of flames, the twenty-seven-year-old lord swung off his mount and looked with shock at Gage's mud-encrusted entourage. "What happened?"

Sir Hayson dropped from his horse. "We were attacked."

Henry looked at their prisoners, his voice angry. "Are these those who attacked you?"

"What's left of them," Sir Wick said.

"Minus Felix," Sir Brent growled from his spot beside Tobin. Bardon moaned from the back of the same cart.

Glancing in that direction, Henry motioned to his squire. "Tad, fetch Madelyn. They have wounded. And you five, take these prisoners and see to it they are well guarded." He looked back to Gage. "How many of your men are in need of tending? And where is Allard? Why did he not lead you straight to Madelyn's home?"

With his own horse blocking Henry's view, Gage felt the reins of Allard's mount dig into his hand like a cord pulling him under water. He swallowed and stiffly swung off Kipper, hitting the ground with a jolt. Pain coursed through his knees and chest, and misery clutched his throat. Unable to form words, he tugged Allard's horse into view.

Henry's gaze traveled from him to the animal to the cloak-wrapped body on its back. The lord's face turned ashen, and he shook his head. "Nay, it is not true. That is not Allard. It cannot be. Tell me it is not true." He pointed at the body. "It cannot be!" he screamed at Gage, his voice shaking. "That is not my brother. Tell me! Tell me that is not Allard!"

Gage miserably met Henry's fear-filled gaze and knew nothing he could say would ease the truth. At his silence, the remaining color drained from Henry's face, and his body rocked. Sir Wick approached Henry, his voice quiet. "Lord Henry."

Henry's chin quivered, and his face flushed. He shoved past Sir Wick and rushed at Gage. "He should have been protected! He was just a boy!" Seizing the front of Gage's tunic, Henry shook him. "You should never have been allowed to train him. This is your fault!"

With mud grating against his skin and his face a hand's breadth from Henry's, Gage absorbed the lord's anger. In a way, it was a relief to have someone express the rage he felt. Sir Hayson yanked Henry off Gage, and Sir Wick stepped between them, a hand pressed against Henry's shoulder. "Stop this!"

Henry shoved Sir Wick and continued to scream at Gage. "We trusted him to you, and this is how you bring him home?" Henry's voice broke, and his shoulders shook. "You promised to watch over him." Shuddering, Henry covered his face with his hands and sobbed.

Gage wished he could join him and let out all his anger and grief, but not a tear rose to his eyes nor a sob to his lips. Instead his agony amassed deep in his soul.

After a moment, Henry uncovered his face. "Who killed him?" he asked, his voice steeped in bitter anger. "Who killed my brother?"

"One of their archers," Sir Hayson replied.

"Which one?"

"He is dead, your lordship," Sir Wick murmured.

"But his master," Sir Hayson offered, "is in the line of prisoners your men took into custody."

Henry clenched his fists. "Then justice will be had." He looked back at Gage. "You have brought my brother far enough. My family and I will see him the rest of the way home. You need not stay to do so. Go on to wherever you will."

The words stung far more than Henry's accusations, for though he'd been called family to Roger's house, Gage clearly was no longer. He'd lost Allard and them too. So it was with death. It was always greedy.

※

Hours later, Sir Wick's voice pulled Gage awake. "Your Highness, it is past tierce." Gage blinked in the daylight streaming in the inn's open window and sat up stiffly from where he had collapsed before the fire in his room the night before. Dried mud fell from his clothes as he stood. His elbow hurt, and his chest and back tightened painfully.

Sir Wick nodded to bread and a bowl on a table. "There is food." The knight departed, leaving him alone to eat. Gage consumed the food, his mind numb.

After a bit, the door creaked. Sir Wick reentered and set a ring of keys on top of Gage's clothing trunk, which had been placed just inside the door along with a bucket of water. Twisting his fingers together, Sir Wick glanced from the trunk to Gage and asked in a pained voice, "Should I . . . attend you?"

It was a simple question, but it felt like a knife blade. Gage looked at the empty bowl in his trembling hand. He wanted to scream and fling it across the room. Something, anything, to express the outrage he felt trapped inside, but instead he set the bowl down. "Nay." He was relieved when Sir Wick simply nodded and left.

Moving across the room, Gage picked up his keys. He had spent most of the night thinking, and in the day's light the decision he'd come to made even more sense. He unlocked his clothing trunk and stared at its contents. Recalling what he needed from it, he shook himself and dug through his tunics looking for clothing that would suit his purposes. His hands encountered a hard edge.

His orders to Bardon flew back at him. He shoved aside his tunics. There lining the bottom of his trunk were the money chests the Blue Crow had wanted. His stomach knotting, Gage yanked out a tunic and slammed the trunk's lid. Locking it, he hurriedly washed and changed as his mind churned. He couldn't go without taking care of those chests.

When he descended to the main floor of the inn, he found Sir Wick waiting for him. It took Gage a moment to find his voice, but he drew air and finally managed to speak. "I require saddlebags," he said in the nobleman's tongue.

Sir Wick ignored the innkeeper, who was busily restocking firewood and couldn't understand them anyway. "Shall I have your horse saddled as well?"

Gage considered the weight of the coins currently hidden in his clothing trunk. "Aye, and tell Tobin all who are able should be ready to depart upon my return."

A frown creased Sir Wick's face. "Shall I have Sir Hayson's horse saddled as well that he might accompany you wherever it is you are going?"

"Nay," Gage said. "You and he are to stay and look to the carts."

"But Your Highness, with respect, I do not think you should—"

"That will be all, Sir Wick."

Frustration and concern collided in the knight's eyes, yet he bowed. "Aye, Your Highness."

A LITTLE OVER a quarter of an hour later, Gage heaved his full saddlebags onto Kipper, then swung himself onto the animal. Disregarding his men's inquisitive looks, he rode from the inn's yard. On his way out of Aro, he borrowed a shovel from a croft and headed north.

When he returned to the inn sometime later, his saddlebags were empty, and there was dirt under his fingernails. Sir Hayson and Sir Wick stood waiting with their mounts beside the loaded carts.

Gage swung off Kipper. "Sir Hayson, take Amos, his cart, Morley, my mount, and Mattson with you to Ulbin. Sir Wick, go to Einhart with Tobin and the rest."

Sir Hayson frowned. "What of you, Your Highness?"

Gage forced the deception from his lips. "I am sure Sir Reid and Sir Brent will soon be capable of seeing me home."

Sir Wick stirred. "Your Highness, I do not think it is wise for you to—"

"The day's light is already half spent, Sir Wick," Gage said. "If you are to make ground, you should be on your way."

"Aye, Your Highness," Sir Wick replied in what sounded more like a deliberation than an agreement. The knight's gaze shifted to Sir Hayson, as if seeking support. Sir Hayson remained silent. Lips pressed together, Sir Wick tried once more. "Would it not be more prudent, Your Highness, if you were—"

"Sir Wick, I have given you my orders."

The knight exhaled and bowed. "And they will be carried out, Your Highness." With that Sir Wick turned and snapped instructions to Amos in the commoner's tongue.

At another time and place, Gage would have been impressed by the mettle Sir Wick showed in being willing to challenge him twice about a decision the knight clearly felt unwise, but at the moment, Sir Wick's interference was a hindrance he could not afford. Had Sir Brent been present Gage had no doubt he and Sir Wick would have stood together in his way, but Sir Wick was the youngest and alone.

Or perhaps he wasn't alone. The bench of old Tobin's cart creaked. The old man's eyes bore into him. Gage's insides tightened. No question filled Tobin's expression. Rather, it was as if the man knew exactly what he was planning. Gage met his gaze, daring Tobin to denounce him. The old man's bony shoulders stooped, and his gaze lowered.

Gage bit his cheek until he tasted blood. He would not be dissuaded. He was leaving. He was done watching other people die under his watch. Never again would he risk other people's lives for the sake of his title.

He waited where he stood until both groups obediently rumbled away. Then he paid the innkeeper, gathered what he needed, and departed.

14

Three days later, with his useless hand tucked under his cloak and the ruby brooch stowed in his satchel, Felix banged his left fist against the stronghold's gate.

The porter opened a small window. "Who is it?"

"The Crow," Felix growled.

The porter closed the window, and after a bit of rattling, opened the people door in the massive gate.

As Felix slipped inside, the porter eyed him. "My lord will want to see you."

Peeling off his satchel, Felix headed toward the hole of a passage leading into the broad base of the fortress's wall. "I will speak with him after I have eaten."

The porter frowned but nodded.

⚬⚬

Felix was still consuming his meal when the baron stormed into the dark quarters built inside the fortress's curtain wall. "What happened? Why are you the only one to return?"

Ignoring the glances from the other men sitting farther down the narrow room, Felix set down his goblet. "The others were killed or captured."

"Captured! By whom?" The lord's shocked expression changed to fear. "What will happen when he hears of this?"

"It changes nothing," Felix said. Grasping a hunk of meat, he bit off a mouthful and chewed. He glanced back at the distraught baron and answered cuttingly, "Cease your distress, your lordship. It will make no difference. He will pay you as usual for providing us sanctuary. That is, unless you wish to end this arrangement."

The baron's voice hardened and heightened. "No, I do not wish to end this arrangement, but what if those who were captured talk?"

"They know the answers they are to give." Felix sipped from his cup and eyed the baron. "Now go about your business, and remember who brought your good fortune. For as it came to you, it could just as easily be taken away, along with everything you hold dear in Edelmar."

The baron's voice took on an edge. "For both our sakes, I hope you are right about his acceptance of his lost men."

Felix set down his cup. "Humiliating the lords, stealing from them, and turning their men against them has yielded information and money, but it has caused those lords to band together. Tearing them apart will only be accomplished by a change of approach. The public hanging of the Blue Crow and his men will only aid this. The lords of Edelmar will assume they have removed the bane of the Crow from their land. Whereas now their troubles will return as something new and unknown." Felix smiled coldly. "So you see, nothing has been lost."

15

Eight months later

THE BANG OF the great hall's doors being thrown open silenced the feast. Gage rose from his place on the dais, his heart pounding.

Baron Roger of Ulbin stormed forward, buckler on his arm and sword drawn. "You have taken my son's life, and for that I will take yours." Stripping off his glove, Roger threw it at Gage's feet. "Will you accept my challenge?"

King Axel rose from his chair and turned to Gage. "Will you fight for yourself, my son, or have a champion fight in your stead?"

His stomach sinking that his father did not question the challenge, only the manner in which he would accept it, Gage retrieved Roger's gauntlet and stared into his good eye. "I will fight for myself. Bring me my sword and shield."

A servant hurried to oblige while those present drew aside the trestle tables. They stood with tankards in hand and eyes bright with the anticipation of combat.

Strapping on his shield and lifting his sword, Gage faced Roger as his father addressed the hall. "Let justice be done."

Roger struck at Gage. Gage heaved up his blade. Their swords clashed with ringing force. The baron whirled his weapon again and again. Gage's arms shook with the vigor of the blows as he blocked each with his sword and shield.

Then Allard lay between them, an arrow protruding from his chest. The squire's eyes fluttered open, and his lips moved.

Lowering his shield, Gage crouched to hear what Allard was saying. Roger thrust with his sword, and the weapon pierced Gage's body.

Gasping, Gage shoved upright, clutching his chest in the darkness. Unbroken skin met his fingers. Exhaling, he sat forward drenched in sweat and shaking.

Around him in the inn, other travelers slept on, their heavy snores stirring the stench of unwashed bodies. Gage rubbed his hands down his face. Sweat continued to pool on his clammy skin.

Weary but knowing from experience he would not fall back asleep, Gage quietly gathered his belongings and climbed to his feet. Straightening his hip-length tunic and twisting his trousers straight, he strapped on his rough leather belt, which held a bone-handled knife and a worn purse. He kept one blade visible, carried another under his clothing with the rest of his coin, and kept a third in his boot.

He shuffled around a straw mattress where Manton, his traveling companion, still slept and left the inn.

※

IN THE COOLER outdoors of Tallus, Gage pulled on his gray cloak and headed along the dark street. He tripped on something as he went. A snort followed by a curse told him he had stumbled over a beggar. He murmured his apology, pulled up the hood of his cloak, and continued on.

He wasn't sure whether it was the news he'd heard the day before, the fact he was within a day's journey of Einhart Castle, or the nightmare he'd just awakened from, but he felt more exposed than he had in months. If the townsfolk or the innkeeper knew the commonly dressed, long-haired, unbathed, bearded visitor in their midst was actually the youngest son of their king, Gage was sure more than the typical ruckus over a prince of Edelmar would have been raised. But he'd been treated the same as every other guest, welcomingly indifferent.

It was an invisibility he had come to rely on and love. Being no one of consequence had its downfalls though, like getting stuck sleeping in a barn or even in the rain because an inn was full and no abbey was nearby, having a peasant send out his hound to chase Gage from a good berry patch, or being forced to pay a greedy gateman double the toll to enter a city. Despite the aid his title could have been in such moments, the advantages of anonymity far outweighed the costs.

The day he'd left Aro, he had bought commoner's clothes and a hat and tucked himself away at an old hunting lodge. For a month or more, he foraged food, ate game, and interacted with the nearest townspeople as little as possible.

Eventually, the silence grew unbearable, and he started visiting the town more often. In time he noticed he could look every townsman in the eye and not be recognized. So, he took to the road, partly out of boredom and partly in the hope of finding Felix and setting at least one thing right.

As a prince he had visited most of the cities and towns in Edelmar, but the more he traveled as a commoner, the more he realized he had not truly seen Edelmar at all.

Living sparingly off his purse and working here and there for a townsman or a reeve in exchange for coin or a meal, he had moved about Edelmar, staying clear of the gentry and nobles and learning to blend in with the commoners.

In a village outside of Rush, he had come across a good horse being sold cheaply by an owner who had no appreciation for its spirit. He'd bought the animal and resold it three days later for a profit. From then on he started buying and selling mounts to earn a living and found he enjoyed the challenge of being a horse trader. He'd lost money once or twice on bad buys and gone hungry a few nights, but for the most part he did well enough to keep investing in new animals. That was how he had met Manton a couple of months earlier.

He'd traveled to Carson for a market that boasted local mounts and had just finished purchasing a hackney when he heard the scream of an angry horse and men arguing behind the town's livery.

"You're going to kill him!"

"It's my animal. I'll do with it as I please!"

The crack of a whip followed, and Gage cringed as another squeal rent the air and hooves thudded wood. The owner cursed, and the whip snapped once more.

Gage rounded the corner expecting to see some wild stallion up on its hind legs ready to trample someone. Instead, to his shock, he found a struggling, skinny horse tied by a half dozen ropes in the corner of a pen. The animal's owner, a heavyset, flat-faced man with squinting eyes, had managed to get a bit in the dark-brown horse's mouth and was attempting to saddle it. The angry, terrified animal laid back its ears and kicked out with its back feet, digging the ropes deeper into its flesh. The owner cracked his whip against the animal's hindquarters.

The creature leapt forward, but caught in the ropes with its feet hobbled, the horse's knees buckled, and it crashed into the dirt.

"Get up, you stupid beast!" the owner yelled, beating the animal further.

A tall, narrow-shouldered observer about Gage's own age with light-brown hair and a scraggly beard, grabbed at the man's wrist. "Leave it alone!"

The older man threw the observer off and cursed. "Stay out of my business, or I'll use this whip on you!" With that he turned back to the animal.

Unable to watch the man do any more damage to the pathetic, half-dead creature, Gage swung himself through the pen's boards. "I'll buy your horse."

The owner's eyebrows lifted suspiciously, and his lips twisted. He pointed to the groaning beast. "You want this monster?"

Gage tried not to look at the animal, which was covered in wounds from the man's abuse. He cringed. "I do. I'll give you two shillings and eight pence for it."

The observer who had tried to intervene bit his lip and looked at the owner. The man sneered. "I'd get more for it if I took it to a butcher."

"With its ribs showing like that? I doubt it," Gage said. "Besides, how would you get it there?"

"Make it four shillin's," the man growled.

"Three shillings. Not a penny more."

The man huffed. "You've got a deal." He snatched the money from Gage's hand and left with his saddle.

The observer, half a head taller than Gage, exhaled and offered his hand. "You have my respect. I'm Manton, woodcarver and game maker."

Gage shook Manton's hand. "Call me Gabriel or Gabe. I'm a seller and buyer of mounts." He glanced at the horse. "Though I'm not sure a mount is was what I just bought."

"He'll make a good mount," Manton said. "I watched him run the pen earlier. Despite how skinny he is, he's solid on his feet—when he's not tangled in ropes, that is."

Gage sighed. "Great, but I'm a seller not a trainer. I can cut him loose and feed him, but as far as seeing him rideable, I wouldn't know where to start."

"I've picked up a thing or two watching horse trainers," Manton said, "and I've got a few days still in Carson. Let me help."

"What would you want out of it?" Gage asked.

Manton nodded to the hackney. "How about a lift to the next town?"

Gage smiled and nodded. "That I can do."

So it was they spent the next several days working together, and Gage quickly discovered that, despite being a carver, Manton was actually quite knowledgeable about horse training.

With Manton's instruction and his hard work, Gage succeeded in convincing the abused horse to eat out of his hand and let him clean its wounds. The horse was still shy of being tacked, but it seemed to know Gage had saved its life. It avoided everyone else but followed him devotedly wherever he went.

Determined to see the animal eventually rideable, Gage and Manton decided to continue traveling together and struck up a mutually beneficial arrangement. As often as he could, Gage provided a mount for Manton to ride between towns, and Manton helped him train Athalos and any other mounts Gage bought.

They'd been on the road together ever since, and Gage would have happily continued that way. But while selling a palfrey the day before, he'd heard a herald announce Edelmar's Noblemen's Feast. Held every five years at Einhart Castle, the feast was where, among other traditions, the king and queen were expected to present their sons before the Edelmarian nobility. It was not a feast one could simply choose to skip.

16

AFTER HIS DEPARTURE from Aro months ago, Gage had expected to begin hearing rumors of his disappearance, but in all his time traveling Edelmar since then, he had encountered not even a whisper. Someone was keeping his secret, but his absence from noble society would by no means remain unnoticed if he failed to attend the Noblemen's Feast, which was but eight days away. Even the thought of attending a feast had him once again waking from nightmares. He wasn't sure who he feared facing more: Baron Roger, Emma, or himself.

Walking alone in the dark, he paused at the well in Tallus's center. Ignoring the bucket attached to the well's crank, he took up a smaller bucket sitting on the shaft's edge and dropped it into the hole. Its rope slithered off the stones beside him, and the bucket splashed into the water below.

Staring into the blackness, Gage wished he could stay as he was—unnoticed, unsought, and unaccountable for anyone but himself. But he knew if he remained absent, when the day of the feast arrived, his family would face an assault of questions. His parents would bear the shame of having to admit they had no idea where he was or what he was doing. Gage could not in good conscience let them be disgraced. He also ached to see them.

Grabbing the end of the rope, he hauled up the sloshing bucket and plunked it down on the edge of the well. He could perhaps manage to attend the feast as Gage. But what would he face if he did? And would he be allowed to leave again as Gabe, a buyer and seller of mounts? Or would he be forced to take back what was expected of him as a prince of Edelmar?

He had thought many times about returning to his life as Gage, but always he found himself caught in the question of how he would live if he did. He would refuse to take on another squire or travel with a retinue. He'd also never accept the lordship of a manor. But no prince lived alone or traveled without an escort. A prince also didn't travel as a commoner and sell mounts to support himself.

Digging his ragged fingernails into his palms, Gage considered for the millionth time any possible existence where he could return to being Gage, be with his family, and yet still remain free of being responsible for anyone else's life.

That day, if not for riding with him, his men would have been safe. The attack on them had taken place because of him, because of his wealth and title. And as a leader he had failed his men. He had valued his pride and money before their lives. Because of him, not everyone had come home. Had he simply surrendered his coin to the Blue Crow, nothing would have been lost that day that could not have been replaced. As a leader, his choices cost other people their lives. Therefore, with or without his title, he would never be willing to lead again.

As Gabe he was free of that burden of responsibility, and as far as he knew there was no law prohibiting him from living as Gabe. But his identity as Gabe ultimately hinged upon no one seeking or denouncing him as Prince Gage. Not to mention, he had never actually sought or received his king's permission to live as he did.

He drew a ragged breath. Dare he return and ask his father for what could be denied? Or was it better to stay away and simply live remiss of seeking permission? Both held risk and loss.

Sighing, Gage scooped cool water from the bucket and splashed it over his face. Standing there with his chin and hands dripping, he wished he could wash away far more than the sweat of his nightmares. Dumping the remaining water into a nearby animal trough, he headed back toward the R&R Inn.

A cheesemaker's shop door opened, spilling light onto the street ahead. Smoke laden with the smell of fresh bread wafted from a baker's shop. Fires everywhere had already been kindled out of the previous day's coals. Gage picked up his pace. Soon all of Tallus would be astir, and so would Manton.

At the wooden silhouette of a cobbler's shoe, Gage turned left down an alley and trekked along a narrow, rutted street with laundry stretched overhead on lines between opposing upper stories. Above a doorway ahead hung the warped and weathered sign of the R&R Inn.

Tallus boasted four inns. The R&R was the fifth. In response, the R&R charged only half as much for a night's stay, thereby managing to entice in enough travelers to keep it and its adjoining stable busy.

Knowing by experience it was easier to tack Athalos when the stable was quiet, Gage headed there first. Opening the building's half door, he stepped inside and let his eyes adjust to its dimness. The stench of horse dung filled his nose. Several animals shifted, rattling the metal rings to which they were tied. One mount snorted and pawed, thudding a hoof against the hay manger that ran the length of the back wall.

Someone yanked on Gage's shirt. Startled, he swiveled around and nearly punched the gray face of a donkey. He sighed and smiled. The animal's nose continued to search him, no doubt looking for handouts. Shaking his head, Gage shooed the animal away and caught its trailing rope.

He re-tied the donkey where its owner had left it the night before and squeezed between the wall and Manton's mule to reach the spot where he'd tied Athalos. Talking to let Athalos know it was him coming, he ducked under the mule's neck and reached for the horse. "Hey, Athalos."

His fingers brushed the animal's taut lead rope, and he feared for a moment he would get bit. "Easy, big boy. It's just me." The rope went slack, and a huff of breath warmed Gage's face. "Good boy. You get enough to eat last night?" While he talked, Gage retrieved his blanket and saddle.

He gently swung both onto Athalos's dark-brown back and shifted them into place. Tightening the straps, he settled his saddlebags on next and secured them. Then he tacked Manton's mule in the growing light.

Buckling the last rump strap of the mule's pack saddle, Gage heard a shuffle at the stable's door. Another traveler entered and headed for a small black-and-white mare tethered four rings down. Gage rechecked Athalos's saddle and tightened it another two holes.

A moment later, Manton slipped into the stable. He frowned over his thin shoulder and scratched his chin through his scraggly, light-brown beard.

"Something wrong?" Gage asked.

Shaking his head, Manton headed his direction and settled his nearly empty packs onto Nigel's back. "I was just wondering who the man is standing opposite the inn. He's no commoner and is clearly keeping an eye out for someone."

Having seen no one when he entered the stable, Gage shrugged. "He's probably just meeting someone."

Manton tied his bags onto his mule. "More'n likely he's a moneylender who's after someone who hasn't paid. You haven't borrowed coin from anyone, have ya?"

Gage chuckled. "Yeah, six shillings last week. Spent them on a new saddle. Can't believe you didn't notice."

Manton laughed. "You eat yet?"

"No." Untying Athalos, Gage ran his hand down the horse's neck and over the scars where the animal's mistreatment would always remain subtly visible.

"We can buy something on the way. Food here doesn't exactly look edible," Manton said, tugging his mule toward the stable's door.

Agreeing, Gage followed Manton outside. With Athalos between him and the opposite side of the street, he glanced under the animal's neck, curious to see Manton's supposed moneylender. Spotting the man, Gage instantly pulled behind Athalos. His heart pounded, and heat rushed through his body. Memories assaulted him. He could see again the sword coming down across the knight's back. Gage's body shuddered. An intense desire to run filled him, but he didn't dare. Keeping behind Athalos, he urged the animal onward. He couldn't be noticed. Not here. Not now.

Ahead of him, Manton bounced twice and hopped onto Nigel's back behind the mule's packsaddle, where there was space since Manton had managed to sell almost all the wood items he normally packed on the animal.

Gage's stomach twisted at the thought of making himself visible, but if he didn't mount, he would risk Manton questioning him and drawing attention. Careful to keep his back to Sir Reid, Gage took a quick breath and swung himself into Athalos's saddle. Figuring his knight's gaze had to be upon him, his heart raced. He held his breath and nudged Athalos forward, expecting to hear his name called out in the growing light of dawn. Each moment that passed felt like a gong proclaiming his identity, but the plod of Athalos's hooves remained the only sound.

Gage's tense body rocked with the beating of his heart. They reached the end of the street. Still no shout came. Slowly, Athalos rounded the corner.

Concealed by one building, then another, Gage exhaled. They passed along a row of houses and turned onto the next street and then the next, working their way through Tallus and away from the R&R Inn. Realizing his fingers were white on Athalos's reins, Gage loosened his grip.

"If we make good time," Manton said, "we can reach Dulcis before sunset tomorrow. There should be a new load of carved goods waiting for us there. Once we pick it up, we can look for a mount and head for Delkara."

"Delkara?"

Twisting on Nigel's back, Manton glanced at him. "I told you I take every other load of goods into Delkara. And this time I plan to attend the fair in Nikledon."

"I remember. I just . . . forgot." Gage's thoughts flew back to Sir Reid. If he hadn't left the inn before the knight arrived, Sir Reid would have spotted him. And then what?

Sunlight glinted off the low sign of a silversmith's shop. Gage swallowed. He longed to believe the knight's presence at the inn was just a crazy coincidence, but he knew it couldn't be. That also meant Sir Reid probably wasn't the only one searching for him. What if next time he was noticed? What would he say? How would he explain himself? Or what if he wasn't noticed? They likely wouldn't look for him in Delkara. But if he left for Delkara without showing his presence anywhere, might they fear him dead? How long had they been searching? Might they already fear him dead? He hadn't ever worried about that because as far as he had known no one was seeking him. But now he knew, and he was intentionally avoiding being found. He told himself that the Noblemen's Feast was perhaps the reason, and maybe they had just recently started looking for him.

Stopping Nigel at a baker's, Manton dropped to the ground. "You want anything?"

No longer hungry but not wanting to raise questions, Gage dug in his purse and tossed Manton a small coin. "What I normally get. Thanks." *And hurry,* he thought.

As Manton bought bread, Gage glanced back the way they had come. Shame overwhelmed him. Disappearing was one thing, but hiding was something else entirely. He heaved a breath. He couldn't do this. No matter how desperately he wished to remain unentangled in his old life, he could not just leave. He needed to speak to his father and put an end to their search and any concerns they might have over his well-being. But to speak with his father, he would have to find an excuse to part ways with Manton. And if he did, how long would it take him to rejoin Manton? A day? Two days? Not until after the Noblemen's Feast? Or would he even be allowed to rejoin him at all?

Gage considered turning around, finding Sir Reid, and telling him to simply deliver a message to his father. But no, better to return of his own accord than be escorted back, for he knew not Sir Reid's orders. He would just have to find a way to part with Manton and deal with this. They would travel through Einhart on their way to

Dulcis. He'd wait until they were in Einhart. That would give him at least the day's ride to figure out what to say to Manton.

17

On the road, Gage and Manton kept their mounts to a trot. They passed through deep forests interspersed with small villages, busy towns, broad meadows, and trickling streams. Eventually, they slowed to give themselves and their animals a rest and began discussing the last place they'd visited and where they were headed next.

Draping his reins on Nigel's neck, Manton rode with his hands on the mule's rump and his body rocking with the animal's stride. "So, you've been to Delkara before?"

Gage raised a hand to block the sunlight suddenly blazing through the trees. "Yes, but mostly just to Duvall," he said, choosing his words carefully. "Once when I was a child, my father had business in Delkara, and he and my brother and I traveled all the way across to the cliffs at the sea."

He remembered cautiously approaching the cliff's edge with Haaken. Their father, close behind them, had chuckled at their gasps when they peered over the edge. It was a breathtaking view, the water so far below. Gage pulled himself from the memory. "How far have you traveled outside of Edelmar?"

"I've been all over Delkara," Manton replied. "Seen a lot of Keric, been up in both sets of mountains, and walked along the sea. I have even stood on the drawbridge overlooking the Valens River in Ithera."

Gage knew the place in Delkara. As a young boy he had stood on that same bridge and been astounded at the thought of always having to pass across such a chasm to reach King Maurice's castle built in the center of the mighty Valens River. He shuddered now at the thought of the rushing water.

Manton squinted. "One place I'd love to see again is Nikor Harbor. It's full of the hustle and bustle of ships and is deep and beautiful. Not at all like the sprawling shallows ships have to navigate to get into Ivenyhan."

Words from the past swept through Gage. *"Lord Borin seeks the king's aid. A merchant vessel from Ivenyhan ran aground."* He saw Haaken packing to follow their father and heard his words. *"I would have liked to have shared your company as far as Aro."*

Gage dropped his hand from blocking the sun and gripped his saddle. If only he'd ridden instead to Ivenyhan with Haaken. If only he had never agreed to take Felix with him. If only he hadn't been such a fool to be tricked by him. If only he had not stopped to help rescue sheep. If only he had just handed over his keys. If only . . .

Willing his mind beyond the haunting words and the never-ending regrets, he recalled his promise to Haaken. *"We shall in a fortnight ride back from the hunt at Blakely together, or else mayhap I will see you before then in Einhart."* Suddenly, everything within Gage ached to be with his family.

"I can't go with you to Delkara."

Manton sat up and pulled Nigel to a stop. "What do you mean?" His voice held confusion and a hint of anger.

Knowing it sounded like he was going back on his word, Gage forced himself and Athalos onward. "I want to go with you, and I will when I can, but I have business I must attend to first." He flinched at the thud of Manton's heels kicking Nigel back into motion.

"You are a buyer and seller of mounts. What additional business could you possibly have?"

Gage exhaled. "It's personal business that I've neglected far too long. I must see to it before going on to Delkara. Perhaps we can meet up again once it's complete."

Manton's tone eased. "How long will it take you?"

"A couple of days. Possibly a fortnight." Gage glanced back, trying to read Manton's expression. His lips were pressed together, and his gaze was clouded, but when he spoke, his anger had disappeared.

"If it's two days, you can find me at Luert. If it's a fortnight, you will have to catch up with me on the first day of the fair in Nikledon." With that Manton urged Nigel back into a trot.

Gage followed on Athalos. "Then I will rejoin you when I can."

Manton scoffed. "And in the meantime, how am I to find someone else to play wari and chess with me?"

Gage smiled. "Maybe you'll have to let them win, as you did the first time I played against you."

Manton slowed Nigel. "I did . . . possibly let you win the first time. But never after that."

Gage chuckled. "No, now you insist I lose because it's better for business."

Manton grinned. "Well, it is."

Glad the tension between them had eased, Gage smiled. "So, I take it woodwork sells well in Delkara. What's the market for mounts?"

Manton settled once more on Nigel's rump. "Packhorses will be a likely buy, along with mules and riding horses. Training and riding anything more than a rouncey though will draw attention, and in Delkara it's best not to draw attention."

"What do you mean?"

"Remember how you told me you sell mounts on the road rather than working directly for a lord because his choices cost you the life of your friend? Well, if you have a disagreement with a Delkaran lord, you don't dare walk away from him or make any such statement. Instead you keep your mouth shut, your head down, and your hands working. Because even more so than here, in Delkara the words and opinions of a commoner mean nothing. And pleading a case against a lord before a lord is a fool's mission. The barons of Delkara are as likely to rewrite the laws as they are to enforce them, particularly when it comes to their own livelihoods. So, like I said, it's best to draw as little attention as possible, even as a traveler."

Gage asked skeptically, "And King Strephon knows this about his lords?"

"King Strephon allows his barons freedom to deal with problems as they see fit."

Months earlier, Gage would have outright rejected Manton's words, but living as a commoner, he had heard and seen enough to now know that the complaints and concerns of the commoners did often carry far less weight than they should have and were at times completely ignored by their lords.

In fact, as Gabe he'd heard grievances against Edelmarian lords that had shocked him. Grievances that would likely have never been spoken aloud had the tenant saying them known their king's son sat listening. He'd also come to learn that most commoners felt they could not bring complaints against their lord to their king, though Gage was certain his father would've wished to know their concerns and would have worked to solve the issues if given a chance. It was likely not much different in Delkara. Few believed their king cared.

Flipping open his saddlebag, Gage dug out his wide-brimmed hat. Every time he wore it he thought of Manton telling him it looked ridiculous on him. That made him smile because Manton's blatantly expressed opinions, whether about hats or lords, was one of the things Gage enjoyed most about him. He loved getting to hear what someone actually thought.

In the short time he'd been traveling with Manton, he'd learned more about people and life than he had in years living as a prince. This was also why he was intrigued by the prospect of going with Manton to Delkara. It was a place beyond Edelmar's borders that he had long wished to explore at whim, but as a prince he'd never had the ability to do so. With Manton he could explore and truly learn about the kingdom.

Struck by a sudden thought, he turned to his friend. "Manton, where do you plan to cross into Delkara?"

"At Clement. It's a lesser toll. And as long as you're not loaded too heavy, it's no extra trouble fording the river than taking the bridge in Awnquera."

Gage was relieved Manton had not said Duvall, which was far too near Ulbin, but regardless his mind ground to a halt on fording the Apse River. He knew it was a calm section of the river, but a recollection of a far less congenial span of the Apse formed a knot in his stomach.

Manton broke off a low-hanging branch and absently tossed it into the woods. "You truly think your business could take you as long as a fortnight?"

"Who knows? I have a feeling resolving the matter might be a bit like trying to sell a rouncey to a man who's looking for a destrier."

Manton laughed. "You've managed that well enough in the past." He mimicked a conversation Gage had had with a man the month before. "It's a solid, handsome thing, quiet at an amble. But it'll take your master for a good run if asked. Of course, you could buy a charger, but you never know what sort you'll get. They can be a handful."

"I think I had him at the line about it being quiet at an amble," Gage said

Manton laughed. "Probably. He didn't look capable of handling a palfrey much less a destrier. You remember that big black charger we found in Orrim?"

Gage glared. "You mean the one you told me you could cure of biting?"

"Hey, we did eventually cure him."

"Yeah, eventually."

Manton half shrugged and half cringed. "When the man said he was a biter, I figured it would be easy to see it coming, like with Athalos. Who knew a horse could be so sneaky?"

Gage rubbed his stomach where he'd had a welt for days. "Sneaky is right. I don't think I'll ever feel the same about big black horses." He could have sworn the horse bit people just for its own entertainment.

Manton frowned. "He seemed so friendly too, letting you pet his head and acting all pleasant. Right up till the moment he dug in his teeth."

"Exactly," Gage said. For some reason the thought reminded him of Felix, which brought him back to all the reasons he'd become Gabe. Becoming a seller of mounts had given him a life again, but he doubted being Gabe would help him convince his father not to mandate his return to being Prince Gage of Edelmar.

18

Hours later the arable land surrounding the city of Einhart came into sight, and Gage drew a fortifying breath.

Like a mountain range looming on the horizon, Einhart's walls, towers, and castle rose into the sky. Streaming from the castle's highest turret, the fully spread blue, white, purple and gold royal standard of Edelmar rippled in the wind. Meanwhile, the billowing sails of two windmills on the opposite edge of the city steadily bowed in graceful homage. Spirals of smoke rose from within the city, and sunlight glinted on the cathedral's crosses and the roofs of Einhart's numerous guard towers.

A strange combination of longing and dread descended upon Gage. The place was home—filled with good memories yet also with the part of him he wished to forget.

Riding a road along the edge of the arable land, they headed for a crossroads where a thoroughfare cut southwest toward the city between fields of barley and spring-planted oats. Tended to by the local peasantry, the hundreds of strip fields surrounding Einhart were laid out like the spokes of a wagon's wheel with the city their center and the woodland their outer rim.

Passing carts and workers, Gage and Manton reached the crossroads. An old woman sat at the intersection with a large wooden bowl half full of chestnuts. Clutching the bowl in a dirty hand, she shook it, sending the nuts clattering against the wood. "Nuts. Buy and eat 'em now or buy 'em and keep 'em for later. You won't find 'em any cheaper in the city, I guarantee."

Gage thought of Haaken. Glazed chestnuts were one of his brother's favorites.

"And will you give me back my coin if I do find 'em cheaper in the city?" Manton asked.

The woman's face wrinkled further. "You buy 'em. You keep 'em."

Manton laughed sharply. "I'll keep my coin instead, old woman."

Gage shook his head in amusement. If he had learned one thing about his traveling companion it was that Manton despised being treated like a fool, and if offered a bad deal, he would subtly or blatantly lay the facts bare. Gage had known people lied and cheated, but traveling with Manton had taught him just how often.

Felix came to mind again. Gage's insides clenched, and he glanced at Einhart Castle. He had no desire to revisit the past. But that was exactly what he was about to do. He had to, for his family's sake.

His eyes followed the trail of people traveling toward what looked like a wall jutting from a cluster of towers built into the city's curtain wall. The third and least-fortified gate into Einhart, it had no drawbridge or moat. Instead, a series of gates and walls with openings on opposite ends forced those entering to wind through a narrow path to access the city while exposed to soldiers from above. As boys, he and Haaken had always called it the maze gate, for it looked like one from the window of the castle's highest turret.

Gage wondered if Haaken might be in that tower now. He could not tell from such a distance, but a longing to stand beside

Haaken filled him. Haaken, the born leader who never failed to live up to all that was expected of him. Haaken also seemed to always find a way to make everyone around him feel capable and wanted no matter their station. But would that still be Haaken's response to him after the choices he had made? Or would Haaken no longer support him?

Gage's gaze slid down the castle's lofty towers, past its walls, through its orchard, and beyond its curtain wall to the strip fields. In one field, plowmen followed teams of oxen dragging blades and overturning fresh dirt. In the next strip, barefoot children ran across plowed ground, shooing birds from newly planted seed. Other fields of oats, barley, and millet were speckled with peasants, and Gage wondered what it was like for them living in the shadow of Einhart Castle. Did it make them feel dominated? Or did they look to the castle with gratitude for its protection?

Manton nudged up beside him. "What do you think? Should we make way for them or stay where we are and see what they do?"

Gage glanced at the road. A stream of men wearing red surcoats and red feathered helmets on swiftly moving mounts had emerged from the maze and were riding toward them. Instantly steering Athalos off the road, Gage dipped his head to hide his face beneath his hat. Manton remained plodding along in the center of the road.

Having thought Manton was joking, Gage stiffened. He saw the first of Baron Alexander's men scowl at Manton, and Gage inwardly screamed at him to move. Though no law in Edelmar commanded commoners to make way for gentry and noblemen, it was an understood courtesy—one that Manton was about to violate.

His chest pounding, Gage watched the legs of the baron's horses prance closer, then past him. He held his breath, expecting a shout or an altercation.

The thud of hooves and the jangle of metal faded. Gage glanced over his shoulder. Manton was riding in the opposite ditch. Reining Nigel back onto the road, Manton grinned at him. "What? You didn't really think I'd go head to head with the Lord of Opes, did you?"

The pounding in Gage's chest slowed. "No, just his men-at-arms."

Manton laughed and flicked his reins against Nigel's rump. The mule took off trotting. Shaking his head, Gage followed.

They quickly covered the remaining distance to Einhart, past carts and peasants, and rode up the incline to the gate at the entrance to the maze. Even on horseback the thick walls rose far above their heads forming a daunting welcome. A welcome that included armed gatekeepers.

"Do either of you have anything you intend to sell within the city?" the eldest gatekeeper asked.

"Not this day," Manton answered congenially.

Gage met the guard's sharp gaze—a gaze that would have been lowered if the man had any idea who he was. "I've nothing to sell either."

"Then no toll is required of you. You may be on your way."

Entering the cobblestone passage, he and Manton headed through the maze behind a man and a boy pulling a handcart full of clay jars.

After turning the last corner of the maze, Gage and Manton approached the mouth of the tunnel that led into the city. Ahead of them the father and son steered their cart with its rattling jars around the holes in the stone where the teeth of the tunnel's portcullis would have embedded. Currently open, the prongs of the lattice gate hung above their heads. Had he wished to, Gage could have reached up and touched the metal barrier.

The coolness of the tunnel emptied onto the crowded, sunlit street of the wool and cloth guilds. The lane greeted them with the rumble of wheels and bartering voices. Gage glanced about the overhanging shops, feeling the warm welcome of the colorful familiarity of the weavers, dyers, haberdashers, and so on. This was his city. Though he'd been sent to Ulbin as a boy to train under Roger, much of his time had still been spent in Einhart. He had always said he had two homes and two families, his and Allard's, but one city. At least that's how things used to be.

His gaze fell to the manure-stained cobblestones and the shadow cast by a distaff-and-loom sign. His horse stopped. Gage looked up to realize a wool man's wagon blocked their side of the street. A man standing in the back of the wagon tossed out yarn to a weaver's apprentice at the shop's door.

Staring at the city's busy street, a thought struck Gage. What if his father wasn't in Einhart? With the feast this close, it was unlikely, but it was possible.

Gage loosened his reins and was about to nudge Athalos around the wagon when a young girl carrying a bundle of feathers burst from an alley and dodged between the back of the wagon and Athalos. Startled, the horse flattened its ears and stretched out its neck. Gage yanked back his reins. Athalos's teeth closed on air where the girl's shoulder had been just a moment before. The oblivious girl disappeared into a hatmaker's shop.

Gage exchanged looks with Manton. He knew Athalos's response came out of fear not malice, but he kept a more wary eye on the alleys and a wider gap between his mount and anyone else foolishly looking for shortcuts.

Eventually, they reached the city's center, where an extensive market of stalls and stands were surrounded by three-story guild halls. Reigning Athalos to a stop near a street-level window where a woman was busy bundling a large chunk of white leather for a customer, Gage waited for Manton to draw even with him. "Here is where we must part ways. Safe journey, my friend."

Manton met his gaze. "May your business conclude swiftly that we might travel together again soon." Hoping that to be true, Gage nodded.

His mind wandering, he watched Manton cross the market and disappear behind a bookbinder's shop. As a boy, he had loved coming with his father to that shop and watching the grey-haired owner, Jeremiah, bent over his worktable. The old craftsman's bushy eyebrows would touch as he concentrated on encasing a new collection of writings in wood overlaid with tooled leather.

Gage had loved seeing the illuminations on the story's pages and the books' intricate bindings. He had wished he could create such beautiful things, but he had long learned he had no skill at artistry. Manton, however, carved the most gorgeous things and patterns in everything from chess pieces to children's tops.

Gage thought again about simply going on with Manton to the fair in Nikledon. He reminded himself that he needed to speak with his parents. And he did long to see them and Haaken, but at what cost? Currently, people flowed around him completely unaware of who he was. They had no interest in him nor did they have any expectations for him. But if he proceeded, that would change.

Pulling his hat a little lower, he glanced at the tanner's window where the woman had just finished with her customer. He bit his lip. "Excuse me, miss. Do you know if the royal family is here in Einhart?"

The woman tucked an escaped brown curl back under the cloth that bound her hair and nodded. "Not often are they, but you've some luck about you. Queen Irena's been in the city for a while, and the res' returned just two nights ago. Or so I hear. Preparin' for their royal feast more'n likely." She leaned on an elbow and sighed. "And what a grand occasion it must be, with all them important people, fine clothes, and pretty things."

A man stepped into the shop behind her. "Sibyl, you selling leather or daydreaming?" Gage recognized the man as the son of the previous owners and was glad for his beard and hat.

Sibyl turned. "A woman can do both at the same time, husband."

"Then ask him if he'd like a new purse, for I can see the one he's got is nearly worn through."

Gage glanced down at the shabby yet still solid pouch hanging on his belt and then nodded at the couple. "I'll keep what I've got for now, but thanks for the information." Lifting his reins, he turned Athalos around and backtracked to a quieter street to take to Einhart Castle.

He had no idea what he would do when he got there. In the past, entering the castle's gates would have been as simple as Sir Brent nodding to the guards as they rode past. But now he was unaccompanied, and if he came as he looked and claimed his title, he'd create a millpond of questions.

He could attempt to proceed as a commoner seeking the king's audience, but if he was recognized, it would result in the same embarrassing display, which would shame his family. Avoiding any public notice in his current state would be best. But how?

As he rode, he came up with a possible solution. He made three stops, purchasing a croissant, a small basket, and some glazed chestnuts. Placing the crescent-shaped bread and the chestnuts inside the basket, Gage found a runner and paid the boy to deliver the items to Prince Haaken along with the words: "A thanks for the abundant fruit you gave last evening."

After following the boy to make sure he delivered the food and message to Einhart Castle, Gage went to find somewhere to wait out the remainder of the day.

19

At dusk, Gage tugged up the hood of his dirty gray cloak and left the corner of the tavern. He passed a raucous table of men drinking after their day's work. Gage tugged open the tavern's door, slipped out, and gratefully let it thud closed behind him. Overhead, thunder rumbled in clouds that had crept over the city, and people hurried along the streets, completing their last chores before curfew.

Swinging up onto Athalos, Gage rode to the corner of the city's stone bulwark where it joined with the wall of Einhart Castle's orchards. He dismounted in the empty lane beside a door that led through the wall into the orchard. Used to allow surplus fruit to be removed from the castle's grounds and taken in carts to the city market, the door was typically kept locked. Hoping Haaken had figured out his message, Gage gripped the door's circular handle and twisted. Its latch held.

Thunder boomed, and the first spattering of rain hit his hood and shoulders. He knocked and waited. Nothing happened. He twisted the handle again and leaned his shoulder into the door, thinking maybe it was just stuck. It held fast, as solid as the stone wall rising above him. Rain pattered harder on the streets and roofs around him. Gage stepped back, his hands shaking. Had Haaken not gotten his message? Had he gotten it but not understood? Or had he understood but chosen not to come?

Standing there staring at the locked door, Gage contemplated the options left to him. At this hour going to the castle's main gate was even more out of the question. But he could not just stay where he was. Maybe he should go to an inn and in the morning catch a servant coming from the castle who could fetch Haaken directly, assuming, of course, that Haaken wasn't choosing to avoid him.

But he knew how servants talked. If he asked anyone to fetch Haaken, half the castle and parts of the city would know about it before Haaken did. He'd fare better marching up to the gate in broad daylight and seeking an audience with his father, but both were likely to bear the same gossip. He didn't even want to consider what people would say if word spread that their king's second-born son was seen seeking an audience before the king looking like a commoner. People would probably think his father had thrown him out because of something he'd done, and he was coming crawling back, which would disgrace his and his father's good names and would make his mother cry.

Gage sighed. "Where are you, Haaken?"

He tried the gate once more, wishing desperately the thing would just unlock and let him through. He dropped his forehead against the door. The cold of the metal strap hinges seeped into his skin.

This was his own fault. If he had just kept one of his royal tunics and his signet ring, he could have simply transformed himself back into Prince Gage and traipsed through the castle's main gate. Instead, here he was beating his head against a servant's entrance.

He slammed his empty hand against the metal and shoved away. He would just have to go to an inn and figure out a different way to get to his father in the morning.

As he turned and headed along the street with Athalos in tow, a voice rang out behind him. "Halt! Who goes there?"

Cringing, Gage obeyed the command. With his back to the voice and water dripping off the front of his hood, he wished he could sink into the ground. This was not the way he had envisioned the night going.

Their horses' hooves clopped on the cobblestones, and Gage wondered how he had missed them coming.

"In the name of the night patrol, turn around and identify yourself," the leader of the guard demanded.

Keeping his head down, Gage turned to face them. A bright flame arched within the lattice of a lantern held by one of the three men-at-arms. Gage frowned. Night patrols were always made up of four men. Then he heard another horse approaching from behind him, and he understood. They had sent a man around to block him in.

The leader was the first to swing down from his mount. "Who are you? And what are you doing at the castle's wall at this hour?"

In response to the man's proximity and challenging voice, Athalos pull backward. Gage tightened his grip on the horse's reins and tried to devise a nonthreatening answer. Rain pinged off the patrols' helmets. The leader's right hand crossed to his sword's hilt. "Answer me!"

Athalos snorted anxiously, and Gage bit his cheek. Knowing no answer that could fix this, he realized he was probably about to see a sword in his face if he said nothing. "I was supposed to meet someone here."

Scorn entered the man's voice. "At this hour?"

Gage kept his voice strong. "I thought the person would have come before now. I beg your pardon. I didn't intend to be here so late."

One of the other men laughed. "Right, and I didn't intend to drink that pint of ale I bought last night at the alehouse."

Gage gritted his teeth and felt heat rise up his neck. "I speak the truth. I meant no harm. Please, just let me be on my way."

The head of the patrol scoffed. "We catch you out late, trying castle gates, and you expect us to let you go?"

Gage realized then that it was far more likely they would take him to a guard tower, detain him for the night as an attempted intruder, and drag him before his father in the morning—or worse, his father's steward. His stomach twisted. It would turn into the juiciest gossip in Edelmar.

The leader turned to one of his men. "Ulrick, bring that lantern. Let us see who this jester is."

Gage stiffened. If he told them who he was, would they believe him? And would swearing them to silence actually work? Or would it just be slightly better than the outcome of possibly not being recognized and being chained up for the night by his father's own guards?

The man holding the lantern stepped toward Gage. Athalos snorted and yanked backward. Determined not to lose his horse, Gage braced his feet to keep Athalos from pulling him over. Distracted by the animal, he didn't see Ulrick reach for him. Fingers wrapped around his arm. Startled, Gage cried out and twisted.

Athalos bolted, wrenching Gage's arm outward and splaying him between man and beast. Gage held onto Athalos's lead. Wheeling at the end of the rein, Athalos squealed and threw a front hoof at him.

Realizing if he did not release the animal, Athalos would likely stop trying to escape and instead charge him and them too, Gage let go.

Athalos instantly pivoted and attempted to dodge past the fourth member of the patrol. The man boxed in the animal.

"Don't!" Gage tried to yank free from Ulrick and prevent Atholos's full wrath from being seen and felt by the fourth member of the patrol, but Ulrick twisted his arm behind him and swung him around.

The flat of the leader's sword smacked the underside of Gage's chin. "Stand! Or you'll wish you had."

Gage stilled, his insides quivering. He waited for the sound of hooves contacting flesh, but it didn't come. Instead, Ulrick lifted the lantern, and the leader reached to pull back Gage's hood.

Gage closed his eyes. Regardless of whether they recognized him or not, there would be no way to prevent the embarrassment they would all face at the end of this.

20

"Stop!" The forceful command came from an overwhelmingly familiar voice.

Gage snapped his eyes open. Emerging from the orchard's door, Haaken threw back the hood of his velvet-lined cloak and raised his lantern, revealing his face and crown. "Let him go."

Stunned, the leader of the patrol lowered his sword and quickly bowed. "Your Royal Highness." The others bowed as well, including Ulrick, who maintained his grip on Gage's arms. Rain assaulted them all.

Haaken's eyes sought Gage's face, still concealed beneath the hood of his cloak, then shifted to Ulrick's face. "I said, let him go."

Ulrick released Gage, but the leader of the patrol was not so quick to give up his prize. "But Your Royal Highness, he was sneaking about trying doors and says he came to meet someone."

"He spoke the truth. He was coming to meet with me," Haaken said. "He has information I seek." Haaken's gaze flicked in Gage's direction and then back to the men. "Now leave us, and be on your way."

"Yes, Your Royal Highness." At the leader's signal, the others, including Ulrick, backed toward their horses.

Gage sighed silently. He waited until the men had ridden off, then glanced at Haaken. With his lantern lowered, Haaken's face was unreadable. Feeling ashamed that he had come in this manner and that he had needed rescuing, Gage dropped his gaze to the cobblestones and for the first time in nearly a year spoke in the nobleman's tongue. "Thank you for coming to my aid."

Haaken's boots stepped in front of him. With rain tapping his hood, Gage bit his cheek and waited for a lecture. Instead, Haaken clapped his arms around him. "I cannot believe it is really you."

Letting the tension ease from his body, Gage returned Haaken's embrace. "I have missed you."

"And I you." Releasing him, Haaken stepped back and for a long moment stared into his face, then shook his head. "The orchard gate, truly?"

Gage cringed. "It seemed reasonable at the time."

"Aye, at the time." Pulling up his hood, Haaken motioned. "Come, before anyone else ventures along."

Searching the dark street, Gage whistled softly. Athalos clip-clopped out of the darkness, reins dragging on the wet cobblestones. Never so grateful for the horse's loyalty, Gage stroked Athalos's damp nose. "Good boy." Leading the animal, he followed Haaken through the gate.

The orchard's trees made a shushing all around them, and the black-blue sky growled as if warning off intruders. Staring at the rising towers of Einhart Castle, an intruder was exactly what Gage felt like.

Haaken relocked the orchard gate, then held up his lantern. Blinking in the sudden light, Gage tipped his head down to shield his eyes. Pained frustration filled Haaken's voice. "I see now why no one knew where to find you."

The shame in Gage's chest tightened. "I am sorry. Had I known earlier I was being sought, I would have sent word."

Unchecked anger rippled through Haaken's voice. "You would have sent word? It has been eight months, Gage. And you did not send word." Gage flinched, but Haaken continued, his voice hard. "When Father and I heard you had been ambushed, we rode with haste to Aro, but you were not there. And when asked, not one of your knights had any idea where you had gone. All the innkeeper in Aro could tell us was that you left of your own accord. We said, 'Mayhap Gage has gone on to Einhart or Ulbin.' But you were not to be found in either place. We thought surely he is somewhere along the way and will show up in a day or so, but you did not. We buried Allard, and still you did not come. The Blue Crow and his men were hanged, and Bardon too we laid to rest without you."

Another piece of Gage crumbled at the news that Bardon was also gone. He closed his eyes. Drawing air, he tried to hold it all at a distance, but it was of little use. It all came loose inside him, laying siege to his soul.

"We figured you just needed time," Haaken said, "that after a while you would come home. But hunts and tournaments came and went, and there remained no sign of you." Haaken's boots paced away and then back. "Christmas and Epiphany went by. I said, 'Mayhap Gage is with friends or with Uncle Elmon.' But when quiet inquiries were made, not a soul had seen you.

"As we looked to Easter, outright fear overcame concern, and your knights petitioned to search for you more thoroughly." Haaken exhaled a shuddering breath. "Father agreed to their request two months ago."

Self-loathing crawled through Gage and wrapped itself around his lungs. Biting his tongue, he watched the rain drip from his cloak and pool at his feet.

Haaken's voice took on ridicule. "Then suddenly here you are, and what do you say? 'Had I known I was being sought . . .'" The disdain in Haaken's voice dissipated, but his anger rode on. "Verily, were I not so incredibly glad to see you, I would pummel you till you could not stand upright."

His chest so tight it hurt, Gage forced himself to meet Haaken's gaze. "I am sorry." He meant the words but knew they fell far short of encompassing what he now realized the months had held for them.

Haaken's eyes glossed, and his voice trembled. "I can scarce believe you are here in front of me, for I have feared more than once I would never see you again."

"Haaken." Swallowing, Gage stumbled forward. They thudded into each other and for a long moment stood wrapped together, soaking up the rain. Relief and shame stung Gage's eyes, and he blinked hard. Turmoil roiled inside him, but so did hope.

Drawing a breath, Haaken released him and clapped his shoulder with an angry shove. "We should get inside out of this rain and find you clean clothes and a hot bath." Haaken wrinkled his nose and moved across the orchard. "For you smell terrible."

Words Gage had said to Allard echoed in his head. *"You smell more like swine than I did. If you want the girl to dance with you, use the bath, and borrow one of my clean tunics."* He saw Allard dancing happily with Emma, then Allard's lifeless eyes.

Gage's body quaked, and the misery and turmoil inside him shifted into a pounding in his chest. His knees began to tremble. He tried to keep up with Haaken, who was already headed toward the orchard's narrow bridge, which crossed to a gate that led into the castle's bailey.

"Could you have been any more cryptic with the message you sent?" Haaken asked over his shoulder.

The unexpected question yanked Gage's mind back to the present. Thunder rumbled, and the rain fell faster. Dragging in air, Gage focused on Haaken. "Well, it worked."

"Aye, if you mean I managed to decipher it," Haaken said. "I knew I had not given anyone fruit last night or any other night. But staring at my favorite nuts and a croissant, it dawned on me that the nuts represented me and the croissant you—the crescent of the second-born. After that I put together the orchard and nightfall. But not until I was here and no one was to be seen did I think of the gate.

"I had to go back then to retrieve its key, a delay that boded ill for you." Haaken eyed Gage through the veil of rain lit by his lantern. "Next time you might consider sending a written message and sparing yourself being stopped by the night patrol." Haaken shook his head. "What were you thinking?"

Gage swallowed before answering. "That I might avoid embarrassing Father and Mother if I had a chance to change before being recognized."

Sighing, Haaken nodded toward the bailey. "If you are to accomplish that, it will take more than just getting past the night patrol."

"I know." Gage attempted a smile. "And if I recall, you and I managed that well enough as boys. Remember how we used to sneak down to the pantry and swipe leftover tarts after feasts? Or that one night when the western barons were all here, and we had to get back to our rooms before Father discovered it was us listening in on them?"

Haaken smiled. "Or the night we snuck out to ride Father's courser, and we both nearly got bucked off, but we made it back to our rooms without anyone knowing we'd been out?"

"Aye, or when we crept up the east tower and dropped bay leaves on the sentries."

Haaken chuckled. "By their faces, you would have thought they were seeing snow in midsummer."

They both smiled, and Haaken nodded. "Let's get you inside unnoticed."

Leaving Athalos tied under a tree in the orchard, Gage slipped behind Haaken into the castle's bailey. He held his wet cloak closed and his saddlebags slung over one shoulder. They eased through the puddles on the steps leading to the courtyard and slipped away from the guards on the wall-walk above. Keeping to the darkness, Gage trailed Haaken's lantern across the bailey's paving stones toward one of three ground-level entrances to Einhart Castle.

"Prince Haaken," a voice called from the direction of the castle's main gate.

Abandoning the shadows behind Haaken, Gage dodged sideways up some steps to the base of the castle's large dovecot and hid beside it. Birds cooed over his head, and rain filled the space around him. The castle's constable, probably on his rounds to check on the porters and see to it the castle was secure for the night, approached Haaken.

Raising his lantern, Haaken conversed with the constable about how good the rain was for the fields and answered several questions about the upcoming feast. The conversation turned to those who would be attending and then to the constable's family and how his children were doing.

With his saddlebags digging into his shoulder and his legs cramping, Gage silently implored Haaken to quit being cordial and get moving. Finally, Haaken wished the man a good night and continued on his way.

Waiting until the constable had done the same, Gage edged out from the dovecot, back down the steps, and circled the kitchen's gardens to catch up to Haaken's lantern. Ahead of Haaken, two chatting scullions exited the lower castle entrance and headed for the nearby woodpile.

Gage crouched beside the end of the gardens and watched them fill their arms with split logs. Pausing, Haaken greeted them both by name and asked if they had any help bringing in the wood to dry by the fire.

They said no, but that they could manage well enough. Arms full, the two headed back inside, and Haaken motioned. Gage forsook the garden and slipped up beside Haaken. Together they entered the castle. The scullions were headed toward the kitchen. He and Haaken turned the opposite direction.

They reached the closest spiral stairs and started up together, only to have to rush back down a moment later to avoid someone descending. Gage scurried deeper down the dark passage, and Haaken paused at the base of the stairs as if politely letting the other person descend first.

Candle in one hand and linens caught up in the other, Addie, a laundress who had been a servant in the castle for as long as Gage could remember, emerged from the stairs. The woman jumped. "Gracious! Prince Haaken."

"Forgive me, Addie," Haaken said apologetically in the commoner's tongue. "I didn't mean to startle you."

She curtsied. "And I didn't mean to keep you waitin'."

"Actually, I have a favor to ask. Will you send Nathanial to my chambers?"

"As you please." Addie bowed and headed off.

Breathing a sigh, Gage carefully rejoined Haaken and followed him up the dark curving stone steps. At the top, Haaken checked both ways and then motioned him onward. They arrived a moment later at the door to Haaken's chambers. Haaken laid his hand on the iron latch and then paused. "By now my squire is likely within awaiting my return."

Gage flinched at the title, and his mind again caved into his memories. His heart beating faster, he nodded farther down the hall, desperate for space to fight what was about to overtake him. "Are my chambers empty?"

"They are."

"Then find me there once you have spoken to Nathanial and devised some errand on which to send your squire."

"Very well." Haaken handed him the lantern.

21

Clenching the light, Gage retreated to his chambers. Images of Allard's mud-smeared face and dead eyes filled his mind. His heart pounding, he entered swiftly and closed the door behind him. The lantern illuminated the all-too-familiar carved furniture, elaborate floor-to-ceiling tapestries, ornate rugs, and large four-poster bed along with his clothing trunk at its end.

Drawn across the room, Gage sank to his knees in front of the trunk he'd last seen the day he'd left Aro. He set down the lantern before he dropped it. Memories slammed over him like the cold water of the Apse and dragged him under in suffocating waves.

He saw Wes grab for his dagger. Sir Brent struck by the first shaft. Amos's fear-filled gaze. The swordsman slashing Sir Reid's back. The Blue Crow's arrogant expression. Bardon hit by the archer. And Allard's lifeless eyes. Their faces, pain, and his panic flooded over him. He couldn't breathe, couldn't think, couldn't reason his way out of it. Reeling, he dragged in air and leaned over. His pounding heart shook his body. With his hands pressed against the floor, he tried to drag himself from his recollections, but they kept coming, bringing with them a crushing sense of helplessness. He inhaled in ragged gasps.

Around him the shadowy forms of the canopy bed, the long tapestries, and the fine fixtures pressed in on him, all reminders of him as Prince Gage of Edelmar. Trembling, he clutched his head and screamed silently. *Leave me be!*

The memories simply struck with new vigor, holding him captive in his mind. Allard's shocked, dead face resurfaced over and over. Gage's hands went cold, but his body burned. He wanted to yank himself away to someplace safe, somewhere he could find peace and freedom again. But this wasn't like his nightmares. He couldn't wake from it.

He'd been here before. Back at the hunting lodge after he'd first left, he'd fought these battles for hours. Eventually, he'd learned to work his way out of them by chopping firewood, walking, hunting, foraging, and ultimately, becoming Gabe. A person so different from Gage, he rarely encountered things that reminded him of Allard. But here with reminders everywhere, it was all fresh and raw again, like it had happened yesterday.

Gage shoved his hands into his hair and curled his fingers tight. His insides ached with a pain that was spread so far and so deep it felt as if it gripped every part of him. Sitting up and tipping back his head, he pressed a quivering hand against his pounding chest and dragged in air.

The latch on his chamber door released.

Jerking straight, Gage stiffened his sweating body. He attempted to even out his breathing and paste on a calm expression, but there was no slowing his racing heart. Fearing if he tried to stand, his legs would crumple, he stayed kneeling and hoped he could bluff his way past whoever it was.

The soft glow of a stub of wax in a candlestick illuminated Haaken's face. "Nathanial is drawing a bath in my chambers, and I sent Joel to fetch some hot cider."

His head aching, Gage closed his eyes, glad it was Haaken and not anyone else. "Thank you." He meant the words, but with his heart still hammering his ribs, he wished instead he was far away on the road with Manton.

Haaken crossed the room. "If you intend to wear clothing from within that trunk, you will have to borrow something of mine instead. Unless, of course, you have its key, for it is locked and has been since you sent it back here."

Sliding his hand down the side of the trunk, Gage rested his fingers on two knots in the wood and pushed. A small drawer containing a key popped out of the trunk's side. Haaken shook his head. "Here all this time I was sure you had the key on you."

Gage scooped it out and inserted it into the trunk's lock. Twisting the metal, he thrust open the lid. Staring at the clothes within, he gripped the trunk's edge and tried to focus only on grabbing an item of clothing. The orange, high-collard tunic he'd worn the second night of the tournament would do. He seized it and pulled. Metal clanked on metal, and his other tunics fell aside to reveal his crown, signet ring, plated belt, and jeweled dagger, still flecked with mud.

Haaken sank onto the end of Gage's bed. "Your crown and signet ring have both been here in your clothing trunk this whole time?"

Focused on extracting the orange tunic from the trunk without falling back into his memories, Gage nodded. "Aye, I left them locked within and sent them here for safekeeping."

"You sent them here for safekeeping?" Haaken shoved off the bed, his eyes flashing and his voice filling with anger. "You could not leave a note, send a message, or say anything about your own safekeeping? But your crown and signet ring, they are of utter importance to you? Clearly, since you locked them in your trunk and left as what, a commoner?"

Gage struggled to his feet, his knees now shaking for an entirely different reason. He could feel Haaken pulling away, and it terrified him. "You do not understand."

The muscles in Haaken's jaw tightened. "Really? Then enlighten me, little brother, to your eight-month absence, where it seems neither your crown nor your title were of any importance to you."

Until that moment, Gage hadn't felt anger. But now it outdistanced every other emotion within him. He pointed at the trunk. "Aye, I left it all behind. And I do not regret it! I am sorry I neglected to send word, but tell me, what was I to say? 'I am well and will return when . . .' when what? When my presence no longer reminds the house of Ulbin excruciatingly of the brother and son they no longer have? When Emma has found another man? When the next tournament comes along for me to, what, win it all? Well, I will not joust again on the morrow, Haaken. I do not want it. Not leadership, not a manor, not a squire, none of it."

Haaken's brow furrowed, and the anger within his gaze dissipated into sympathy. "Gage," he murmured, "you battled with a man who long flaunted his ability to strip noblemen of wealth and men. Your encounter with him cost you much. But you brought the Blue Crow to justice. More than one lord breathed relief at that accomplishment."

His mind spinning with everything wrought by that day, Gage shook his head and dug his nails into his palms. "I did not bring in the Blue Crow. Allard delivered him to justice, and for that he received an arrow through his chest." Gage ground his gaze into Haaken's. "So pardon me if I do not share any regard for that accomplishment."

Haaken blanched. "I did not mean to imply . . ." Pausing and drawing a shuddering breath, Haaken paced away, then turned back toward Gage. "I simply meant the Blue Crow's inability to harm anyone else might be of some comfort to you, if you let it."

Images swallowed Haaken's words, and Gage dragged a shaking hand across his mouth. "Prithee, just let us not speak of it."

The light of Haaken's candle flickered across the tapestry of a grand hunt and flashed in Haaken's eyes. "I understand not wanting to speak about it, Gage, but you need to speak of it. For despite the time you have spent away, clearly, you have not dealt with it."

"I am dealing with it," Gage snapped.

Striding forward, Haaken snatched up Gage's crown and signet ring and shook them in his face. "Not like this, Gage. Not by leaving behind who you are!" Haaken thrust Gage's crown and ring back into his hands and pinned Gage with a forceful look. "It is not God's will that you abandon what He has given you. So, fight to thrive, and don't ever stop." With that Haaken turned and left.

The reality of his brother's words brought a strange calm that settled Gage's anger and slowed his heartbeat. Haaken was right. He would fight to thrive. And he had, as Gabe.

22

Gage bathed alone in Haaken's chambers, grateful to have no one attending him. Once he was finished, he pulled on the soft orange tunic, then washed his commoner clothes and hung them in his room to dry.

When Haaken returned, Gage's dark hair was just beginning to curl. He tied back its damp mass with a strip of leather and attempted to smooth his wrinkled tunic. He looked at Haaken. "Well?"

Haaken's expression tightened. "I spoke to Father."

Gage stiffened. "What did you tell him?"

"Only that you had returned and would come to speak with him yourself. He awaits you in the solar."

⁂

The family's private living area, the solar, offered a place away from servants' ears, and Gage was grateful for the choice. Yet as he reached the door, dread filled him. Taking a deep breath, he entered.

Flames in the hearth reflected off silver candle fixtures, shone over the smooth carved table and chairs, and sent shadows dancing into the distant passage leading to his parents' bedchamber.

His father rose from a chair set between a shelf of books and a table holding a stone chess set. "Gage." Striding forward, his father embraced him. His broad hands shifted from Gage's back to his shoulders and held him out at arm's length. Concern furrowed his father's face. "You are well? No harm has come to you?"

Forcing himself not to look at the floor, Gage took a breath. "Nay, Father. I am well. Prithee, forgive me for not sending word months ago."

His father's hands dropped, and his voice lost its protectiveness in grieved anger. "Numerous times in the last months, I considered sending every knight and men-at-arms in Edelmar out looking for you. Had I not known you left the inn in Aro of your own will, I would have done exactly that. But clearly you wished to be alone, so I stayed your knights from going after you and honored your choice, thinking surely my son would have the sense to return sooner or later. Were I aware just how much later, I would not have stayed my hand."

His father's anger took on new depth. "It is one thing to leave for a month or two. It is another to disappear for eight, Gage. Do you not have any idea the concern and distress you caused? What with unknown parties causing issues amongst the lords and you still unaccounted for, there were far too many possibilities. I finally allowed your knights to search for you because we had begun to fear your absence was no longer of your own choosing." Moving toward the fire, his father stared into the flames. "That was two months ago."

Gage swallowed hard. "I know. Haaken told me. I am sorry."

His father looked back at him. "You could have contacted us, Gage. Left word with someone, anyone. When I think of how many countless nights—" His father's hands clenched, and his eyes closed.

Gage recognized the action and knew if he waited, his father's next words would be what King Axel of Edelmar thought best to say, not what he wished to say. Gage opened his mouth to break the silence, figuring he deserved his father's unbridled rebuke. But before he could, the king heaved a sigh and took a seat in one of the nearby chairs. Fists uncurling, he motioned to Gage. "Sit."

Relieved to obey, Gage sank into a chair. Firelight glowed between them. His father's eyes were gripping, and his voice held quiet potency. "Where have you been all this time?"

His skin prickling, Gage answered slowly. "Mirus, Carson, Decoro, Orrim . . . a lot of places."

"But not here or to Roger in Ulbin. Why?"

"I . . ." Gage couldn't draw forth the words.

Leaving his chair, his father paused again at the fire. "You traveled to these places not as a prince of Edelmar."

Gage swallowed. "Did Haaken tell you that?"

"Nay, but had the second-born son of the king been in those places, the barons would have known, and the news would have made its way to me." His father's voice tightened. "Instead I heard nothing of you. So, unless you are lying about where you were, you traveled not as a prince and remained remarkably undetected in whatever attire you chose." Heat swept up Gage's chest and neck as his father heaved a breath. "What am I to do with you, Gage? A manor awaited you, and eight months ago I would have given it to you readily. But now—" He scrubbed a hand across his mouth.

Gage wanted to scream, *Just say what you are thinking! Say I cannot be trusted to lead. Say I failed. Say I cost Allard his life. Because I already know it. That is why I am here and why I cannot stay.*

His father sank back into his chair. "Why have you returned now, when for months you clearly chose not to?"

Gage inhaled slowly. The all-too-familiar pressure of his title, the expectations, and his wish to prove himself swirled within him. But instead of driving him into a panic, he heard Haaken's words

"Fight to thrive." The fear in him shifted and fed his determination. He had tried and failed to meet their expectations, but divided from those expectations, he was free. He had no doubt his father would give him a second chance, but he didn't want one. He took a breath. "I returned, Father, because I knew you would need an explanation as to why I will not be at the Noblemen's Feast. I came to tell you I do not want to be lord of a manor. Neither do I want to return to Ulbin nor live as a prince." Amazed he'd said the words aloud, Gage was petrified of what would happen now that he had.

His father sat perfectly still. Silence pressed around them for a mortifying length of time. Gage gripped the arms of his chair and tried to read beneath his father's grieved expression to prepare for what might come next. Finally, his father spoke. "If you are sincere in what you have said, then what *do* you intend to do with yourself?"

Gage replied with as much strength as he could muster, "I wish to continue traveling as a commoner."

A cringe crossed his father's face, and Gage feared he'd reached the end of his forbearance. He expected resistance, but instead his father offered a quiet response. "How will you support yourself?"

"The same way I have been ... by training and selling mounts."

"Why?" His father's voice took on the full weight of his authority. "Why forsake your title and land and choose the life of a commoner when anyone else in your place would rejoice at the opportunities that lie before you?"

Gage felt like he'd just been slapped. "Opportunities? Opportunities for what, Father? For more pain and loss? I have made a life for myself as a commoner, a life I love. A life where I have no need to require my own protection at the cost of anyone else's lives or to lord over my friends." Even as he said it, Gage wished he could snatch back his disdain-filled words, for they startled even him.

To his astonishment, his father's expression softened, and his voice became gentle once again. "Gage, the death of someone close to you is not easily borne by anyone. But do not let your grief become a reason to walk away from who you are. Years ago when I held your baby sister in my arms and watched her tiny body breathe its last breath, I wrestled too. I questioned who I was and if God was judging me for something I had done. I wanted an explanation and a way out of the pain. But God will walk you through, Gage. Grief is part of life. Accepting that and living through it is a path by which we learn to truly live and truly love.

"Haaken traveled that same path when Novia drowned, questioning and wrestling with God until he finally found life again resting in our Almighty Lord. You must do the same, Gage. Surrender your grief to God, for only in Him will you find peace."

Gage did not bother telling his father that he had long ago given up believing in God. Instead, at the moment he felt an overwhelming fear that his concerns about returning were about to become a reality. "Father, I have found peace and freedom traveling as a commoner. Prithee, do not take that away from me. Allow me to continue living as I wish."

"Gage, you are a prince of Edelmar, playing at being a commoner. For how long will you truly desire such a life? You speak of it as freedom, but such a life bears a cost I do not think you understand."

Panic and anger stirred within Gage. He already bore a cost, but it was that of being Gage, not Gabe. "Father, prithee do not forbid me this."

As a knight he had sworn an oath of fealty to his king. He would not break that vow, and as a son he would not dishonor his father. But where that might leave him terrified him, for he already knew what being back did to him. "Father, I cannot stay. Prithee, let me go. Call off the search, and allow me to return to living as I have been."

"I believe neither you nor I would wish such a decision be made in haste." His father replied slowly, "Therefore, I will take time to consider and pray over your request. Then I will answer you."

Grateful his father had not given a straight-up no, Gage nodded and kept silent, knowing there was no argument he could make now that would speed up his father's decision.

His father stood. "Your mother was eager to see you but agreed to tarry below in the hall until you and I had spoken. Will you see her now?" Gage nodded his agreement, but he felt wrung out and exhausted. If speaking with Haaken and his father could bring such turmoil, he worried what facing his mother would do. But it was too late to change his mind.

※

Rolling a chess piece in his hand, Gage looked up when his mother swished into the room, her purple satin skirts flowing around and behind her. The firelight glinted on the gilded pins in her coiled silver-black hair. Her strong features, diminutive smile, and warm brown eyes welcomed him. "My son." Her voice sounded strained, but she lifted her hands to his cheeks and drew his face down to kiss his forehead.

"Mother." Gage smiled and hugged her. "You are well?"

She leaned back and caught his gaze. "Do I look unwell?"

He laughed. "Nay, Mama."

"Good." She patted his flat belly. "And you? Are you eating enough?"

He smiled and wrapped an arm across his stomach. "Aye, Mama." His father and Haaken entered. His mother and father exchanged a look. Gage's smile slipped away. He prepared himself for a deluge of new objections to his request, but his mother simply swept herself into a chair and nodded to Haaken. "Tell him of Sir Reid."

At the shift to news, Gage frowned. "What of him?" He wondered if somehow Sir Reid had beat him back to Einhart Castle from the R&R Inn.

Haaken brightened. "Sir Reid has finally asked Baron Ogden for Lady Cathleen's hand."

Gage pictured Sir Reid and Lady Cathleen's elated smiles at Nardell but also Emma and Allard laughing as they danced together. He gripped the back of the closest chair. Haaken frowned. "You do not look pleased?"

Gage shoved away the images and forced a smile. "Nay, I am overjoyed for them."

His mother glanced between the two of them. "I wish my own sons were thinking of such things as marriage."

"Irena," their father chided.

Her eyebrows lifted. "Well, I would like to have grandchildren. Is that such a bothersome request?" A second look passed between his parents, and with it Gage saw a flash of grief cloud his mother's face. She lifted her chin, the strain returning to her voice. "I think I shall do some stitching. Axel, will you add another log to the fire? Mayhap you boys would like to play chess."

Gage realized then that somewhere between the hall and the solar, his father must have warned her to ask him no questions. Normally, his mother would have sought to glean all she could about his adventures, and he would revel in the telling and laugh as she gasped at his accounts of being nearly wiped from his horse or taking a tilt without a single hit. He mourned the loss of her inquiry but was also grateful for it, for she would have been hard pressed to glory in his recent ventures. But still, he wished to tell everything to them, as if the recounting of his last eight months could somehow bridge the gap that was growing between them. But he had a feeling it would just make the gap bigger.

His head aching, he sat down at the chess table and looked at Haaken, inwardly begging him not to refuse. "Will you play a round with me?"

Haaken move to join him. "Indeed."

23

STARTLED AWAKE BY a nightmare, Gage rose from before his bedroom's empty fireplace. He opened one of the chamber's windows and stood in the cool air waiting for the trembling in his hands and chest to fade. Slowly, dawn cast its scarlet hew across the horizon.

The evening before, playing chess with Haaken and being with his parents, had felt oddly normal, but then he'd returned alone to a room he had last shared with Allard. Nothing had stopped his memories then, and he'd spent half the night struggling to survive them until he finally fell into an exhausted sleep.

Still dressed in his orange tunic, Gage listened to the hearty "Dong, dong, dong," of the church bells announcing the day. He wondered where Manton was. Probably just rising in some small village between Einhart and Dulcis.

A knock sounded. Gage turned. "Come in."

Haaken entered. "Good, I was hoping you were already up. I sent one of the stable hands to bring in your mount, but he will not let the man near him."

Having forgotten about Athalos, Gage hurried past Haaken. "Nay, he does not take kindly to being approached by anyone else. I will see to him."

"Be quick about it." Haaken called after him. "Mother has requested the two of us break our fast with her in the solar."

Slowing, Gage glanced back. "Where is Father?"

"Praying in the chapel."

Praying. So his father had meant what he had said about wanting time to consider and pray about his request. Gage wondered skeptically how praying over a decision could make any difference, but he also worried what difference it might make.

Heading to the orchard, he brought Athalos through to the stable, stripped his tack, and fed him, all while ignoring the questioning glances he caught passing among the stable hands.

Dusting hay off his clothes, he returned through the castle's great hall to make his way up to the solar—a decision he quickly regretted. Servants eating to one side of the massive stone hall respectfully bowed their heads to him, but the moment he passed, he heard quiet chatter behind him. His chest tightened, and his heart pounded.

His anonymity was indeed gone. Everywhere he went and everything he did was observed, murmured about, and questioned behind his back. He started up the spiral stairs near the dais and halfway up caught himself against its curving stone wall. His legs trembled so badly that he could not make the next step. He sat down to keep from falling and pressed a hand against his chest.

He smacked his fist against the wall. Channeling his anger, he shoved himself back to his feet. Using both hands to steady himself, he forced his legs to carry him the rest of the way up the stairs.

⚬⚭⚬

HE ARRIVED IN the solar to find Haaken and his mother waiting for him at the room's board, where a meal had been spread. Two servants stood nearby ready to fetch anything else they might request.

Gage returned his mother's warm greeting and kissed her cheek before settling on the bench. He was surprised yet grateful no other guests were staying within the castle. It meant they could dine privately without needing to entertain anyone.

His mother reached her hands out to him and Haaken. They obliged her as they had as children by placing their hands in hers. Bowing her head, she prayed. "Lord God, I thank You my two sons are seated again beside me. May Your hand be upon each of them, may they walk always according to Your ways, and may Your grace and wisdom abound toward us all, especially Axel. Bless us and this food, Almighty Lord. Amen."

Gage opened his eyes and began to eat. He chewed slowly, savoring the taste of the spices, the perfectly boiled egg, and the softness of the honey-sweetened bread.

Haaken, with a butter-coated knife in hand, looked at their mother. "Did Father say how the meeting with Baron Alexander went?"

"Baron Alexander of Opes?" Gage asked, recalling his and Manton's near encounter with the lord on the road the day before. Nodding, Haaken kept his gaze on their mother.

"He is not pleased," she replied, "but he has agreed to wait for the feast to address the issue."

"What issue?" Gage asked, noting Haaken's worried look and remembering something his father had said about issues amongst the lords.

His mother delicately spooned a scoop of egg. "The baron is being accused of having sent several knights to seize a handful of cattle from Baron Ogden's herdsman. Alexander claims none of his knights were responsible nor did he order any cattle taken on or off his demesne. But when Baron Ogden sent his sheriff to investigate, two of Ogden's cattle were found in one of Baron Alexander's barns."

Gage blinked. "That does not make any sense. Why would Baron Alexander steal another lord's cattle?"

"He would not," Haaken said. "But it is his word against Baron Ogden's."

"In the last several months," their mother explained, "a number of other similarly odd offenses have created discord amongst the lords. Messengers have been waylaid and their messages stolen by knights displaying Baron Blakely's coat-of-arms. Two barons have been turned back on the borders of Leland's manor by guards claiming to serve Roderick. Boundary stones on Lord Orrim's land were moved, and now Baron Alexander is accused of stealing cattle and having knights he has not knighted."

Haaken turned to address Gage. "Father has banned the lords from laying any charges against each other until all complaints can be discussed at the Noblemen's Feast with all lords present, though whether or not this will help reveal the true sources and motives behind these incidences is yet to be seen."

Gage hoped desperately he wouldn't be around for the feast, but Haaken's words reminded him of the grievances he had heard from commoners. He had planned to share them with his father, but hearing about the lords made him realize why many of the commoners' grievances existed in the first place. He also realized the issues at hand were probably more than enough of a burden upon his father's mind.

"Gage?" His mother's voice sounded expectant.

Realizing he must have missed something, Gage looked up. "Pardon?"

"Your knight, Sir Wick, returns to Einhart on the morrow to report to your father. I was asking if you would not mayhap wish to entertain him for a meal? I am sure he would be pleased to see you."

Gage dropped his gaze to his food. "Aye, mayhap."

His mother and Haaken's conversation turned to preparations for the feast. Gage was again listening absently when he heard Haaken say, "Gage and I can take the piece to him."

Gage looked up. "What piece? To whom?"

24

An hour later, Gage stood in a silversmith shop watching Haaken unwrap a large silver plate supported by a curved stand. Haaken held the piece out to the master silversmith. "Can you make two more to match this?" he asked in the commoner's tongue. "They would have to be done in six days."

The man wiped his hands down his leather apron and took the item, turning it over in his calloused hands. "Her Majesty wants them exactly the same?"

Haaken nodded.

"This I can do." The smith set the silver plate on his worktable. "I'll deliver them to the castle myself when I'm finished."

Haaken smiled. "Thank you. My mother will be very pleased."

"It is I who am pleased to do work for Her Majesty," the smith said with a bow.

Gage exited the shop ahead of Haaken, a bitter taste in his mouth. He had never detested seeking anyone's service before, but as he watched the craftsman snap to attention at their presence, bend over backwards to meet their requests, and promise to see personally to this or that need, he keenly felt the derision of it. It was as if they, the high class, were doing such a favor to request a service from the lower class, and the lower class were supposed to be thrilled to oblige. They made a good show of it too, but he now knew how fast those smiles disappeared and what sort of comments were made the moment a nobleman departed a shop. And on the street, no matter where they went, Gage felt eyes watching them.

Four men-at-arms, Haaken's squire, and a servant trailed behind them. Their presence—for guardianship and the convenience of carrying their purchases—made Gage's stomach churn.

Haaken glanced over at him. "I know new plates are a trifle, but I like how buying them puts food on a craftsmen's family's table and coin in their purse. Such is the way buying and selling ought to be. Do you not agree?"

Feeling as if Haaken's words carried more than met the eye, Gage stopped mid-stride. "Did Father put you up to this?"

Haaken paused, his smile turning into a frown. "Why would you think that?"

Noting a woman with a young daughter curtsy and go wide of them, Gage reminded himself that he was standing in the middle of Einhart and should keep his mouth shut. He also needed to avoid the sellers he had encountered the day before lest Gage and Gabe meet. His face hot, he strode past Haaken. "Forgive me. I mistook your intent."

"Gage?" Haaken jogged to catch up with him. "What is bothering you?"

"Nothing."

Haaken's voice took on a tinge of anger. "Do not tell me 'tis nothing."

"'Tis not the place to discuss it," Gage replied, highly aware they were being watched.

"Discuss what?" Haaken's gaze narrowed. "What exactly did you and Father talk about last night?"

The moment they returned to the castle and he was free from Haaken's questions, Gage retreated to his own chambers. But once there he had nothing to occupy himself. He paced like a penned mount. When he could bear it no longer, he went to find his father. He searched the castle, the guardhouse, the stables, and finally asked a servant where the king might be found. The servant directed him to the castle's chapel. Gage frowned. Was his father really still praying?

He entered the chapel quietly and eased the door closed behind him. All within was still, as if the air itself was enraptured amid the glorious columns and soaring colored-glass windows. A sunbeam streamed through the numerous exquisite panes, casting images from every portion of the Scriptures in a majestic display across the oak benches that lined the building's center.

In the back of the chapel, spiral stairs led up to balconies lining the chapel's nave while straight ahead down the central aisle past the benches and pillars stood the altar in the chancel.

Covered in pure white linen, the altar held two gold-leaf candlesticks, a gilded chalice, and a golden plate. Above it in the beautifully painted apse hung a cross. Three strides from the altar rose the stairs to the pulpit upon which the priest stood, so his voice might reach all present. Gage had listened many a time to that viewpoint. Always the priest had sounded so confident in his words, as if he really believed what he read was true.

Gage would admit that being within the building did evoke awe, but he did not attribute that to the presence of an all-powerful God, capable and desirous of intervening on humanity's behalf. He believed the feeling came from the architecture alone.

Dedicated to the idea of the cross, the high-ceilinged building was designed to elicit a feeling of reverence. Two areas expanded outward from the long nave just before the altar, forming the transept—the arms of the cross. These quiet recesses displayed their own secluded corners and offered places where one might stay and pray more privately.

It felt strange to troop down the center of the building to look for his father, so Gage strode down the left edge of the chapel instead. He passed gilded depictions of biblical scenes sculpted into the stone walls and heard a low murmur from the south side of the building.

Crossing through the benches, he approached the right side of the transept. There in its depth, his parents were seated next to each other on a stone bench while Haaken stood before them. Gage backed away. "Forgive me. I did not mean to interrupt."

His father's strong voice stopped him. "Gage. Stay, what we speak of concerns you. I have made a decision about your request."

Gage's heart beat faster. Uncertain from his father's gaze if that decision bode good or ill for him, he searched Haaken and his mother's faces, hoping for clues. Haaken looked just as hurt and angry as he had earlier, and his mother stared pensively at her hands folded in her lap.

His father rose from the bench. "You still wish to return to traveling as a commoner?"

Gage swallowed. "I do."

Emotion rattled Haaken's voice. "You cannot be persuaded?"

Gage cringed. "Nay. This is what I want, Haaken."

His father said, "Then I would have you know 'tis no flippant answer I give you. 'Tis one debated at length and wholly lain before God."

Sweat dampened Gage's hairline, and his heart began to pound.

"Gage, your title is yours by birthright, not appointment. It cannot be removed nor surrendered by you. You are a prince no matter how you live." His father sighed. "But no law prohibits you from laying aside all expression of your title. Therefore, if you wish to travel as a commoner, you have the right to do so."

Hope and fear mingled inside Gage. "I have the right, but have I your permission?"

"Nay."

Feeling as if everything inside him had suddenly been ripped loose, Gage quaked. "I do not understand."

His father eyed him. "I will not give you my permission to travel in this manner, for I do not advise this choice. But nor will I prohibit you from making it."

Gage exhaled in utter relief. "Then I may go?"

"I am not finished," his father replied sternly. "If you choose to travel as a commoner, the responsibility of that choice is yours and yours alone. Do you understand?"

"Aye, Father." Being responsible for no one but himself was exactly his desire.

"Then understand this as well. If you travel as a commoner, the laws of the land will apply to you as if you are truly a commoner. And if any one of us comes across you in our travels, we will respect your choice by treating you not as royalty but as a commoner. Do I make myself clear?"

Swallowing, Gage glanced at Haaken, who would not meet his gaze. Gage looked back to his father, feeling remorse but also resolve. "I understand."

"For one year only I give you the freedom to make this choice and travel as a commoner," his father continued. "When a year is through, you will return hither to Einhart, and you and I will speak again about this matter."

His mother's soft yet assertive voice joined the discussion. "And if you change your mind before a year's time, you are welcome at any point to return to living as a prince of Edelmar."

He nodded. "Thank you, Mama."

"And as our son," his father added, "you are always welcome here at Einhart Castle, regardless of what means you choose to live by. Just prithee, come and go with caution. For if on the road any suspect you are a prince, you may not be safe."

"I will be careful, Father."

His father cleared his throat. "There is one more condition. You must carry your signet ring with you." Gage opened his mouth to object, but his father raised his hand. "I have already taken the liberty of hiring a saddler to create a concealed pocket in your tack. You will have a place to store it safely and out of sight."

"That way, to communicate with us, you can send a message with a normal seal on the outside but with the seal of your signet ring within," his mother explained.

"Or you can send chestnuts and a croissant," Haaken quipped.

Gage looked from Haaken to his parents. "Thank you." His liberty to live as he wished was not limitless, but to his utter relief, it had been granted.

25

Before dawn the next morning, Gage left Einhart Castle through the orchard gate, dressed again in his common clothes and gray cloak. He had said his goodbyes by candlelight in the solar. Upon reaching the stable, he discovered his parents had provided much more than just a hiding place for his signet ring. Another set of saddlebags had been added to his tack. They contained dried meat, cheese, bread, and a number of smaller bags of grain. His waterskins also sloshed with liquid. Feeling blessed and a bit ashamed, he rode through Einhart with his hood low.

Only once he was out the other side of the city's western wall and trotting toward the fields with a steady trail of peasants did he look back. He squinted into the sun tearing open the eastern horizon. After exhaling, he breathed in a full breath of fresh air, nodded his farewell, and touched his heels to Athalos's sides.

※

Gage reached Luert by late afternoon and started searching for Manton. He checked every tavern, stable, and inn but found no sign of his friend. Had he missed him? He calculated the days since they had parted. Manton had said he planned to cross at the ford, and Luert was the only way to the ford from Dulcis. There was no way he could have already come and gone.

Trying to convince himself he was just too early, Gage refilled his half-empty waterskin, browsed the local shops, checked out the two horses for sale in town, and ate a late meal from his saddlebags. He had started the day so relieved and happy to be back on the road, but now, leaning against the rough wall of a thatcher's storehouse, breathing in the dusty scent of drying straw, and eating alone, doubts crept in.

He stroked Athalos's neck. Sunlight pierced the lowest branches of a beech tree wedged between a chandler's shop and a butcher's shop down the street. Squinting at the descending sun, Gage knew he needed to find a place to settle for the night. He missed the teasing debate he and Manton often had about where to stay. He sighed. He'd forgotten how much he disliked traveling alone.

Delaying until just before dark, he procured a spot at an inn that was an improvement over the R&R in Tallus.

Only gentry and nobles experienced the sundry qualities of inns, things like a bed to themselves, a stocked fire, and a good meal. For everyone else, an inn was simply a place to sleep free from rain and the risk of being attacked in the night by wild animals. Sharing the space was anticipated. A fire was not. Rooms were too cold or too hot and almost always crowded.

Sleeping in a room full of strangers had taken some getting used to, but Gage had eventually adapted to it by reasoning they were not strangers, just fellow travelers wishing for the same thing he did—a solid, uninterrupted night's sleep.

Eventually, a crowded inn had become comfortable to him, much more so than some of the other lodging he had experienced traveling with Manton. Manton would willingly seek a night's stay from almost anyone and knew a number of families and business owners in different villages and towns. Before traveling with

Manton, Gage had stayed with herdsman here or there or occasionally in barns with field workers, but never had he thought to intrude upon a family's home.

Several of his first experiences staying with families Manton knew had been so awkward Gage had considered parting ways with him. Slowly, however, he learned how to keep out of a family's way and yet still be helpful and the kind of guest they wouldn't mind having back. Carrying water, entertaining little ones, sharpening tools, milking goats, pulling weeds, and chopping firewood were all ways he'd learned to help. While staying with families, he had also discovered much about the lives of the lower class he'd never known before.

He'd been surprised at first that people with no extra money and so little space were willing to take in guests, but Manton brought news from other places, entertaining stories, a helping hand, and gifts of wooden toys. And it always seemed the families considered them more blessing than burden. Gage had come to realize news and entertainment were a valuable commodity among the lower class.

As part of the royal family, receiving information was something he had taken for granted. Word was expected to arrive hurriedly by the hooves of lathered horses or by the wings of pigeons. The latest and biggest happenings in Edelmar were always known by them within days, never longer than a month.

But the common people might go years without hearing word that a cousin had died, a friend had gotten married, or a baby had been born. Travelers became news carriers, gratefully welcomed in to tell what they knew and be told news to pass along.

Knowing what sort of news to collect and share was a tricky endeavor when one was unfamiliar with what was expected, but over time Gage had learned to discern the information the lower class hungered for and how to accumulate it in the places he and Manton visited. It was not hard considering the taverns and inns where Manton sold his games were perfect places for gleaning information.

Tonight though, Gage did not listen in or chat with his fellow travelers. He was in no mood, for without Manton, concern ate at him. He could still buy and sell horses, but he was not sure he had a good enough eye for knowing the training they would require to make his money back. And he was certainly not sure whether or not to go on to Delkara alone.

Lying in the dark with eyes wide open listening to the mix of snoring around him, Gage thought through his options. Was this truly the way he wanted to live? He recalled his mother's offer about being welcome to return before a year's time. He could change his mind. But if he did, what then? Return to Einhart? To what, panicking in the halls and second-guessing himself while servants looked on and whispered behind his back? That was no life.

The common people struggled to survive, but at least among them he too was free to struggle without feeling a fool. As a commoner, life was raw no matter how one looked at it, and it was acceptable to be wearied by it. Most of all, they did not expect much. Never did they assume any of their own had what it took to run a manor or lead knights into battle. Instead, they embraced the ordinary. They didn't look to the past but lived in the moment, seizing each day as it came.

It was a life he had come to love. Even if it meant sleeping every night in a dark inn with twenty snoring strangers, he would choose it over ruling a manor any day.

26

Gage woke to those around him moving about and collecting their things. He blinked. It was dawn. Not once in the night had a dream yanked him awake. Exhaling happily, he rose with renewed determination and pulled on his boots. With or without Manton, he would go on to buy and sell and explore Delkara. He could travel the neighboring kingdom with far less concern about being recognized, for what little anyone in Delkara had seen of him had been mostly when he was no older than a page.

※

In the first glorious rays of the sun, Gage headed toward the town's wide main road to find a street seller he had seen there the day before. The seller sat outside a tavern with her young daughter sleeping in the shade beside her and a collection of baskets spread in a semicircle before her. She had radishes, garlic, leeks, dried dates, dried figs, and fresh figs, for sale. Amid all were bay leaves to keep the insects away.

Knowing the ripe figs had to be from the spring crop, which did not usually have as rich a flavor, Gage chose the dried figs instead. Left in the sun for four to seven days to dry, they were chewy and sweet. He paid for a handful of the fruit and moved down the street to dig in his saddlebags in search of the hunk of cheese his parents had provided.

"Tell me you paid a reasonable price."

Looking up at the sound of the familiar voice, Gage laughed. "Manton. I could've sworn I searched all of Luert for you."

Manton attempted to stop the short yet powerfully built horse he rode. His reins tightened, catching and lifting the animal's long flaxen mane. The horse fought his grip. Twice Manton forced the animal to back up before getting it to stand still, all while maintaining his hold of Nigel, who was fully loaded and trailing on a lead behind him. "I stayed with a friend in the village on Lord Nolan's manor and left early this morning."

Manton's chestnut mount tucked its head, flicked its flaxen tail irritably, and began to paw. Gage nodded at the animal. "Did you pay a reasonable price?"

Manton grinned. "How much were your figs?"

Gage laughed and stuffed them into his saddlebags. "Not near a penny to what you spent on that animal, I'm sure. Were you planning on selling it yourself?"

Manton shrugged. "I figured I'd rather ride than walk to Delkara. And I knew you'd catch up with me eventually. Besides, the man was desperate to get rid of him. He took the first price I offered. I've no doubt you can sell him for a good profit once he's had some training."

Gage eyed the mount. "He's got a good build and isn't bad looking. I supposed I could take you up on the offer."

Manton rested an arm on his saddle. "I take it then your business in Einhart is settled?"

"It is."

Manton eyed him. "Then as long as you agree to lose to me at checkers, chess, and wari whenever I want, we have a deal."

Laughing, Gage nodded.

※

BEFORE LEAVING LUERT they stopped at each tavern and inn. Manton sold one gameboard, two sets of dice, and a few replacement checker pieces. Then they headed for Clement. It rained on the way, and Gage took charge of Nigel, leaving Manton free to deal with the new mount, which Gage dubbed Chester.

Just before nightfall they dripped their way into the gates of Clement and took lodging at the Wallmon Inn, which was built directly into the city's outer wall. The common room's window opened just below the battlement, and from it they could see to the White Fortress. It was situated on the opposite side of the road from Clement and two hundred paces from the Apse River, which formed the border between Edelmar and Delkara. Constructed of cream-colored stone, the fortress had a barracks, a four-story tower, a stable, and a yard but was not large enough to serve as a castle. Therefore, the Lord of Clement maintained his own fortified manor to the north of Clement but in general kept about six knights and three dozen soldiers garrisoned within the fortress.

The fortress served as guardian of the ford since no walls or gates closed off the crossing on the Edelmarian side. A barrier-free crossing was an odd choice but one Gage's father had once explained, saying the kings of Edelmar wanted people to know they were free to come and go. Thus the White Fortress stood on one side of the road and Clement on the other, leaving between them an unbarred passage to and from the ford as a symbol of goodwill to all.

Gage happened to know that tunnels ran to the fortress from the basement of King's Tavern and from the lowest level of the lord's watermill, both of which were inside the walls of Clement. The tunnels provided a means by which messages and additional soldiers could be sent to the fortress without anyone being the wiser. Gage had been inside the tunnels once with his father and once with his knight, Sir Wick, whose father was the Lord of Clement.

Every once in a while a young lord would question why in a time of peace the lords of Edelmar maintained so many soldiers. Without fail, a gray-haired baron would tsk and quote an old saying. "Everything is hard won by someone at some time. Enjoy peace, but keep both eyes open and a sword ever handy." It was a mindset Gage dearly wished he had heeded. For when the memories of the ambush came, he always recalled with burning clarity the moment he had unstrapped his sword.

"Gabe, you paying attention?"

Manton's words jerked Gage's gaze back to the candle and chessboard in front of him. "Sorry." He reached to move a pawn but then remembered he was supposed to be losing for their audience. Scrubbing his chin, Gage took out Manton's rook with his knight, knowing it would cost him his queen.

The pudgy salt merchant looking over Manton's shoulder lifted his eyebrows but remained silent—unlike the long-legged traveling minstrel, who hummed several happy notes and bumped Manton's arm.

The scribe in the corner observed their game with curiosity while sharing bread and cheese with his wife and four little ones. The couple had come to the city looking for a place to set up shop, and Gage hoped they found one, for the man's family looked thin and travel worn.

"He's going to lose," the female spice seller stated from where she sat at the end of the board just inside the candlelight. With features like a worn grindstone, the woman had appeared absorbed with sorting the bottles and dried plants within her satchel.

Propped near the window, a beekeeper from Weldon lowered his flask with a slosh. "Which one of 'em?" he asked.

The spice seller snorted and shoved her gray-brown braid over her shoulder. "You can't tell?"

With amusement playing at the corners of his mouth, Manton took out Gage's knight. Gage decided to shift the game to keep Manton and their observers guessing. He struck with his last bishop, taking out a pawn and throwing Manton's king into jeopardy.

Frowning as he waved away a fly, Manton slid his king over a square. Gage swung his bishop forward, greedily removing a pawn. Seizing the opportunity, Manton wiped out Gage's queen. The minstrel cheered at Manton's success, only to instantly shush himself while glancing apologetically toward the scribe's wife and her sleeping baby.

Manton cornered Gage's king in his next two turns. Gage threw up his hands in defeat and surrendered the board to Manton, who offered to play someone else.

His work done for the night, Gage willingly stood from the bench to let the minstrel take his place. As he moved away from the table, the spice seller's green eyes pinned him. "You play your game well."

Gage smirked and tipped his head to her. "Thank you, my lady."

She thwacked his leg with the back of her hand. "Don't be pompous. I meant it."

He stepped out of her reach and commented accusingly. "So did I."

A smile replaced her scowl, and her eyes and hands swept to her satchel. Withdrawing something, she revealed what looked like short pine needles pinched between her fingers. She held up her hand. "Smell."

Eyeing her, Gage leaned forward and sniffed. The savory scent of rosemary flooded his senses, reminding him of so many wonderful feasts. "Oh." He sighed happily.

She stated a price. He frowned, and she chuckled. "There's more than one way to play your kind of game." Realizing he had been taken in as easily as a gudgeon, Gage laughed.

"Who in heaven's name would be out traveling at this hour?" the beekeeper asked, staring out the window. Curious, Gage and the salt merchant joined him at the opening to observe a lantern-carrying rider making his way past the city. "Looks like he's heading for the ford," the beekeeper said.

"Not at this hour," the salt merchant replied. "Edelmar may not have gates to close across the ford, but Maneo will be locked tight. He must be going to the fortress."

In the dark below, the rider shifted his lantern, and Gage caught sight of his face and the coat-of-arms on his saddle. Gage pulled away from the window and recalled his mother's words from two days before. *Your knight, Sir Wick, returns to Einhart on the morrow to report to your father.*

If Sir Wick was supposed to have been arriving in Einhart the day he left, why was he there outside of Clement? He must have arrived early in Einhart and reported to King Axel first thing. Then he would have been told the search had ended, and after that Gage's father would have done the logical thing. He would have sent Sir Wick back to his previous post at the White Fortress. Which meant, Sir Wick could easily be part of the guard at the ford in the morning.

Wearing common clothes and a hat, Gage had passed unrecognized by many an Edelmarian lord with whom he had talked and dined but never face-to-face with one of his own knights. Persuading Manton to choose another route now would be impossible, and his reasons for making the request would be completely unexplainable. He'd either have to stay behind or take the chance and hope Sir Wick would not be at the ford his first day back.

27

That night, Gage tossed and turned in the inn's lower room. He wondered where each of his other knights were now, which brought him back to the Blue Crow's attack, hearing and seeing everything. Novia's face flashed into the mix of the dead. Gage shoved himself up from the straw mattress, inhaling rapidly. Why Novia?

He knew why. The answer flowed just past the city, its fierce current turning the lord's watermill. Heaving a breath, he dropped back down and wrestled onto his other side.

"Will you please settle down over there?" the beekeeper hissed from the opposite end of the room. "You're making so much noise."

Gage gritted his teeth and forced himself to remain still. Closing his eyes, he fixed his thoughts on Delkara—the one place he might yet find freedom.

☙❧

Morning arrived with little rest, for despite having finally fallen asleep, Gage had dreamt the spice seller had announced him to be Prince Gage and then called through the window to ask if Sir Wick recognized him. Sir Wick had stormed the inn, and Gage had been desperately trying to explain why he could not return with him to Einhart when Manton began yelling "Liar!" loud enough for all of

Clement to hear. At that point, Gage had mercifully bolted awake in the dark to the welcome sound of snoring.

With light finally seeping in the street-side windows, Gage did not know which he feared worse, being recognized as Gabe or as Gage. As he rose he wished for the first time that he was neither.

Manton wasn't in the inn. After checking the stable to confirm Nigel and Chester were still there, Gage returned to dine with the other guests. Manton would show up eventually.

The innkeeper's wife, a short, wiry woman, served them rye bread and cracked wheat boiled in goat's milk and chatted freely with the spice seller, who seemed to be a regular there. After his nightmare, the two women chatting with each other disturbed him.

The beekeeper added honey to his food, but Gage finished the bland mixture and distractedly chewed the last of his bread while the scribe and innkeeper discussed empty shops for rent within Clement. Gage paid the innkeeper and exited the common room to descend a city tower to street level. He re-entered the inn's stable, which was three floors directly below the common room he had just left.

Built of the thick stone of the city's wall, it remained cooler in the summer than those constructed of wattle and daub but was dark and dank. Raising the wick on the stable's lantern, Gage ignored the rodents and cockroaches scurrying away and distracted himself from what lay ahead by working with Chester. He handled Chester's feet, bridled him, brushed him, and then made him step this way and that until he was assured the animal would perform any ground action asked of him.

Manton entered carrying a pigeon-sized package wrapped in cloth. "Sorry about the delay." He stuffed the parcel into his personal pack. "You ready to go?"

Running a hand down Athalos's scarred shoulder, Gage distractedly opened his mouth. The nobleman's "aye" rose to his tongue. Catching himself, he switched to the commoner's tongue. "I'm ready."

His entire being screamed to the contrary, but what else could he say? *"Actually, I've decided we should enter Delkara using the bridge in Awnquera. See, there's this knight at the White Fortress I'd rather not cross paths with, and because of this girl I once knew, I really don't want to wade through the Apse."*

"Good, then let's get moving," Manton said. "A ropemaker friend of mine lives on the other side of Maneo. We can spend the day in the city and then hopefully the night with him and his wife to get the lay of the land before deciding where to go first in Delkara."

Intentionally trailing behind Manton through Clement, Gage pulled his dark hair loose from the leather strip binding it back and tugged his hat low over his eyes. He knew it would make no difference if he came face to face with Sir Wick, but at a distance it might be enough. He swatted at flies swarming up from animal refuse and wished for the cover of the previous day's rain or at least the half-light of dawn.

Instead, they passed through Clement's massive wood-and-iron gates in full sunlight and turned right toward the ford. A breeze rustled the ash trees along the road, blowing away the city's smells and its clamor. The ford was not yet visible through the trees, but the White Fortress loomed ahead.

A peasant, wet up to his waist, drove several oxen toward them on the road followed by a man on a mule who looked to be a lord's bailiff.

Easing Athalos out of the driver's way and farther from the fortress, Gage felt his heartbeat quicken as they passed its gates. He kept his head down and rode with what Baron Roger would have described as a disgraceful slump—a form no one would associate with a knight, let alone an accomplished jouster.

He hoped Sir Wick was in the fortress and not at the ford. Their mounts meandered down a curving hill to an opening in the trees where beyond a sandy bank stretched the Apse River. Its wide, glinting surface flowed quietly past. Hints of the water's strength rippled around a basket anchored mid-river, swelled at the ends of Maneo's palisades entrenched deep in the river's edge, and heaped about the legs of a fishmonger casting a net into the downstream current.

The tall timbers of Maneo's palisade—jutting like spiked arms from the city's stone walls—were gray and tilted, but they remained a solid barrier between open land and the ford, forcing travelers to pass through Maneo, the second of three border crossings between Delkara and Edelmar.

Inside the stakes on the Delkaran shoreline, two children played in the reeds while above them an old woman sat weaving baskets. Finished versions were piled around her for sale. Twenty paces to her left, Maneo's huge round gate gapped open, its thick edge hanging above the swiftly receding ground.

Two soldiers and the city porter loitered within the tunnel behind the gate, but it was not the guards on the Delkaran side that concerned Gage. He hurriedly studied all four of the young Edelmarian soldiers standing near the river's edge. He recognized none of them.

Two of the soldiers hung off to the side while the other two, one bearded and one not, argued with a brawny stump of a man who was dripping wet and holding an armload of cabbages. The bearded soldier speaking with the cabbage man raised his voice and pointed toward the river. "You got your cart stuck in there. You get it out!" Gage realized then that what he had thought to be an anchored basket belonging to the fishmonger was actually a sunken handcart bobbing with vegetables.

The cabbage man gestured angrily. "I told you, the wheel's come off. If you'd just help me, we could get it out."

"I'm not sending soldiers to get soaked and possibly pulled away by the river to rescue your vegetables. You risked the ford. You deal with the consequences."

Air squeezed from Gage's chest. Perhaps fording the river wasn't such a good idea. But Manton was already addressing one of the other soldiers. "My companion and I seek King Axel's permission to cross into Delkara."

"You'll just have to wait," the soldier said.

Seemingly unperturbed by this response, Manton pulled Chester to a stop. He immediately repeated the action when the animal forged ahead the moment he loosened his grip. Chester fought the reins, twisting his head, but Manton kept them tight. Finally the horse stomped back a step, his flaxen tail swishing irritably. Manton released the reins.

Gage sympathized with the horse. He didn't want to stop either. And being delayed for no apparent reason only exacerbated his impatience. Had he come as Prince Gage, the soldiers would have snapped to attention at his arrival, offered him swift accompaniment across the river, and even announced his presence on the far side. He was glad not to receive such notice, but being left waiting was not exactly the inattention he had hoped for either.

Apparently sensing his angst, Athalos sidestepped behind Nigel. Gage laid a hand on the animal's neck to calm the horse and himself. "Easy, boy."

Still arguing with the soldiers, the cabbage man dumped his armload of vegetables. "Then I'll leave it in the middle of the river!"

The bearded soldier thrust a finger at him. "You do and I'll fine you for obstructing the ford." The other soldier murmured something to the bearded soldier, who nodded. "Tell him there's a man who can't or won't move his cart."

The soldier nodded and headed past them. "Sir Wick was always good at dealing with these sorts of things," he said over his shoulder. "Hopefully, he still is."

His heart suddenly pounding, Gage glanced back toward the fortress. How long would it take the soldier to fetch Sir Wick? Could they be across the ford before then?

"Arms," the bearded soldier said as he approached them.

Frowning, Gage looked at Manton. He thought for a moment the soldier was asking if they were carrying weapons, but then he watched Manton raise his hands to show the back of both wrists. Gage understood then and did the same. They were looking for brands. Free men could cross borders as they pleased. However, any person who bore a mark received either for debt or theft required their owner's permission, either in person or in writing, to travel. If they didn't possess their owner's permission and were discovered off their owner's land, it was the duty of any lord's man to detain that person and see him or her returned to the master to whom they were branded.

The soldier nodded. "Are you simply visiting, or do you plan to buy and sell while in Delkara? And do you intend to return to Edelmar by day's end, or will you be staying longer in Delkara?

"We intend to travel to sell at the fair in Nikledon," Manton said. "And we'll possibly be returning over a different crossing."

"Then you will require papers." The soldier motioned to Nigel. "And I warn you, a pack mule carrying goods will cost you extra in tolls. You also cross the ford at your own risk. Particularly where your goods are concerned."

"I understand." Manton splayed open his coin purse.

"What do you carry for trade?"

"Carved goods. I can open the packs if you wish."

Gage inwardly groaned at Manton's suggestion and silently exhorted them to hurry it up. The soldier checked one of the packs on Nigel, accepted Manton's toll, and then approached Gage. Athalos laid back his ears and turned his neck. Gage pulled the horse's head straight, but the soldier stepped back and eyed him. Cringing, Gage quickly dismounted. He didn't have time for trouble, not with Sir Wick headed his way. Stepping away from Athalos, he handed the man his toll and turned back to his horse.

"Wait."

With both hands gripping his saddle, Gage paused, his legs trembling. He wanted to scream at the soldier but instead glanced over his shoulder. The soldier nodded to his saddlebags. "None of your packs carry any goods you plan to sell in Delkara?"

"No."

"Then you are—"

"Stevenson," a voice said.

The soldier snapped around. "Yes, sir."

Gage faced his saddle, his heart pounding. He recognized the voice, but it wasn't Sir Wick's.

"You have a problem with a handcart?"

"Yes, sir. I—"

"You what? Thought I would come and handle the situation for you?"

"No, sir. Well, yes, sir. He says that he—"

"Have you finished with these two?"

"No, sir. I was just about to give them their Edelmarian papers and let them depart."

"Then suppose you do so before they start growing moss."

Gage smirked and cringed. He definitely knew the voice. Sir Wick had introduced him to the knight at the White Fortress a year and a half earlier. The knight's name was Sir Hedrick. He was a practical, level-headed commander who tended to be a bit hard on his men but did his job well.

A scuffling sound preceded a hand bumping Gage's arm. He flinched and turned just enough to realize it was the soldier handing him a piece of paper. The paper bore the royal seal of Edelmar and said in a flowing script that most commoners didn't know how to read, "This Edelmarian traveler crosses Edelmar's border by leave of His Majesty King Axel of Edelmar."

Gage folded and tucked the paper into his purse and swung up onto Athalos while haphazardly gathering his reins and trying to keep his head down and his hair in his face. Manton secured his own papers and steered for the ford, trailing Nigel. Gage tapped his heels into Athalos's sides to catch up.

"Wait," Sir Hendrick called out. "Have we met before?"

28

Gage sighed. Of all the people he had crossed paths with in the last eight months, of course a knight he had only met once would be the one to remember him. Lifting his reins to turn Athalos, he opened his mouth to reply.

"It's possible," Manton replied. "I've been through a time or two. I'm the son of Brit from Dulcis."

"Ah, then I have seen you before," Sir Hedrick called back, "but it was John Miller's son from Luert I was thinking of. Any relation?"

Gripping Athalos's reins, Gage stared ahead, breathing heavily. Manton twisted further in Chester's saddle and shook his head. "No, we're carvers not millers."

"Well, you never know."

"True," Manton said with a laugh.

"Safe journey."

"Thank you." Manton lifted a hand in farewell and released Chester, who had begun to paw the water impatiently. The horse splashed deeper into the river, and Manton freed his feet from his saddle to be able to jump off in a hurry if need be—a wise precaution for anyone trailing a packhorse whose lead might be lost or whose packs might come loose. But Gage left his feet in his stirrups, for he had no intention of setting foot in the Apse.

Athalos must have sensed his fear, for the horse hesitated at the water's edge. Gage tried to encourage him. "Come on, boy." Snorting, Athalos splashed one hoof down, then the next, and finally trekked full force into the river after Nigel. At each of the horse's high steps, water splashed Gage. He swallowed and steered Athalos around the sunken handcart with its floating vegetables.

Through the moving water, Gage saw where the sandbar dropped off. He kept to its center but missed a hole in front of him.

Athalos sank up to his chest, and cold water rushed about Gage's ankles. He stifled a gasp. The water soaked into his boots. He clutched his fingers into Athalos's mane. Snorting, Athalos lurched up out of the hole and tossed his head. Droplets spattered Gage's face. He closed his eyes and tried to keep his breathing steady. They were already more than halfway across. He just needed to stay calm and make it all the way.

Athalos snorted and stopped moving. Gage opened his eyes and tried to urge the horse forward without loosening his grip. "Go on, boy. Walk on." Athalos threw his head.

"We haven't got all day." Manton called back teasingly from the shore.

Shaking so badly he could barely grip with his knees, Gage kicked his heels into Athalos's sides. One of the children playing in the reeds tossed a rock into the shallows to the right of him. It sank in a gurgle of bubbles and disappeared into the river's grip. Beside it the current snagged weeds and splayed them out like the locks of a woman's hair. Wanting nothing more in that moment than to be far, far away from the river, Gage rammed his heels into Athalos's sides. "Come on."

Athalos reared. Hands bound in the horse's mane, Gage held tightly to Athalos's rising body. His own body swung into midair. Not out of his saddle but not in it either, he hung there.

For a split moment, black spots spread across Gage's vision. He feared he might pass out, then Athalos dropped, and Gage hit the saddle hard. Water drenched his face, legs, and arms.

He wasn't fully upright, but he clung to Athalos regardless. Beneath him, Athalos leapt the last several lengths through the water and surged up onto the shore. Manton pulled in front of them. "Whoa!"

Athalos jerked to a stop. Staring at the solid ground below him, Gage drew a ragged breath and shakily pushed himself up from Athalos's neck. He unwound his fingers from the animal's thick brown mane and wiped his face.

"Your approach was admirable," Manton said with a chuckle. "But your ending needs work. I thought for sure you were going to end up wading the rest of the way."

"Not in the Apse," Gage replied without looking at Manton. Ignoring the staring children, the old woman's frown, and the smirks of the Delkaran soldiers, he steered Athalos toward Maneo's gate. He expected the porter to rise and demand a toll, but no one said a thing as they rode through the tunnel-like opening leading into Maneo. Gage straightened upon exiting the tunnel, and water rolled out of his hair and down his face. He wiped it away.

To their left, a handful of soldiers loitered at the base of a sentry tower that bulged from the city wall. A sliver of light shown between it and a line of houses squeezed together along that side of the street. Opposite the guard tower, a muddy lane ran beside the city wall to their right. The lane was half blocked by crates and broken barrels, likely a dumping ground for the long, low building full of shop windows, which crowded its side of the street. The building butted up against taller shops with second floors that protruded over the road. The design gave the occupants more space upstairs but made the road feel close and enclosed, which was even more true since the road, despite being broad enough for four horses to ride abreast, was barely open enough to drive a cart through.

The area was cluttered with people and filled with goods and produce hanging from stands, stacked on barrels, and displayed on boards. Women and shopkeepers chatted, children clung beside their parents, and men hawked or delivered goods. Meanwhile, geese wandered underfoot, and dogs sniffed over heaps of moldy produce discarded beside doorways and in alleys that exuded a stench strong enough to fill the street.

Gage drew a happy breath anyway. Despite Sir Wick and the Apse River, he had made it to Delkara. And no one here knew him as Gage or Gabe—not the man carrying a wooden yoke with two dangling buckets, not the maiden with a basket of eggs, not the seller of vegetables, not the soap maker, and not the page carrying a loaf of bread who hurried along the lane ahead of them. Keeping Athalos close to Nigel's rump, Gage absently avoided the gauntlet of fixtures and overhangs around him and followed Manton into Maneo.

IN THE HEART of the city, they stopped at a large tavern. Gage headed inside while Manton worked to free his saddlebags. The place was a square, squat building with a thick door, solid floors, and dim lighting. Gage's toes squished soggily in his boots as he headed for a board. He settled in a corner and pulled his boots off under the table.

A middle-aged woman with hollow, flushed cheeks and wispy hair thrust up the rumpled sleeves of her dress and asked what he wanted. He answered, then inquired if she knew of anyone locally who was buying or selling mounts.

She placed her hands on her hips. "Hmm . . . I expect Tom's probably got a couple of horses for sale. He's over on Solder Lane, next to the smithy."

She took a step away then turned back. "And Peter Wells. He's always got a young thing or two. None of 'em rideable yet though. He don't train, just breeds 'em and sells 'em, mostly to the manors here about for plow horses."

He smiled. "Thank you." It seemed buying and selling mounts in Delkara would be much the same as it was in Edelmar.

29

After his boots were somewhat dry and his stomach full, Gage followed the sound of a smith's hammer to Solder Lane. He rode the three horses Tom had for sale but didn't like the look or the price of any of them.

Tom's broad hand scrubbed his bristled chin. "Well, you can check out the two fillies Wells has, but I'm guessing they're a bit heavy for what you're looking for. You might talk to Mark Potter though. He bought a six-year-old gelding last year and doesn't like it. Said he'd rather have a mule."

Following Tom's directions to their place, Gage found the potter's wife and children at work in the pottery shop painting bowls. She said her husband and eldest sons had just left to make a delivery and wouldn't be back for a few hours. Gage explained why he'd come, and she showed him the horse but wasn't sure what price her husband wanted. Once he'd seen the animal's hooves and legs, Gage didn't need to know its price. He nodded his thanks and moved on.

At vespers he met back up with Manton at another tavern on the west side of the city, and together they rode to Maneo's heavily guarded west gate. Two of the twelve guards there were busy searching the cart of a man entering the city. The other guards checked his and Manton's Edelmarian papers and then waved them on.

Glad not to have had to pay a toll to enter or leave the city, they passed peasants working in fields and rode into the hush of the forest beyond. They hadn't traveled far when Manton slowed at a massive oak tree and turned just beyond it down a footpath cutting steeply through the woods.

Gage hesitated at the top of the narrow dirt path littered with pinecones. "Where are you going?" The trees on both sides of the path were so thick that nothing but spindly undergrowth grew beneath their branches.

"It's a shortcut to the manor where my friend lives," Manton called over his shoulder.

Gage frowned and eased Athalos down the path. With pine branches brushing at him, he kept one hand up to protect his face and leaned back in his saddle. "How long of a shortcut?"

Manton laughed. "Not far."

A moment later the ground evened out, and the trees thinned. After a short ride along a winding path, they left the forest behind and came out into evening sunlight. On the other side of fields of beans, millet, and beets was a large cluster of thatched wattle-and-daub cottages. Smoke curled from their chimneys.

He and Manton crossed the fields on a worn path and came around past the manor village. Behind each home were small fenced-in crofts for gardens and animals. Gage spotted chickens, geese, and pigs.

A woman with her hair wrapped in a cloth and dirt smeared across her cheek came from a croft carrying a basket of carrots and radishes. A little girl toddled beside her gripping her skirt. The mother turned back to a young boy. "Kalik, don't forget to water the animals."

"Yes, Mama."

Seeing Gage and Manton approach, the woman averted her gaze and stepped into her home. She was likely about to prepare an evening meal for her husband and older sons, who would return from the fields at sundown.

In front of another home, an old man with swollen knees sat whittling. At the end of the lane, past a woman carrying water, the manor lord's dwelling could be seen. The large stone house and chapel rose between two big beech trees. The lord's granaries, barns, sheepfold, ovens, and forge stood not far from the house inside a line of ash trees that surrounded an orchard grove.

Encircling the manor were more fields, some with peasants spread across them. The strips stretching south had been left fallow, but the other two thirds were green with crops. Beyond them was a meadow used for winter hay and waste ground where animals grazed during the summer months.

Manton turned Chester and rode parallel to the manor's tree line toward a set of cottages near the woods at the end of another village lane. He dismounted outside the last two cottages. "Kenley, you home?" he called out.

Through the second cottage's window Gage saw someone rise and head for the open door. A blond-haired peasant with a thick, straight nose and cheeks that bulged under his eyes as he smiled ducked out the entrance. "Manton! It's been too long." The fellow was probably about Manton's age.

"I know. Sorry about that." Manton gestured toward Gage. "Kenley, meet my traveling companion, Gabe."

Having just landed on his feet next to Athalos, Gage stepped away from the horse to greet Kenley. A woman in a green dress with long braided brown hair and a baby on her hip stepped from the first of the two cottages. Manton grinned. "This is Kenley's wife Heather. With a little one I haven't met yet."

Kenley's cheeks bunched even further. "This is Tate."

"Hi, Tate." Manton touched the little one's hand. The baby turned and buried his face in Heather's shoulder.

"He's a little shy," Heather said, smiling.

Manton laughed. "They usually are at that age."

"Will you stay the night?" Kenley asked.

"Only if it won't be a problem."

"It's not," Kenley said. "There's space enough for both of you in my shop, and you're welcome to join us for an evening meal. Our lordship is currently in Phenes."

"His bailiff oversees the manor then?" Manton asked.

Kenley nodded. "And no doubt already has a tankard full of the lord's wine. We will be left in peace, I assure you."

Gage wasn't sure why peace needed to be assured. Lords typically didn't intrude upon the privacy of their tenant's homes unless there was trouble with their labor or their taxes were left unpaid. But perhaps their manor lord took more interest than most.

"Are we your first stop in Delkara?" Heather asked.

Manton nodded. "We crossed at Maneo this morning."

"Did you have any difficulty coming or going from the city?" Kenley inquired.

"None," Manton replied. "They looked at our papers is all."

"Good. That bodes well for your travels."

Manton nodded. "We can hope. In whatever case, I'll take it any day over having to unpack my goods to convince some cynical guard that all I owe them is a normal toll."

"True," Kenley agreed. "Once you see to your animals, come inside, and we can discuss more of what news you carry and what news you seek. I don't have hay, but if you have hobbles, you can let your animals graze."

30

Gage deposited his saddlebags and saddle at the second cottage where Manton had already dumped his own tack. The sun had slipped behind the trees, and a gentle wind made the green dusk feel cool after the hot day.

The tinkling of bells drifted across the fields. A white-and-black flock of shorn sheep led by a shepherd ambled toward the lord's sheepfold. Serfs trailed in from the fields. Voices floated from the manor's barns as three milkmaids appeared, each carrying buckets. Smoke wafted from the manor's kitchen, bearing the tantalizing smell of roasting meat.

Gage's stomach growled, and Manton chuckled. "Hungry?"

Gage smiled. "Apparently."

"Come on." Manton headed into the lantern-lit interior of the ropemaker's home, and Gage followed.

A large table filled the center of the straw-strewn dwelling. Gage stepped next to it to give Manton enough room to close the door. As Gage did so, he bumped into a string of onions hanging down the wall and knocked his foot against a propped washtub. The tub wobbled noisily against the wall. His cheeks warming, Gage steadied it and shuffled past it, only to find himself trapped at the end of a shelf rising up to the ceiling and extending all the way to the corner of the cottage. Its boards held everything from cheese to spools of rawhide. Dangling from the cruck in front of it were all kinds of dried plants and flowers.

Eyeing a square of open floor between the shelf and the fireplace jutting from the middle of the next wall, Gage considered ducking under the drying plants to fit himself into the space but stayed put. He was worried he might upset the bucket of water on a stool near the fire or knock loose one of the hanging pots, pans, and utensils protruding from the mudded wall.

Tucked beside Kenley, Heather shifted Tate farther up her hip and bent to stir the contents of a pot hanging from a swivel hook over the fire's glowing coals. Trying to decide what might be inside the pot, Gage eyed the table that dominated the space. On it was a cluster of clay jars crowded amid a stack of bowls with spoons, a handful of eggs, a heap of pea pods, a pitcher of some dark liquid, a lantern, a knife, a half loaf of dark bread, and a pile of leafy stems, which looked like the tops of parsnips.

"It's ready." Heather handed Tate to Kenley. He motioned Gage and Manton toward a smaller square board positioned against the same wall as the door. A plain pottery cup containing a handful of wildflowers decorated its surface along with a clay candlestick holding a stout, half-burned candle, which was likely tallow.

While Gage and Manton moved past the door toward the small board, Kenley navigated beside a stack of wood and a lumpy bedspread with a worn wool blanket. The bed, clearly built to fit the space, hugged the corner of the cottage beyond the fireplace and the next wall. Off its end, wedged in the opposite corner and turned sideways, so it could still be opened, was a dark wood trunk.

Holding Tate in one arm, Kenley slipped around the edge of the square table to settle on the trunk. With his free hand he dragged the small table in on top of him, exposing two mid-sized barrels tucked under it.

Manton chose the barrel closest to the wall and repositioned it as he sat down. Noticing Manton catch himself against the wall when his barrel shifted, Gage smirked and made sure his own barrel was set evenly before trusting his weight to it.

At the fireplace, Heather drew the pot out of the coals, then ladled a thin pottage into four wooden bowls. She ferried them to the small table and slipped in beside her husband on the trunk.

Kenley began to eat, and Manton did the same. Heather frowned and gestured to Gage's bowl. "Please, eat."

He realized he had been waiting for someone to say grace. "Sorry, it's been a long day."

Heather smiled. "Then a good night's sleep is what you need. Someplace where the floorboards do not vibrate with snoring."

Gage laughed at her description of an inn and nodded. "I look forward to it."

After that the thunk of their spoons on the wooden bowls, the pop of the fireplace, and the cackle of chickens outside were the only sounds until Manton set aside his empty bowl. "So, tell me, what have I missed in Delkara?"

"You've been gone awhile," Kenley said with a note of reprimand, while still bent over his own bowl.

Manton shrugged. "Business elsewhere took longer than expected."

Kenley looked up and wiped his mouth. "Anything exciting?"

Manton laughed. "No, but I did bring you a package from Clement. I'll fetch it." Scooting his barrel backward and standing, Manton headed outside.

Kenley glanced at Gage. "How long have you and Manton traveled together?"

"About two months," Gage replied.

Kenley rocked Tate, who was beginning to blink sleepily in his arms. "You are from Edelmar then?"

"I am."

"What's your trade?"

"I buy and sell mounts."

"How'd you meet Manton?"

Finding the questions intrusive, Gage decided to shift the conversation's focus by asking questions of his own. "In Carson. How did you meet him?"

Kenley studied him for a moment. "Through a mutual friend."

The door creaked, and Manton returned carrying the package Gage had seen him stuff in his saddlebags in Clement and a smaller object, which Manton handed to Heather. "For when Tate gets a bit older."

She displayed a short wooden top in her palm. Its surface swirled with delicately carved patterns. "It's beautiful!"

Manton chuckled. "He'll probably drive you crazy spinning it on the board while you're trying to get things done."

"Ah, but I won't mind." She kissed Tate's little head and leaned to place the top beside a tiny silver box and a carved stag on a narrow shelf above the bed. "It will sit beside your other present until he is old enough to appreciate it."

Manton set the package in front of Kenley.

Kenley nodded and set it aside. "You will find trade in Delkara more difficult than the last time you were here."

"What sort of difficulty?" Manton replied lightly. "Are people not buying, or are they buying elsewhere? Or are the places to sell just more difficult to sell in?"

"More the lords are becoming leery of travelers, particularly since there has been an increase in attacks being made upon them on the roads. From what I hear, just three weeks ago a large shipment of Baron Bertram's grain being transported out of Lyster on its way to Nikor Harbor was attacked and taken by a group of well-armed commoners."

Feeling like he'd been rammed off a mount, Gage's body swayed and his insides twisted. The lords of Delkara were being targeted and attacked by commoners like he had been. But how could that be? The Blue Crow and his men were dead. He swallowed hard and tried to make sense of what he was hearing. Could there really be more than one group bold enough to steal from barons? Apparently there was.

Kenley continued, as if discussing nothing more concerning than the previous week's weather. "Not even one attacker was caught."

"I can imagine Baron Bertram was none too happy," Manton replied.

"From what I heard, he brought in men-at-arms from five different manors to track them down. Nine such raids have taken place in the last six months."

Gage wished he hadn't eaten. "These attackers," he asked, "they are targeting only lords?"

Kenley's gaze flicked from Gage to Manton, then back to Gage. "When those lords are traveling with goods, yes. The attackers believe the lords are unjustly abusing their authority and that the goods the lords are transporting rightly belong to the people."

Gage drew air. Apparently, he and the nobles in Edelmar had mistakenly assumed the Blue Crow's men were an isolated group. Felix was still free, but clearly people other than him and the Blue Crow were using such lies to also justify thievery and murder. His stomach twisted tighter. Whoever these other rebels were, they needed to be stopped. But how? From the sound of it they had been openly attacking the lords of Delkara for the past six months, and they still hadn't been caught, which didn't bode well for their actions and influence being stamped out any time soon. Which meant more attacks would likely come and possibly more lives would be lost.

Panic spread through Gage. The lords needed people on the lookout for these rebels, people the rebels wouldn't suspect. A thought stirred within him. They needed the help of commoners. He opened his mouth but then remembered he wasn't in Edelmar anymore. He was in Delkara with no authority and supposedly no reason to do anything about a rebellion. The Delkaran lords clearly knew this group existed and would no doubt do what was necessary to protect themselves and to capture the rebels. He need not concern himself. The rebels were the Delkaran lord's problem. He was simply Gabe, a seller of mounts from Edelmar. Besides, him getting involved wouldn't change anything. It would just make him and anyone with him a target, something he had sworn never to do again. It was far better if he just continued as he was and stayed out of it. If he happened to learn anything helpful, he would pass it along to a Delkaran lord. But dealing with these rebels was their responsibility, not his.

"King Strephon is still saying he desires to support the commoners despite these attacks." Kenley added, "He's provided the resources to build a new mill in Burnel, and I've heard he has been improving the roads along several major trade routes. He also had new wells dug for travelers between major cities."

"Meanwhile," Manton said, "I'm guessing his lords have free rein to go after those behind the attacks, in order to root out, and round up all those involved."

"They do."

"Have any attacks taken place in the last few days?" Manton asked.

Kenley scoffed. "I may serve an old and not-very-landed lord, but if you recall he's not exactly favorable toward his tenants coming and going at whim, particularly not now. So I wouldn't exactly be the person to ask."

"Forgive me," Manton said. "I should have remembered."

"No need to apologize. I don't know current news, but I do know where you can go to find business. Travel north to Asplin and then to Lapidus. Both are known to be good places for trade. But be aware, many lords have men-at-arms patrolling the roads. Being stopped and questioned is likely, and having yourself and your things searched is possible. If you can weather such encounters, you should be able to travel just about anywhere in Delkara and find good trade."

Gage frowned at the idea of being searched, but Manton accepted the information as if it were not at all disturbing. Thinking it through, Gage supposed it was a small price to pay for traveling safely and anonymously. And he hoped it led to the Delkaran lords catching the rebels.

Kenley stood. "It's getting late. I'll show you to the shop."

Lighting a tallow lantern, he led them outside. Crickets chirped, and the horses grazed noisily. Taking a deep breath of the cool night air, Gage scooped up his tack and saddlebags and carried them into Kenley's shop, which smelled of dried plants. The smoky lantern illuminated the shop's walls, which were covered in bundles of cord and coiled ropes of different lengths and thicknesses.

Kenley set the light on a waist-high surface beside a hand crank, a large hackle board that looked like a hedgehog, and two rope tops with wooden handles and grooved, cone-shaped heads.

Kenley ducked under four hemp cords stretched across the room between two shoulder-high stands. He moved a stool, a distaff full of hemp fiber, and its neighboring spindle of cord to the corner and motioned to the two wooden stands. "Just give me a moment to move these."

"May I help?" Manton asked.

Kenley nodded. "If you don't mind grabbing the traveler. I've just strung it and the strand twister, so I'm not worried about undoing any work." He motioned Manton to a stand with a single hook on one side and a crank on the other.

Manton carried it toward the space Kenley had just cleared. Meanwhile, Kenley collected the stand with a large gear at its center connecting four smaller gears with hooks, all of them turned by a single handle in the back. Ropemakers used the strand twister to twist each individual cord, then the traveler to turn all the cords together. A rope top was used to wedge the rope tight while the traveler was cranked. In this way, the pre-twisted cords were turned against each other, so the force of them attempting to unwind served to bind them into a single rope.

"You can sleep on the dried hemp if you like," Kenley said, pointing to a huge heap of plant stocks stacked against the far wall. The stems were split open, revealing their fibrous insides. "They've been broken but not scutched yet, so feel free to crash around on them all you like." They nodded their thanks to Kenley and settled for the night.

With the information shared at dinner still racing through his head, Gage reminded himself that, as commoners, he and Manton would be of no interest to the rebels. But when he finally drifted off, the nightmares still came.

31

Awake before anyone else, Gage was glad they'd planned an early start. Eating before first light, they headed out. Late morning clouds rolled across the sky and rained on them as they rode.

The day's long wet journey north brought them to a guard tower outside Asplin's city gates. They were questioned about where they were from, but after showing their Edelmarian papers and paying a minimum toll, they were let inside the city. They slept that night at the shop of a papermaker—another of Manton's acquaintances—and went about their business in Asplin the following sunlit day.

Manton headed off to the taverns and inns, and Gage plied his own trade. He bartered and bought for a good price a partially trained small bay gelding with white facial markings. He briefly considered taking the horse over Asplin's bridge back into Edelmar, but having heard nothing more about any attacks, he met back up with Manton that evening instead.

They stayed a second night with the bustling papermaker. The man's large shop boasted heaps of raw pulp, two vats of water heated by huge fireplaces, numerous molds and deckles, sheets of felt to place between wet paper, a large screw press for squeezing water out of the paper, and a web of lines for drying finished paper.

Bedding down in the shop's storeroom on the third floor, they had slept well the first night after a rainy day but roasted the second night. Still, it was far superior to an inn.

The following morning they helped the man with several chores, and Manton handed the papermaker a cloth-wrapped package. In return, the man gave Manton two folded pieces of paper and wished them a safe journey.

☙❧

Over the next two days, taking turns working with Smudge, the new bay, and Chester, Gage and Manton traveled west toward Lapidus and deeper into Delkara.

They were a good way into their second day on the road toward Lapidus when a company of men-at-arms came thundering upon them from behind. Gage dropped his gaze to avoid making eye contact with the first rider who galloped past. He was followed by a mounted company of over a dozen heavily armed and armored soldiers. They all bore the coat-of-arms of Asplin—a beech tree in the center of a shield with a javelin and a woodsman's axe crossed over its trunk. Gage hoped that if they were riding in response to an attack they got there in time to catch every last rebel involved.

A few hours later, they encountered three commoners walking the road. Manton didn't offer them a greeting, so Gage did, but they acted more startled than appreciative and gave little to no response in return.

In Edelmar, Gage had learned that common travelers who encountered each other often struck up conversations, asking those they came across where they were coming from, what news they had, and freely returning the same. It was a custom that Manton usually embraced with gusto, but not in Delkara. It was neither appreciated nor reciprocated. Gage wasn't sure why, but since he was the stranger, he followed their lead and at the next encounter exchanged nods but said nothing, which seemed to be received better.

⟡

Reaching the carved outer palisade walls of Lapidus, they each paid a toll and rode into the city's first layer. They passed through another palisade of tall timbers and through two sets of stone walls to reach the part of the city where they were headed. Gage had been to Lapidus as a boy, but having watched Manton at work, he had a completely new appreciation for the city and its two biggest trade goods: woodwork and stonework.

All of Lapidus seemed to be either sculpted or carved. Its shops, taverns, stables, guild halls, and homes were all constructed of a dark stone that reflected the sun's light in flecks of silver. Meanwhile, the buildings were roofed and embellished with wood of all types and textures, including beautifully crafted doors, thick shouldering beams, elegant shop signs, lathed railings, hewn steps, and carved doorframes. Rooflines displayed lines of tree rings and amber beads gleamed in the knots of beams and doorframes. With designs and patterns everywhere, the city was an artisan's paradise that smelled of damp rock and wood sap.

Turning down one such fragrant street, they stopped at a cooper shop belonging to a widow, who Manton informed Gage was named after Delkara's queen mother, Annalee Marjorie. The cooper widow's husband had passed away six years earlier, but the spry women had kept the shop going with the help of her two sons, Jordan and Derik.

It was a good-sized place filled with the scent of freshly cut wood. Metal hoops hung on one wall, uncut wood leaned against another, and a third wall boasted stacks of finished barrels and buckets. The middle of the shop was covered in wood shavings, benches, and tools.

Marjorie immediately invited them to stay with her and her sons while they were in Lapidus. They accepted, and during the evening meal, which was prayed for by one of the sons, there was much conversation about business in the town, on the road, and at the upcoming fair in Nikledon. The Cooper brothers also hoped to attend the fair, and the four of them discussed the possibility of camping there together. Little was said about the state of Delkara, and nothing was spoken about any attacks.

As the evening transitioned into candlelight, the sons worked on barrels, and Manton embellished chess pieces while they all swapped stories of travel and trade. It was a pleasant evening of food, company, and laughter, and by its end, Gage had come to very much like the family. He also dared to hope the situation in Delkara was like the Blue Crow—a problem that needed to be dealt with but not the kingdom-wide rebellion Kenley had made it sound like.

THE NEXT DAY Manton took advantage of a market day in Lapidus, and Gage found a buyer for Chester. He sold the horse for triple what Manton had paid for the animal. Less than an hour later, he reinvested a third of that money, purchasing a pack mule from two men who had just arrived from Phenes with a string of them. Gage saddled the mule and tested its rideability. Finding it decent, he took it to the opposite side of the city and made a good profit reselling it as a mount.

The rest of the day he spent outside the city training Smudge. He returned to the Coopers before dark and gave Manton the coin he'd originally paid for Chester plus a little extra for the find.

※

THE FOLLOWING MORNING in the pale light of dawn, Gage helped Manton secure a large barrel of wine—a gift from the Coopers for Manton's father—atop Nigel's packs. Then Manton mounted Smudge, and Gage swung onto Athalos. They departed to hearty waves from the sons and a blessing from Marjorie.

They took the main road west toward Phenes, planning to head south to Umbra. The road cut through thick forests with numerous trails and side roads dividing from it, but the main route was wide and tall and easily traveled.

At midday they came across one of King Strephon's new wells. They stopped to eat beside it and were joined by a religious pilgrim traveling in the same direction. In contrast to all the other travelers they had encountered, the pilgrim was quite friendly and talked enough for six people, all about eternal life, old relics, and living out one's holy salvation in fear and trembling.

Finishing their food quickly, Gage and Manton mounted up and hurriedly outdistanced the man, who was on a pilgrimage to St. Jude's Monastery in Koth. He was going to study copies of the holy writings, which he claimed were utterly fascinating.

"I'd say he was a bit cracked," Manton said once they'd decided it was safe to slow to a walk.

Gage laughed. "He was definitely ... devoted."

"Devoted, is that what you call that?"

"Well, not exactly, but Christianity isn't all bad," Gage said.

"Oh, please, tell me you don't believe any of that stuff."

Waving a fly away from his face, Gage shrugged. "No, but I've heard my fair share of it."

Manton eyed him. "I try and stay away from it." He tapped his temple. "It does something to you, up here."

Gage rolled his eyes. "Not all who believe in God are crazy."

"True," Manton said, snapping off a branch that was encroaching on the road. "There are those like the Coopers who believe it but don't push it on others with every breath. They're regular folk with just a few stricter principles that they thankfully keep mostly to themselves."

Gage frowned and wondered if that was really all religion was—a few stricter principles.

"What?" Manton asked.

Gage shook his head. "Nothing. I agree. I'd much prefer the Coopers over our latest company. Though you never know, because—" He mimicked the pilgrim. "If only you could read the Holy Book for yourself, it would transform your life. It would help you to see things you've never seen before."

Manton snorted. "Exactly, and lack of sleep and a couple tankards of good ale'll do the same."

Gage bent a finger at Manton, once more mimicking the pilgrim's voice. "You shouldn't get drunk, young man, you shouldn't."

Manton shook his head. "I swear, I was so close to telling him all he might see if he didn't stop talking. He's fortunate you finished eating when you did because I don't know how much longer I could have kept my mouth shut." Manton laughed.

"I did think your silence unusual," Gage said. "A commendable show of restraint on your part to be sure."

Manton accepted the compliment and shrugged. "Well, it's not like it's his fault. We all need to believe in something."

Manton's words echoed in Gage's head. Stroking Athalos's neck, he watched the animal's scars ripple and thought of his father's words. *"Surrender your grief to God, for only in Him will you find peace."* His family had always had something to believe in. What did he believe in? A year earlier he would have said honor, justice, and a solid weapon. But now he had no idea.

32

"Could be trouble ahead." Manton's half-joking observation broke through the quiet slosh of the wine barrel, which had filled the last hour or so of their travel.

A dozen soldiers loitered in the trees at the merging of the road that Gage and Manton were on with a road running southeast toward Umbra from Phenes. Gage frowned. "Why are they out here and not at Phenes's city gate?"

"Probably to keep an eye on more travelers," Manton said.

Letting their mounts maintain their pace, they approached the soldiers. The men all bore upon their tabards a half shield with a stag's head on one side and a tower on the other. Gage guessed the coat-of-arms belonged to Phenes, but he couldn't remember for sure.

Most of the men leaned against trees, their hands resting casually on their swords. Only one man, his helmet glinting in the sun, stood at the edge of the road as if attempting to look official while instead appearing hot and excessively bored.

If their orders were to scrutinize and search travelers, they should have been making their intentions and authority known by blocking the road, but instead the soldiers stayed in the shade and seemed to take no particular interest in them.

Finding this odd, Gage thought of something his mother had said: *"Messengers have been waylaid by knights displaying Baron*

Blakely's coat-of-arms. Barons have been turned back by guards claiming to serve Roderick. And now Baron Alexander is accused of having knights he has not knighted."

What if these men were not soldiers but rebels waiting to ambush someone? Gage reached for his knife but then thought better of it. If they were rebels, his knife wouldn't stop them, and if they were soldiers, reaching for a weapon would make him look like a rebel. He exhaled slowly and reminded himself there was no reason for either group to take any interest in him as Gabe. Still, his heart pounded.

Ahead of him, Manton tugged Smudge left toward Umbra. Gage followed but glanced fleetingly toward the men. The "ching-ching-ching" of something striking metal rang mutedly through the trees behind the soldiers. Trailing unhindered after Manton down the road, Gage breathed easier but wondered what was causing the noise.

Manton ambled along on Smudge until the soldiers were out of sight, then pulled Smudge to a stop. "Did you hear that sound in the woods?"

"The clanging?" Gage said.

Manton nodded and dropped to the ground. "Let's go see what it is."

"What about the soldiers? I'm pretty sure they're there to keep people away."

"They'll never know," Manton said.

Gage glanced over his shoulder.

"Come on, don't you want to know what they're guarding?" Manton said. "We can tie our mounts in the woods and double back on foot through the trees. We'll just grab a quick glimpse of whatever it is and then come right back. News to pass along."

Gage scrubbed a hand through his beard and across his mouth. It was risky and stupid, but at the same time he was incredibly curious. Already leading Nigel and Smudge off the road, Manton glanced back at him. "You coming or not?"

Tipping his head from side to side, Gage heaved a breath and made up his mind. "I'm coming." Careful not to leave an obvious trail, they led their horses into the woods far enough so they could just see the road, then slipped back through the trees.

The forest air was muggy, and insects assaulted them in clouds. Trying to be as quiet as possible, Gage ignored the buzzing pests alighting on his arms and face and crept along behind Manton.

Up ahead he saw movement and the glint of metal. The clanging rang more clearly. Lifting a finger to his lips, Manton pointed left. Circling bushes and sidestepping young saplings and downed branches, they corkscrewed their way toward the sound.

"Get those axes over here!" a voice bellowed. "You three, start on the next line. I want this section finished before nightfall."

Manton motioned, and Gage eased closer behind a tree. Through the undergrowth he saw a wagon of logs, two men bent swinging axes, and a soldier standing between them with a crossbow slung at his side.

Hunching, Manton crept forward and dropped to his stomach to worm his way through a patch of ferns to a big rock to get an even better view. Too curious not to follow, Gage crawled up beside him.

Stretching left of them was a freshly cleared, two-cart-wide trail through the woods. In front of them, the next portion of the trail was in the process of being cleared by peasants. Men and women hauled away felled trunks and tree limbs. Others hacked at stumps, splintering them into shards that could be pulled out and removed. The resounding ching came from where a peasant swung a chisel at a large rock that jutted into the path. Gage found it strange to see women in the midst of the workers, their dresses dark with sweat and their faces weary from exertion.

"Keep it moving!" a soldier yelled, trekking toward a worker who had let his ax rest on the ground.

The peasant swung up his tool. "I need water."

Pivoting, the soldier whistled and motioned. Following the gesture, Gage noted the workers on the far side of the lane digging at the edge of a hill that spilled into the cleared ground. Amid the moving bodies, a young girl emerged. No older than seven, she carried a large bucket. Her thin arms strained with the weight of it, and her body rocked back and forth in a strange gait. As she headed toward the soldier, Gage spotted the cause of her amble. Air rush from his lungs. She was hobbled with shackles. Fury and confusion rose within him. Why was a child chained?

The girl made it to the soldier, who motioned her on to the peasant. The worker reached out and shakily drew a ladle from the bucket. Gulping the water, the man dropped the ladle back into the bucket and wiped his chin with his other hand, revealing locked around his wrist a metal fetter with a ring protruding from it.

Gage swiftly checked the other workers. Every one of them, male and female, had at least one wrist or ankle bound by metal. He noted then that the soldiers, two of whom held the leashes to dogs, were not watching the forest for threats to the workers; they were watching the workers. This was not a bunch of lord's peasants sent out by a reeve. They were prisoners. Swallowing, he grabbed Manton's sleeve and mouthed, "Let's go."

Manton eased back from the rock. Bent over double, they crept from the spot. The moment they were far enough away not to be seen or heard, Gage straightened fully and ran. Reaching their mounts, he grabbed Athalos's lead but paused to catch his breath.

"What have they done?" Gage asked.

"Cut a new road, it looks like."

Startled that Manton seemed unconcerned by the state of the people, Gage drew a breath. "I meant the prisoners. There are women and children in their midst."

Manton jerked Smudge's reins loose and pulled the animal toward the road. "They participated in attacks against the Delkaran lords," he replied flatly.

Gage stopped so abruptly that Athalos's head bumped into his back. All those people were rebels? His heart pounded. There were three times as many men in that work party as the Blue Crow's group. And there were women and children. How could that be? Had those women and that girl really been involved in an attack against a lord? She was just a child, but she was shackled like some dangerous criminal. A new wave of anger and indignation rose up within him, but then he remembered Wes. He himself had justly seen a child bound beside the Blue Crow.

Light-headed, Gage gripped the top of Athalos's neck. If so many rebels, children included, had already been captured, and attacks were still taking place, the rebellion was far more widespread and far more dangerous than he wanted to consider.

※

FELIX LINGERED IN the great hall waiting for the lord by one of the fortress's huge fireplaces. The nobleman finally descended into the hall. His tunics and trappings having become even more lavish in the last several months, he waved away the two servants following him and approached Felix. "You wished to speak with me?" His pompous tone failed to hide the fear in his voice.

"Keep me waiting so long again, and next time he will hear of it," Felix replied.

The nobleman's lips tightened together, and his finger jutted at Felix, though it trembled. "Tell him I made a deal with him, not you. You are his pawn. I am a lord of Edelmar. I will finish whatever it is I need or wish to attend to before seeing to you."

Ignoring the insult and not bothering to remind the man that even a pawn could be deadly, Felix waited a moment before speaking. The lord's delusion of self-importance was needed, so he allowed him to feel like he yielded control. "I came to inform you a message has arrived by pigeon. You, me, and your full retinue are to travel to Nikledon. We are to be there over the fair. It will present the perfect opportunity to discuss future arrangements."

The lord twisted his hands together. "Nikledon?" Turning away, he paced. "With all the rebel attacks that have taken place in Delkara, is he sure that is a good idea?"

"You are an Edelmarian."

"Yes, who has watched similar attacks take place in Edelmar. Is not concern something I would feel were it not for my relation to you, or in Delkara perhaps because of my relation to you?"

"Travel as you will, " said Felix, "with a guard or without, but the meeting is not a request. You will attend. That is, as long as you wish to remain part of what is to come."

The lord absently turned the heavy silver ring on his finger and nodded. "I will inform my marshal of my plans to travel to Nikledon for the fair."

"Then I shall send a message confirming your intentions to accept his request."

"Yes, do so." With that the power-hungry fool turned and fled up the steps away from the great hall.

Stretching the fingers of his marred hand, Felix heard the soft trailing voices of women entering the great hall from outside. He smiled at the sight of the lord's daughter crossing the room while talking over her shoulder to one of her maidens. Intercepting her path, Felix greeted her by name.

33

Hours after their foray into the woods, Gage and Manton left their mounts in a dark meadow and hiked on foot into a manor village. Manton knew a man there who welcomed them in for the night. The free lodging meant sleeping under the man's table, but Gage was so exhausted he didn't care where he slept as long as he didn't have to do so upright. But once he was wrapped in his cloak in the dark, he couldn't sleep. Instead he thought about the rebels and wondered how many more there were in Delkara and in Edelmar. How had a rebellion based so wholly on lies grown so broad?

As he considered Manton's comments about the lords, he supposed it wasn't really that strange. Lies and partial truths were just as easy to spread as the truth, and people were often willing to believe the worst of others, particularly if they'd had bad experiences with others in similar positions. Still, stealing from and attacking lords hardly seemed worth the risk. However, he recalled that was exactly the rebel's point: taking the risk of turning the lords' own men against the lords and proving that the noblemen's only real power came from the people, which in a way was true. But without the lords, the commoners would lack land, order, justice, and protection. Neither side was intended to stand alone or to use their position to destroy the other. And if serfs or even freemen thought they could act in opposition to sworn oaths and the laws of the land, they deserved whatever punishment they got. Gage only hoped that everyone who was part of the rebellion would soon be discovered and punished without it costing the lives of any more good men.

He fell asleep clinging to this hope and woke within the lingering clutches of a nightmare. He rolled over, his body stiff and his teeth aching.

"We should get going," Manton said out of the darkness. Gage wasn't sure why Manton was awake so early and intent upon leaving, but he was more than willing. He gathered his things, and they crept out of the village in the dark and rode on to Umbra, eating from their saddlebags as they went.

⸻

Umbra was a town surrounded by fields and pasture land grazed by sheep. Originally built around a manor village, the town had shallow stone barriers, narrow, convoluted streets, and nearly all wattle-and-daub homes. Goats wandered atop the old village walls, eating people's laundry. Dogs rooted through discarded produce, and roosters crowed from crofts and rooftops.

The lord's manor on Umbra's southern side seemed to cringe away from the town, but despite the appearance that the moss-covered town had nothing of value to offer, the dyers, spinners, felters, and weavers of Umbra were known far and wide for their high-quality woolen goods.

According to Manton, Umbra also had a few other treasures to offer, like a quaint village green at its center, quality food, and a good well. Gage and Manton filled their waterskins at the well, let their mounts drink, and then parted ways, agreeing to meet up again at the Roast Hen cookhouse on the west side of the village green.

At vespers, after an unsuccessful day of work, Gage entered the Roast Hen and found Manton already there. They ate a hearty meal together, and then discussed where they would stay the night and where they would head next.

Manton knew a local felter who might have space for them for the night and suggested that the following day they make their way along what the locals called "the ridge path" to Burnel, a town on the Plene River.

Interested in seeing the new mill King Strephon had reportedly built in Burnel, Gage agreed to the route.

They exited the Roast Hen and were headed toward their mounts, only to find three men-at-arms awaiting them. The soldiers bore Umbra's mauve-colored anvil-and-fleece coat-of-arms, and their expressions were hard. Gage's insides churned. What did they want?

"You two are visitors to Umbra, are you not?"

"We are," Manton replied. "We're travelers, planning to attend the fair in Nikledon."

"Your mule is heavily laden, and the fair's not for a good number of days. What are you carrying?"

"Carved goods. We thought we'd make the most of the trip and buy and sell around Delkara as well as at the fair."

"You don't mind if we check your packs to confirm you speak the truth?"

"Be my guest," Manton said with an indifference that surprised Gage. "Do you wish to search them yourselves or would you like me to unload them?" Manton asked.

"My men will see to it." The soldier pointed with his chin. "What of the barrel? Does it also hold carved goods?"

"No, it's a gift of wine from a friend here in Delkara to my father." The slosh of the barrel being shaken by one of the other soldiers punctuated Manton's words.

"Where are you traveling from?" the soldier asked as his men unlaced the other packs to check their contents.

"Dulcis in Edelmar."

The leader's fingers tapped his sword. "And your companion? Is he a carver from Dulcis as well?"

Gage opened his mouth to respond, but Manton was quicker. "He is a buyer and seller of mounts from Carson."

Gage blinked. He'd never said he was from Carson.

"We have our Edelmarian papers with us," Manton continued. "And if you wish further confirmation of my trade, I have a letter written by the lord of Dulcis praising my family's shop and wishing me successful trade at the fair in Delkara. I carry it with me as a reminder of my family's high hopes for this journey." Manton pulled the folded papers from the coin purse tied at his belt and handed them to the soldier.

Surprised by the news that Manton's family's shop was so highly praised, since Manton had never boasted about it, Gage curiously watched the soldier skim the letter. Looking taken aback yet satisfied, the soldier refolded the papers and returned them to Manton. He checked Gage's Edelmarian papers and then nodded to them both. "Safe travels." With that the soldiers completed their minimal search and departed.

Tucking the letters away, Manton tied up his packs, mounted, and scooped up Smudge's reins. Swinging up beside him, Gage could only think how grateful he was that Baron Evan of Dulcis had such high regard for Manton's family.

"There is an inn here where I might be able to sell a boardgame or two," Manton said. "Would you mind if we settled there tonight? Last I remember it was reasonably priced."

Since Manton didn't usually pass up an opportunity to stay somewhere free, Gage eyed him. Either Manton felt he could sell enough at the inn to make up for whatever they'd paid to stay there, or he wasn't certain his friends would host them. Not wanting to push the issue, Gage shrugged. "As long as 'reasonably priced' doesn't mean anything like that inn in Bentley."

Manton grimaced. "Absolutely not."

"Good, because rats running across my face in the night is not an experience I'd like to repeat."

"Nor I." Manton shuddered. "And believe me, falling through floorboards into their nest is an experience I'd love to forget, though the look on that innkeeper's face when you demanded every guest's money back was something I won't forget."

Gage wasn't sure whether to take Manton's comment as a compliment or a complaint. "I figured we all deserved our money back."

"We did, but normally we'd still have walked away empty handed. You telling him you'd report him to the local lord if he didn't repay us was brilliant. I would never have thought of threatening that, nor would I have ever expected it to work."

Gage frowned. "No one should have to pay to sleep like that. That inn deserved to be burnt. And honestly, the local lord should have been the one held accountable. A lord should know the conditions of the shops he rents and the way his tenants are living in them."

Manton snorted. "Yeah well, their kind don't pay attention to the living conditions of their tenants, and they certainly don't stoop to set foot in such places to spend the night. No, as long as they get what they want and aren't given any trouble, they don't care about us."

Gage knew Manton well enough to not hold the words against him, but the them-versus-us mindset still left him unpleasantly trapped between Gabe and Gage.

34

Gage found the ridge path to Burnel just as challenging to navigate as his and Manton's conversation from the night before. Little more than a hunting trail through the forest and still wet from a night's rain, the path was, according to Manton, a shortcut with a great view, but Gage was still skeptical on both counts.

Forced to dismount at times to get under low branches and around fallen trees, they slowly worked their way up an ever-increasing incline. Cresting yet one more hill, they finally came out of the trees. Gage pulled Athalos to a stop and stared. "Wow."

He could see all the way to the cliffs of Nikor, which made up a good length of the Delkara and Keric border. The Nikor River was hidden within the cliffs, whereas the Plene River, which started somewhere in the cliffs of Nikor, wound out into Delkara toward them. The river curved through the distant walled-city of Nikledon, churned Burnel's two waterwheels, and flowed into Lake Plene. The emerald trees, green fields, indigo lake, and shimmering river contrasted gloriously with the bright blue of the cloudless late-morning sky.

Manton chuckled. "Now do you understand why I like coming this way?"

Trying to absorb as much of the view as possible, Gage nodded. "It's beautiful."

Standing there, Manton stifled a yawn.

"Feeling your early morning, huh?" Gage teased. "What were you doing up so early anyway?"

Manton stiffened. "I, um, had some unfinished business to attend to, but I didn't realize I woke you when I left. Did you manage to go back to sleep? Or were you still awake when I got back?"

Confused that Manton seemed so concerned about waking him, Gage shrugged. "I don't remember you returning, so I must have fallen back asleep."

"That's good." Manton kicked Smudge into motion. "Come on. If we want to make it to Burnel with time enough to do business before dark, we best get moving."

※

AFTER SWEATING ON the trail for another several hours, they finally descended into the outskirts of Burnel, a sprawling medium-sized town busy with activity.

"It looks a lot different from the last time I was here," Manton said as they steered along a crowded yet wide street bright with new paint. A blue shield standard with a waterwheel and a cluster of wheat on it hung from large guild halls and flew above newly constructed towers leading to a keep in the middle of Burnel. Soldiers occupied the keep, and all about the town they intermingled with the townspeople.

A group of soldiers exited a shop ahead. One of them caught hold of a maiden passing by them. He spoke some comment to her. Turning red, the girl twisted in his grasp. The soldier swiped something from her basket, then let her go. The others laughed, and she hurried off.

Watching this exchange and steering wide of yet another cart heavy laden with sacks of grain, Gage gritted his teeth and wished he could reprimand the soldiers. Instead he turned to Manton. "Let's go see the new mill."

※

Built below the old mill, the new mill was a broad, squat structure with a ramp from the river leading up one end and a huge waterwheel partly sunk in the river by its back side. Workers came and went through the mill's massive doors. It appeared finished on the outside, but the inside was apparently still under construction.

In the river, walls had been built around the mill's wheel. A parallel wall hugged its side, acting as a protective barrier. Above the wheel, perpendicular walls created a sluice, limiting a part of the river's expanse while raising its depth.

The headrace flowed into the upper side of the wheel about halfway up, filling buckets, not blades, on the waterwheel's rim and turning the wheel back and downward. The lower tailrace rushed out from under the wheel, bubbling and gurgling. The sound muffled the rumble of turning gears inside the new structure.

The old mill just upstream had an undershot wheel, which required no change to the river and meant only its base rested in the current. It also turned backward but with less efficiency. It was clearly still in use as a mill though, for peasants unloaded carts of grain outside it while other workers swung the sacks onto their backs and carried them inside. No doubt somewhere up on the old mill's second floor, a miller was supervising the grain being fed from a hopper down between two grindstones.

"The new mill doesn't look like a grain mill," Gage said. "What do you think it will be used for?"

Manton squinted at it. "I don't know, but you can be sure the toll for using it will be high."

"Why assume the tolls will be high?" Gage asked, frustrated.

A coldness entered Manton's tone. "Because this is Delkara."

"What is that supposed to mean?"

Turning Smudge, Manton looked back over his shoulder. "You haven't seen much of Delkara yet. Once you have, you'll understand."

Fighting the desire to contradict Manton's statement, Gage swallowed and kept quiet. He didn't understand, but he wanted to, because Delkara was indeed a mystery to him.

35

Business in Burnel was good. Gage sold Smudge for a high price and purchased two new mounts—a donkey that was perfectly sound once its hooves had been cut and its bridle adjusted and a light-gray mare that rode well but had no ground manners.

With the sun setting over the river at his back and the two mounts on leads behind him, Gage pulled Athalos to a stop in front of a pair of tall arched gateposts. Its iron gates looked in on a large monastery tucked in the trees behind a stone wall on the eastern edge of Burnel.

Manton had said to meet up with him at sundown outside Aqua Vivus. Thinking the place a tavern, Gage had eventually asked for directions, which had led him here. Chiseled into the side of one of the gateposts was a cross and the Latin words *Aqua Vivus,* "Living Water." A cord ran up the posts to the arm of a small bell hanging within the gate's arch. Figuring Manton planned on traveling from there to wherever they were staying, Gage kept his distance to avoid attracting the attention of the monks coming and going within the monastery's grounds.

Dismounting, he tied the donkey to Athalos and did ground training with Chalk while he waited for Manton. Gripping the horse's lead line, he flicked the rope against the mare's chin. Snorting and lifting her head, the mare flattened her ears. Gathering the end of the rope in his other hand in case she rushed him, Gage continued thwacking the rope against her chin and saying, "Back up." Finally Chalk leaned back. Gage instantly stilled the rope to reward her move in the right direction. "Good, girl. Now back." He bumped the rope into her chin again. A moment later, he got another lean, and on his next attempt, he got an actual step back.

It was sometime later when he took two steps backward and Chalk backed up two steps as well, perfectly mirroring his behavior. Someone clapped.

Embarrassed, Gage looked around. It was Manton standing in the lane with Nigel's lead draped over his shoulder. "Well done. I like her already."

"Good, because she's your ride to wherever it is we're staying."

Manton nodded to the darkening expanse of the monastery. "We're already there."

"You're not serious."

Manton chuckled. "Relax, we're spending the night, not joining the choral service. Besides, it's cheaper than the inn."

Gage frowned at Manton's words. Yes, the church's hospitality was free, but it was customary for all who were able to give alms in exchange. Not to mention, Manton had never expressed any interest in staying at a monastery or an abbey before. "You're sure?"

Manton laughed. "I promise it's safe. I've come and gone from this place before, and the wrath of God has never struck me dead." Offended by the implication that he might be the kind of person who would or should be worried about God's wrath, Gage searched for a response that would make it clear that wasn't his concern, but before he could think of anything, Manton pulled the gate's bell cord.

The bell clanged loudly, and a middle-aged monk with tonsured hair and long pale robes exited a nearby building. He approached and opened the gate. Hiding his hands within his long sleeves, he greeted them with a weathered smile. "I am Brother Barnabas. How may I be of service?"

"I wish to speak with Prior Joseph and ask that we might be allowed to stay as guests for the night," Manton replied respectfully in the twilight.

"Guests are always welcome. Come. I shall show you to the stable where you may leave your animals, and I will let our prior know you seek to speak with him."

Closing the gate behind them and leading them past extensive gardens, beehives, a smithy, carpenter shop, and mason's shed, the monk showed them into a large barn where two young monks were shoveling manure.

Brother Barnabas pointed to an empty corner of the barn. "You can settle your animals here, and I will send someone to show you where you may sleep."

The barn smelled of dust and hay and housed two horses and a half dozen mules. Gage tied Athalos next to Nigel while Manton secured Chalk and found a spot for the donkey.

Starting to unload Nigel, Gage pulled free the ropes binding the wine barrel. He caught it as it rolled loose but didn't fully anticipate its weight. He lifted a knee to help support it, adjusted his grip on it, and lowered it to the floor with a sloshing thunk. He exhaled, glad he hadn't dropped it. Manton joined him, and together they finished stripping the packs off Nigel.

Taking up the saddlebags they needed and storing the rest near their mounts, they warned the two young monks to stay clear of Athalos and then followed another monk out a side door and along a stone path.

Their guide led them past a collection of buildings and around a line of trees. Gage stopped mid-stride. Before them in the dusk amidst a once-beautiful garden was the blackened rubble of what had been the end of a building. Heaps of stone and charred wood were scattered between the remains of two walls, which looked like they had been the exterior of a room just off the monastery's chapel. The smell of ash still hung in the air.

"What happened here?" Gage asked.

"A fire in the scriptorium," the brother replied. "It burned our books and writings, including all our copies of the Holy Scriptures. We mourn far greater the loss of these than that of the building. Three of our brothers have gone to Koth in hopes of procuring a new copy, but if one is not available, one will have to be made. We are not at a total loss though," he said, his tone lightening, "for Brother Philip can quote whole books of the Holy Word. Over this eve's meal he—"

"Manton." A sturdy older monk with a well-kept silver beard and short tonsured hair strode toward them. His expression was welcoming and warm. His dress was identical to the other brothers except for a fist-sized wooden cross swinging on a cord against his chest. He greeted Manton with a hearty embrace. Gage stepped back, stunned by the familiarity between the two and wondering how they'd come to know each other.

The monk nodded to him. "I am Prior Joseph."

"I'm Manton's traveling companion," Gage replied as the other monk slipped away.

"Yes, that I gathered," the prior said with a smile. "Though I'm surprised to find Manton traveling with anyone. He's always saying he lives better alone."

Manton shook his head. "Don't start on me, Joseph."

The prior lifted a finger. "Ah, but one of these days, you will see what you have been missing. And you will regret the time you have spent running from our Holy Lord."

Manton smiled. "Well, until such a time, I'll enjoy my freedom from the rules of your spirituality."

"Not rules, my friend, commands given by our God, who created us to live in a way that pleases Him and brings life and peace to ourselves and others."

"And that peace, is that sooner or later?" Manton nodded to the shadows of the burnt building. "Because it doesn't seem to be working for you. Am I not right that this fire was no accident?"

Confused by Manton's accusation, Gage looked from the building back to the monk. For a moment, grief weighed on the prior's posture and voice. "No, it was no accident, but such is the cost of truth." His mournful expression dissolved, and his shoulders straightened. "As Scripture says, we present ourselves to God as workers who need not be ashamed. For we rightly speak truth. In Paul's second letter to Timothy, he warns of a time when people will not desire the truth of the Word and will instead seek those willing to speak lies. We will not be those who speak lies."

"Then it would seem the peace you speak of does not exist."

The prior held Manton's gaze. "It is a spiritual war, not a physical battle. Every man, both common and noble alike, is a slave to darkness until he surrenders to God."

"Not a physical battle?" Manton scoffed. "Tell that to those fighting the lords. Or to those who ordered this fire started."

Staring at the rubble, Gage wondered if those who would set fire to a monastery and those who attacked the lords were not one and the same.

"Of course the spiritual affects the physical," the prior replied.

"Now you're contradicting yourself," Manton said. "But why not? Your religion's full of contradictions. He's a God of justice who hates the wicked. No wait, He's a merciful God who loves everyone."

Gage glanced at the prior, worried he might take offense, but the monk just sighed. "Manton, what you see as contradictions are simply the stunning nature of an incredible and complex God. You do not understand who He is because you deny His authority and doubt His existence. Everything would become clear if only you realized and accepted how much God willingly endured to fulfill His justice against evil and prove His love to humanity."

"Isn't it in your own Scriptures," Manton said, "where three men are saved by your God from a fiery furnace after not bowing to a false god? If that God is real, where is he now?"

"My friend, do you sell a gameboard the same way every time?" the monk asked.

"No."

"Well, neither does God rescue His people the same way every time." The prior eyed Manton. "You might also consider God rescued those three men from that fire not for their own sake but for the sake of the people and the ruler who had thrown them into that furnace to begin with."

Gage remembered this story from those his parents used to read to him and Haaken in the solar when they were boys. He had been enthralled by the story and others from the Scriptures, but he hadn't thought of them in years.

"I thought we had an agreement not to discuss spiritual things anymore," Manton said, clearly annoyed.

Prior Joseph smiled. "We did agree not to argue about such things, but somehow you always start me preaching at you. How is that?"

Manton's lips twisted into a tolerant smile. "Perhaps because you fall into it too easily."

The monk shrugged. "What can I say? It's the life I have chosen."

"But one I have not," Manton said flatly.

Prior Joseph's eyebrows lifted. "True, but something here does have you curious." The monk gestured around the monastery where newly lit lanterns spread light across the grounds.

Manton scoffed. "And what's that?"

"To many it would be God's forgiveness, His love, or perhaps His goodness. But to you it is the strength of God's presence in us here. His Scripture is being silenced, and you know it's not because it lacks power but because it has it. God does exist, and He is at work."

"I'll believe it when I see it," Manton said.

"Someday you will. I only hope it is before you stand before our Holy God on Judgment Day." The prior sighed and turned to Gage. "What of you, Manton's traveling companion? Do you too say, 'I'll believe when I see?' Or do you believe without having first seen?"

Gage shifted his saddlebags, which were digging a dent in his shoulder, and shrugged. "I don't know."

The prior's brown eyes held his. "Then you are of the lost who has yet to have the veil of blindness removed from his eyes. Seek, and you will find. Knock, and the door will be opened to you."

The steadiness within the prior's gaze reminded Gage of Haaken, but the man's words disturbed him and stirred questions within him that he did not want to answer.

36

In the silence of the night, the prior's words echoed in Gage's mind. *"Do you too say, 'I'll believe when I see?' Or do you believe without having first seen?"* Gage tossed and turned, trying to push the questions away. He fell asleep hearing, *"Seek, and you will find. Knock, and the door will be opened to you."*

Dreams came. He was sitting with his father. "How can you not see, Gage?" his father asked. "God is in control. Surrender to Him, and He will give you peace."

Allard appeared next with an arrow in his chest and his eyes closed. "Life and death are before you. Can you not see God holds them both?" a voice said.

In the next moment, a hand descended upon Gage's throat, crushing his ability to breathe. A fire rushed toward him. He thrashed and shoved himself upright.

He woke in darkness.

When the pounding in his chest finally subsided and the sweat on his skin had dried, he laid back down and sleeplessly awaited the dawn.

⚬⚭⚬

Gage woke Manton early. They left alms, packed their mounts, and while the bells for prime rang, they slipped from the monastery.

Buying food in Burnel to break their fast, they ate as they rode and departed Burnel by means of a road leading north around Lake Plene toward Ivett.

Just beyond the road's first bend, they were stopped by five soldiers sweating in the sun beneath a blue Burnel standard. As in Umbra, Manton answered their questions and again handed over the letter from the Lord of Dulcis.

The lead soldier, who wore no surcoat over his armor, probably because of the heat, read the letter and viewed their Edelmarian papers but still ordered their belongings searched, which they were told to unload from their mounts.

Getting yelled at for Athalos's aggressive behavior and biting his tongue twice to keep from commenting on the soldier's rudeness, Gage barely managed to stay polite while the soldiers poked through the contents of every pack and saddlebag they carried. He was amazed Manton remained so calm, but then again, as a commoner, avoiding the consequences for mouthing off to a soldier was probably well worth it.

Eyes downcast to keep his annoyance from showing, Gage shoved his things back in his bag. When he and Manton had finished repacking, the leader returned their papers. "We're looking for thieves and can't be too careful. Safe journey."

It took Gage a good way around the lake to unclench his fists. By that time, with no trees for shade, sweat trickled down his forehead, and flies buzzed around him.

Swapping the donkey's lead into the same hand as Athalos's reins, he wiped his face and watched a large bird fly out of the reedy expanse filling the northern end of Lake Plene. Gage followed its flight over the road and noticed the top of a construction crane jutting out of the trees ahead to their right. It was an odd location for a crane considering they were a long way from Burnel and still quite a distance from Ivett.

It turned out to be a treadwheel crane, which functioned by means of one or more people walking within its wheel to turn a rope about its thick center shaft. The rope lifted or lowered the crane's load depending on which direction the walkers went and was being used in a large clearing to stack enormous logs. The huge trees had been stripped of their branches and filled the expanse around the crane.

The ground amidst the log piles had been turned to mud by wide-wheeled wagons, and Gage noted the ruts all turned down a road leading into the forest. "Where does the road go?" he asked.

"To the road from Deubor toward Phenes," Manton replied.

Gage pictured the map of the three kingdoms his father kept. "I bet this wood is from that new road we saw being cleared outside of Phenes." He thought of Burnel's new mill. "That's why they're stockpiling the logs here. You remember the ramp off the new mill? I bet they're planning on floating these logs right to it."

"Would you like to evaluate how long it will take to cut them too?" Manton asked, kicking Chalk into motion. "Or can we get moving, so we can stop baking on this road?"

"But the sun is so pleasant," Gage said.

Manton swung his reins at him. Laughing, Gage ducked. The lines missed him and came back around to slap Chalk's side. The mare bolted sideways. Jerked from his saddle, Manton landed in a heap in the middle of the road. Shoving himself up, Manton glared at Chalk.

Gage couldn't help but laugh. "That's the easiest I've ever seen you come off a horse." Since they often rode mounts with unexpected tendencies, they'd both gotten used to occasionally being bucked off or thrown, but neither of them had ever come off simply by means of a sidestep.

Manton snatched up Chalk's reins. The mare lowered her head, as if apologizing, and Manton shook his head, then began to laugh too.

Gage joined back in. They were both still laughing when a mule cart trundled around a curve ahead. The driver looked at them as if they were fools, which only made them laugh all the harder.

"So, are we staying at Ivett or just passing through?" Gage asked when he'd finally caught his breath.

"I know a fletcher and his family who will welcome us for the night," Manton said. "He's a good man and a true craftsman with a barn, a large shop, and six children so far. His wife is Marjorie's eldest daughter and sister to the Cooper brothers in Lapidus."

Gage grinned. "Then I think I will like them."

※

LIKE THEM HE did, for Ian and his wife, Wilona, had raised a merry household. Their eldest child, a boy of fourteen, was apprenticed to a smith down the street but lived at home along with their five girls and the newest member of their family, a chubby little boy, who was passed from sister to sister faster than anyone could keep an eye on him. As such the evening meal was a happy mass of confusion.

"Why can't I have more bread?" one of the little girls asked.

"Because there isn't more," replied Jubilee, the oldest girl.

"Yes there is. It's right there."

"That's only the basket. Thomas ate the last slice."

"No he didn't," one of the others piped up. "Sylvia did."

"I did not. Esther had it."

"She shared it with Papa," Thomas said.

"And how have your travels been so far?"

Gage looked at Wilona, who he realized was asking him the question for the second time. "Sorry. Our travel has been good."

She smiled. "It's a little overwhelming, but you get used to it."

"Traveling?"

She laughed, sounding exactly like Marjorie. "No. My children. But I suppose traveling might be as well."

And so the evening went, until finally the children were sent or carried to bed and just the adults remained in blessed silence. Ian sank down with a sigh.

"How is business, Ian?" Manton asked.

"Well, I've found someone to collect feathers for me and another who is now supplying me with ash wood. And with Thomas working at the iron smiths, I easily have all I need to make everything from heavy bolts to throwing arrows. Most of my time though is spent on hunting arrows, which Jubilee helps me with now. A couple of months ago, I was whipping feathers on after gluing them with pine pitch, and she says to me, 'Papa, I think I could sew that on faster than you.' I handed her the arrow and linen, and sure enough, she can. Now she helps me all the time."

Manton laughed. "I could see her opening up her own shop someday."

"I'd rather have her happily married, thank you," Wilona said.

"Well, yes, happily married, with her own shop, like her grandmother."

Wilona smiled. "And how is my mother?"

Gage excused himself, letting Manton share the news from Lapidus, and headed to bed in the shop's storeroom.

Gage woke in the morning from a dreamless sleep to find one of the Fletchers' little girls sitting an arm's length away, watching him. He closed one eye and stared at her, then switched eyes. She giggled.

"Is Manton already awake?" he whispered.

She rose up on her knees and looked over at Manton. Sitting back, she shook her head.

"Are your parents awake?"

Her chin rose, but then she paused as if trying to remember. She finished the nod.

"Are they up?"

She nodded again.

"Then I suppose I should be too." Looking about, Gage frowned. "Where are my boots?" She shrugged mischievously. He eyed her. "Do you know where my boots are?"

Giggling, she leapt off the floor and disappeared down the stairs. Flinging off his cloak, he chased after her.

✿

After tracking down his and Manton's boots, Gage ate with the family. He left Manton still talking with them and went to saddle their mounts. Once finished with that, he started loading Nigel. Crouching, he bent to heft the wine barrel. He swung it easily onto Nigel's back and frowned. He could have sworn it had been heavier at Burnel. Tying it down, he tugged its ropes to make sure it was secure. The wine sloshed, and the ropes held. He shook his head. It was strange how expecting something's weight could make it feel lighter. There was probably a lesson in that somewhere, but he didn't bother to consider it further.

Gage returned to the Fletchers' shop and watched Manton deposit three gifts—a wooden peasant girl and two pretty tops—into the children's eager hands. Then they said their goodbyes, and he and Manton headed west to the large city of Deubor. They paid their tolls, showed their papers, were thankfully not searched, and spent two nights with a reticent mason and his wife, neither of whom seemed keen on conversation. Business in Deubor was good though. Manton sold a number of boardgames, and Gage made a profit on his donkey and bought two mules.

On their way southeast to Legan, trailing their mules, they crossed paths with a middle-aged baron and his retinue bearing a yellow-and-white quartered coat-of-arms with red back-to-back standing lions. It was the first Gage had seen of any of the Delkaran nobles.

The eight knights and dozen men-at-arms with the baron carried swords, shields, and crossbows, and even with his eyes downcast, Gage noted that while they passed, the baron's hand rested upon his sword. Gage figured he'd probably travel the same way if he still rode as a nobleman and was glad he did not.

※

In Legan, Gage parted with Chalk for a good profit and one of his mules for a decent price. That meant the following day Manton was left riding the last of the two mules, the one they'd taken to calling Sulky because the animal's ears were always drooped to the sides.

They headed for Nikledon but ended up in an inn in a small town waiting out a storm. While playing boardgames and discussing their hopes for the fair, they happily discovered the innkeeper held a wealth of information about the event.

※

On the following day, they reached Nikledon and in sunny weather searched for the best place to sell during the fair. They found the spot they wanted—high ground east of the heavily walled city at the edge of a huge green meadow reportedly used for the fair. The spot was near the route coming from the city gates and had tree cover. But with the fair still a number of days away, they chose to visit a few more places before settling at the fairgrounds.

Along the Plene River, Gage tried Coley's famous cabbage pottage and slept soundly under the stars in a peasant's fenced croft.

He bought two more horses in Coley the following day, both of which he knew he could sell for a higher price once they put time into them. Then he and Manton journeyed east to Lyster.

Clouds rolled in, and rain began to pelt them. They answered questions and paid their tolls at Lyster's gates, then urged on their mounts and trotted to a tavern that Manton knew of not far inside the city.

37

Water dripped down the tavern's chimney, causing the fire behind Gage to hiss and smoke. Studying his scattered chess pieces, Gage attacked and captured Manton's pawn. Placing it at the side of the board, he folded his arms upon the table's roughhewn planks. He was glad to be indoors and close to the heat wafting from the rock hearth, even if the place stank of barley and soot.

Manton struck with a knight, taking one of Gage's bishops. A murmur rolled through their growing circle of spectators. Gage uncrossed his arms. Manton already had five of his pawns and both of his knights. His remaining bishop was close to capture, and his king was at risk. He made a show of shifting a rook across the board and in beside his king.

The tavern's door creaked, letting in a gust of damp air. A blocky man with a full beard and thick hands pushed back the hood of his wet tunic. Curly locks hung about the man's shoulders, and a frown wrinkled his pockmarked face. He jutted his chin at their table. "What's this?"

"They're playing a game of strategy," said a thin-faced patron sitting alone, who had shown interest in the game until the rules were explained. He glared at them. "Trouble if you ask me."

The grisly newcomer gestured to the tavern's keeper. "A tankard." Exchanging a coin for a large pewter cup, he headed for their table.

The place closest to the fire was immediately vacated, and the bench Gage had shared with four other peasants groaned under the man's weight. The newcomer downed a swig and then nodded at them. "What's the aim?"

Pulling back his knight to remove Gage's invading pawn, Manton did little more than glance at the man. "Winning is the aim, and you win by capturing or cornering your opponent's king."

The tankard suddenly looked malleable in the man's hand. "What you speak of is a dangerous thing." At the man's tone, those hovering at the edges of the gameboard drifted away while those sitting shifted uncomfortably.

Gage looked at Manton. The newcomer wore common clothes but clearly had authority, which meant he was most likely a reeve, responsible for the labor due in the manor fields belonging to the baron of Lyster.

"Children who play blind man's bluff aren't blind, nor is a man dangerous because he plays chess," Manton said.

"These days anything can be used against a man." Plunking down his tankard, the reeve stood. "You and your game had best move on."

Manton held up his hands. "I'm simply a carver trying to make some coin. This place has welcomed me before. If not this game then let me show you another. Perhaps you would prefer wari or draughts?"

The man placed both hands on the table. "I said, move on."

"Where would you suggest I go?"

Not sure if Manton was being serious or sarcastic, Gage glanced between the two.

"There are taverns in Delipp. Why don't you go there?"

A disgruntled edge entered Manton's voice. "That's a day's journey from here."

Gage blinked. The man couldn't really be serious, could he? After all, it was just a boardgame. The man stared back at Manton, and those about the tavern watched the altercation with wary gazes.

"If I pack my wares, may I at least stay in Lyster till the rain lets up?" Manton asked.

"Fine," the man growled. "There's an inn on the other side of the city, Dawn's Rest. If you keep your games to yourself, you may spend the night there. But you'd best be gone from Lyster before first light."

WRAPPING HIS CLOAK about himself, Gage hurried through puddles and across mushy ground to catch up with Manton, who was already slinging his bag of boardgames back onto Nigel.

With water dripping off the edge of his hood, Gage ducked around two other horses to pull Athalos's reins loose. "What's his problem anyway? Like you said, it's just a game."

"No," Manton said. "It's more than a game. It's the idea that a commoner could use strategy to trap a king."

Gage stilled. As a nobleman, he had played chess all his life. Never had he considered it through the eyes of a commoner or a king. He frowned. "Will you stop selling chessboards in Delkara?"

"Oh no," Manton said. "I'll still sell them. I just won't sell them in Lyster."

At Dawn's Rest they kept to themselves and departed the following morning for Delipp.

"Were we planning to go to Delipp," Gage asked, frowning as they rode along the soggy road, "or are we following the reeve's instructions?"

Manton glanced sideways at him. "You really think I'd go to Delipp because some reeve told me to?"

"No."

Manton chuckled. "Then you know me well. Delipp simply offers a hopefully profitable way to circle back to Nikledon."

Gage gestured onward. "Then to Delipp it is."

Unlike most large towns, Delipp was not surrounded by open ground; instead its fields were tucked and scattered throughout the forest. The town's crops flourished due to an extensive watering system that flowed down brick-lined ditches that ran through the woods and into the fields.

Gage remembered seeing the system long ago as a boy, but as they rode past one such ditch, he marveled anew at the ingenuity of its design. Whoever had first built Delipp had done so atop a gushing water source. Then they had followed the natural downward course of it and cleared fields wherever they found good ground and could channel the water.

The road into town paralleled one of these gurgling waterways. He and Manton followed the ditch up to where it channeled through Delipp's wattle-and-daub walls. The walls' mudding was cracked in places and falling out of the woven sticks.

"Not exactly the most secure defense," Gage commented.

Manton shrugged. "It serves its purpose."

Stopping at the gate, they paid their tolls, answered questions, showed their papers, and entered a mucky, foul-smelling street. The locals manned their shops and went about their business as if the swarms of flies and slimy ankle-deep ruts were normal. After so much rain, they probably were.

Tempted to lift a hand to his nose, Gage wondered where the fresh watercourse had gone. Listening, he discovered it tucked under timbers lining one side of the street.

Riding parallel to the wall, they eventually turned up a sloping street that led to the town's highest ground—a large square with big oak trees and grass in its middle.

Directly to their left, constructed against a large guild hall at the west end of the dirt square, stood a stone basin that Gage remembered seeing as a boy. At the top of the basin was a statue of a nymph riding a water horse, and filling the basin was the town's endless bubbling water source, which seemed to surge up from nowhere. It overflowed the back of the stone basin into the channels, which took the ceaseless stream throughout the town and out into the fields.

Opposite the basin on the east end of the square rose the towers and steeple of a huge church. Shops bordered the rest of the square while four roadways entered it—two on either side of the basin, like a tree's roots sunk deep on either side of a stream, and two coming from opposite directions just before the end of the square, like branches holding up the church.

Manton pointed halfway down the south side of the square. "The chandler's shop is where we're headed. Friends of mine own it."

Dismounting at its candlestick sign, Gage entered before Manton. He inhaled the soft, sweet scent of beeswax and sighed contentedly. "Now that is a smell I could smell all day."

The wiry, gray-haired owner coming from the back of the shop smiled. "I just finished dipping a new batch." He pointed to the lines of golden-colored candles hanging from a wooden frame over a vat. Another frame sat beside it, dangling dozens of empty linen cords waiting to be dipped in the vat of wax built above an enclosed fireplace, which looked like a baker's oven. It was used to heat the wax into a liquid.

The newly dipped candles gleamed, while the rest, hanging by their strings throughout the shop from poles and overhead beams, were dull in comparison. Gage inhaled their sweat honey scent once again. There were short, fat candles with multiple wicks, tall candles with single wicks, twisted candles, candles with pretty designs in their wax, and just inside the door in a neat, dangling row were dozens of candles all dyed different colors.

"They do smell good," Manton said, entering behind Gage, "but candles aren't the reason I came."

The shop owner's thin face burst into a smile. "Manton! Here I was starting to wonder if you'd lost your wanderlust and settled down somewhere."

"Not likely," Manton said, giving the man a hug. He gestured to Gage. "Evan, meet my traveling companion, Gabe. Gabe, meet Evan Chandler an old . . . family friend."

Evan's eyebrows lifted. "And how is your father?" Manton shrugged. The chandler gave Manton a disapproving look. "Have you not seen him any time recently?"

"Not in two years," Manton said, "but Victor said to pass along a greeting if I saw you."

Evan tsked. "You and your pa could have made a good team."

Manton snorted. "Yeah, but it'd only have lasted until I learned to use my fists and tongue as well as he uses his."

"Eh." Evan threw up a hand, then eyed them both. "Will you and your friend stay for supper? Tilda'll be making something soon, and Georgie and Jack are visiting from Claustrom. Jack is attending to business but should be back by tonight."

"I was actually wondering if we could stay a bit longer than that," Manton said. "Maybe a day or two?"

Evan shrugged. "Got a full house, but if you can find a spot, you can sleep in it."

⚬⚬

Since the Chandlers had no barn, Gage and Manton took their mounts down the street to a livery stable, warned those there to stay clear of Athalos, and headed back to the Chandlers.

"You really haven't spoken to your father in two years?" Gage asked Manton on the way.

"No, he's an arrogant man who despises everyone but likes having someone around to blame for his problems."

"I'm sorry. I guess I just assumed—"

"Assumed what?" Manton's eyebrows lifted. "That I had some great happy family at home but decided to travel the three kingdoms anyway? Well, I do have a great family." Manton grinned. "They just happen to be spread across the three kingdoms."

⚬⚬

At the meal that night, Gage was lost in thought considering his own family. His mother's words about writing swirled through his mind. He was thinking about the ring hidden in the underside of his saddle and what he might write when Manton's laugh pulled him back to the story Georgette was telling about the day her husband, Jack, had accidentally left their croft's gate open and let their nanny goat loose.

"Then the darn thing heads right under a wagon. I'm trying not to get run over, so I cut around behind. But she's not on the other side. I'm standing there thinking, where'd she go? Then I look. She's still under the wagon, trotting along, pulling cabbage out of a hole in its floorboards.

"I can't get to her because the wagon's still rolling, and I'm thinking, if I tell the driver, 'My goat's eating your cabbage. Can you please stop your wagon?', he'll laugh his head off, then make me pay for the cabbage. So, trying to think of a way to get to her, I'm trailing along after him, hoping he doesn't notice me ducking and peering under his wagon." Shaking her head, Georgette pointed to her very pregnant self. "And of course, I wasn't like this then."

Manton laughed. "So, how did you get her back?"

"Finally, the driver had to stop to let someone else pass, and quick as I could, I dove underneath and dragged her out." Georgette, as tall as her father but with her mother's heavy figure, giggled. "I'm sure I was a sight, but at least I got my goat back."

Tilda sighed and shook her head, "And this is the daughter I raised."

Evan patted his wife's shoulder. "Just remember she's already happily married."

"Yeah, and that my husband was the one who let the goat out," Georgette responded indignantly.

They all laughed.

38

That night Gage and Manton settled on the first floor while the family occupied the second floor. Staring up in the dark at candles he couldn't see, Gage longed to sit at a meal with his own family, hear their stories, and laugh with them. Careful not to bump into Manton, he rolled over and laid his head on his arm.

Still awake what felt like hours later, he heard a thud, someone shuffling about, and then Evan's loud whisper. "Jack? Is that you?"

"Yeah, it's me," a deep voice replied.

"Where have you been? Georgie and Tilda have been after me since supper wondering where you'd got to."

"Mud made the going slow."

"I figured. Couldn't have picked a worse time."

"Wasn't up to me."

"Well, come get some sleep."

There was more shuffling and then the creak of wood as the two men ascended the stairs.

Rolling over, Gage closed his eyes once more and thought of the nights his father was supposed to return but hadn't and how his mother would wait up for him. As he pictured her waiting, he thought of how much he missed everyone he cared about, including those at the house of Ulbin. With this came a piercing pain and a reminder of all the reasons why he chose to stay away. It was safer, for everyone.

※

THE NEXT MORNING after chopping firewood, Gage crossed paths with Manton, who was carrying a basket of chunked beeswax to the front of the shop. Evan gestured to them both. "Come eat."

Having met Jack while helping with chores, Gage sat opposite him at the morning meal. Solidly built with an intelligent face, dark hair, and a quick smile, Jack was as friendly as his wife, though a bit less talkative.

Once they had eaten, Gage and Manton checked on their mounts, then returned to the square as the church's bells clanged for terce. Shops were open, and stall owners displayed their goods in the shade of the big trees. People got water from the square's basin, talked, bought produce, called greetings, and haggled prices.

Gage and Manton purchased, among other things, smoked meat, cheese, and lentils to refill their food supply for the fair. They had been warned by the innkeeper outside of Nikledon that every shop owner in Nikledon would raise their prices during the fair, so they should buy anything they could ahead of time and bring it with them.

Having done so, they were just returning to the Chandlers' shop when someone from the road near the south side of the water basin yelled, "Watch out!" People screamed.

"Get out of the way!" someone else shouted.

A rider on a flying mount tore through the mingling buyers and sellers. People dodged, animals squawked, and somehow the rider made it across the square.

Yanking the animal to a stop, the man lunged off, bolted up the church's steps, and disappeared inside.

Another ruckus arose near the water basin. A collection of peasants with bows and swords strapped to their backs dispersed hurriedly through the startled and disgruntled townspeople.

A thunder of hooves was heard next, and a mass of armored horsemen bearing spears plowed into the market.

Chaos ensued. People screamed and rushed out of the way. Others fell. Produce was trampled, and animals were lost. In the hurried press, many of the townspeople tried to flee toward the opposite end of the market.

Spurring their mounts forward, six of the forty or so horsemen—bearing a red standard with a blue chevron above a hound with a ring of keys in its teeth—galloped past where Gage and Manton stood and toward the church, cutting off the people's retreat.

Other horsemen took up positions at each of the square's exits. The rest dismounted and used the shafts of their spears, held in both hands like shields, to drive the people together under the trees.

Before Gage's stunned mind could decide why soldiers who were clearly not in service to the local lord were invading the square, Manton grabbed his arm and pulled him into the Chandlers' shop.

Evan paused while hoisting a rack of candles. "What's wrong?"

"Soldiers are corralling people in the square," Manton replied hurriedly.

With a startled expression, Evan looked at Jack and pointed. "Go out the back."

"Where are Tilda and Georgette?" Manton asked.

Evan dropped the rack of candles. "Upstairs."

"I'll go," Jack said.

"No," Evan replied.

Setting down the supplies they had just bought, Gage looked at Manton. "What's going on?"

Manton turned. "I'll—"

A soldier built like a bull barged in the shop's front door. "All of you. Outside!"

Four other soldiers followed him into the shop. "You heard him. Out!" Seizing Manton's arm, one of the soldiers propelled him toward the shop's front door.

"Get moving." A gauntleted hand shoved Gage from behind. Startled and confused, he twisted to glare at the soldier. The man smacked him in the back of the head. "I said out the front!"

Staggered by the unexpected blow and angry, Gage lifted a hand. The soldier grabbed his wrist, twisted his arm sharply behind his back, and steered him out into the square. Another soldier brought Evan out behind him.

Before Gage could even think to resist the soldier's hold, he was thrust into the frightened crowd of townspeople amassed around the trunks of the square's trees. A townsman and Manton caught him as he stumbled into them.

Gripping Manton's arm, Gage straightened, his heart pounding and his mind spinning. He met Manton's fury-filled gaze and felt the same. Irate expressions stirred in many of the faces around him, but everyone stayed where they were.

Who were these soldiers that they thought they had the right to disregard basic human decency? And what possible reason could they have for dragging people from their shops?

Gage searched for the Chandlers. Evan hadn't been tossed on top of them. He could only assume the soldiers had inserted the man into the crowd someplace else. Other townspeople were driven toward them, but two peasants were separated off and hauled toward a knight.

The knight dismounted, accepted a handful of bows and swords from the soldiers who had brought the two peasants, and gave the soldiers rope in exchange.

A cry from a butcher's shop across the square swung Gage's focus back to the Chandlers' shop. He spotted Georgette being led by an arm toward the crowd. Her gaze caught on the peasants the soldiers were binding. Staring in horror, she tripped on the rutted ground and fell. Her legs tangled with those of the soldier leading her, and he too fell.

Cursing, the soldier struggled to his feet and kicked Georgette's pregnant belly. "You stupid wench! Get up!"

Gage's body went cold, then flushed with an even deeper anger. Manton shifted forward, but a townsman seized his arm. "Don't. You'll only make it worse."

The grasp of a soldier, however, did nothing to stop Jack. The man ripped free of his escort and plowed headfirst into the man who was about to kick his wife again. Wiping the soldier out at the knees, Jack pinned the man down, tore off his helmet, and punched him in the face.

Tilda came up behind them, helped her daughter to her feet, and fled with her into the crowd. The townspeople opened to the two like a door to a wounded traveler and closed about them protectively. Unfortunately, Jack was too far away to reach.

He immediately released the soldier, but it didn't matter. Three other soldiers seized him. Gage cringed. He knew Jack would be dealt several blows to remind him of his place before they deposited him into the crowd.

Instead, the soldiers beat Jack into the ground.

Gage covered his mouth and felt Manton turn to stone beside him. The sickening thud of the soldiers' fists and boots could be heard as they struck Jack again and again. Amid the crying women, whimpering children, and muttering men, an angry murmur arose from the townspeople.

"Stop it!" Georgette screamed. "Please, stop."

Gage's body rocked at her cry. Someone had to do something. Jack lifted his head, only to be struck again in the face. The soldier Jack had punched coiled back his gauntleted fist.

"You four, see to your orders!" bellowed a knight bearing the same coat-of-arms as the rest.

Backing away and leaving Jack lying there broken and bleeding, the four dispersed to the edges of the square, where other soldiers were still dragging occupants from their houses and shops. Most people fled into the crowd willingly. Anyone who resisted was met with swift, brutal force.

Furious over all he was witnessing, Gage inhaled in relief when two more riders entered the square. The blue-and-red trappings of the foremost rider's horse and his ostentatious armor declared the solid-built, bearded young man to be a nobleman. His squire was the second rider, a youth wearing the surcoat of the hound with a ring of keys in its teeth.

Gage assumed the lord's presence would bring restraint to the soldiers' actions, but the young noble just watched as the soldiers finished brashly pulling people from their homes.

"Why isn't he stopping them?" Gage murmured in angry disbelief.

"Because that's Bertram," Manton growled, "Baron of Lyster."

Gage blinked. "He can't be the baron of Lyster. He's barely older than I am."

"He's twenty-three," a townsman muttered. "Baron Markus died two years ago. Thus Bertram, his eldest son, became Lyster's lord."

"If he's truly Lyster's lord, then what is he doing here?" Gage asked. "He has no right to cross into another lord's lands and seize and detain his tenants."

The townsman beside Gage snorted. "Try telling him that."

"When it comes to the lords, Gabe, right versus ability are two different things," Manton said.

Feeling patronized and reprimanded, Gage stirred angrily. He had the right to tell Baron Bertram exactly that, but just as Manton had said, right versus ability were two different things.

Swallowing, he glanced at where Jack still lay, heard the murmuring anger around him, and wondered if Baron Bertram cared anything for the respect of the people.

"Silence!" a knight bellowed.

39

FLINCHING WITH THE crowd, Gage glanced at the knight and noted three more commoners had been added to those the soldiers had separated from the townspeople. They were lined up on their knees with ropes around their necks and their arms bound behind their backs. A set of guards stood behind them, swords drawn.

Gage listened as the knight rode over and reported to Baron Bertram in the nobleman's tongue, which the townspeople couldn't understand. "My lord, we have found five of the attackers. But we tracked four more here from the woods, where they were dividing up the remainder of what was taken. One is within the church. The three others we are still trying to find. What are your orders, my lord?"

"Retrieve the one from the church of course," Baron Bertram replied as if the knight was daft. "And find the rest." Scowling, the baron kicked his mount forward. "People of Delipp!" he called out condescendingly in the commoner's tongue. "You have enemies of Delkara in your midst." He pointed to the kneeling peasants. "These men fled here after attacking my men and my wagons. They thought to make a mockery of a lord and will be punished for it—as will anyone who is found helping them."

The fact that the bound men were rebels changed Gage's feelings toward them. Even his outrage over the soldiers' despicable actions lessened somewhat at the realization that they were pursuing rebel thieves and murderers.

"No! You cannot take me!" a man screamed from the direction of the church. People twisted trying to see what was happening. Gage already knew, but he rose on his toes anyway and watched as a struggling commoner was dragged down the church's steps. A priest followed the arresting force, shouting. "You cannot take him! He has claimed sanctuary. You must respect the holy ground of the church!"

With a rattle of metal, Baron Bertram spurred his mount around the crowd. He yanked the animal to a stop at the church's steps. "Stand aside, priest. This man is a traitor to the crown. He has no right of sanctuary."

Gage wasn't sure if this was legally true or not, but in Edelmar when the right of sanctuary was claimed, most lords dared not deny it.

The priest stepped into the soldiers' path. "It does not matter what he has done," he sputtered. "You cannot trespass on holy ground and deprive a man of his right of sanctuary."

With a rush of hooves, another contingency of horsemen, all bearing light-green livery, rode into the square. An older man drove his white horse from the mix and out in front of Baron Bertram. "What is happening here?" he demanded in the nobleman's tongue. Hair and beard metal-gray beneath a hat embellished with white feathers, the older lord wore a long dark tunic over which was strapped a maroon scabbard that carried a sword with a gilded hilt. Though it had probably been ten years since he'd met the man, Gage recognized the baron as Lord Hadrian of Delipp.

Despite his younger age, which should have required a tone of humility, Baron Bertram answered the Lord of Delipp sharply in the nobleman's tongue. "I am arresting those who attacked my wagons last night."

Lord Hadrian glanced at the man held upon the church's steps, then toward his gathered and guarded townspeople. His face darkened further. "Baron Bertram, you have come seeking wrongdoers, but I take offense that in so doing you have corralled my people like animals, defiled the church, and desecrated a man's right of sanctuary."

Baron Bertram cursed and kicked his horse forward. "You dare reprimand me, old man? 'Tis your townspeople and priest aiding these thieves. Take a stronger hand, Lord Hadrian, or it will be taken for you. Now tell your priest to return to his church, and remind him it is King Strephon, not God, who rules this kingdom."

Gage blinked. Never in his life had he witnessed a younger lord express such blatant disrespect for an older lord nor such disregard for his authority. Expecting to hear Lord Hadrian tongue lash Baron Bertram for his insolence, Gage was stunned to hear the older lord instead appeal to wisdom. "Baron Bertram, the church here has complied with all of Strephon's wishes. This trespass is not about rebellion but tradition. So prithee, allow this man to return to the altar that the church and people might yet be appeased. Do so, and I promise I will bring this man to you bound on the morrow without the riot you will have on your hands if you take him in this way."

"If this is what you fear, old man, then you indeed have no control over your people." The younger baron shook his head scornfully and wheeled his horse. "I tell you, let the people attempt a riot. They can learn respect at the hands of my men." He motioned to his soldiers, who shoved the rebel to his knees and bound him like the others.

A seething murmur erupted amidst the crowd who, having understood nothing of the lords' exchange, had no idea of the baron's threat. Shouts of wrath were hurled, and the priest hurried toward Lord Hadrian. "Your lordship, please, you cannot allow this."

Gage cringed. Even if Lord Hadrian chose to stand in Baron Bertram's way, it was clear the baron planned on doing whatever he wished regardless. And since the baron's entourage was an army in comparison to Lord Hadrian's paltry retinue, the only real question was how bad Baron Bertram's retaliation would be if anyone took action against him.

More shouts arose. "You can't take him! He's claimed sanctuary!"

Stirring into action, Lord Hadrian wheeled his horse and pointed up the steps. "Go back to your church, priest." Then he turned to his people. "All of you, be silent. You think this is an outrage, but it is not. This man does not deserve the right of sanctuary. The Lord of Lyster seizes men who have stolen from their lords and broken their vows of fealty. They are traitors to the crown, and the baron is here to restore peace. Therefore, if by the hand of any one of you violence erupts against him or his men, I will see that person flogged. Now stand fast, and let justice be done."

A quiet murmur of angry questions circulated through the crowd, but to Gage's relief, the townspeople stayed where they were, and no further resistance was made.

When the last of the rebels had been found, Baron Bertram galloped from the square, followed by his squire. His soldiers lifted their spears and, watching their backs, departed with their nine prisoners in tow. The moment they left, Lord Hadrian and his retinue retreated in the opposite direction.

Standing amidst the townspeople, Gage stared after the lords, feeling both shame and anger—shame that they represented the leadership of the lords and anger that their leadership had caused so much harm.

Those around him slowly drifted back into motion. People trailed to their shops or collected goods that had been knocked off carts. Others helped up the injured, and several rounded up loose animals. Voices were hushed and strained. The soldiers of Lyster were gone, but the entrapment, confusion, and fear they had brought to Delipp still clung to everyone.

40

Back in the Chandlers' shop, Gage glanced at Evan, who sat hunched beside the wax vat. The man's hands were knotted and his eyebrows smashed together. Tilda and Georgette were upstairs tending to Jack. Meanwhile, Manton paced below the shop's candles, looking as if he might tear something to pieces. No one spoke. What was there to say? A force had demeaned and abused them, and nothing could change that. If the baron's men had asked for their aid or had even the decency to announce their intentions, it might have been different. But the townspeople weren't given the chance to comply, let alone help. Instead, they'd been treated as mere chattel, tossed aside so a search could be done more effectively.

But unlike clothing or goods, a man thrown down didn't rise the same. Obedience by abuse worked, but Gage's father had described it accurately: *"Force can achieve a momentary compliance, but in the end abuse reaps a hostility far more dangerous than lack of compliance."* Gage now personally understood this. Had he the opportunity, he'd have happily smashed Baron Bertram from his horse with a lance.

By allowing the soldiers' actions and their brutal punishment of anyone's resistance or even Jack's defense of his wife, Baron Bertram and his knights had destroyed the respect and trust of the commoners.

Yet as much as Gage fully felt the situation from where he stood outraged as Gabe, he could not dismiss what he knew as Gage. He knew the horrors the rebels were capable of. He also knew what it was to watch them take something precious from you and get away. And deep inside he also knew far too well how much Baron Bertram wanted and needed to succeed in capturing them.

This wasn't the first rebel attack Baron Bertram had endured. Gage couldn't fathom surviving such an experience more than once. Perhaps it wasn't so strange that the young baron and his men were so aggressive toward the commoners. After all, the lords' inability to tell which commoners were loyal and which weren't was exactly what the rebels used to their advantage. As a lord, it was too dangerous to trust everyone, but suspecting everyone wasn't a solution either.

As he considered this, Gage realized the paranoia on Baron Bertram's part was probably exactly what the reeve from Lyster had been trying to warn them about. It also seemed to be something Lord Hadrian knew. Why else step aside to protect his people from the baron and then fail to stay to assure them that what had taken place at the baron's hand was unacceptable and would be dealt with? Instead Lord Hadrian had acted as if Baron Bertram was untouchable. And with this as their example, it wasn't hard to understand why the townspeople believed he was. What recourse did they have? They could not confront Baron Bertram themselves. And if their lord would not do so, what was left to them? It was proof of Manton's assumption that the lords did not care, and this more than anything infuriated Gage.

Perhaps an appeal could be made to King Strephon. But would Strephon listen? And would he do anything about it? Gage had met Strephon as a boy, but since Strephon was quite a bit older than him, they'd interacted very little. Gage recalled his uncle Elmon's words from the feast, "Strephon's rule has no doubt been a difficult one. Many said he was not ready to take the crown." But Manton's friend had said that despite the rebels' attacks, King Strephon desired to support the common people.

Manton's words from the day they'd spoken about traveling into Delkara resurfaced as well. *"King Strephon allows his barons freedom to deal with problems as they see fit."* This time Gage heard the words with his naivety stripped away. But had not his own father done the same thing? He too had bequeathed the lords of Edelmar the right to deal with the Blue Crow as they saw fit.

No doubt both kings assumed their lords would go about such a pursuit honorably, and a man's lack of honor wasn't always seen by those who appointed him. Thus, one lord's actions was not proof of his king's intentions.

Therefore, if King Strephon was informed of Baron Bertram's actions, he may in fact curb the lord's conduct. But who of the townspeople of Delipp would dare inform him? Who would make such a journey to stand before their king and report a neighboring lord's misconduct, particularly when they believed it would make no difference?

Gage sighed. Most lords were not at all as they were accused of being. They did care, and their people did matter to them. Even Lord Hadrian, despite his shameful retreat, had shown that he cared about his people. Sadly, to his people, who had understood nothing of the nobleman's conversation, his care had come across as him standing with Baron Bertram.

If both sides understood more about the other, a lot might change. They needed someone who could bridge the gap between them, someone capable of seeing and speaking for both sides. The thought that he could fill such a role sunk through Gage's skin and clung to his bones. He killed the thought before it could go any further. He was not that person, and Delkara wasn't his kingdom. He, Prince Gage, wasn't even supposed to be there. He was just a commoner from Edelmar traveling to Delkara, and as far as he was concerned what happened there and who the lords were was none of his business. He had come simply to sell his mounts at the fair and then return to his own kingdom. And that was what he intended to do.

41

In the following day's setting sun, Gage marveled at the transformation of the road into Nikledon. Brightly painted wagons, well-dressed merchants with carts and tents, and an excess of hawkers with bundles of goods were scattered along the road's edge like an endless flow of color leading into the meadow where the fair was to be held.

At the fairgrounds newly constructed stalls were being decorated while more wagons rolled in, hauling additional wood. Excited children raced about while their parents and older siblings pitched tents, set up makeshift shops, and unpacked campsites. Two multi-colored pavilions, one the blue and green of Nikledon and the other with vertical stripes of blue and yellow, claimed the far side of the meadow. Scattered about the rest of the space were the smaller tents of sellers.

Having paid their tax to sell at the fair on their way into the meadow, Gage and Manton headed to the spot they hoped to occupy for the next several days. They both groaned. It was already taken.

With regretful glances, they passed the perfumer settled there and headed to the next-closest expanse of trees to claim a spot with at least some shade.

The drifting smoke from numerous fires smelled of pottage. Gage's stomach grumbled. With only an hour or two before dark, food would have to wait.

Swinging to the ground, Gage listened to the clink of tent stakes being driven, the thwack of wood being unloaded, the bray of a mule, the happy shrieks of children, and the pop and snap of their neighbor's fire.

The first thing Gage did was string a picket line between trees for their five mounts while Manton unloaded them. On Sulky and one of the other mounts, they had brought hay from Delipp and downed wood they had collected on their way. With no tent, they were counting on good weather. The Cooper brothers had promised them space in their tent in exchange for saving them a spot, but with the fair still two days away, they were on their own until the Coopers arrived.

"You want to start the fire or fetch water?" Manton asked.

"I'll start the fire."

Manton headed off, and Gage scraped out a firepit and cracked twigs into a pile. Then he took a thick stick and headed to where their neighbor, a cloth merchant by the look of his goods, was stirring a pot hung over his own campfire. Gage approached with a smile. "May I borrow from your flames?"

Dressed in a clean shirt and trousers with neatly trimmed hair and beard, the man gestured welcomingly. Crouching, Gage poked his stick into the fire. "Thank you. I'm Gabe. My traveling companion's Manton. If you need a hand with anything during the fair, just let us know."

The man studied his face as if to confirm Gage meant the offer, then nodded. "I'm Liam."

Smiling, Gage lifted his stick, now bright with yellow flames. "Thank you, Liam."

※

Having fallen asleep listening to a mother singing a lullaby to her little ones a couple of tents away, Gage woke to the clatter of wood being unloaded. With his cloak still wrapped about him, he rose stiffly.

Stepping around Manton and nodding sleepily to Liam, he headed off to get water from the stream, which cut through the backside of the meadow.

Returning, he found Manton nursing their fire back to life. They boiled water for a breakfast of cracked wheat and raisins.

Around them the meadow came alive as others stumbled from their tents and wagons. On the far side of the meadow, two men—clearly in service to the local lord—pounded stakes and strung rope around a good-sized area, probably portioning it off for competitions.

Trying not to think about the possibility of there being archery, a mêlée, and possibly even jousting, Gage ate his food and determined which mount he would work with first. The mare still needed work on her ground manners, and Black could use some work picking up his feet.

※

Throughout the day while working his mounts, Gage watched the meadow fill in with more tents, booths, the beginning of a stage, and a sheltered platform from which the nobility would watch the competitions.

The Cooper boys arrived late that night, and he and Manton helped them pitch their tent. Jordan, the elder of the two brothers, had brought a lute. So, that night they laughed and sang to music.

The next morning the workers were pounding away on the stage before dawn. By sext the middle of the meadow had filled with stalls and tents, and by nightfall the only open spaces left were the wagon routes in and out of the meadow, the competition area, and a half-moon stretch in front of the stage. It felt a lot like a tournament settlement, except those present were not soldiers and knights but peasant families, merchants, shop owners, and travelers.

Six more large colorful pavilions had also gone up. Gage recognized Umbra's, Burnel's, and Asplin's colors amid the mix but was relieved to not see the lord of Duvall's pavilion because several of the Baron Hewitt's knights could recognize him.

Leading Black and Sulky back from the stream, Gage admired the weaponry in a bladesmith's stall. A collection of plain and detailed swords hung on the walls, and an assortment of daggers and knives lay on the stall's board.

Five booths later he passed a tent holding a collection of covered cages that squawked and chirped. Hunched cleaning an empty enclosure, the seller scooped a coil of fur from his arm and placed it up on his shoulder. The small brown animal turned around and eyed Gage. Gage grinned. It was a monkey. Dragging his gaze from the unique sight, he clicked to his mounts.

"Did you hear?" Derik asked when Gage arrived back at their campsite.

"Hear what?" Gage said as he tied up the two mounts.

"There's to be a dance tomorrow after the first full day of the fair is complete."

A dance instantly brought to mind memories of Allard and Emma. Gage turned away and grabbed the water bucket. "Great."

"You aren't excited?" Derik asked.

With his back to the brothers, Gage shrugged and felt his stomach knot.

"Have you ever been to a dance before?" Jordan asked.

Gage shook his head. It wasn't a lie. He'd never participated in a commoners' dance. They were not the elegant affairs of the noblemen's class. They were loud events full of brash gaiety and often accompanied by enough alcohol to drown a cow. Judged as the foolish indulgence of the common people, the activity was frowned upon by the more proper noblemen and their wives. But what did that matter now?

"He's never danced before." Derik looked at Manton in disbelief. "Where did you find this poor traveler?"

"Apparently, in a very dull town," Manton said

Derik chuckled. "Well, I guess we'll just have to see how well he keeps his feet. You two do have clean clothes for the fair, yes?"

Manton shook his head. "No, we thought we'd wear these clothes for another month at least." When Derik eyed him, Manton chuckled. "Of course we have clean clothes. We're going upstream tonight to bathe and change."

Gage stroked Black's neck. As Prince Gage of Edelmar, he'd dressed for so many events. Always there had been a strength and certainty in pulling on his royal tunic and placing his crown on his head. As a commoner it was so different. Longing and dread clashed within him. What was he doing here?

The answer stamped beside him. Exhaling, he patted Black's shoulder and smiled. He was selling mounts, and as a seller of mounts, he had absolutely no reason not to thoroughly enjoy the fair and dance his heart out.

42

The fair started the following morning with the arrival of Lord Nikledon's entourage. Announcing the lord were riders and heralds in blue-and-green tabards carrying flags exhibiting Nikledon's coat-of-arms. At the flag's center was a halved shield, one part blue with a gold upright lion and the other part green with a black eagle. The heralds trumpeted their glistening instruments.

Setting aside his food, Gage rose along with Manton and the Cooper brothers and watched the procession of young and seasoned knights, squires, and pages of barely seven trek through the meadow toward the competition grounds and colored pavilions. In the procession's center, a lord's stately dark mount caparisoned in bright blue and green foamed at the mouth and trotted on a tight rein.

The lord seated upon the mount wore a lavish hat, a tunic with fur trim, and gold chains draped across his shoulders. But no silver ran through his hair, and no aged wisdom wrinkled his bow. Rather the lord appeared to be Haaken's equal in age. Gage wondered where the Lord of Nikledon was that his son rode in his stead on the day of the start of Nikledon's fair.

The Lord of Nikledon's absence didn't delay the festivities though, for the moment the procession passed, the sellers stirred into action, and Gage happily joined them.

Derik and Jordan stacked their barrels and buckets, and Manton uncovered the wooden items he had unpacked on a board. A large variety of whistles, tops, figures, and gameboards were all spread for buyers to see. Gage untied Black and headed where animals were being sold.

In the rising sun, everyone's goods were proudly displayed and even oiled to make them glisten. Flags flew, voices carried, and excitement filled the air.

※

Two hours later, Gage had sold Black for twice what he'd bought him for and had a possible buyer for Sulky trailing him back to their camp.

The merchant wiped his brow and nodded to the crowded lane and busy sellers. "This is the most people I've ever seen at the fair. The Lord of Nikledon boasted he would bring in more sellers this year, and it seems he did so. Many are not Delkaran though. Like that one." He said to Gage and pointed to a stall of rugs and pottery. "See the patterns? You won't find anything like it in the three kingdoms. Whoever the seller is, they came by ship."

Gage found the man's knowledge intriguing. "Do you know why the Lord of Nikledon is not in attendance?"

The merchant eyed him quizzically. "Did you not see him and his procession pass through the grounds this morning?"

Slowing to avoid a small child who was running to catch up with his parents, Gage frowned. "I thought that was his son riding in this morning."

"Baron Selwin? Yes, he was the son of Nikledon's lord, but Lord Terryn passed away several years ago. Selwin is now the Lord of Nikledon."

Taken aback by the news, Gage was about to ask more about Lord Terryn's passing when a wagon trundled toward them. They ended up on separate sides of it, and it took several moments for him to find the merchant again after the crowd washed back together in its wake. By that time they were almost past their campsite. Gage caught up to the man and pointed. "The mule is over here under the trees."

※

THE MERCHANT HADN'T been convinced Sulky was worth what Gage was asking, but three hours later, Gage sold his mare for a hefty purse, which he quickly tucked out of sight under his tunic. He came back to the campsite to find Jordan manning the Coopers' wagon. Derik was nowhere in sight, and Manton was busy talking to two men who didn't look interested in buying anything.

About the same height, both men wore rough tunics, thick belts, knives, and wary expressions. One had dark hair and a full beard. The other was clean shaven with light-brown hair.

Passing them, Gage crouched to scoop from the water bucket and noted the clean-shaven man eye him and shift his hand to his knife. Curious to know why the man was concerned by him, Gage wiped his chin and approached. "I'm Gabe. I've been traveling with Manton for the last couple of months. Is there a problem here?"

"There's no problem. These are friends of mine," Manton replied, "Arron and Michael of Dinslage."

Arron, the cleaner shaven of the two, eased his hand off his knife. "You're from Edelmar?"

"I am."

The other man's dark eyes swept over him.

"You sellers or buyers for the fair?" Gage asked, trying to ease the tension he felt from them.

"A bit of both," Arron replied.

A young mother and son approached the board of toys and games. Michael nodded to Manton. "We should be going."

The two departed. Watching them go and Manton focus on his customers, Gage untied Sulky and started toward the selling ground. He was wading through the bustling lane, listening to the distant cheers coming from the competition ground, when he heard a female voice yelling, "Gabe! Gabe!"

Frowning, he searched the crowd for a woman who knew him as Gabe. He saw her, dodging this way and that toward him. Somehow she reached him without knocking anyone over with her large satchel. Gage laughed. "What are you doing here?" Her shiny gray-brown braid was grayer than he remembered, but her eyes were livelier.

She straightened to her full height, which was just above his own. "I don't call myself a seller of spices for nothing." She flicked her hand disdainfully at Sulky. "But here I thought you were a horse trader, not a seller of these obnoxious, flea-infested things."

"I sell mounts, my lady."

She responded to his snarky comment the same way she had back at the inn in Clement. She thwacked him.

Gage chuckled. "How have sales been for you?"

"Good. Very good."

He bowed in mock deference. "Well, may it continue to go well for you."

She curtsied back. "The same to you."

Shaking his head in amusement, Gage was about to bid her good day when he was suddenly pushed backward by people hurriedly making way for riders coming down the lane. Gage tried to steer Sulky sideways and winced as the animal stepped on his foot. He was elbowed by someone. Gage shuffled his way backwards to avoid stepping on others as he angled the mule off the road. A mother with two children hastily pressed in on top of him. The woman gripped her daughter's and son's shoulders. "Keep your heads down, and stay quiet," she whispered, then tipped her own face toward the ground.

"Make way!" a voice yelled.

Pressed against Sulky's furry chest, Gage glanced toward the lane, wondering why all the panic. He spotted the lord's coat-of-arms—a dog with a ring of keys in its teeth. Something akin to fear traveled through him. He dropped his gaze.

Only once Baron Bertram and his retinue had passed did Gage realize he was holding his breath. He exhaled and watched the mother also relax and let go of her children. Slowly, everyone eased back onto the road.

Gage stared after Baron Bertram of Lyster's retinue. No one like that should be allowed to rule. Tugging Sulky back into motion, Gage headed for the selling ground.

≈

Hours later, Gage returned with Sulky still in tow. He'd gotten plenty of offers for the mule but none as high as he wanted.

At their campsite he ate with the others and listened to their day's stories and told a few of his own, like bumping into the spice seller from Clement. Then they prepared to head to the dance.

They'd just left their campsite when quick music burst to life from near the fair's stage. Clapping and cheers exploded a moment later.

Cutting between tents, the four of them reached the area near the stage. Torches encircled a swiftly moving mass of weaving and ducking people with broad smiles and excited faces.

"I think I'll just observe at first," Gage said.

"Oh no you don't." Manton, Jordan, and Derik grabbed him and pulled him into the bouncing feet, flying bodies, twisting arms, and thunderous assault of hands, feet, and faces.

Gage instantly lost track of them and found himself turned and twisted by other dancers, who swung him about in a chaotic whirl. A pretty lass swept by, catching his arm and spinning him. A little boy, too short to reach Gage's elbow, grabbed his hand in small fingers and tugged to get him to turn. Gage did and was snagged by an old woman with missing teeth, who grinned like a little girl. She hooked her bony elbow into his and flung him into full motion. His feet flying, Gage caught the arm of someone else and laughingly embraced the music and chaos.

Crossing paths eventually with each of his friends, he found them smiling like fools and realized he probably was too. He and the spice seller ran into each other not long after. "Hey, hey!" he shouted and then hooked arms with her and swung her about merrily, only to be snatched away by the next person and the next.

Eventually, he stumbled away from the twirling mass. Standing with others who were watching or, like him, trying to catch their breath before diving back in, he smiled at the joyous crowd spread before him. It did look disreputable, but it was also a wonderful means of entertainment.

43

Shaken awake by Jordan at dawn, Gage groaned. "I don't think I've ever been so tired in my life."

The other three laughed and began rising.

"Does anyone remember where I put my shoes?" Derik asked as he searched around Gage's saddlebags and through a pile of clothing.

Manton yawned. "I think they're by the fire."

Stumbling out of their tent with the others, Gage splashed his face with cold water and started on the chores.

After breakfast, the others set out their goods, and Gage set off again with Sulky. He got the price he wanted for the mule two hours later. With nothing else to sell, he decided to see the rest of the fair.

As he wandered about, he discovered he recognized faces all over the place. He exchanged smiles with the others sellers he had whirled about with the night before. It was as if they now shared a delightful secret.

Passing stalls displaying women's gloves, ivory combs, shawls, and jewelry, he thought of his mother but saw nothing that was quite right for a present for her. He bought a handful of candied oranges and munched on the sweets while wandering by a troop of musicians and jugglers. Their performance was good but nothing like what he had seen at Nardell.

A distant clash of metal came from the competition grounds. He considered going that way but instead went back to shopping. He passed a few lords and ladies out amongst the stalls with their men-at-arms and servants. Like the rest of the commoners, Gage gave them their space.

Eventually working his way all the way out to the roadway, he slowed at a wagon to look over the seller's pewter bowls, plates, spoons, trinkets, and candlesticks. Then a hawker's goods spread on the ground beside the wagon caught his eye.

On a blanket before her lay a vast collection of seashells of all sizes, colors, and shades. They were some of the strangest, most beautiful things he had ever seen. After much deliberation Gage selected two shells that closed tightly together. They had a white frilly texture on the outside and a smooth dark purple on the inside. Gage knew his mother would love the shells and asked the seller how much she wanted. She named her price. He haggled her down to half that.

With the shells in hand, he headed back toward the fairgrounds, past baked items, honey sweets, tunics, masks, and musical instruments.

At their campsite he ducked into their stuffy tent and dug through his saddlebags, which were the only set in the tent. The others left theirs under the wagon, but Gage wanted his out of sight of passersby and within reach at night. Pulling out one of his shirts, he wrapped the shells in it and tucked them back into his saddlebags.

༺⚬༻

That evening after dusk, Gage followed Manton and the Coopers to the area where the dance had taken place, but this time they sat in the worn grass at the back of the crowd facing the stage.

Gage scanned the area. Groups of families and friends were clumped everywhere, talking or simply waiting for the first play. The arriving lords and ladies took their seats inside a nearby open-faced pavilion. Their attendants stood or sat outside the tent.

The baron of Nikledon arrived, and the moment he gave a signal, actors rushed out onto the stage in wild colors and launched into their show. At the end of it, Gage clapped heartily with everyone else. The two performances that followed were both short yet good. The fourth was a tragedy and terrible, and the fifth was so bad it was amusing.

The sixth play was slow in arriving, but when it did, Gage found it familiar. A child adopted by a princess grew up as royalty to people not his own. His own people were slaves to those who had adopted him. The grown boy, watching his people at work one day, saw one of his fellow countrymen being abused and killed the man abusing him.

As the actor playing the abuser fell to the ground, a murmur moved through the crowd, and a commotion at the nobles' pavilion drew Gage's attention. Baron Selwin emerged from the pavilion speaking to one of his knights. Several other lords joined him looking agitated.

Wondering what had them astir, Gage glanced about. Seeing nothing out of the ordinary, he turned his attention back to the stage and told himself that whatever the issue was, it was their problem, not his.

The scene on the stage had transitioned to the wilderness, where Moses now herded sheep. Having seen this mystery play before along with a number of other stories, Gage wondered how they would depict the burning bush.

A man crouched behind a bush wearing dark clothing and unfurled strips of gold and red cloth and swung them into motion. Eyes widening, the man playing Moses pointed, but not at the bush. "They're coming!" he yelled.

Instantly, all the actors scattered across the stage. Soldiers rushed up the steps, grabbing some of the performers but missing others. They dragged the actors they had seized from the stage. Those they missed leapt into the audience and took off running.

Moses was one of those who made it off the stage. Jumping over an elderly man's lap, he called for pardon as he went. Moses was a lance's length from where Gage and his friends sat when a soldier hurled a knife at the actor's back.

Gage gasped. In utter clarity he saw the actor's face and heard his cry as he tumbled forward and crashed to the ground with the knife sticking from his back. The actor struggled to get up, but the soldiers were already upon him. They hauled him off the ground and in the process knocked off his head wrap, revealing tonsured hair. Horrified, Gage thought the soldiers would immediately let go and back away, but they simply turned and dragged him through the crowd. Thunderstruck, Gage stared after them.

"Silence!" The boisterous voice hushed the murmuring crowd.

From near the pavilion, Baron Selwin addressed the crowd. "Please accept my sincere apology for this unfortunate display. These men have broken Delkaran law. Justice has been done. Please sit."

At his words, many in the audience returned to the ground while those still standing looking confused or angry were quickly pulled down by those around them.

"Start the next play," Baron Selwin commanded.

A new collection of actors was shoved out into the torchlight. With frightened expressions, they launched into their performance.

His stomach roiling, Gage rose and fled through the tents.

By the time he made it back to their campsite, he had managed to keep his stomach from revolting but only barely. Sinking to his knees at their fire, he swallowed and lifted his shaking hands over the coals. Moses's face filled his mind, and Baron Selwin's words rang in his head. *"Justice has been done."* With what he had just seen, he doubted that was true.

Someone touched his shoulder. He whirled.

"Are you all right?" asked Liam, the cloth merchant.

"No, they arrested the performers of a mystery play!" Still in shock, Gage motioned back toward the stage. "One was a monk. The soldiers put a dagger in his back. They said they'd broken Delkaran law."

"Most likely they were part of those standing against the lords," Liam said. "In my opinion, their actions have brought nothing but bloodshed. They attack, and the lords retaliate. It's futile and foolish. A monk should have known better than to join their ranks."

Gage inhaled. He agreed with Liam. But did that justify the way the Delkaran lords were going after the rebels? Was what happened at the play really justice? Perhaps there hadn't been another option or opportunity to take down those particular rebels. Or perhaps the lords had done so onstage intentionally as a warning to others. As Gage thought about it, he realized Moses might not have even been a monk. His tonsured hair could have been a disguise the man had used during an attack upon one of the lords, possibly even Selwin.

With such widespread rebellion taking place and the barons desperate to put an end to the rebels attacks, he couldn't blame them for being desperate and at times overbearing, particularly when they had no idea who in a crowd was their enemy and who wasn't. It was terrible but necessary.

Gage swallowed. Was Edelmar headed for the same fate? He hoped not, but if the Blue Crow's men weren't the only ones, what was happening in Delkara could very well be happening in Edelmar.

43

The next morning, Gage returned with a bucket of water to find the Coopers and Manton talking about the plays. "Why even attempt to perform a mystery play?" Manton asked.

"You're not a Christian," Jordan replied. "You wouldn't understand."

"You're right. I don't understand how you can act like a mystery play is important when there are so many other things to concern ourselves with," Manton said.

Not wanting to think about the incident, Gage slipped away from their campsite to wander the booths he hadn't gotten a chance to see the day before. He hoped to find gifts for his father and Haaken and at least bring back something cheery with him.

He strolled through stalls all morning and at sext bought a meat pie and ate it while watching a sword walker climb a ladder of blades. He returned to viewing booths as the sun began its descent.

He glanced over one seller's gold and silver goods, admiring the unique necklaces, cloak clasps, rings, and women's hair pieces. He shifted to turn away, but a brooch at the back of the board caught his attention. It was a circle of gold with four blood-red stones. Such a piece was probably common. There had to be hundreds similar to the one Felix had stolen off him. But with such a specific design in the gold?

In the days after the tournament while it had still been in his possession, he had become well acquainted with the pattern engraved around the brooch's gold circle. Trying to breathe, he stood rooted to the spot. It couldn't be the same brooch, could it? Perhaps James had bought a similar piece from a smith who had made several. But what if it wasn't a similar piece?

Once again feeling Felix yank it from his tunic, Gage drew a shuddering breath. His mind spun with the possible implications. He had to know.

"Can I help you?" the seller asked.

Gage ignored the man's tone, which suggested Gage couldn't afford anything in the stall. "Yes, may I . . . may I see that piece?"

The seller held it in his palm, so Gage could see it. The design was definitely the same. Gage's stomach knotted. "Can you turn it over, please?" Looking at him strangely, the man did so. On the back was the trailing end of the design and the small sharp divot in the gold, just as Gage remembered it.

Feeling both hot and cold, Gage jerked his gaze to the man's face. "Where did you get this?"

The seller pulled back his hand. "Someone sold it to me. Why? What concern is it of yours?"

"When and where did they sell it to you?"

At Gage's forceful question, the man glared. "Today, around terce."

Lightheaded, Gage gripped the edge of the board. Could it be that Felix was there? "Who did you buy it from?"

"We didn't exchange names."

Gage forced himself not to seize and shake the man. "Did he have a crippled hand?"

"Heavens no. It was a woman. A noble lady."

"A noblewoman?" Then Felix had sold it, but maybe there was still some way of finding him through the woman. Gage met the seller's gaze. "What did this noblewoman look like?"

The man squinted. "Tallish, pretty thing. Brown hair, netted. She was wearing a pale-pink dress with silver trim."

"Thank you." Gage turned to leave but then paused. "How much for the brooch?"

"You wish to buy it?" The seller's disbelief was evident.

Gage nodded. He knew as Gabe he could never wear it and that it was foolish to spend the money, but it belonged to him.

The man named his price.

"Is that what you paid her for it?" Gage asked, his tone taking on an edge. Looking embarrassed, the man shrugged. Gage named a lower price.

They bartered forcefully, and finally the man nodded. "It's yours." He lifted a finger. "Provided you actually have the coin to pay for it."

Gage took his purse from under his shirt and dished out the coins. He didn't care that buying it meant he would have to scrimp later; he wasn't walking away without what belonged to him. Closing his fingers about the brooch, he left the stall determined to find the lady who had sold it. If he found her maybe he could find Felix and at least do something to help fight the rebellion.

He searched every row of booths and swung past the nobles' colored pavilions. They were all open, their doors pulled aside to let out the heat. Several lords were within, as were a few servants and six ladies, none of whom wore the dress described.

He thought of the sheltered platform where the nobles watched the competitions. Gage worked his way through the crowd to the ropes to get a clear line of sight to the platform beyond an archer match.

His gaze swept the nobles seated upon the grandstand. One of the women wore pink, but it was dark pink with no trim. Clenching his fists, Gage twisted his way back through the crowd.

He rechecked the stalls, tents, and booths and even followed the wagons out to the road but saw no noblewoman in pale pink. He headed back through the meadow, his mind spinning. Perhaps she had gone into the city, or maybe she had changed her dress.

He altered his course and headed back toward the seller to ask more questions.

45

Gage was halfway back to the stall when he stopped in his tracks. A noblewoman stood at a hatmaker's booth. Her brown hair was netted, and her pale-pink dress with silver trim brushed the ground. A man-at-arms stood a stone's throw from her and a female servant stood beside her, holding the lady's purchases and shifting as if tired of standing.

Gage angled toward the noblewoman. He wasn't sure what he was going to say, but he had to know how she had come to possess his stolen brooch.

He was five strides away when she turned from the hat seller. Her face became visible, and Gage felt like he'd been kicked by a horse.

How could it be her? She had stood opposite him at Nardell. She had seen the brooch. She knew it belonged to him. His stomach twisted. Had she known of the Blue Crow's plan to attack his men? Was she part of it? Could she have masterminded the ambush? The possibilities tipped his world.

Feelings that had settled deep inside him after Allard's death shifted within him. Like an hourglass turned upside down, he felt his anger pour through him. He stepped into her path, his heart pounding.

The gray-green eyes that had risen indifferently to his upon Lady Agnes introducing them at Nardell didn't bother looking at him now. Natriece merely flicked her fingers. "Step aside, peasant," she said in the commoners' tongue. "I don't want whatever it is you're selling."

Gage turned over his hand to display the brooch. "What if I'm interested in what you are selling?"

Looking down to what he held, she recoiled and tried to step away from him.

Gage seized her arm, not hard enough to hurt her but with enough force to keep her in place and force her to heed him. He noted the man-at-arms move toward them. Gage shifted so that Natriece's body blocked the man's view. "Get rid of your guard, and tell your servant to take your purchases back to wherever it is you are staying," he murmured. "Do it now, and we will talk." He released his hold and stepped away from her.

Her eyes avoiding his and her hands knotting into shaking fists, she turned and addressed the man-at-arms and her female servant. "Hugh, please accompany Mia with my purchases back to my tent. Mia, await me there."

Looking happy to comply, the girl curtsied. "As you wish, my lady." The guard looked less pleased but complied.

The two disappeared into the crowd, and Natriece's lithe figure turned back toward Gage. Eyes flashing, she moved as if to march past him but then paused beside him. "He gave it to me," she said sharply in a hushed tone. "I have the right to do with it as I please. If he's angry, tell him to speak to me himself."

Gage frowned in confusion. "Who gave it to you?"

Her gaze flicked. "Felix, of course."

Gage flinched and snapped back. "Then you know him."

"Of course I do, fool. Didn't he send you?" At this she met his gaze.

Disdain filled Gage. "No, Felix did not send me."

Natriece blinked. Confusion rushed across her face. "Then who—"

"Where is Felix?" Gage asked, too angry to care about her apparent misperceptions.

Staring at him, Natriece's face went pale, and she lifted a hand to her mouth. "You! What are you doing here, of all places? My father said King Axel announced you were traveling. But in Delkara? I never would have ... And your clothes, why are you—"

Realizing she had finally recognized him, Gage breathed the first threat he could devise. "Speak my name aloud, and I swear I will see you stripped of your title." Natriece closed her mouth but continued to stare at him, her eyes wide. Not sure who she had thought he was yet not caring, he spoke with quiet force. "Felix?"

This time at his mention of the name, Natriece trembled. Clearly now grasping the situation within the context of who stood before her, she looked up at him with pleading eyes. "Please, I swear I had nothing to do with taking that brooch."

Beguiled by her looks and disgusted by her words, Gage attempted to contain the rage he felt. "You said Felix gave it to you. Why would he do that?"

Her face flushed, and her eyes dropped. "It was meant as a token of his affection."

"Affection?" A whole new level of fury spread through Gage. "Then you know him well."

"No!" Her eyes leapt to his.

Incensed by her denial, he held up the brooch. "Felix took this from me as a price," he whispered. "He would not have given it away lightly."

Natriece glanced about, then back at Gage. "And he did not," she said, her words strident. "But regardless of his feelings for me, I abhor him. Why else would I sell it?"

"To hide your connection to him."

Her eyes pressed closed, and she exhaled a shuddering breath that made Gage's heart clench. "I admit knowing where it came from was part of why I wanted it gone." She opened her eyes and met his gaze. "But I sold it to spite him. To bury it would have been safer, but I wanted to take the coins and throw them in his face."

Gage stared into her wild gaze, forced himself to not be taken in by her, and said scornfully, "If that is true, then tell me where I can find him, so I can see him hang."

She looked around, frightened. "He's no longer here, but his men are. I thought you were one of them following me."

Gage stiffened. The thudding in his chest became a pounding awareness of how close he'd come to finding Felix. Then another thought struck him. Natriece was a noblewoman of Edelmar, and Felix was a rebel who apparently spent enough time around Natriece to fancy himself in love with her. Both were in Delkara at the same fair, and she knew Felix's comings and goings. Repulsed at the thought, Gage stared at Natriece. "Are you traveling with him?"

"No. Yes." She cringed. "It's not what you think. If I had a choice in the matter, I'd be as far from him as possible." Her eyes skidded this way and that. "Please, if any of Felix's men see us, it will be bad for us both. We cannot keep talking like this."

Gage noticed the hat seller eyeing them. They had indeed attracted attention. "Follow me," he commanded quietly. "If anyone asks, I'm a seller of mounts taking you to see a palfrey."

Keeping an eye on Natriece until he was certain she truly intended to follow him, he led her down the lane toward where he had earlier sold his mounts. As he went, his thoughts wound around what she had said about Felix having his own men. Had he collected them since the ambush? Or had there always been more rebels with Felix? Did Felix lead just one group in Edelmar or more than that? Were there other leaders, other groups? Who did they answer to? Did they answer to anyone? How were their targets chosen?

Gage didn't know the answers to any of these questions, but what he did know was that the rebels were crossing borders and growing in number. They had to be stopped. But how? Which side was the beautiful Lady Natriece truly on? And how much did she know?

He veered in between stalls and the sellers' tents, searching for a place they could talk unobserved. Natriece willingly followed him down the footpaths amid the canvas walls, guy lines, and tent stakes.

If she truly wasn't traveling with Felix by choice, then Gage was missing something. Someone else had to be part in all of this, someone with power over Natriece, someone who was either working with Felix or under his control. How else could Felix fancy he had the right to bequeath a token of affection to a nobleman's daughter?

A nobleman's daughter. Gage's breath caught. He paused behind two empty tents and turned on Natriece. He needed to hear her say it to actually believe it. "Who is it who connects you with Felix?"

Natriece swallowed. "Felix has at least two dozen men who answer directly to him. And always there seemed to be more available. He himself answers to someone, but I do not know who." She declared all this with frightened determination, as if willing Gage to accept her words and turn his focus to them.

Gage gritted his teeth and forced aside the desire he felt to come to her aid and believe every word she spoke. "Answer my question."

"And if I do?" she asked angrily. "Who will protect me?"

Gage stiffened. He was thankful for her anger for had she begged him to protect her he may in fact have pledge himself to the task. Instead he embraced his own anger. "Answer my question, Lady Natriece, or I'll drag you back to Edelmar myself and throw you before the royal court for aiding a murderer."

"Is that what you think? That *I* am aiding Felix?"

He callously met her gaze but felt his heart twist.

"You are mistaken. I am not helping him." She spoke boldly, but then her shoulders shook. Blinking rapidly, she turned away from him.

Gage gripped her arm, holding her in place for more than one reason. "Tell me what I wish to know."

She turned her shimmering gaze back to him. Her voice contorted with shame as she nodded at the brooch, still clutched in his fingers. "Too long has that served as a symbol of my cowardice."

He swallowed. "Then speak."

Tears crested in her eyes, and she struggled to draw air. "Please, just promise me he will not be hanged."

Gage's torment rose with full force. "Do not negotiate with me."

Tears drifted down her cheeks, and her brow furrowed in pain. Her voice shaking, she spoke as if to herself. "Truly, I cannot save him from his own folly nor myself." She lifted her wet chin and swallowed. "For a heavy sum, he agreed to provide provisions and a place for them to stay. That was all. It was an agreement made long before . . . before Nardell. Only shelter and food, at least, that was the deal made."

Gage closed his eyes and felt her words tear through him. It explained so clearly the Blue Crow's ability to vanish and why no search had ever discovered him. No lord would think it necessary to search another lord's fortress. He met Natriece's tortured gaze, and for a moment his fury overtook the strength of her feminine presence and tears. "Who made the deal? Say it aloud."

More tears ran down her face. "My father, Lord Gregory, has aided and hidden Felix."

Feeling like screaming, Gage scrubbed a hand down his face and growled. "Why? Why would he do such a thing?"

"Because the deal he made is a large, ongoing source of coin," she answered painfully. "At first it was just a place to stay and supplies. When it became more than that, it was too late for him to go to the other lords. They would have found him guilty."

"Because he *is* guilty."

Natriece's gaze dropped. "I know."

Gage took a breath and turned away from her, trying to think past the allure of her grieved presence and the rage churning within him. Knowing a lord was involved was so much worse than just knowing there was a group of angry rebel commoners. But at the same time, it meant there was a place Felix was certain to eventually be. And once Felix had been caught, perhaps he could be used to take down other parts of the rebellion.

"What will you do with me?" Natriece's words, full of uncertainty and pain, drew Gage's attention back to her. Her gray-green eyes searched his.

46

Staring at Natriece as she stood vulnerably awaiting his judgment, Gage felt the full power he held over her. The rage in him wanted to destroy her, but the knight in him wanted desperately to save her. And regardless of either he still needed her. "You will go to my father and tell him what you have told me."

Natriece's fingers clutched her pink skirt. "Please, no. You still don't understand. I can't. I was given freedom here at the fair because they assumed there was no one for me to tell. But in Edelmar . . ." She shook her head. "Outside of Veiroot's walls, I am never let out of their sight. If I cross them, there are consequences. At Nardell had I said more than five words to you, one of them would have intervened, and it would not have ended well for me. They claim it's for my protection . . ." Drawing a breath, she continued, her voice shaking. "I cannot leave to speak with your father. They would stop me."

At this revelation, her former poise struck Gage as the regal facade of a noble mount that looked free but was in reality held back by a vicious bit. She couldn't run away. She stood now at his mercy, but even now he wasn't the one holding the reins.

He clenched his fingers. The brooch's clasp and rubies dug into his palm. She hadn't killed Allard and Bardon, but she had known where Felix was and that Felix was responsible for their deaths—if not before, then without excuse the moment Felix had handed her the brooch. She claimed to be under their control, and he wanted to believe her. But surely she could have found a way to say something.

The reality of her silence spread hatred through him, but the longer he stood there grappling between his anger and the fear in her eyes, the more he pitied her. But even that turned back to anger, because he had also once pitied Felix. Natriece too could be lying. There may not be any real threat to her life. But the brooch *was* real. So, regardless of whether she was telling the truth or not, she was his link to Felix. Besides, if she was lying, why sell the brooch? Why tell him about Felix or implicate her father? Every piece she'd shared made too much sense to be a lie. But that scared him too. Because if Felix had become so brazen as to give Natriece the brooch, he must believe his advantage strong indeed.

"If you intend to condemn me, then do so," Natriece said with a tight edge to her voice. "I have waited long enough for this to be over." Gage opened his mouth to respond, but before he could, she straightened her shoulders. "And whether I am condemned or not, for the sake of Edelmar, I will help you finish this." Bewildered, Gage stared at her.

Glancing about, she stepped close to him, her gray-green eyes bright with purpose. "Felix has been meeting with people here at the fair and is currently headed to speak with someone else here in Delkara. If what I overheard is true, he will be bringing a lot more men back with him to Edelmar. Meanwhile, my father and I will return in two days' time escorted by his men. They will await Felix at my father's stronghold.

"I don't know how long it will be before Felix returns, but with him gone, his men at ease, and my father unsuspecting, an Edelmarian force could be within the gates of Veiroot before a single man thought to raise his weapon. Once inside, the space in which

Felix's men are staying could easily be barricaded. Trapped within, their hunger would drive them to surrender. You would need only then quietly await Felix's arrival to achieve a full victory." She drew air and looked at him expectantly.

Gage stepped back to be able to think and breathe. She'd clearly spent substantial time considering ways Felix and his men could be conquered, and her plan seemed sound. "All of Felix's men will be at Veiroot until Felix returns with more men?"

"Yes."

"And your father's men-at-arms will not resist the arrival of an Edelmarian lord with a large armed retinue?"

"They would have no reason to. Nor is my father such a fool as to start a war with Edelmar's royalty. So you see, at your command, it would be a simple matter."

Her statement "at your command" jarred Gage back to reality. There was no question Lord Gregory had to be dealt with and Felix and the rebels stopped, but Gage wasn't the person to command anything. Even if he still had men to command, he would not risk them on her word, which may or may not be true.

Natriece huffed. "Well? Why do you just stand there as if I've suggested something impossible? You are Pri—" She caught herself, turned red, and finished with less force. "You must respond."

All the reasons Gage had walked away from his title rushed through him. There was far too much possibility of her information being a trap, but there was also too much at risk to ignore it. So, what was to be done? His mind raced. He thought of a solution. If he rode for Edelmar immediately, he could tell his father everything Natriece had told him along with what he had learned while traveling through Delkara. His father would know how to proceed wisely and how to deal with everyone involved.

He met Lady Natriece's anxious gaze. "Felix will see justice."

Her relief was visible. "Thank you." He swallowed. He wasn't sure whether to feel ashamed that he didn't trust her, glad that she felt he had helped her, or terrified that he might be playing right into her hands. She nodded to him. "I should return to my tent before they begin to search for me."

Fear turned within Gage. "If anyone asks, tell them you met a seller of mounts who showed you a palfrey. Do I make myself clear? Because if I hear even the smallest rumor of me and you meeting here in Delkara, I will denounce you as a traitor and use this as the proof to hang you." He tipped the brooch.

Natriece's regal facade slipped coolly into place. "I would not dare breathe a word of this. Nor would I risk my life or your success. Destroy Felix, for both our sakes."

"Indeed." He stepped away from her and nodded. "Since you are not interested in the mount I have for sale, my lady, I will be on my way." With that he trekked off at a swift pace. He continued until he was out of sight. Then he ducked between two tents and paused to pin the brooch under his shirt beside his belt.

He looked about. Convinced no one was watching and that Natriece hadn't attempted to follow him, he cut between the lines of tents and the back of the stalls. If Natriece spoke the truth—and even more so if she were lying—he needed to leave the fair immediately.

He moved quickly across the fairgrounds but drew to a stop at the back of a tent beside the lane opposite their campsite. Two dismounted riders were speaking with Manton. Trying to decide if it was possible Natriece had already told Felix's men about him or if they had found out who he was from the hat seller, Gage stayed hidden behind the tent.

Lifting their hands in farewell, the two riders turned and mounted. They were Manton's two friends from Dinslage. Breathing relief, Gage waited until they were gone and then crossed the lane and hurried forward. "Manton, I need to talk to you."

Manton glanced from Gage to their tent and then back to Gage and gestured. "I'm headed to get water. Come. We can talk on the way."

It suddenly occurred to Gage that he couldn't just tell Manton he was leaving, not without Manton asking why, and he couldn't share his reason. Therefore, he needed another explanation. He took a breath. "No, I'll wait for you to come back." The delay would give him time to come up with an answer. Manton shrugged reluctantly and headed off.

Waiting until Manton was gone, Gage ducked into the tent. Grabbing his cloak and his few other belongings scattered about the tent, he packed them into his saddlebags.

Rising to his feet, he drew the bags up with him. As he did so, they bumped Manton's wine barrel, which they'd been using to set their lantern on at night.

The barrel tumbled over with a sloshing, hollow thunk that revealed its open end and empty interior.

Befuddled, Gage tipped the wine barrel upright. Its inside was indeed dry. He swiveled it toward the tent door to get a better look.

It sloshed.

He blinked. The barrel was empty. He studied its interior. Its inside was straight up and down, not rounded like the outside. He rocked the barrel. Liquid sloshed again.

Twisting the barrel over, he felt the cork still wedged in the cask's side. The only explanation was that there were two separate compartments built into it. The center of the barrel, accessed through the top, and the outer edge, still holding liquid, accessed through the cork. Clearly, the barrel had been made to transport something undetected. But what?

The barrel barely weighed anything now, but he remembered it being heavy in Burnel. Something must have been removed, but what and when? What was Manton transporting that he didn't want anyone to see?

Gage picked up the barrel's lid and wondered if it could be opened and closed multiple times or just once.

Turning the lid in his hands, he ran his fingers over dozens of tiny dents in the wood. It looked as if dozens of sharp points had been propped on it—or in it.

He eyed the barrel's length. Arrows. It was the perfect length for arrows. But why secretly transport arrows? And regardless, what would Manton want with arrows? He had never heard Manton talk about hunting, and any other use for arrows would not be something any commoner would—

Gage sucked in air and stared at the barrel. One group of commoners would and did use arrows for more than hunting. And they would not want those arrows seen. They would also not want to purchase the arrows in their hometowns.

Manton was smuggling for them.

Gage stumbled to his feet and away from the barrel. He shook his head. Manton couldn't be part of the rebellion. The more he thought about it though, the more pieces fell into place, and the more the pounding in his chest increased.

The packages and information Manton had received and passed along and the people they had stayed with—the Coopers, who'd made the barrel, and the Fletchers, who'd likely made the arrows. How many times had the items in the barrel changed from one thing to the next? How many meetings at taverns had even been about selling boardgames?

How had he missed it all? It had been at the edge of everything. Still, he hadn't seen it. He pressed his hand to his forehead. They'd passed through Lyster just before an attack, and Jack had come into Delipp to the Chandlers shop after curfew, the same night Baron Bertram's wagons were ambushed.

Gage's mind reeled at the reality of it. That was how the rebels were staying one step ahead of the lords, with smugglers and spies carrying on everyday lives. People no one would ever suspect. And he had called them friends.

He had been deceived, again.

His head spinning, he grabbed his saddlebags and fled from the tent. He had to go before Manton returned because if he didn't leave now, he wasn't sure what he would do.

With shaking hands he cinched Athalos's saddle, latched the horse's bridle, and tied on his things as quickly as he could. Flinging back Athalos's reins, he went to mount.

"Where are you going?" Manton's voice froze Gage in place.

His heart pounding, he swallowed hard. "I'm leaving." He had forgotten about coming up with an explanation, and he didn't dare delay now to invent one, else he find himself instead confronting Manton and the Coopers. Pain coursed through him. He had liked them, all of them. And he had believed them. But they had also believed him to be just a commoner from Carson.

He clenched his jaw. Why had Manton asked him to come along, and why had they welcomed him into their homes? Had they thought they could bring him over to their way of thinking? Well, they were wrong. He was Prince Gage of Edelmar. He would never be one of them.

He swung onto Athalos.

"I don't understand," Manton said. "Where are you going? I thought you wanted to talk."

Gage gripped Athalos's reins and looked at the ground for fear that if he looked at Manton everything inside him would spew forth. "I don't have time. I must go." Athalos snorted and sidestepped, sensing his mood.

"Gabe, wait! Are you coming back?"

"I must go."

Intensity colored Manton's confused voice. "How will we find each other again? Please, if nothing else, delay a moment and talk to me."

Gage swallowed back words that rose on his tongue. It was fortunate for Manton that he had bigger concerns and didn't dare take the time to find absolute proof of Manton's dealing with the rebels to reveal to the baron of Nikledon, else he might have delayed to do just that. "I cannot take the time." With that Gage released Athalos. The horse leapt into motion.

"At least tell me where you're going!" Manton called angrily after him.

Gage answered silently without looking back. *Home. I'm going home.*

47

Gage passed blindly through the fair's booths, wagons, and people as loss made its slow decimating path through his mind.

Finally through the crowds and on the empty main road, Gage let Athalos explode into a full run and felt anger shred through his grief. He drew a breath from the wind whipping past his face. First, he would take down Felix, and then he would go after every last rebel, even if it meant he had to march an army into Delkara to do so. Even if it meant bringing in Manton and the Coopers. Even if he had to drag them out of their homes, even if . . . His thoughts spurred onward. He knew he didn't truly mean most of what was pulsing through his mind. But at the moment, he was too angry to care.

The more he thought, the more his body coursed with pain, and the more he wanted to scream it all out. There was no safe place. No safe person. Nowhere that lies and betrayal could not find and destroy him. Nowhere he could be free of pain, loss, and regret.

His body contorted forward in the saddle, but he couldn't release his emotions. Athalos slowed, and Gage considered other ways he could end his turmoil. Gasping, he pictured each person he cared about and shoved back the emotions tearing him to pieces. He pictured each person—Haaken, his mother, his father, his knights—and he reminded himself that he held information they needed. He inhaled and returned his focus to the road ahead.

He had been in such a hurry to leave for Edelmar he had made no rational plan as to how he would get there. He had taken the main road out of Nikledon, heading northeast. A good choice, but upon his observation of the sun's position, he realized he had only about three hours of light left. There was no way he would make it to Lyster before dark. There had to be smaller manors or hunting shelters ahead. If not, he would sleep in the woods, because there was no way he was going back to Nikledon.

He urged Athalos back into a gallop. Hooves thudding on packed ground, Athalos snorted and threw his head. Gage embraced the horse's speed, but upon rounding the next curve, he yanked back on Athalos's reins.

Two knights, four horsemen, and five footmen blocked the road ahead.

Athalos jarred to a stop, and Gage tightened his knees to keep his seat. Straightening, he stared at a drawn sword and two crossbows.

"Stay where you are," a middle-aged knight rasped, his thick chin and nose jutting from between the gorget of his neck armor and his orange-plumed helmet. His surcoat bore black battle-axes crisscrossed on an orange shield, a coat-of-arms Gage remembered seeing at the fair. The other knight had no visible coat-of-arms but wore chainmail and a breastplate with an open-faced helmet that closed about the knight's high cheekbones and emphasized his deep-set eyes.

Easing his hands off Athalos's reins, Gage shifted his gaze from the two knights to the bolts loaded on the crossbows, then beyond the horsemen to where a family was busy reloading their goods into a wagon. The soldiers were searching travelers.

The thick-faced knight gestured to him. "Dismount and empty your saddlebags."

Taking a breath, Gage swung off Athalos. The aim of the weapons followed him down, reminding him far too much of facing the Blue Crow's men.

His heart pounded, and his knees trembled. He gripped Athalos and stiffened his body, willing himself to be calm. He just needed to be patient and polite. Then he would be on his way again.

Two of the foot soldiers circled down the road behind him while another moved to take hold of Athalos. The animal immediately laid back its ears. The soldier reached for Athalos's reins anyway. The horse snapped his teeth at him. The soldier leapt backward, cursing.

Gage snagged Athalos's bridle before the horse could lunge after the man. "He doesn't like other people," he said hurriedly.

"Leave the horse!" barked the older knight with the thick nose, who was a good ten paces away. His fleshy gaze swung to Gage. "Get your saddlebags off the animal."

Gage nodded and, with fumbling fingers, worked to untie the straps from his saddle. When they were finally loose, he pulled both sets off Athalos's back.

The knight gestured for him to pass them to a blond foot soldier. Figuring that submitting to their search would be easier and faster than debating the need for one, Gage handed over his bags.

The soldier took them and headed to the side of the road. Setting down the first set, the soldier yanked loose the second set of saddlebag's laces and dumped out both bags.

Gage's flint, dishes, candles, knife, tinder, Edelmarian papers, and food all clattered out. The last item hit the ground, and the soldier checked over the bag, then crouched to paw through the pile.

Meanwhile, the younger knight with the high cheekbones strode forward. "Everything else you have on you, your money purse, knife, all of it, strip it off, and hand it over."

Gage stiffened. "Why?"

The knight's deep-set, steel-colored eyes dug into his. "Are you refusing a command?"

Reminding himself commoners didn't ask questions, Gage lowered his gaze and shook his head. Taking off his belt, he passed it to the knight along with his second hidden money purse and second knife but left the brooch pinned beneath his shirt and the knife in his boot.

Eyeing him, the knight opened the top of Gage's purse and dumped the coins into his hand. "Nothing here." Pouring the large clinking handful back into the purse, the knight tossed the pouch onto the pile the soldier had already rummaged through.

The blond soldier seized Gage's second set of saddlebags and emptied them out the same way he had the first.

Hearing the soft crunch of something breaking, Gage flinched. The soldier unwrapped a shirt to reveal the seashell Gage had bought for his mother. It lay in six pieces. The soldier tossed it aside without even a pause.

Gage clenched his jaw to keep from spouting a demand for an apology. After all, it was possible to search a person's things without destroying them. But clearly they did not care.

"I found something." From the bottom of Gage's rumpled clothing, the soldier withdrew a roll of dark leather bound with a tie.

Staring at the unfamiliar item, Gage felt his stomach turn and his mouth go dry. "That doesn't belong to me. I've never seen it before." Even as he said it, he knew it sounded like a lie.

"Open it," the knight commanded, his steel-gray eyes flicking to Gage.

The soldier loosed the tie, and the leather roll fell apart. Large gold coins in a long stack lay in the dark leather.

"Exactly what we were looking for," the soldier said triumphantly, his voice tinged with anger. He bunched the hide, sending the coins turning in the leather. They were nothing like any gold pieces Gage had seen before. They were thick, with a ram's head on one side and something written in Latin on the other. Gage caught only the words *amare* "to love" and *discat* "learn" before the soldier closed the leather over the handful of wealth.

"Looks like we found our thief," the knight said.

"What? No! I'm no thief." Embarrassment heated Gage's neck and face. "I've never seen those coins before. And I certainly didn't steal them."

The blond soldier snorted. "No, they just happened to end up in your saddlebags."

Gage's mortification twisted into panic. As sure as he knew the cold force of the Apse River, he knew they wouldn't believe him. But that did not stop him from desperately attempting to persuade them. "I didn't know those coins were in my bag, and I swear I had nothing to do with stealing them." His heart thudded in his chest so hard he felt he'd tip over. How *had* the roll of coins gotten in his saddlebags?

"Seize the thief," the knight commanded.

The two soldiers who had been hanging back came at Gage from behind. Fear screamed at him to run, but instinct reminded Gage of the crossbows. With nowhere to go, he pled with the knight. "No! Please, someone must have put those coins in my saddlebags during the fair."

Suddenly, he thought of the barrel. He realized it was possible the stolen coins had been smuggled to the fair by Manton—though the barrel had been empty, and Manton had been getting water. Perhaps Manton had just received the coins or stolen them and had meant only to store them in Gage's bags temporarily until he could place them in the barrel and smuggle them away from the fair.

Gage met the knight's hard gaze. "My saddlebags were in a tent only a few came and went from. I can help you find the real thief."

The soldiers' hands latched onto Gage's arms as the knight responded. "Your kind is all the same: lying, thieving wretches who can be dealt with by nothing less than a hearty whipping. And upon the return of this gold, a whip will take from your back retribution and from your mouth the true names of those rebels who assisted you in stealing it."

Gage's body turned cold. He had to think, had to find a way out of this. If he was already thought a liar, surely telling them he was a prince of Edelmar wouldn't help. He needed some other way to convince them he neither needed nor wanted to steal gold. He thought of his signet ring. They would just assume he had stolen that too. Appalled, he realized there was nothing he could do or say that would change the situation. He tried to swallow, but his mouth was dry.

The knight motioned. "Take him to the manor."

Pulled forward by two sets of hands, hope flitted through Gage's mind. A manor lord could not sentence him until he had been tried, and he could be convicted only on the testimony of two or more witnesses. No one had seen him steal anything, so he could not be convicted of theft, and before a court he would have the opportunity to explain his innocence.

But all that would take time. His thoughts spun with Lady Natriece's words. "*I don't know how long it will be before Felix returns.*" Time was not something he could presently afford to spend, not if he wanted to stop Felix.

He dug in his feet and looked at the pudgy-faced, middle-aged knight who hadn't said a word since the beginning of the exchange. "Listen to me, please. I'm not lying. Someone else put that gold in my bags. You must believe me. I hold no allegiance to any rebellion against your master or any other lord. I pledge to you on my life that I am not a thief. Send someone with me if you must to confirm my identity, but please let me go. I will meet you again at whatever place you say and at whenever time you ask to set right this misunderstanding, but you must let me return now to Edelmar for the sake of King Axel and the lords of Edelmar, for I have information they need. Check my papers. You will see I am Edelmarian."

Squinting angrily, the steel-eyed knight stepped closer. By the look in his eyes, Gage anticipated the knight's next action, but held in place, he could do nothing to stop it. The knight's fist slammed into his stomach. The blow folded Gage. He tried to gasp, but air wouldn't enter his body.

Someone kicked out his legs. He landed on his knees, still trying to inhale. With his arms turned behind him, his body contorted forward.

Stinging coursed through the back of his head, forcing him to tip his face skyward. His vision blurred with tears. The knight's wavering form stood above him.

Helplessness blazed across Gage's body, darkening his sight. Air burned through his chest. He inhaled furiously and tried to bring his head forward, but the knight still held a handful of his hair.

Blinking liquid from his eyes, Gage met the knight's hard gaze, greedily gasping air that was still far too hard to get. "If you are truly from Edelmar, thief, you should have stayed there." With that the knight let go, raised his fist, and swung.

Pain exploded across Gage's face. He took two more blows and then blacked out.

48

A THUNDERING HEADACHE greeted Gage when he woke. He groaned. He felt like he had been unhorsed in a tournament and then trampled. He tried opening his eyes to orient himself. His right eyelid fluttered up, but his left eyelid felt thick and would only open a slit. His head aching, he recalled the pounding he had received from the knight, which explained the pain in his face. He ran his tongue along his cheek and encountered a collection of cuts inside his mouth.

He exhaled and without moving looked around. Blinking painfully, he stared at dark hay, a wall, and the legs of horses illuminated by lantern light. A set of boots passed by where he lay on his side, and he vaguely heard someone talking. He was in a stable. But where?

Cringing, he tried to drag his hands from above him, but something held his wrists. He painfully turned his head and caught a glimpse of scraps of hay dangling in spiderwebs, the rungs of a ladder leading up through a hole in a plank floor, and a wooden wall.

He tugged his hands and heard the rattle of chain. He blinked at metal cuffs around his wrists and twisted his neck. A loop above him in the wall clanked. He yanked hard against the links of metal and the padlock fastening him to the ring. They held fast.

Breathing heavily, he absorbed the reality that he was chained. Panic stirred within him. He had never even been locked in a room before. How long had he been there? And where was he? Was this the manor of the lord whose gold had been stolen? Would a court be called right away, or would he have to wait until the next time court was held?

He couldn't afford the delay. He would also prefer not to have to publicly announce his title to prove he had nothing to do with the rebels or their stolen gold. There had to be a faster, less humiliating way of dealing with this than standing before a court. But what if there wasn't? Or what if the lord of the manor didn't believe him?

At least theft was not a hanging offense, like acts of violence. And if no one believed him, at worst he could send someone to collect the coin he had buried outside of Aro to pay retribution for what he had supposedly stolen. Though if they truly thought him a rebel, theft may not be the only charge laid against him.

He swallowed and told himself to not panic. Even if it wasn't the only charge, there would be a way to deal with it.

A horse snorted, and the lantern light dimmed. The voice of a young man drifted to where Gage lay. "Peter, quit dawdling, and finish feeding the mounts before we miss supper."

"Who is he do you think?" a second voice asked.

"It doesn't matter. He's not our problem. Are you finished?"

Gage gingerly tipped his head to look toward the light. Two forms stood between him and a lantern hanging between the stalls. "Yeah, I'm done," the second voice answered.

"Good." One of them took up the lantern, and they headed from the barn. Shadows crept in, leaving Gage in the dark.

He was clearly on a manor, and it was after nightfall, so it had probably been only a few hours since the incident on the road. That meant he was likely still within a day's ride of Nikledon and a long way from Edelmar.

He breathed past his pain and frustration. The only way he was likely going to get out of this quickly was if he could convince the manor lord he was trustworthy and not a rebel. Ironically, the only way he could think to do that was to admit he wasn't the person he appeared to be. Such information would best be shared with just a lord and would be far less mortifying than standing to explain himself in court. It was probably also the only way he was going to get back to Edelmar in time to stop Felix. And he had to stop Felix.

Felix. Perhaps that was the answer. If he told the story of what Felix had done and who he was and why he was trying to stop him, perhaps he could gain not only the lord's trust but maybe even his help.

Using the chains, Gage pulled himself to a sitting position. The moment he did, his head felt like it would split in half. He grimaced. If ever he got his hands on that knight, the man would seriously regret beating him.

Propped against the wall in the dark and listening to horses munch hay, Gage gently ran his fingers over his tender, puffy face. All the damage seemed to be under his skin.

He lowered his hands and considered the fastest way to get an audience with the manor's lord. He could yell and hope someone came, which was likely to make his headache worse and possibly get him struck again.

He thought of the knife in his boot. Pulling up his leg, he searched for it. It was no longer there. He sighed. He could wait for morning and make his request in a reasonable and less irritating fashion, which might mean receiving a more favorable reply.

Not feeling particularly patient, he contemplated yelling anyway. But in the end he thought better of it and eased himself onto his back to rest.

49

Gage woke still in the dark and listened to voices. Breathing the putrid stench of horse pee, he caught the glint of lantern light through the barn's wall and the scuffing clatter and jingle of people at work outside. A door creaked open. Several attendants entered. They deposited lanterns around the barn and began saddling horses.

Squinting in the light, Gage called to them. "Is the manor lord awake? I need to speak to him." They acted as if they could not hear him. He tried a different approach. "Tell him he will want to know what I have to say."

One of the attendants glanced in his direction but scooped up the next saddle. Annoyed, Gage raised his voice. "I know you aren't all deaf, so one of you go tell your lord the favor of the King of Edelmar could be upon him if he listens to me."

The attendant who had glanced his way eyed him and led a horse through the lantern light and out of the barn. Gage recognized the horse as belonging to the knight whose fist he would dearly like to break.

The attendant was back a moment later to tack a second mount, this time with a harness. Realizing they were preparing for the departure of a large party, Gage opened his mouth to try again.

Just then the nearest barn door thudded on its hinges, and the steel-eyed knight from the road stepped through, followed by three other knights, a squire, and two of the foot soldiers from the road. Each knight wore armor, swords, and daggers. Two of the knights were middle-aged. The third was young, probably knighted within the last year.

They headed for their horses while the knight from the road paused inside the door. Handing something to one of the two foot soldiers, he nodded to Gage. "Bring him."

"As you wish, Sir Jarret."

Gage grabbed the chain's lock as if the action might prevent them from moving him somewhere he did not want to go. "Are you taking me to the lord of this manor?"

His eyes narrowing, Sir Jarret trudged toward him. Gage quickly removed his hand and ducked his face away. "Please just let me speak with the lord of this manor." Keeping his head down, he waited. The knight turned and tromped out the door.

The soldiers unlocked the padlock, and the chain and ring above Gage rattled, then pulled tight. The first foot soldier backed away holding the links like a lead line. Refusing to be treated like an animal, Gage did not rise at his tug. "I'm not moving till I get a response."

The second soldier grabbed him by the arm and hauled him to his feet. "You already got one." Propelled by the soldier's hand and pulled by the chain, Gage was dragged forward and outside. He drew an acidic breath of cool, torchlit air.

Despite his pounding head, he gaped at the mass of horses, men, and wagons spread across a large yard formed by hewn-rock walls and heavy timber gates. Torches fizzled while servants busily thudded sacks, barrels, and chests into creaking wagons. Pages and squires held the armor, saddlebags, and weapons of knights, who donned their gear and tied down their packs. Horses snorted and shifted. Foot soldiers strapped on shields and clapped on helmets. Others thunked arrows or bolts into quivers and cranked crossbows or restrung longbows.

Gage had seen many a lord load to travel but never anything like the group assembled before him. It looked like an army, not a retinue. Dawn was not yet even a line on the horizon. So, where were they going? And to what purpose?

A hard jerk from the foot soldier slammed Gage's wrists together and pulled him off balance. He stumbled along the side of the barn.

The soldier turned at the end of the building and yanked Gage with him. Already struggling to keep his balance, Gage tripped. His shoulder clipped the corner of the barn. He staggered off the building and would have lost his feet altogether if the other soldier hadn't seized his arm again. Fingers dug into his skin and steered him passed the barn and into a murky darkness that spread like patchwork between it and the next building.

Gritting his teeth, Gage spotted Sir Jarret's form ahead and resisted the urge to physically or verbally protest the soldier's painful grip. The knight preceded them between two more buildings. Swallowing, Gage risked a question. "Are you taking me to the lord of this manor?"

"No," Sir Jarret replied without turning. "You are being taken to the smithy, where you will be marked and then delivered to the one you stole from."

It took a moment for Gage to fully comprehend Sir Jarret's words. When he did, he snapped to a stop. "You can't do that!"

Fingernails bit into his arm, and the chain went taut, dragging him back into motion. His knees threatened to drop him, and his chest pounded. Marking shouldn't have even been a possibility. He was supposed to have had time to defend himself before getting even halfway to a ruling of guilt, let alone being forever branded a thief. It was unlawful to condemn anyone before he or she stood before a court, and only upon an establishment of the person's guilt and his or her lack of ability to pay retribution could the person be punished by the irreversible fate of marking. Once marked, he would be owned and forever seen as a thief.

"You cannot just mark me!" Gage's voice came out shrill. "It's against the law. You must bring me before a court." They continued to ignore him.

Trembling, Gage inhaled sharply. Digging in his feet, he grabbed the chain and twisted hard against the soldier's grasp, forcing them to momentarily heed him. "If nothing else, I have the right to stand before your master and dispute this claim laid against me. Mark me before then, and you will be guilty of injustice."

At his words the two foot soldiers hesitated. Sir Jarret turned, his body a dark form. Gage swallowed to return moisture to his mouth. "Ask the lord of this manor. See if I'm not right."

"Stolen gold was found in your possession," Sir Jarret said. "Your guilt is indisputable. If there is any injustice, it is that you were not caught and punished sooner."

Gage's stomach dropped. He shook his head and twisted his wrists angrily. "I didn't steal anything! You cannot mark me for something I didn't do!"

"Enough! Get him moving."

The metal cuffs dug into Gage's wrists. He fought back. "You can't do this!"

The foot soldiers dragged him onward. A whoosh of sparks, blown into crimson by the bellows of a smith's forge, lit the inside of a building ahead.

Gage spoke fiercely. "You have no idea who I am." He wanted to scream, *"I am Prince Gage of Edelmar."* But as much as he had once feared the authority behind his title, he now feared it would bring nothing but laughter.

Nearly to the smithy, he tried one status lower in a last desperate effort to reach the knight. He switched to the nobleman's tongue. "Cease this folly! I tell you I am the son of a nobleman. Heed me! For I have stolen nothing, but I do have words your lord will dearly wish to hear. Take me to him before you do something you will regret."

Swinging around, Sir Jarret grabbed the front of Gage's shirt, yanked him forward, and slammed him against the wall of the smithy. Gage lost his breath on impact and stared at him, stunned.

The knight thrust his armored arm up under Gage's chin and squinted at him, his face half lit by the forge. "Who is your father then, hmm?" he asked in the nobleman's tongue. Staring into the man's furious, gleaming gaze, Gage swallowed against the rough pressure of the man's chainmail and hesitated. "I didn't think so," Sir Jarret said, contempt suturing his voice as he switched back to the commoner's tongue.

"Baron Roger of Ulbin," Gage said. He cringed as he said it, for he doubted Baron Roger would still offer him such a status, but it was as close to the truth as he dared go.

The knight's eyebrows lifted, and his voice filled with derision. "Baron Roger of Ulbin? Well, next time I see him I'll be sure to tell him I sent his thieving son to a new master." With that Sir Jarret turned to the soldiers. "Secure him, then unlock his right hand."

Shocked and outraged, Gage tried to grab for the knight's dagger. Sir Jarret rammed him harder against the smithy wall. His wrists were yanked sideways. Gage squirmed under the knight's hands. "No! Let me go!"

The padlock clicked, no doubt fettering him to another loop of metal meant for tying mounts. "He's secured."

Spitting a curse, Sir Jarret shoved away from him.

Gage's head hit the building, but he didn't care. With his right hand free, he twisted his left wrist in the metal and yanked hard. He jerked to a painful stop. Panic flooded him.

Beyond the soldiers' dark forms, the smithy's bellows whooshed. Snapping, yellow specks flew into the air. Beneath them red coals sizzled, casting an eerie glow on the blacksmith's pitted face.

With no way to escape, Gage pressed back against the building, his breath coming in bursts and cold sweat dampening his neck.

The blacksmith reshuffled a brand in the glowing coals and heaved again on the bellows. Blue dagger-like flames spewed up.

His stomach churning, Gage reached out with his free hand, searching for anything he could use as a weapon. The closest soldier seized his arm, twisted him around, and thrust him face first against the building.

With the wall scuffing his bruised skin and the chain digging into his side, Gage writhed. "Get off me!"

The blacksmith pulled the glowing brand from the fire. "Hold him still."

Sir Jarret and the second soldier stepped back toward him, and despite Gage's furious attempts to thrust them all away, they pinned him, wrestled the palm of his right hand against the building, and gripped his fingers to leverage his wrist flat.

"You can't do—"

The blacksmith shoved something into Gage's mouth. A thick cloth full of soot pressed against his tongue, making him gag. He tried to spit it out, but Sir Jarret clamped a hand over his mouth.

The smith lifted the scarlet metal of the glowing brand toward his right arm.

Trapped, all Gage could do was flee inside. Sweat soaked his shirt and trickled down his back. The brand passed by his face.

Gage sucked air through his nose and pressed his eyes closed.

Raw heat seared into his wrist.

He screamed.

50

In the ascending dawn, Gage kicked the boards of the wagon and curled his fingers and toes to keep from crying out.

He had been jostling along with a collection of barrels for almost an hour, but the pain of the burn was still intense. It throbbed like the brand was still blazing into his skin.

They hadn't re-fettered his right wrist, but his left wrist was shackled to a metal loop secured through the wagon's right wall.

The wagon rumbled over another set of holes. Gage braced himself and placed his hand high on his knees to reduce its pulsing pain. In the day's growing light, he bit his tongue and stared at the mark scorched into his flesh. The outlines of a ball-and-chain flail and a loaded crossbow were seared into his skin. The two weapons' handles crisscrossed at the top of his hand.

Gage let his head thud back against the wagon's boards. Even if he could convince whoever the gold had been stolen from that he wasn't guilty of stealing it, it wouldn't change the fact that he would still forever bear the mark of a thief. It was a shaming that couldn't be reversed, altered, or outrun.

Gage swallowed the bile that rose in his throat. Not only had Sir Jarret destroyed any chance he had of making it back to Edelmar in time to warn his father, the knight had also take his honor and his freedom.

Feeling as if he were about to go insane or explode thinking about it, Gage shoved himself upright to see the dim road upon which the wagons and the guard traveled. Day had come, but the sun remained hidden in clouds.

The large company around him rode in close formation. Foot soldiers walked the road's center between horsemen riding nose-to-tail under bowed branches. More soldiers trudged beside each cart and wagon, their faces grim and their lips closed.

The wagon that Gage sat in was near the center of the entourage, which was made up of probably close to 100 soldiers guarding 15 or so wagons. Birds chirped, harnesses and bridles jangled, axles and wheels groaned, and saddles creaked, but not a word was spoken. Gage straightened further. Silence within such a big company did not happen by chance. It had to have been ordered. But why?

He glanced at those closest to him. The knight he had been handed over to, Sir de Lane, rode two horses from the wagon with his squire beside him and his eyes on Gage.

Gage jerked his gaze away. Anger raced through his body. He looked at the other horsemen. Their hands held lances or rested upon swords' hilts, and their eyes observed the woods.

Their numbers, their weapons, and their quiet passage suddenly made sense. They were guarding a lord's envoy of supplies—the ideal target for a rebel attack.

Gage shuddered but then realized that despite being among a lord's guard, he was still dressed as a commoner. From what he knew of the rebels, they didn't target commoners. Which meant in his current state, if rebels attacked the entourage, they might actually help him. Until they found out who he really was. Then they would probably kill him.

Gage considered what awaited him ahead regardless. Sir Jarret's words echoed in his mind: *"A whip will take from your back retribution."* Gage pictured the shackled rebels hacking away at stumps and Moses with the knife in his back. Dread trailed through him along with a swell of helplessness and anger.

The rebels were responsible for all of this. They'd ruined his life as Gage, and now they had also managed to destroy his life as Gabe.

He could beg for his freedom and try to prove his innocence, but he knew exactly how unlikely it was his words would even be considered, let alone believed. To all of Delkara, he was a rebel, shackled and marked, with a voice that meant nothing and no one to speak for him. He would be a slave with no rescue. No one even knew where he was.

Even if Haaken or his father looked for him, they would never think to search for him at a lord's manor in Delkara, just as no one had thought to search for the Blue Crow in Veiroot. He would live being punished for supposedly being a rebel thief while Felix would slip freely back into Edelmar with more men to do whatever he pleased.

Gage's father's warning of him not understanding what he was asking for to live as a commoner spiraled through his thoughts. His father had been right. He had had no idea. Hopelessness choked him. He couldn't live as a slave. Wretched irony struck him at the thought, though, for he had once been convinced he could not live as a prince, and now he would give anything to have even one man do as he commanded.

He recalled Haaken shoving his crown back into his hands. *"Not like this, Gage. Not by leaving behind who you are! It is not God's will that you abandon what He has given you. So, fight to thrive, and don't ever stop."*

He had fought to be Gabe, but being Gabe had failed him too. And this time he couldn't create a new identity to run to and live out. He couldn't fix this, couldn't change it, because unlike every other time in his life, no decision lay before him. All choice had been taken from him.

Regret so strong Gage could taste it twisted into turmoil inside him. His father's words filled his mind. *"Surrender your grief to God, for only in Him will you find peace."* He was a prisoner on his way to a master. It wasn't peace he needed but freedom. But there was no freedom to be had either. He had tried to find freedom by embracing a new life, and in the process he had blindly followed a rebel through two kingdoms and was now condemned for being part of the very rebellion he despised. If there was a God, he was either cruel or incapable, for why else allow all this when all Gage wanted was to avoid doing harm and to stop Felix from destroying any more lives?

His father's words pulsed through his thoughts. *"Surrender it to God."* Gage kicked the barrel next to him. What good could surrendering do? Surrender couldn't get him out of this mess. Besides, he wouldn't surrender. Not to God. Not to anyone.

The chain binding him to the wagon mocked him. Surrendered or not, he wasn't in control. He was a mere slave to the owner of whosever's mark he now bore. Fear churned within him. He couldn't be a slave.

Prior Joseph's words gripped him. *"Every man, both common and noble alike, is a slave to darkness until he surrenders to God."* Gage knew in Scripture darkness symbolized everything contrary to God. But he had never believed it was something humanity could be in bondage to. Rather he had always been convinced mankind's evil actions were what made up the darkness.

Scripture also said God was good and taught good. But if God didn't exist, what made an action good versus evil? Gage didn't know the answer, but regardless of what he believed, he was and would still be a slave to a lord. And the answer to some stupid religious question wouldn't change that.

51

The wagon rolled to a stop. Fear coursed through Gage. He sat up to see his surroundings. They were not at a manor but in an open stretch of grassland tucked into a sort of dell. The horsemen wordlessly dismounted, and the foot soldiers quietly sat down to rest.

Servants set up metal tripods and began stacking kindling under them. They were stopping to eat. Gage's stomach grumbled. He tried to remember when he had last eaten. It had been at the fair, which felt like a lifetime ago.

From where he sat chained, he could see probably half the men in the assembly. They varied vastly in age, armor, and weaponry, but as Gage looked around, he noticed something even odder than their silence. Not a single coat-of-arms was visible anywhere. He searched once more. Not one surcoat or uncovered buckler was distinguishable as belonging to any particular lord. So, whose manor had they been staying at? And whose supplies was he sitting beside? He glanced again to the mark on his wrist. Were the rebels only attacking specific lords? Was that why the company rode without identification? Or was there some other reason?

"Watch out!" someone yelled at the edge of the gathering. A dark-brown horse, ears flattened, burst into the mix of men.

A handful of foot soldiers leapt to their feet, and two horses veered sideways. "Careful," someone warned, "he's vicious."

Gage drew a happy breath. Athalos! He pressed his lips together and tried to whistle, but his mouth was too dry to make a sound.

Trailing a broken rein and blowing loudly, Athalos trotted among the men, who scattered away from him.

Sir de Lane lumbered to his feet and cursed. "That stupid beast just won't quit following us."

Not caring how stupid the man thought his loyal horse was or what it would cost him, Gage opened his mouth to yell for Athalos. Before he could, a wagon driver cracked a whip in Athalos's direction. The horse bolted, tearing into the trees and disappearing from sight.

Feeling like he had just been punched, Gage dropped back against the wagon. Dully, he watched the men go back to preparing their food. The smoke from a fire drifted past him, bringing the scent of cooking vegetables. Gage's stomach growled again, and he tried to swallow. His tongue felt thick and his throat raw.

Quiet murmuring took over the camp. Bowls were passed around. Sir de Lane received one along with a chunk of bread.

Eyes fixed on the knight, Gage felt his stomach tighten. Sir de Lane glanced his way. Their eyes locked, but the knight simply continued eating.

The chain behind Gage rattled. He had leaned forward and hit the end of it. Biting his tongue, he closed his mouth and waited.

Eventually, he realized it wouldn't matter how patiently he waited. No one had any intention of bringing him anything to eat. He twisted his wrist in the metal cuff and kicked at the closest barrel. Stubbing his toe, he inhaled a sharp breath. What did they want him to do? Beg? He gritted his teeth. He wouldn't do it.

By the time he watched them pack up, his resolve wasn't quite so solid. Part of him had still hoped once they had all eaten they would give him something. But Sir de Lane continued to ignore him, and everyone else acted as if he were invisible.

Before long most of the horsemen were mounted. His head aching and fighting both pain and hunger, Gage finally succumbed. When the knight's young squire moved past the wagon, Gage spoke, his voice grating. "Water. May I please have water?"

The squire looked at Sir de Lane. "He's asking for water."

Sir de Lane frowned, and for a moment Gage thought the man would refuse him even water, but the knight tugged out a waterskin and tossed it into the wagon. Gage grabbed it with his free hand. He winced as the skin on his wrist tightened. Too thirsty to let the pain stop him, he pried opened the waterskin with both hands and poured its contents into his mouth. The water was hot and bitter. He downed it anyway, then drizzled the last drops into his mouth and let them soak into his dry tongue.

He lowered his head. "Thank you." The moment the words left his mouth, he inwardly berated himself. Why in the world was he thanking the man? He ground his teeth and reminded himself that his mother and Lady Agnes had taught him chivalry. Therefore, it was simply his own nobility speaking, not any expression of his indebtedness to the knight.

It wasn't long before Sir de Lane and everyone in the company was mounted, but they held their places. Gage was wondering why when he heard a commanding voice address them. "Keep your eyes open and your mouths closed. And remember, if so much as a handful of grain is lost this day to those wretches, you will each be held responsible."

Knights shifted in their saddles, and Gage spotted the owner of the voice—a thick necked man with a chiseled face and wide-set eyes. He wore dark, engraved armor with a peaked helmet and rode a red sorrel bearing a full black leather harness with no coat-of-arms. Not certain if he was just a knight or actually a lord, Gage listened as the man continued. "Stay close to your parties, and watch for anything out of the ordinary."

A second, thinner rider in plainer but well-fitted armor kicked his mount up beside the man. "Remember, they mean not just to take goods but also to inspire further rebellion," he said. "Do not let them succeed. If they come, make them pay for their mistake."

The hair on Gage's arms rose. That voice. He squinted at the rider's back. Why did he know that voice? The rider's brown hair was tied back below an open-faced helmet, and he held his reins in his gauntleted left hand while keeping his right metal-gloved hand close to his body. Gage's skin prickled further. Felix? No, Felix was a rebel commoner traveling to meet and bring back men to attack the Edelmarian lords. He wouldn't be riding as second in command of some Delkaran lord's military force. And he definitely wouldn't be telling them to make the rebels pay if they came against them.

The thick-necked rider wheeled his mount. "Move out." The thinner rider beside him turned to follow.

Staring at a clean-shaven, angular face as thoroughly burned into his mind as the mark on his wrist, Gage's body swayed.

Felix kicked his mount and rode after the other man.

◈

It didn't matter that it had been almost a year since Gage had seen Felix. The effect was like reliving every nightmare he'd had since the day of the ambush. And this time the panic and rage didn't come from without like it had the moment he'd seen Felix standing beside the Blue Crow. This time it burst forth from a place within him, rooted to every corner of his being. He had so often envisioned Felix's hanging, it was as if he had convinced himself Felix was already dead or else would drop dead the moment he set eyes on him.

But Felix was very much alive.

Gage twisted his wrist hard in the shackle. His lungs refused to take in air. Despite being right in front of him, Felix was completely beyond his reach. Enraged, Gage's heart pounded. He had been trying to get to Edelmar to stop Felix. But insanely, here they both were in the same company, he chained as a supposed rebel thief and Felix in a position of authority.

Gage shook his head, trying to clear away enough of his fury and confusion to think. How could Felix possibly be masquerading as a knight? Or *was* he masquerading? Who was Felix really?

The questions spun Gage's world. None of it made sense. Which side was Felix on? Was he a rebel commanding knights? Or was he a rebel deceiving knights? Or was Felix actually a knight going after rebels? There was one other option. Was the company even lord's men at all?

They had to be. Felix himself had just warned them about the rebels, and they had come from a lord's manor. But they bore no coat-of-arms, and they could have manipulated another lord as they had Lord Gregory.

The wagon lurched and rolled back into motion. Gage leaned forward, his head pounding. He stared at the mark on his wrist. They couldn't be rebels because rebels would not have marked him a rebel thief. But if that was true, and he was surrounded by men loyal to a lord, then who was Felix? Did it matter? Even if he knew, he couldn't do anything about it.

But it did matter to him. It mattered so much he felt ill at the reality of not knowing. He inhaled and forced himself to start back at the beginning of what he knew for certain.

He knew Felix had been part of the attack on him and his men, had stolen his brooch, had been at Veiroot, had given the brooch to Lady Natriece, and had been reportedly headed from the fair to collect more men to take back to Edelmar. But now Felix was in a position of authority over a troop of men having come from a lord's manor, transporting a lord's goods, and trying to avoid the rebels. So, Felix was either lying again and had, as a rebel, somehow deceived his way into command, or he was actually a knight who was secretly a rebel. That meant Gage couldn't denounce him without announcing himself as knowing him, and that wasn't likely to end well. For one thing, who would believe him over Felix? For another, if he called attention to himself as a threat to Felix, he'd make an easy target chained to a wagon.

52

By the time the light of the gray day was dwindling, hunger and thirst had overtaken Gage's thoughts of Felix. He was wondering instead whether or not he would be given food when they arrived wherever it was they were going.

The wagon rocked to a halt. The riders and foot soldiers paused. To their right a wooded hill pressed against the path. On the left a grassy stretch of land sprinkled with rocks and trees led to the edge of a ravine. The drop-off of its wide crevice was visible through the trees at the edge.

Gage figured this stop was also planned, but then the knights and foot soldiers began shifting. Sir de Lane drew his sword. "Eyes sharp," he commanded quietly.

Others reached for their weapons. The horsemen steadied their lances, and the foot soldiers pulled out bolts and set them to their crossbows. Horses that had been calm all day sidestepped and rattled their bits. The men stared up into the leafy undergrowth to their right.

Abrupt cries of alarm, pain, and chaos jolted everyone. They came from up ahead.

"They've attacked the front of the line!" someone yelled.

Sir de Lane brandished his sword. "Foot soldiers, guard the wagons! Horsemen, with me!" He and the other men-at-arms kicked their mounts out onto the grassy edge and thundered ahead and out of sight.

The nerve-rattling cries of men, the clang of metal, and the scream of horses reigned beyond the wagon where Gage sat chained. His heart racing, he twisted to look over the barrels, but all he could see was the driver's head and shoulders and the sky.

The foot soldiers continued to eye the trees, their expressions anxious.

"Bring them in closer," one of the soldiers called, waving to the carts and wagons spread down the road.

They rumbled forward, and more soldiers filled in around them. Up ahead the sound of fighting continued.

"They will handle this," the soldier said. He sounded like he was trying to convince himself as much as reassure anyone else.

The cries and clash of weapons ceased, and a shout went up. "Don't let them get away!" The pounding of hooves faded, and silence stretched. The foot soldiers remained in place, white-knuckling their weapons. The quiet ahead thickened, and the soldiers began to murmur amongst themselves.

Watching the tops of the trees on the forested hillside, Gage saw a branch move, then the tip of an arrow. His heart skipping, he cried out and ducked. The whiz of flying shafts and the thunking of them battering men and wagons made him gasp. Amid shrieks of pain, the men around him screamed at each other to take cover.

Wedging himself as far down in the wagon as he could, Gage jerked when a bolt smacked into the top of the barrel above him.

The foot soldiers' numerous crossbows released, and more cries were followed by the whiz of arrows.

A horse squealed, and suddenly the wagon Gage was in lurched to the left and burst into motion. Swinging straight, it picked up speed. Its wheels rattled over rough terrain, chattering Gage's teeth and causing the barrels to clunk into each other. What was the driver doing? Gage brought up his head. He could no longer see the driver.

Slamming into a barrel and jiggling on the floorboards, he looked back. The wagon's driver was sprawled dead on the road beside wide-eyed foot soldiers left in the open with arrows showering down upon them.

The realization he was chained within a runaway wagon hit Gage at the same time the wagon's wheel thudded hard over a rock. He crashed into the wagon's side.

Trees growing ever closer to the road flashed by. Smaller saplings slapped the wagon's underside. Cries of "Watch out!" burst from soldiers as the wagon flew between them and bigger tree trunks. Somehow the wagon cleared them all and careened onward.

Gasping at the impact of the wagon's haphazard path and fearing what might come next, Gage grabbed the wagon's edge and held on tight. Powerless to reach the horse's reins, he looked about for help. All he could see while bouncing around and clenching his teeth were the wagons, carts, and men he was swiftly leaving behind. No one cared about the runaway wagon. They were too busy fighting for their lives.

The wagon flew over more rocks and roots and passed foot soldiers crouched within the leafy limbs of a huge downed tree that looked like it had just been dragged off the road. The men knelt beside their fallen companions, reloading crossbows. Gage swallowed and hoped the horse was taking him away from the battle and not into it.

The wagon veered again. Gage braced himself and stared at startled horsemen galloping along the road that he and the wagon had just vacated. On the wagon's opposite side, tree branches screeched against the wagon's underside. Gage turned that direction.

He saw green leaves, then nothing. No ground. Just air.

The ravine!

The wagon's first wheel fell off the edge, and Gage's insides fell with it.

The next wheel went. And the entire wagon, dragged forward by the frantic horse, tipped sideways.

Gage clutched its side and watched in panicked slow motion as the barrels slid across the wagon. They cracked into the wagon's side, shifting its weight. The wagon lurched the rest of the way off the ravine's edge and began to roll.

"No. No. No!" Clinging to its wall and the chain, Gage heard the wretched cry of the horse and the creaking and snapping of the wagon's contorting form.

Floorboards tilted out from under him. The hollowness of falling filled him. Tree trunks came out of nowhere. The wagon slammed into them. Wood shattered, the barrels disappeared, and Gage's left arm flew up over his head.

He jolted to a swinging stop and screamed in pain.

53

Swinging over sloping ground that dropped off like a castle's curtain wall, Gage watched and heard the thwam, thunk, and crack of barrels ricocheting down the incline below him. Suspended in the air, his wrist and shoulder throbbing, Gage tipped his head back to figure out how he was still alive and not flying after the barrels.

The wagon's mangled form squeaked and groaned above him. It was caught lengthwise between the trunks of two large ash trees. In front of the wagon, the horse swung dead, strangled by its own harness.

Gage's stomach heaved.

More wood splintered, and the wagon lurched. The realization he could still join the barrels at the bottom of the ravine jolted Gage to action. Breathing hard, he reached up with his free hand to see if he could somehow get himself loose from the chain and climb up it, but the cuff digging into his skin was not coming off.

Grimacing, he looked for other options. The tree trunk to his right was close. If he swung, he might be able to grab it and reach its branches.

Preparing for the pain he was about to cause himself, Gage bit his tongue, pulled up his legs, and flung them out. The chain thunked, and his body rocked forward. He reached out but wasn't close enough to get a solid hold of the tree.

With the cries of battle coming from somewhere above him and the creak of the wagon ready to come down on top of him, he flung his legs out again and again. His body swung, but he could not get his arm far enough around the tree to keep himself beside it. He tried once more. This time he grabbed for the tree with his legs instead.

Hanging there with his legs hooked around the tree's trunk and his arm still chained above his head, he took a breath. His chest pounding, he concentrated on getting ahold of the branch, which was still a hilt's length out of his reach.

Seizing the chain in both hands, Gage hauled himself up it while the wagon creaked loudly. His left shoulder screamed its objections, but his mind's demand for survival outweighed its sharp complaints. He scooted his legs up the rough tree trunk to match the height of his arms. Bracing himself, he let go with his inside leg and carefully lifted it up toward the branch. Gasping, he managed to curl his heel over the tree's limb.

Spread across the three supports, he held his breath, released his other leg, and flung it up toward the branch. His ankles locked together. He inhaled and immediately grabbed the branch with his right hand to let the pressure off his aching shoulder. The mark on his wrist pulsed painfully.

With his legs and one arm wrapped around the branch, Gage gritted his teeth and glanced at where his left wrist was still attached to the wagon. He drew a steadying breath. Now what?

His arms trembled. He stared at the wagon. It was missing its left side, back wall, and half its floor, and more boards looked ready to give way any moment. He couldn't get free from the chain, but he might just be able to get the chain free from the wagon.

Using his legs to hold on, he hoisted and rotated his upper body sideways to wrap both arms over the branch. With the chain looped around the branch with his arms, he let go with his legs.

For a moment he hung there staring at what was left of the wagon. His body shook. What if he lost his grip and hit the end of the chain? He doubted the boards would hold him a second time. He swallowed and adjusted himself on the branch. Knots in the wood bit through his shirt into his chest and arms.

Curling his legs, Gage flung his feet outward, smashing his boots into the top board of the wagon's right wall, where the metal loop tethered him to the wagon. The wagon groaned, but the board held. Gage kicked at it again and again, ignoring the wagon's creaking.

In a matter of moments, he was breathing hard and sweating profusely. The board looked less solid but still held. Gulping air, he heaved another kick into it. This time he heard it crack. But just then something else cracked. The wagon shifted and started to splinter loose.

Oh, bad. Bad. Bad! Gage kicked frantically at the board. But the wagon was already sliding. He grabbed the chain so the part of it that was looped around the branch was locked in his grasp, then swung his legs up around the tree limb and clung to it for all he was worth.

The chain snapped tight in his fist and dug into the branch, then amazingly, it swung loose. Gage gulped air. His shackle dangled the chain and only a chunk of board.

The rest of the wagon completed its screeching descent and exploded into kindling below. Feeling even less secure than he had moments before, Gage tightened his hold on the branch. He was grateful to be alive and free from the wagon, but staring at the incline below, he realized he was still a prisoner. The ground was too steep to climb, and descending it looked just as dangerous. The grassy edge of the ravine was above him by the height of three men. The tree was his only option. It seemed sturdy enough and had plenty of branches.

Forcing himself to move, Gage shakily twisted his way up over the branch. He bit back a cry as he bumped his marked wrist in the process. Working his way to his feet proved even more difficult, but he managed to clamber his way upright using the tree's trunk for balance. Once standing, he climbed onward, making sure not to catch the trailing chain and board below him.

He drew even with the ravine's edge but realized he would have to go higher if he hoped to make it to the flat ground, which was still a good horse-length from him.

Climbing farther, he reached a point where the tree no longer felt stable but where he figured he could jump and clear the distance. Staring at the edge below, the steep gap of the ravine between him and it and the ground he hoped to land on, he drew several breaths.

He wasn't positive he could make the jump, but he was positive he didn't want to stay in the tree. From what he could tell from his vantage point, his runaway wagon had blown past the entire company of foot soldiers. This left him beyond the fighting, which was a relief since the last thing he wanted to do was risk his life, only to get himself killed by the rebels or the soldiers.

He eyed the ground he needed to hit. Trying to convince himself it wasn't that far, he attempted to picture it as just the last six steps of a stairway. An easy distance.

Gage wrapped up the chain and held the chunk of board, so it would be out of his way. He shifted his feet on the narrow branch. Knowing logic was never going to persuade him to do something so insane, he reminded himself he'd be a fool to stay where he was. Taking a breath, he picked the spot where he hoped to land and leapt.

The ground rushed at him.

He hit hard. His legs crumpled. He rolled to alleviate the pain of the impact, then stumbled to his feet.

He saw a soldier down the road pressed behind a tree, trying to reload his crossbow. Before the soldier spotted him, Gage limped across the road into the underbrush. He headed uphill, figuring traveling away from the road was better than staying near it.

He made it over the hilltop, but by then his knees were trembling so badly he stumbled and fell headlong. The chain and wood flew from his hand and landed before him. For a moment Gage lay in the leafy foliage, his insides quivering. Drawing a breath, he shoved himself out of the dirt and to his knees.

Fifty paces ahead of him, a horse stood in the underbrush, its saddle empty. Rejoicing at the sight, Gage struggled up. He retrieved the board and chain and lurched toward the animal, hoping his legs would get him to it.

Six steps later, he stumbled into the middle of five soldiers, four mounts, and three masked commoners all sprawled dead in the undergrowth.

Gage's body heaved at the sight. He bent beside a tree, expelling what little was left in his stomach. Shaking uncontrollably, his legs crumpled beneath him. Clearly the horsemen hadn't had the upper hand that they had thought.

His head swimming, his throat burning, and his mouth dry, Gage inhaled shallow breaths. He knew he had to get to the horse to avoid being the next casualty of the battle, but his legs wouldn't cooperate.

He placed his palms in the dirt and forced himself to crawl through the carnage. A waterskin looped over the saddle of one of the dead horses caught his eye. Cringing at the thought but desperate, he diverted toward the mount. Pulling the waterskin loose, he turned away and drank, emptying the waterskin. A moment later, life flowed back into his limbs.

He rose carefully to his feet. Spotting the horse still ahead, he took several steps in that direction. Then he stopped short. It was Sir de Lane. The knight lay on his back with an arrow protruding from between his armor plates and his eyes staring up through the trees.

Gage inhaled sharply. Allard's face flashed through his mind. He didn't want to feel anything, but grief rushed up his throat and choked him. Tears pooled in his eyes. He tried to force the emotions from a year earlier back into the depths of his soul, but somehow encountering Felix and then seeing this senseless slaughter made that impossible.

Anguish ripped through him, and tears escaped down his cheeks. How could people be alive one moment and dead the next? It wasn't fair. There was no chance to say goodbye or say how sorry he was. They were just gone. He would never again laugh with Allard over an awkward exchange or share a knowing look over a long dinner. He wouldn't see Allard become a knight or watch him marry Emma and have children who would've called him their uncle. He'd taken a boy as his squire, and he'd brought him back to his family as a body wrapped in a cloak.

Fresh tears burned down Gage's face. Blinking, he stared at Sir de Lane and wondered who would receive the knight's body. Who would grieve his loss?

Crawling forward and reaching out his marked hand, Gage closed the knight's eyes. At least whoever came for him, whether family or not, would not be haunted by his eyes as he was by Allard's.

Kneeling there, Gage pictured Felix crouched beside Emerett's campfire, his brown eyes downcast in feigned incompetence.

Gage exhaled his tears and inhaled fury like the dust from a dry, desolate field. The rebels would pay.

He shifted to grab the chain and board he trailed but then paused at a realization. Sir Jarret had given Sir de Lane the key to the shackle. Feeling like an actual thief, Gage succumbed to the circumstances and searched the knight's body. In the growing gloom, he finally found the key in a pocket in the seam of Sir de Lane's jerkin. Clutching it, Gage bent to twist the shackle on his wrist to get to its keyhole. That's when he heard voices coming up the hill behind him.

Abandoning his efforts to rid himself of the chain, Gage stuffed the key into his boot and hurriedly searched for the horse. It had wandered a fair distance deeper into the woods. He threw himself after the animal.

No matter how hard he pushed his exhausted body, he could not catch the beast. Every time he got close, the horse picked up its pace until it had outdistanced him.

For what felt like the hundredth time, Gage watched the infuriating animal angle its path and trot out of his reach. A moment later, it bashed through the undergrowth ahead out onto a rutted lane and took off at a run.

In despair, Gage realized the horse had pushed a long way through the woods yet had come back to the same road and was now probably headed home, which was apparently somewhere ahead.

Gage sank to his knees in the trees beside the road. The ground was flat leading up to the road, but on the opposite side, he could still see the drop-off of the ravine.

Hooves pounded toward him. Gage lifted his head, thinking the horse was returning. But there were too many hoofbeats.

He saw the knights and horsemen just as they saw him.

Gage's fingers went cold, and his mind screamed. Leaping to his feet, he whirled and ran.

Six steps into a jumbled sprint, something nicked his left knee. Pain buckled his stride. Gage cried out and dropped.

Landing in a heap, he clutched his stinging leg.

The riders swooped into the trees, and before Gage could right himself, he was surrounded by their horses' legs.

54

Lying on his side, Gage lifted his chained hand. His legs felt like wilted cabbage, and the pounding in his head reverberated like a ringing bell. Blood from a gash in his knee covered his fingers, and fear clung to him like sweat.

One of the armored horsemen dropped to the ground and nudged Gage's leg with his toe, as if evaluating a downed animal. "You nearly missed him."

Hissing air, Gage clenched his teeth and shoved himself to a seated position.

"Sir Treyson said to stop him, not kill him," another rider answered while tucking a bow over his shoulder.

"That I did," said the commanding voice Gage had heard earlier in the dell. "Though I thought we'd found a rebel attacker we could get answers from, not Sir de Lane's escaped prisoner. The question now is, is he worth dragging back with us?"

Several of the riders chuckled.

Twisting to look up at Sir Treyson, seated on his red horse, Gage drew a sharp breath. On the mount beside the knight sat Felix. Felix's gaze moved scornfully over Gage but took no particular interest in him.

Gage knew his long hair, beard, and dirty clothes had vastly altered his appearance, but still, the reality that Felix didn't even somewhat recognize him was like a firebrand tossed into the dry field of his fury. Every day since the ambush he had remembered Felix, but Felix had simply forgotten him.

The other horsemen were seeking rebels, which meant Gage could still accomplish at least one thing while he yet drew breath. He inhaled and spit past the rage burning in his chest. "You wish to know my worth, Sir Treyson? Then let me reveal to you a betrayer in your midst. The man who sits beside you. He is a traitor to Edelmar and Delkara and is responsible for the murders of more than one lord's man."

Sir Treyson's expression darkened. He glanced at Felix, looked back to Gage, and then burst out laughing. The others joined him.

Gage stared at the men. The fools didn't believe him. He clenched his jaw, but then his indignation turned to ash in his mouth. Felix's gaze, devoid of amusement, was focused on his face. The man dismounted, drew a sword with his good hand, and approached where Gage sat, still clutching his knee. His brown eyes narrowing, Felix spoke with a chillingly calm curiosity. "Where are you from?"

Gage remained silent. Felix pressed the sword's edge to Gage's throat, daring him to stay silent.

Angling up his chin to avoid being sliced by the blade, Gage glanced at Sir Treyson hoping to find help. The knight looked willing to let Felix do whatever he pleased. Panic stuck in Gage's gut like a caltrop. He felt as incapable and powerless as he had the day of the ambush. This realization re-ignited his anger and steadied him. He would not let Felix win. Not again. "I'm a seller of mounts from Carson."

He thought he'd see confusion in Felix's eyes. Instead there was a flash of recognition, and Felix smiled. "Sir Treyson, feel free to ride on and leave me to deal with this one. For I believe he will indeed prove useful. We will rejoin you when you return this way with the wagons."

"Very well. He's all yours." Sir Treyson spurred his horse toward the road. The others followed, taking Felix's mount with them.

With the encircling horsemen gone and the rush of their horse's hooves fading, Gage swallowed hard. Though they too had been a threat, they had also been his only protection.

55

Felix flicked his sword down to Gage's chest and scoffed. "I hardly believe it. You, the whelp of a prince, who last I saw sprawled in the mud. How long have you been following me?"

Gage blinked at the question but answered boldly. "Long enough." Wishing he had any kind of weapon, he watched Felix's eyes drift over his clothing and the shackle on his wrist. "Your journey, it would seem, has been eventful."

Running with Felix's assumption and hiding his mark, Gage lifted his shackled wrist and shrugged. "You mean this? It got me where I needed to go."

For a moment Felix's eyes wavered with uncertainty. Then they hardened. "You came all this way and dressed as a commoner for what? Revenge? Or were you truly attempting to seek justice?" Felix smiled scornfully. "Because it would appear you are as incapable of that as you are at protecting your own men, spotting the lies of a lowly servant, and keeping track of your tournament prize. Then again, winning the tournament was always destined to be your demise. And you made so many mistakes. Mistakes you still seem to be making, for I do not believe you intentionally got caught in order to confront me. So tell me, Prince, why did you come to Delkara? Were you seeking information, proof, or just someone to blame for your own gullibility?"

"I came to stop you," Gage growled, wishing his facade had lasted longer but too angry to let it go.

"You came to stop me? Alone? How did you find me? And who all have you told about me? Did you send word to your father informing him I've gathered a new force of men who even now are headed for Edelmar?"

Gage flinched at the news that the men were already on their way to Edelmar. Felix smiled. "Ah, then you didn't know that. Well, let me assure you, Your Highness, we will bring Edelmar to her knees one way or another. And having you in our possession will bring us an advantage indeed."

Shaking and furious, Gage wished again he had a weapon. "You're a snake."

"Crow, actually, is what they call me." Felix circled behind Gage, trailing his blade around his shoulder and across his back. "The Blue Crow is dead, no thanks to you. But the Crow lives on and always will."

Trying to resist cringing in response to the blade's path, Gage clenched his fist around the chain dangling from his shackled wrist. The wound inflicted upon Sir Reid's back at the ambush filled his mind. The chain's links bit deeper into his fingers, and suddenly it occurred to Gage that he *did* have a weapon.

Felix chuckled behind him, "You really thought you could take me down by appealing to Delkaran justice? Clearly you're as naïve and gullible as the day we met. You've no idea what real power is, but you will learn. Now get to your feet."

Gage seized the rage and fear blazing through his chest and overrode the pain that threatened to shred his strength. "The day we met, Crow, you were on your knees begging. And you will be again!"

Lunging forward, Gage spun around and whipped the chain with its chunk of board like a flail toward Felix's head.

Taken by surprise, Felix flung up his sword. He managed to protect his face but got his weapon wrapped in the chain. With the metal links encircling Felix's blade and hilt, Gage yanked, thinking to use the chain to drag the sword out of Felix's hand. But instead of resisting his pull, Felix charged him.

Reeling backward, Gage lost his footing and fell onto his back. Felix paused above him to rotate the blade in his left hand. This and the man's seething expression were enough of a warning.

Gage rolled sideways.

Felix drove his sword downward. Still wrapped in the chain, it stabbed into the ground where Gage's shoulder had just been. Staring at the quivering blade, Gage scrambled backward, kicked at Felix's gauntleted hand on the weapon's hilt, and hauled on his chain, trying to free himself.

Cursing, Felix stomped Gage's left arm. Gage cried out and with his free hand seized Felix's armored ankle just as Felix pulled his sword loose.

Throwing his body sideways, Gage wrenched Felix's foot toward himself and kicked at the man's other leg. Felix's body twisted and toppled backward. He thudded to the ground with a loud clank of armor and a whoosh of expelled air.

Determined to keep him down, Gage clambered on top of him, mobility being the one advantage he had without armor. With one knee on Felix's chest and the other pinning down the man's arm, he seized Felix's good hand and pried at the sword locked in his fingers.

A growl burst from Felix's lips, and he heaved his chest upward. Thrown off balance, Gage rolled off him and crashed headlong into ferns. He glanced back over his shoulder in time to see Felix raise his sword to swing at him.

Yanking his arms up, Gage curled his body. The blade hit his side, chiming against the chain trailing over his body from his wrist. Gasping in relief and panic, Gage did the only thing he could think to do. He grabbed the chain and swung it and the board over his shoulder as hard as he could at Felix's upper body.

His first swing clanked against armor, but his second made a thud and brought a bellow from Felix. Hoping that would slow Felix down, Gage scrambled to his knees and crawled as fast as he could through the underbrush. His injured knee landed on the trailing chain. He cried out and crashed to his chest.

Lying in the dirt, Gage remembered all the times he'd come off a horse while practicing jousting. Knights often took a moment to get back on their feet after being unhorsed, but Roger had always said to him, "You're not practicing to compete. Your practicing to live. Now get up! Before your enemy is upon you!"

Metal clanked behind him. Gage glanced over his shoulder to see Felix on his feet, his face filled with rage. Bruised, breathless, and in pain, Gage scrambled up and broke into a limping run.

Two steps in he tripped over a downed tree limb and sprawled. The limb he'd caught was about as thick as his fist and twice his length with a forked end, the perfect weapon.

On his knees, Gage seized the limb in both hands and turned it toward Felix, who was rushing at him. Couching the branch like a lance, Gage lurched to his feet. He ignored the pain in his knee as Roderick would have done and charged. Felix anticipated the hit to his chest and adjusted his sword.

Gage knew that if Felix managed to deflect the branch's end their combined momentum would bring his unarmored body directly into the path of Felix's next sword thrust. He kept going and did two things he'd never done jousting. He used both hands on his weapon and at the last moment dropped his weapon's aim below his enemy's waist.

Felix hacked at the branch's forked end, but because of its lower angle, he succeeded only in knocking its point of impact even lower. Driven by Gage's full body weight, the branch plowed into Felix's right leg and slid down his armor. It caught on his greaves and thrust his leg out from under him.

Felix staggered and hopped on one leg for two gigantic steps, then crashed headlong. The freed branch snagged into the ground with a cracking sound and jarred Gage to a painful stop. Felix grunted behind him.

Breathing hard, Gage glanced over his shoulder. Felix was already struggling to his knees to rise once again with sword in hand. Shifting his fingers on the branch, Gage yanked its broken end from the ground, hefted it, and swung it like a longsword at Felix's helmeted head. The resounding thud knocked Felix sideways. The man's slack body rolled flat. Felix lay there on his back with his arms splayed and his head lolled.

Inhaling a ragged breath, Gage cautiously approached him. Felix appeared to be unconscious. Gage slammed the branch down on the man's chest just to make sure. Felix didn't even twitch. Taking no chances, Gage straddled Felix's chest with his full weight anyway. He pinned Felix's arms under his ankles and yanked the sword from the man's loose fingers.

Felix's eyes flickered, and he stirred back to consciousness. Seeing Gage, he immediately began to struggle beneath him.

Gage drew up Felix's sword and held its tip above the gap between Felix's gorget and helmet. Felix stilled. Gage had reached this point of a killing strike hundreds of times before in training but had never before completed the thrust.

In the deepening dusk, Felix's brown eyes in wide pools of white stared at the weapon's tip. The man's gashed forehead, scuffed cheek, and bleeding lip elicited no sympathy from Gage. He tightened his fingers on the sword's hilt and prepared to drive it home. But instead of seeing the man he wanted to kill, he saw eyes full of life.

He fought his hesitation. Felix deserved to die. He should have hanged months ago with the Blue Crow. Because Felix had lived, more people were dead. What Felix had started needed to be finished.

The desire to simply kill him burned through Gage's being, but their fight was over. He held Felix's sword. There was no threat left to justify him taking Felix's life, only taking him into custody. But in a moment of fury, Gage could finish all of it here and now. No one would know how it had happened. It would simply be over. Or would it?

No amount of time, money, wishing, regret, or revenge could give back the lives already gone. Grief and anger twisted inside him. Killing Felix wouldn't change the losses, but it would avenge Allard and Bardon's deaths and perhaps finally let Gage be rid of his nightmares. He slid the sword's tip to Felix's throat.

Allard's young face and cheerful voice filled Gage's mind. *"I will tell them Prince Gage of Edelmar is a good man, worth following into the mud."* Gage choked on the words and felt his eyes burn. Was he a good man, worth following? Would he still be a good man if he did this?

Bombarded by turmoil, Gage wished to heaven and earth he could just drive home the blade and end Felix. He clenched his teeth.

Why? Why was it wrong to kill Felix there himself? Why couldn't he just decide for himself that it was right?

In answer, he saw Jack being beaten into the ground, Moses stabbed in the back, and himself marked. Some things were simply wrong no matter what. And if he and every other person alive could at any time simply choose for themselves whether something was right or wrong, the results would be utter mayhem.

He drew a breath. But Felix was going to be hanged. That was justice. So perhaps it wasn't wrong to end him now. Gage longed to embrace this thought. Prior Joseph's words swirled through his mind. *"It is a spiritual war, not a physical battle."* Gage didn't understand this, and he wished he could just block out all the objections running through his head and do what he desired. He tightened his fingers about the sword's hilt.

Felix shifted beneath him and tried to twist his arm free from Gage's ankle. Infuriated that the man would attempt to utilize his hesitation, Gage raised the sword, seized the pauldron piece of Felix's armor, and wrenched Felix over onto his face. Gage dropped his weight down again this time onto Felix's back. He pried the man's helmet off, and raised the sword once more. At least now if he drove the blade home he wouldn't see Felix's eyes.

Felix grunted beneath him and tried to push up with his good hand. Gage jammed his weight down harder. "I will kill you."

"Then do so," Felix spat into the ground, "and we can both burn in hell."

At Felix's words, it was as if Gage could feel the fire already consuming him. More of Prior Joseph's words haunted him. *"Every man, both common and noble alike, is a slave to darkness until he surrenders to God."*

Gage's arms trembled. He didn't know what he believed about God or hell, but he knew the pain and anger trapped inside him demanded a response. Yet he had a feeling if he did what he desired and murdered Felix, that darkness would indeed own him, and perhaps he really would burn in hell.

His father's words the night they'd spoken in the solar again brushed his mind. *"Gage, surrender your grief to God, for only in Him will you find peace."*

He looked at the sword in his hands. Surrender to God? He couldn't. Surrender meant defeat. Failure. Surrender wasn't something knights did. But his father had surrendered to God. So had Haaken. They had both surrendered, and they both seemed to have found peace. This thought melded with each of Gage's emotions until everything he felt was one huge mass slamming around inside him, and he couldn't take it anymore.

With a cry of frustration and rage, Gage drove the sword down so hard its impact jarred his body. Felix gasped in shock, then breathed in shuddering breaths that puffed dirt against the blade buried in the ground a finger's breadth from his cheek.

Leaning over the sword's hilt, Gage exhaled. Killing Felix would've been the same as Sir Jarret branding him without giving him a chance to speak to a lord. No matter the proof of guilt, it wasn't justice. He yanked the sword loose. Felix would still pay for his crimes. Gage would make sure of that, even if it meant hauling him all the way back to Edelmar. How to get across Delkara to Edelmar was the question though.

As Gage thought about this, he realized that thanks to Sir Jarret's shackle, Sir de Lane's key, and Felix's armor, he not only had a means, but he also might not have to take Felix that far at all. He could trade clothes with Felix, and once the lord's company had passed, he would lead the man back to the closest manor. For he had a feeling convincing a Delkaran lord of Felix's allegiance as a rebel would be much easier once he himself looked like the knight he was and Felix looked like a commoner. Even if Felix did speak or accuse him, no one would believe the man, just as they had not believed Gage.

Digging in his boot, Gage withdrew the key. Unlocking and removing the shackle from his wrist, he stripped off Felix's gauntlet and closed the metal bracelet around Felix's left arm, taking control of his good hand.

"What are you doing?" Felix growled.

Gage gripped the chain and board with his left hand and, with the sword in his right hand, removed his weight from Felix's back. "Giving you what no one gave me. Now get up. You're coming with me."

Felix rose stiffly and in the darkening woods turned toward Gage. His brown eyes were a mixture of anger, relief, and scorn. "Are you really such a fool to think you can march me out of here? Or have you forgotten there's a whole company of soldiers coming this way?" Felix nodded. "Even now one approaches."

Stiffening, Gage listened.

Sure enough, a horse was approaching.

"Over here!" Felix yelled.

56

Yanking Felix close, Gage pressed the sword against the man's throat. "One more sound, and I will kill you."

Gage looked at the road, searching for the rider Felix had alerted to their presence. The hoofbeats slowed, and he spotted the mount's dark legs through the gloom of the trees. The animal stood stock-still, as if its rider were holding it in place trying to decide if he had actually heard something or not.

Felix shuffled his feet, causing a rustle. Gage slid the sword along Felix's neck. The man flinched and stopped moving.

The rider still did not alight or call out. Instead his mount made the loud huffing sound horses make when they are nervous yet being territorial.

Finding this odd, Gage was struck by a thought. He whistled softly. Snorting, the animal trotted forward and stuffed its head through the foliage.

"Athalos!" Overjoyed, Gage pushed Felix out onto the road in front of him. Athalos backed away, huffing.

Gage shook his head. "You crazy thing, you really are following me." With a horse, he could transform himself fully into a knight.

The chain slackened in Gage's left hand. He eyed Felix and gave the links a sharp tug. "Let's go."

Felix used his upper arm to wipe away the blood trailing into his eyes from his gashed forehead and snarled. "Where will we go? You're in the middle of Delkara."

"To wait out the entourage," Gage replied, "then travel back to someone who will believe me when I tell them you're a rebel who likely helped plan today's ambush."

Felix looked befuddled. "You think I helped plan today's ambush?" The man's frown dissolved, and his mouth dropped open. "You still don't know," he said with amused disbelief. "How is that even possible? You've tracked me halfway across Delkara and gotten yourself captured and branded a rebel thief, but still you don't know."

Feeling like he'd dodged a mace but been hit by a rock, Gage stiffened. "What are you talking about?" At his angry tone, Athalos snorted and backed even farther away.

Straightening, Felix shook his head. "Nothing."

Gage growled and jerked the chain to bring Felix closer. "Tell me!"

"How about I show you instead!" Felix rolled down the chain, kicked Gage's injured knee, and smashed his armored back into Gage's chest. Felix then grabbed his branded wrist, pinning them together.

Hissing air, Gage cried out and heaved on the chain. He attempted to swing the sword, but with Felix's armored back pressed against his chest and the man's fingers clasped around his right wrist, he couldn't maneuver the weapon far enough around to strike anything but air.

Felix threw his head backward, clobbering Gage in the nose. Roaring in pain, Gage somehow managed to hold onto the chain, but he felt Felix's fingers tear the sword loose from his hand. Felix shoved away from him.

Blinking rapidly, Gage felt the chain pull and glimpsed Felix turning on him. Sword in hand, Felix rushed him and swung. Gage tried to block him using the part of the chain he still held, but still half blind, he missed blocking the blade.

The weapon sliced into his chest and across his shoulder. Gage gasped. A deep chilling pain followed the sword's path. He pressed his right hand to the wound. Seeing Felix preparing for another swing, he heaved on the chain with all his strength.

Dragged forward onto the dark road, Felix fell to his knees but still managed to slash the blade at Gage's legs.

Gage retreated backward. The sword missed.

Felix smacked the blade into the ground, needing the support of his good hand to shove himself back to his feet.

Feeling his body waver, Gage gritted his teeth to stay upright and stumbled forward onto the weapon, pinning it to the ground.

Felix tried to yank the blade up, but under Gage's weight it only grated in the dirt. Felix let go and braced himself on the ground. With warmth trickling through his fingers, Gage glared at the man. "You're done."

Felix shoved up and threw his left fist at Gage, opening his fingers as he did so. Dirt flew at Gage's face, peppering his eyes. He gasped and blinked rapidly. In the next moment, Felix ripped the chain from his fingers.

Worried Felix would finish him off now that he was loose, Gage felt for the sword under his foot. Brushing at his stinging eyes with his left hand, he grasped the sword's hilt with the slippery fingers of his right hand.

Squinting and blinking, he heaved up the blade and fell over. To his relief Felix wasn't standing above him. The man had instead fled toward Athalos.

The horse tried to spin away, but Felix seized the animal's trailing reins. Jerked around by the man's grip, Athalos's shifted from fleeing to flattening his ears.

The horse's warning went unheeded. Felix reached for the saddle. Athalos swung his head, mouth open. Seeing the horse's teeth coming, Felix punched the horse's cheek.

Athalos jerked his head away, and Felix used the opportunity to heave his armored body into the saddle.

The moment Felix landed on the horse, Athalos threw his head and squealed.

"Oh no you don't." With a look of furious determination, Felix slammed his heels into the animal's sides. Athalos didn't bolt forward. Instead he coiled—body arched, neck curled, and ears pinned.

Gage sank back. Blood from the slice across his chest and shoulder seeped down his shirt. He knew Athalos too well to doubt what would happen next. And at the moment, he was content to let the horse punish Felix for his stupidity.

Athalos exploded off the ground. Shock on his face, Felix grabbed for the saddle and was amazingly still mostly in it when Athalos landed his first leap, but the horse wasn't finished.

Squealing and bucking hard, Athalos bounded across the road. Felix flew forward in the saddle. Athalos knocked Felix between his neck and the saddle twice more. Having gained momentum, the animal launched into a rear. Rising, the horse reached fully vertical and kept going.

Gage watched in stunned silence as Athalos tipped backwards. Felix's body separated from the saddle and slipped into the air. Off balance, horse and man descended backwards together. Felix fell hidden behind Athalos's dark body.

The horse's massive frame crashed into the grass, and a man's cry echoed. Athalos's long legs flailed sideways for a moment before the horse managed to roll and leap back to his feet.

Gage stared at where Felix should have been. There was no sign of him. Stumbling to his feet, Gage grabbed the sword and stumbled across the dark road. His breath caught. A bent line of grass led off an edge and into nothingness.

Dropping to his knees, Gage crawled forward and looked over into the dark ravine. He spotted Felix's body far down at the bottom.

Trembling and suddenly cold, Gage sagged backward away from the edge. Sitting there, he felt Athalos's breath on his neck. He climbed unsteadily to his feet. Clutching his bleeding wound and standing beside his once again docile horse, he closed his eyes and leaned against Athalos's side.

Feeling both thankful and horrified, he murmured in the nobleman's tongue, "Just or not, the price of his crimes has truly been paid." And if he didn't get out of there, he would be branded a murderer as well.

He scooped up Athalos's reins and tried to mount. The horse's saddle slid sideways. The cinch had torn through. With no way to repair it, he had no choice but to strip the saddle off—a painful process that caused more blood to saturate his shirt.

Dumping the saddle, he was about to leave it behind when he remembered his signet ring. Dragging the tack over, Gage removed the ring and, wiping the blood from his hand, slid it onto his finger. Using the saddle as a step, he heaved himself onto Athalos's back.

He nudged the horse with his heel. "Come on, Athalos," he murmured. "We've got to go before the soldiers come."

His head pounding, Gage couldn't have heard if anyone was coming behind him, but the fear of following hoofbeats assaulted him over and over. Meanwhile, the fingers of his right hand were slick with blood, and his left hand rested between Athalos's shoulders and clutched the reins.

He knew he needed to get off the road to avoid being found by the soldiers, but he also knew his only chance of getting anywhere was if he stayed on Athalos.

Spotting a gap in the dark trees ahead, he felt hope. It was a trail, tall enough for a horse and decently well used. It looked similar to the shortcut that he and Manton had taken to reach the manor outside of Maneo.

Turning Athalos into it, Gage lowered his hand from his aching shoulder and gripped the horse's mane. He hoped the trail led to a village or a manor but wondered if anyone would actually risk aiding a marked man bleeding from obvious sword wounds. Probably only someone interested in turning him in for a possible reward. The farther he went though, the more he realized he didn't care why someone might help him; he just knew he needed help.

Unbroken darkness filled the woods around him. Winding on and on along the path, his hope of arriving anywhere faded along with his strength. He could see no candle's flame or fire in any direction, only an empty, endless forest.

He should have stayed on the road and let the soldiers find him. But after what had happened to Felix, they'd probably have just killed him or left him to die.

Weariness drifted over him like a fog. He told himself to stay focused, but when even the jarring pain of Athalos's steps began to dull, he knew he was losing the battle.

No longer capable of holding up his weight, he wavered forward. His face brushed the roughness of Athalos's mane. Somewhere in his mind he was aware that falling off Athalos meant wolves would likely find him before morning, particularly with the scent of blood he was literally trailing.

His body rocking with Athalos's steps, Gage felt his life slipping from his grasp. Prior Joseph's voice floated through his mind. "*God does exist, and He is at work.*"

Gage's fingers fell from Athalos's mane. "If you truly exist, God, please help me."

A Scripture inscribed on the wall of the church in Ulbin entered Gage's fading thoughts. "*I am the light of the world. He who follows Me shall not walk in darkness, but have the light of life.*"

"Prithee, God, give me Your light."

Gage was no longer conscious when his body slid from Athalos's back and thudded to the ground in the vast forest far from Edelmar.

Discussion Questions

1. Gage questions his decision to pull up his lance at the joust. Have you ever had a right decision result in negative consequences? Has this ever made you wondered if the decision was still right? (In Acts the Apostles face brutal consequences for doing what God asked them to do. Acts 5:29 tells us why.)

2. Because Gage allows Felix to travel with his retinue, does this make Gage responsible for the ambush?

3. Have you ever been told by others or by Satan that someone else's choices or the evil that someone else did was somehow your fault?

4. Gage rightly takes responsibility for those he's leading, but he wrongly takes responsibility for the evil actions of other people. What was the truth he should have told himself about the ambush?

5. Was it right or wrong for Gage to walk away from his life as Prince Gage?

6. When things are hard or cause us a lot of pain, it's easy to want to run from the challenge of overcoming what we're facing. Have you ever had something really hard or painful make you want to run away?

7. Gage buries his pain rather than dealing with it, which results in that injury remaining unhealed. This choice and its consequences make him blind and vulnerable to much of what's happening around him. Have you ever held onto grief or pain and buried it like Gage does? What were the results?

8. Gage thinks a knight who admits injury makes himself a disgrace. Is this really a right and good mindset to have? How does Roderick, Gage's jousting opponent, prove this mindset wrong at the feast?

9. What do you think might have happened if Gage had been willing to stay and admit his pain and deal with his grief with his family and friends after the ambush?

10. If you were in King Axel's place would you have allowed Gage to continue traveling as a commoner?

11. How do you think Gage would have responded had his father forced him to stay?

12. Gage traveled with Manton for months, but how much did Gage really know about Manton?

13. Have you ever been burned by someone you befriended and chose to trust? How might the situation have been different had you first learned more about the person?

14. How did Gage's own deception play into the situation he found himself in with Manton?

15. Have you ever misrepresented yourself and then found yourself in a position where your own lies ensnared you into further trouble? (Proverbs 29:24)

16. What were some of the wise principles King Axel passed along to his sons? What kinds of wise principles have those around you passed on to you?

17. Gage grew up hearing about God but believes that God doesn't exist. Why? What has happened in Gage's life that made him question God's existence?

18. Have you ever encountered events in your own life that made you wonder how an all-powerful, loving God would allow such things to happen? How have you responded? Have you trusted in who God is like Haaken and Axel? Or have you rejected God like Gage? (Book 2 will address this topic further.)

19. Gage makes many of his decisions from the principles his father taught him, but because he doesn't believe in who God is and in what God says is right and wrong, he finds himself often conflicted about the decisions he's making. How does knowing God's Word is true help you make decisions more confidently?

20. Why does Prior Joseph's conversation with Manton disturb Gage so much?

21. Have you ever had God put His finger on an issue in your life that you are struggling with? When God does this, do you listen and respond to Him or do you run away? (Jonah 1-4)

22. How do you think Gage's journey may have been different had he sought God's help along the way?

23. Do you believe God can use even our wrong choices to accomplish His purposes?

24. Gage faces consequences because of the decisions he's made, and he waits for the last moment to cry out to God. Do you think God still listens even when we've ignored Him for so long?

25. Have you ever felt like you were beyond saving? (Moses was a traitor, a murderer, an exile, and a rebel leader, and God loved him, saved him, and powerfully used him.)(Exodus 2-12)

26. Gage's journey isn't over and neither is yours. So learn from the mistakes you have or will make, run to God, and live your life in His love, power, and grace.

Acknowledgments

My deepest gratitude goes to my family for being a wonderful part of my crazy life as an author and for loving, helping, and supporting me through the ups and downs of my writing projects.

I would also like to thank everyone else who helped during the different stages of creating this specific book, particularly BriAnn Beck, Rachael Lofgren, Luke Franklin, Victor Michlik, Colton Anderson, Oren Printy, Kaben Hoffman, Kate Ophoven, Patricia Mueller, Nancy Bjorkman, Kevin Miller, and everyone at my publisher.

"Without counsel, plans go awry, but in the multitude of counselors they are established." Proverb 15:22

Books by Given Hoffman

Contemporary Suspense
The Eighth Ransom

Medieval Action/Adventure
The Tournament's Price
The Rebel's Mark

Nonfiction
The Voices of the Pioneers: Homeschooling in Minnesota

Visit GivenHoffman.com to learn more.

The Rebel's Mark

MARKED
Book 2

PAIN FOUND GAGE in the endless darkness like an arrow hitting its mark. It pierced deep into his chest and shoulder, decimating the calm where his mind had been floating.

He cried out and tried to struggle away from whatever was causing the excruciating pain. Hands gripped his arms, holding him in place, and a male voice spoke sharply. Gage's muddled mind could not put meaning to the words nor could he draw himself out of the darkness to successfully resist the person's hold. The pain increased and was forced deeper into his chest.

Unable to escape the overwhelming agony, Gage screamed. His mind mercifully drew him back into unconsciousness.

When Gage could next perceive anything, the intense agony had settled to a heavy ache in his chest and shoulder while other pain drifted to his attention. His wrists throbbed, his body burned, and his pounding head assaulted him in waves.

He tried to recall what had happened to him, but no matter where he searched in his mind there were no answers. He encountered only a suffocating heat from which he could not wake. Panic filled him. Why was he so hot? And why couldn't he remember?

Fatigue and a frightening sense of vulnerability filled him. He fought to recall any memory to hold onto, but no matter how he tried to seize what he knew was there, it vanished from his grasp like steam. The fire consuming him hurled him anew through pain and weariness.

Hours or perhaps days later with the inferno burning through his body, Gage heard the echoing glory of angelic singing.

He wondered if perhaps he was dead. But if he was in heaven why was he trapped in the fires of hell? And if he was in hell why the angelic choir? A fresh wave of heat shredded his thoughts. Only an urgent sense of fear and a need to escape remained, but Gage could not recall of what or why. Perhaps if he could somehow force his mind to identify where he was, he could remember, but focusing on anything other than his boiling exhaustion proved too grueling a task. Swept away, he wandered in distorted dreams.

Eventually the stifling heat diminished, and Gage's ability to think returned. But weariness continued to battle against him every time he tried to gather his thoughts.

Worn out by the struggle, part of him longed to embrace the cooling emptiness and simply let himself drift, but another part of him screamed in stubborn rage every time a memory came and then slipped from his grasp.

Somehow the knowledge of needing to warn someone stayed, but he could not grasp who. Then he saw Haaken and heard his brother's teasing voice. *"Or you can send chestnuts and a croissant."*

Warmth threatened to carry the thought away, but Gage seized the recollection and zealously guarded its ragged edges. He repeated the words over in his mind and slowly the memory of his conversations with Haaken and his parents before leaving Edelmar became fuller and more defined. His memories spread out from there, regaining ground across Delkara.

He broke free of the steamy fog in his mind like a traveler bursting from a hot swampy dell to a mountain's crest where the air is cold and the view stretches to the horizon, but the view he encountered made him wish he'd stayed in the dell.

He remembered traveling with Manton across Delkara, buying and selling mounts at the fair in Nikledon, spotting his stolen brooch, talking with Lady Natriece, finding out Manton was a rebel smuggler, having Sir Jarret discover stolen gold in his saddlebags, and being branded a thief by the knight. The permanence and judgement of what Sir Jarret had done drew back to the surface Gage's anger, fear, and humiliation. He was a marked man and there was nothing he could do to change that.

Somehow he knew that wasn't the only thing he had to fear though. Sir Jarret had put him in a wagon to be taken to his master, and their wagons had been attacked on the road. But what had happened after that? Who had brought him to wherever he was now? The rebels? Or the soldiers?

Forcing his thoughts past the warmth lingering in his body, Gage pushed his senses beyond the chaos of his mind to what he could glean of his surroundings.

He lay on what had to be straw. A thin material separated him from it, but the chaff pricked through to his skin and did little to pad the hard surface beneath. It also smelled dank like molding grass. Drawing a full breath, Gage realized he was shirtless. But something was wrapped tightly over his chest, and there was pressure around his wrists. His heart beat faster. He wanted to move his arms to discover exactly how firmly he was tethered, but just then a sound like cloth fluttering in the wind filled his ears. A scuffing followed, and a young male voice close beside Gage snapped his mind into focus. "You see! He doesn't seem to burn as hot with fever as he did before."

A cool hand touched Gage's forehead, and his insides jumped. "You are right," a quieter male voice said. "It does seem he's not as hot as before."

"Is it certain then that he will live?"

"Only God knows who will live and who will die. Now, get on with you. I will keep the next watch," the older voice said.

Gage wanted to stir to prove to them he was alive, but then fear made him realize maybe he didn't want to reveal to them his awareness, for his bound wrists and the pain he remembered from earlier made him wonder if perhaps they valued his well being not for his sake but for their own.

Were they servants of his new master, told to report if he survived? Or were they soldiers needing him to live so they could put him back in a wagon and deliver him to their master? Or were they rebels, hoping he lived so they could use him as a pawn in their war against the nobles?